The Righteous Sin

By G.I. Berry

B.O.S.S. Publishing

Copyright

The Righteous Sin
by G.I. Berry
First Edition 2015
©Text Copyright 2007
Edited by Andrea Paul
Published by B.O.S.S. Publishing ~ www.boss-publishing.com

For information address B.O.S.S. Publishing at
4820 Walden Lake Point
Decatur, GA 30035

Publisher's Note: This is a work of fiction. Names, characters, places and incidences either are the product of the author's imagination or are used factiously, any resemblance to actual persons living or dead, business establishments, events or otherwise are purely coincidental.

For information regarding special discounts for bulk purchases, sales, promotions, speaking engagements and or book clubs, please contact us by email at: sales@boss-emag.com or visit www.therighteoussin.com

Manufactured in the United States of America

ISBN: 978-0-9863559-4-3
Library of Congress Control Number: 2015956712

10 9 8 7 6 5 4 3 2 1

Dedicated to

Sophia Morgan-Genus
For never losing faith in me

*What would you do if
you were not afraid?*

Chapter One
The Second Baptism

"Are you ready, my dear?" The Pastor said proudly with a broad smile on his face.

"Of course," snapped Sister Georgina, angry that this man was asking such a stupid question. He had known her all her life and knew just how much she had longed for this moment to arrive. Her salvation was on the line and he should know better than to waste time engaging in trivial small talk. Her soul was being saved and she had every right to demand a solemn atmosphere to reflect the serious nature of the commitment she was making. *The Pastor just needs to hurry up and get on with it,* her thoughts continued.

Sister Georgina had been about twelve weeks old at the time of her first baptism. Naturally, she couldn't remember anything about the commitment she had been forced to make. However, now eighteen years old, she was fully conscious and wanted to relish every moment of the glorious ritual. She wanted the world to know that from this point on, it would be her lifelong goal to be a good Christian woman. Sister Georgina loved the Lord and could not remember a time in her young life when she didn't, so this public declaration of her faith was a very serious moment, indeed. It was one she wanted to cherish and remember for the rest of her life.

"Are you ready?" The Pastor repeated cheerfully, clearly having ignored the vexed look on Sister Georgina's face after his first attempt to lighten the mood.

Unable to help herself, she cut her eyes at him in a dramatic attempt to indicate her disgust and said as calmly, but as sarcastically as possible, "Yes, of course. Why else would I be standing here, Pastor?"

Sister Georgina wondered briefly about what happened to the many complaints she had submitted to the leadership committee regarding the Pastor's lack of professionalism. Hearing a few coughs and murmurings from the congregation quickly returned Sister Georgina to the present. From that moment, she decided that nothing was going to ruin her special day.

She had been preparing for months; spending hours researching the finer details of the baptism ceremony and fantasizing about her moment in the spotlight. While she stood in front of her church family, Sister Georgina reflected on her life and allowed her mind to review her years of hard work.

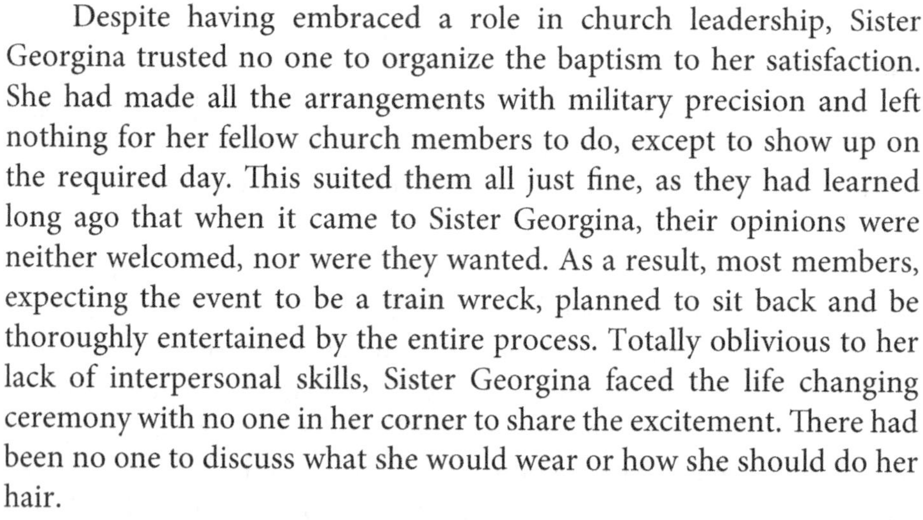

Despite having embraced a role in church leadership, Sister Georgina trusted no one to organize the baptism to her satisfaction. She had made all the arrangements with military precision and left nothing for her fellow church members to do, except to show up on the required day. This suited them all just fine, as they had learned long ago that when it came to Sister Georgina, their opinions were neither welcomed, nor were they wanted. As a result, most members, expecting the event to be a train wreck, planned to sit back and be thoroughly entertained by the entire process. Totally oblivious to her lack of interpersonal skills, Sister Georgina faced the life changing ceremony with no one in her corner to share the excitement. There had been no one to discuss what she would wear or how she should do her hair.

Never seeing the value in paying attention to such trivialities, her personal self-care had always being the furthest thing from her mind. It was only after forcing herself to accept that a new outfit was required, she reluctantly spent hours at the local thrift stores until she found a hidden gem. It was an elegant, all-white, ankle length dress. She ignored the scripted apology from the volunteer cashier about not having her size because she was confident that she could make it work.

The dilemma about what to do with her hair had also been resolved when she considered an off-white headscarf, found at another thrift store, to be a perfect match to complement her outfit. She could then focus her attention on what she considered to be a more important use of her time. Including, practicing holding her breath under water (achieving a personal best when she hit the two minute mark), as well as standing ceremoniously in wet clothes in her bathtub, much to the annoyance of her siblings who seemed to always want to use the toilet whenever she rehearsed. Then, she imagined stepping down from the alter like an Olympic gold medalist, being greeted by crowds of well-wishers, and having to enthusiastically shake the hands of those who naturally wanted to offer their congratulations.

Her prepared five page testimony, which had been scaled back from its original ten pages, had been carefully read and reread before being loaded onto the overhead projector to be shown over brunch when the formal ceremony had concluded. It would *obviously* receive a standing ovation, warranting its reprint in the next edition of the church's newsletter. With everything in seemingly perfect order, when Sister Georgina woke up on the morning of her baptism, she felt excited, confident, and ready for the day ahead, as her imagination had already declared the event to be an overwhelming success.

However, in spite of all her planning, she actually found herself rushing around before even leaving the house that morning. The two-and-a-half hours she allocated to get ready flew by with several unexpected events delaying her departure. Firstly, after many failed attempts, she had to accept that the zipper on her dress could not do its job without assistance and reluctantly decided to locate some safety pins. But, as they were not where they should have been (in the sewing basket next to the cabinet by the fridge), she had undertaken a frantic search though the house, during which she accidentally bumped into the kitchen table, spilling the contents of her father's half-empty coffee cup left from the night before onto her beloved outfit. Without becoming emotional, Sister Georgina diligently continued her hunt until the elusive packet of safety pins were found tucked neatly behind some discarded mail in one of the kitchen drawers.

She then dealt with the second incident by wetting the edge of the kitchen towel with water and cleaning up the stain on her dress until she felt it was hardly noticeable. Although these mishaps had stolen more of her precious time than she had anticipated, having resolved them to her approval, it was an elated Sister Georgina who rushed out of the house that Sunday morning to change her life.

Refocusing her attention on the purpose and reverence of the service, Sister Georgina returned her thoughts to the present and stood with confidence at the front of the church. Feeling dressed to impress, like a bride on her wedding day, she felt special and truly deserving of claiming her place in the afterlife. Knowing that her salvation was going to be assured shortly, meant a broad smile unexpectedly appeared on her face, despite the air of seriousness she had so desperately wanted to create. Realizing that her lapse in composure was on public display, Sister Georgina mentally reprimanded herself, adopted her usual frown, and symbolically brushed non-existent wrinkles out of her clothes in a feeble attempt to hide her embarrassment.

"It's okay to allow the joy of the Lord into your heart," the Pastor said enthusiastically and loud enough for the rest of the congregation to hear when he noticed the smile disappear from her face. He then gently placed his hand on her shoulder and smiled encouragingly, looking out towards the congregation for them to be impressed by his talent at being compassionate. Annoyed, Sister Georgina, in an exaggerated gesture of disapproval, aggressively shook his hand off her shoulder and gave him no reciprocal smile. The Pastor, oblivious once again to the negative social cues coming from Sister Georgina, saw it as an opportunity to give a spontaneous testimony.

"It's okay, my sister. Allow the joy of knowing the Lord to shine outwardly! You know, I allow myself to feel joy every time I feel the warmth of the sun on my skin, or marvel at the individuality of a snowflake. The Lord sends us signs of his greatness everywhere we look. Our job is just to recognize his miracles every minute of the day. As I was walking here this morning with my dear wife, who you all know I love so much... Well, she was by my side and when we stopped at the crossroads- you know the one at the corner just before you get to the chicken place on Martin Luther King Boulevard. There is a bent signpost. You know, it looks like it's been that way for quite some time because it is all covered in dust and grime."

Before continuing, the Pastor paused and took his time to survey the entire church hall to ensure that all eyes were on him.

"I am sure someone must have reported it to the council, but if they haven't repaired it by next week we will contact them ourselves. We have to make an effort to keep our community looking smart. So, where was I? …ah, yes, the signpost. We spotted a large black spider weaving its web in the bend of that signpost. My darling wife and I stood there in the crisp morning air and watched as it majestically weaved its intricate web. We couldn't help but see evidence of God's presence! My wife, of course, was scared. She doesn't like spiders, never have. I am the one, who goes into the bathroom with a cup to catch them and relocate them into the yard. But, that's what husbands do, of course. As I… "

The Pastor, who had been forcibly evicted from his amateur dramatic group as a young man for consistently disregarding directorial instructions and taking center stage, found he was able to indulge his narcissistic compulsion in the ministry. He had inherited the position at the tender age of thirty-two, from a distant uncle who had unexpectedly been required to take a ten year, all expenses paid vacation, courtesy of the United States Government. Despite having no previous interest in religion, let alone any formal academic training, he happily accepted (as having the captive attention of an audience was a requirement of the position). He had never bothered to find out the reason for his uncle's incarceration, but was clear that on his release he would not be returning to his former position at the pulpit.

Regardless of the fact that the Pastor had just given a two hour sermon, if the cluttered pulpit did not need to be rearranged to set up the medium sized, blue, plastic wading pool that served as the church's temporary baptismal, he most likely would have gone on for another couple of hours. So, while the stage was being set for Sister Georgina's big moment, the Pastor reluctantly made small talk with individual members of the church as the organist gave a back to back rendition of the church's favorite hymns. When the service had resumed, as if he needed a 'fix' for his addiction to having an audience, the Pastor seemed determined to divert attention away from the baptism onto himself and stood in front of Sister Georgina continuing his unsolicited testimony.

"…I cannot understand how anyone, seeing a spider weave a web, does not reach the same conclusion that we do…how can they not acknowledge God's presence in this world? I am so grateful every time I get up in the morning. I feel so blessed to know my life's journey is to spread the message that God is alive and present in our lives, no matter how dysfunctional we may think it is." He gave a hearty laugh and then paused for breath before shifting his attitude to highlight the seriousness of his message.

"I absolutely believe that my submission to the Lord gives me the strength to say and do extraordinary things, take this morning, for example, when we saw that spider…"

He stopped mid-sentence again, not because he finally acknowledged Sister Georgina's disapproval or the bored looks on the usher's faces as they stood waiting patiently to exercise their duties, but because Mrs. Cartwright was waving frantically from the back of the church to get his attention. It was her usual signal to let him know that brunch would be ready soon. Members of the congregation, who also knew what she was relaying to the Pastor, began picking up their belongings to ensure they would be first in line. Knowing that he now had a restless audience and remembering that young Sister Georgina had a tendency to be obsessive about her faith, he shifted his attitude and attention once again.

"Next time, my dear family, I will tell you about our morning walk, but for now, let's focus on officially welcoming our sister into the beloved arms of our Lord and Savior," he said as he motioned graciously to Sister Georgina.

As they stood next to the makeshift baptismal pool, the Pastor performed his duties in a manner that would make even John the Baptist proud. Sister Georgina soon forgot about her irritation with him and embraced the historic moment. Being baptized meant everything to Sister Georgina. Her physical submersion in the baptismal waters represented her total commitment to the Lord. It would wash away her sins, giving her a fresh start to walk the journey of life.

How easy my life will be now, she thought to herself. *All I have to do is live in submission to God's Truth and his blessings will be showered on me. Simple.* This time however, her smile could not be contained.

The blessing that Sister Georgina was secretly looking forward to the most was a husband. Yes, of course, having children and the promise of eternal life were high on her list, but they had become incidental to the intimate relationship she would legally be able to experience with a husband. Unlike those in her senior high school class, she had proudly maintained her virginity and would do so until she married.

Now, she was finally of an age to marry and experience the joys of married life. Or in other words, finally have sex, she was expecting to receive a proposal in the immediate future (despite not having a potential suitor in sight). She did not tell anyone of this secret desire, believing her thoughts to be "un-Christian-like." She chose instead to suppress them; having concluded that the best time to settle down and build her happy home life would be after graduating with her college degree. In the meanwhile, she would dream of her husband and future family. He would naturally want at least three children. If they were financially secure, they would have perhaps four or five. She would most likely do her graduate courses as a part-time student, as nothing would interfere with her obligations to her family. Although, she could barely wait for her dreams to materialize into reality, she decided to channel her energies into successfully representing her Lord and Savior. Her earthly sacrifices guaranteed her happiness and would be evidence to non-believers about God's blessings.

"Others will be so envious of me and my family," Sister Georgina said to herself confidently. "But, all they have to do is follow my excellent example and they, too, would be similarly blessed. After all, the Truth is the Truth," she gloated. Sister Georgina was secure in the belief that the Truth was on her side.

And, so, it was with total trust that Sister Georgina stepped into the shallow water and willingly contorted her body to lay flat on the bottom of the improvised baptismal pool. She held her breath and tightly shut her eyes as the two male ushers continued to fill the pool with lukewarm water from their hoses to ensure that Sister Georgina was completely covered. Feeling relaxed, she lay peacefully holding her breath under the water, pleased that her unorthodox preparations had paid off. Even though her water logged ears could only make out odd words as the Pastor said the blessing, she treasured the ritual and the peace that came over her as a result. Regardless of the ceremony's obvious flaws, she chose not to worry about the things outside her control, like her natural hair covered tightly by its wrap and how it would look when she came up out of the water or her unflattering coughing or sputtering as the water invaded her throat. When she stood up, she really felt as though she had actually been reborn. This time she had no choice but to allow the flow of her unexpected and uncontrollable tears to fall freely down her face. She was so happy. After all the time and effort she had put into making this moment a reality, she wanted it to last forever. So, as if in a feeble attempt to stop the passing of time, she graciously rejected the outstretched hands of the Pastor and ushers to step out of the pool and into dry clothes. Instead, she stood defiantly in the water, choosing to ignore the 'what is she doing now' comments and loud sighs of pity to provide the much anticipated entertainment the congregation had been expecting.

It was not the sight of the soaking wet, overweight, eighteen-year-old with her twisted head wrap revealing her matted unkempt hair, dressed in a disheveled ill-fitting outfit that was held together by several large unsightly safety pins and was covered with visible brown stains (along with some that could not be identified acquired from the towel she had used to clean her dress) who stood boldly before them that prompted the whispers from the congregation. It was because no one had *ever* seen young Sister Georgina so emotional and they had no idea how to handle this unusual turn of events. So, when their applause of support for her tears faded before going silent, as if in unison, they overlooked the final particulars of the ceremony and started to sing the closing hymn.

By now, the smell of Mrs. Cartwright's famous Sunday brunch had wafted into the hall and most members were no longer interested in the ceremony. The Pastor, strongly motivated by his desperate need to avoid the intense emotionality of the situation, hurried the process along by creatively jumping to the last verse of the closing hymn and the congregation gratefully followed his lead. He then ended the ceremony with a quick prayer before leading his flock to the cafeteria for their weekly indulgence in a soul food banquet. The ushers were therefore left with the responsibility of dealing with Sister Georgina who continued to refuse their gentle encouragement to step out of the pool. After much consultation between themselves, they decided to wrap towels around her shoulders, discreetly place a chair by the pool, and quietly went about their chores. Sister Georgina, although, fully aware of the happenings around her, chose to ignore them because unbeknownst to everyone, she was using the opportunity to reflect on her childhood and youth that had led to her landmark decision.

Her greatest influence was her late mother, to whom she would be eternally grateful for raising her in Truth. Words could not express how much she admired her mother's unshakable faith. It had given her short and difficult life, meaning, stability, and structure. Seeing her mother kneel each evening at her bedside, giving thanks to the Lord, was undeniably one of Sister Georgina's most consistent and pleasant childhood memories. She would watch in awe as her mother was never fazed by the daily struggles of raising eight children and being the wife of a non-believing husband. Sister Georgina loved hearing her mother sing as she hand washed the clothes of everyone in the house. After her mother's death, Sister Georgina would speak proudly of this to illustrate a Godly attitude to her Sunday school children, despite the challenge of first trying to inform her young audience that there was a time before washing machines and dryers. But, when she had tried to follow her mother's example and sing while she hand-washed a couple of her delicates, she had quickly become frustrated by the menial process. She found herself programming the delicate cycle on the washing machine and never used it as an example in class again.

Sister Georgina's love of her mother had risen to new heights when she witnessed the inevitability of her terminal illness. As far as Sister Georgina was concerned, her mother prepared to meet her maker with dignity and grace. The details around when or how she got the news that her mother's cancer had spread were sketchy. She was about six years old at the time and all she could remember was that everyone had to be quiet. In her young mind, her mother was in bed for what seemed like months, being waited on by her father. He had surprisingly stepped up to the plate and took care of the household, despite his limited capabilities in this area. It had taken this crisis for him to be involved in the day-to-day activities; for up until that point, he preferred to sit and vegetate in front of the television whenever he came home from work. But, now it was a painful, albeit, comforting sight to see her father carrying her mother to the bathroom. His attempts to cook were even stranger and Sister Georgina remembered looking forward to the bland tasteless dinners she would have at school to avoid his lumpy sweet potatoes and uncooked collard greens that would be displayed on her plate in poorly designed smiley faces. Her father's feeble attempts to cheer up his family were futile as nothing could shake the deep sadness everyone felt as they waited patiently for the inevitable.

The silence was eventually broken after weeks of tiptoeing around the house by the sounds of her mother singing again. It was a signal that they could all go back into her room, sit on her bed, and hear her beloved "back home" stories. However, this time it was different. Her mother told Sister Georgina and her siblings with a genuine smile that she was getting ready to meet her Lord and Savior. She was so sorry to be leaving and would not be around to see them all grow up, but she trusted that her departure was God's will and He knew what was best. She was not afraid and they should not be also.

She chose to celebrate the little time she had left with her children. She laughed at their endless "knock knock" jokes and listened to how their days had gone at school. She would tell the children their favorite stories, read passages from the Bible, and share her hopes for their futures. Sister Georgina's mother helped them plan her funeral, choosing hymns and Bible passages to be shared amongst her loved ones. She even invited the local florist to the house and put in the order for the flowers. Her mother made the entire process painless for her family, wanting to care for them, even beyond her death. The dignified acceptance her mother showed during her last days despite her intense pain made Sister Georgina in awe of her mother's never failing faith. The bar of how a believing woman should conduct her life *and* death had been set extremely high and Sister Georgina was determined that her faith would be just as strong. Like her, Sister Georgina would dedicate her life to be of service to others, endure difficulties in silence, and strive to be a good servant of the Lord. Yes, she knew it was going to be tough, but witnessing her mother's example throughout her life, she, too, wanted to be a positive influence on others.

Sister Georgina had received confirmation to follow her mother's path only a few months after the funeral when her father had accidentally called her by his wife's name. Sister Georgina had settled a dispute between her younger siblings as her mother would have done and it had delighted her father. He quickly apologized, realizing the insensitivity of his remark and returned to making dinner for his children (overlooking their lack of appreciation for his culinary skills). Unknowingly, his slip of the tongue made a lasting impression on his young daughter who had taken it as confirmation that she had stepped into her mother's shoes and was on the path of righteousness. She could ignore the *I am so sorry for you* looks from outsiders and the fact that people did not want to talk about their loss, or even how quickly someone had taken her mother's seat at the back of the church. She reminded herself that all she needed was to walk with the Lord and everything would be alright. From that moment, Sister Georgina remembered making the decision to throw herself into church life, believing that with their help, her goal of following in her mother's footsteps and being a true servant of the Lord would be achievable.

———————⁓———————

Her mother had found their church home when she came to the United States from Jamaica in the early 1950s. Her welcome had been a cold one. Nothing had prepared her for the loneliness and poverty she experienced. Before arriving in the 'land of opportunity,' she excitedly ran to the post office, as many others did, every Saturday morning to hear the Postmaster read letters from those who had moved abroad or passed away. The post office was second only to their church for being the focal point of the remote village's hub of activities. Some thoughtful person had decided to build the small wooden hut under the shade of several huge trees. It had no formal hours, though villagers would know it was opened for business when its shutters were held ajar by a pole. The hut was strategically situated on the dirt road where people gathered to get a ride into town, a two hour drive away. Whether or not people had plans to travel or mail to send and collect, it had proven to be an ideal place for the villagers to just hang out.

Her mother's back home stories usually referred to something she had seen or heard while hanging around the post office. It was a time before television and movie theaters, so people gathered there to be entertained, to catch up on the latest happenings in the village, or to simply be around others. Even though the informal communication network meant news traveled fast, people still felt the need to formally post birth and death notices, engagements, and wedding dates on the large wooded sign post that had been erected outside the post office entrance. Her mother had said it made everyone feel like royalty posting their news on the gates of Buckingham Palace.

On either side of the sign post were benches for people to sit and watch those who went in and out in silence. A few fruit and vegetable vendors had set up shop to sell their produce to the lingering crowd.

"Definitely, no chips or candy," her mother would tell the children since it was a time when people waited patiently for their meals to be cooked and served at specific times. On seeing her children's horrified faces, she would quickly tell them that buns and cakes were offered if someone had baked and wanted to share.

The bus stop, she told them, wasn't really a bus stop; it was just a clearing for cars or trucks to park safely a little way from the post office. It could be seen from the benches and it was where people sat while waiting for a ride into town. There were only a few people in the village who had cars or trucks, but they gladly gave rides to anyone who needed one. It wasn't unusual to see people packed tightly into cars or hanging off the back of a truck. More often than not, the drivers and their occupants would get out of their vehicles and join conversations outside the post office, not being in any particular rush to get anywhere. This informal community center was always a buzz of activity and was what Sister Georgina's mother liked to talk about the most. Her children loved to see her smile and the excitement she clearly felt as she shared her stories, so they loved hearing them no matter how many times they had heard it.

Every Saturday morning, she hurried to complete her chores and rush down to the post office. She had deliberately neglected to tell her children that apart from church on Sunday and bible class on Wednesday evening, it was one of the few occasions she would be granted permission to be away from her abusive caretakers. Silently watching the crowds milling around the post office in her usual spot underneath one of the large trees that shaded the area, she felt free and happy. It was a place where she could see and hear the postmaster clearly, but could remain hidden from any unscrupulous eyes that may report her obvious excitement to her caretakers. Some folks listened to the BBC world news on the battery operated radio that would be hanging from one of the poles that kept the shutters open. Others would play dominoes or just wait for the post office to officially close its doors whenever the last person left. It was then that the postmaster would come outside and read the letters that had been addressed to 'Everyone'.

In his strong Jamaican accent, the Postmaster would ask enthusiastically, "everybody ready?" After wandering around the grounds giving his salutations to the gathered crowd, he would bring out his large, regal chair from inside the post office hut and settle himself right next to the sign post. With no particular time frame or order, he would pick one of the letters and begin to read it out loud. Some weeks, there would be as many as ten, but on others there would be just a couple.

Mimicking the Postmaster, Sister Georgina's mother began, "this one's from Mistah Johnson. 'Membuh? …he usta live up yonduh by the

Chard's farm. He modah and fadah must get this letter aftuh we finish, eh." The children would light up and try to hold back their laughter at their mother's deepened foreign voice.

Information about the author's previous place of residence and their family were always provided, no matter how many times they had previously written. The Postmaster would read the letters slowly and deliberately, repeating any new phrases or names he knew the audience had not heard before or felt would be difficult for them to pronounce. Once read, the letters would be posted on the notice board; until family members or the natural elements, such as the sun, rain, or insects would remove them. Despite the bustling environment in which the letters were read, Sister Georgina's mother's imagination would whisk her off into the worlds of the United States, Canada, and England. Her dream to relocate (and she had no particular preference as to where), was never just an option. Relocation meant escape; escape from her daily abuses, poverty, and sense of hopelessness.

Not wanting to upset her children, Sister Georgina's mother had always purposely left out the painful details of her past. However, as the children got older, they somehow sensed its omission and could read between the lines of the sanitized version she told them. She had willingly shared that their grandmother had died while giving birth to her and as a result, never had any information about her father-their grandfather, or extended family background to share with them. Thoroughly ashamed of the scraps of information she did have, she chose instead to be tortured over the decades by keeping it all a secret and living in fear that someone in her family would find out. Sister Georgina's mother died with the knowledge obtained about her heritage desperately pieced together from overheard conversations from the villagers outside the post office or her abusive caretakers. Mainly, that her mother, just after celebrating her thirteenth birthday found out that she was pregnant. The identity of the father remained a mystery, although some people speculated that because of the close attention paid to her by the local Justice of the Peace and the headmaster of the village's small school, that one of them was believed to be the father. However, as both the men were married and had families, they had no intention of leaving; they seemed unusually relieved when she died from complications during childbirth.

The child (Sister Georgina's mother) was then given to a local family who was childless. Unfortunately, soon after she was sent to live with them, the family conceived, not once but twice. This meant Sister Georgina's mother was no longer wanted and unable to give her back to the hospital, the family raised her as an unpaid servant to care for their household and biological children. No matter how hard she tried over the years to push her traumatic childhood memories to the back of her mind, she could never forget the physical and emotional abuse she suffered at the hands of her caretakers. She used to think that the beatings from the biological children were the worse, as she was never able to hit them back. If she tried she would have been beaten twice as hard by the adults. Initially, she was thankful when the physical abuse decreased as she got older, but soon wished it would return, seeing it as more tolerable than the emotional abuse. Being told she was ugly, useless, and would amount to nothing, all day every day, eventually wore her down until she internalized it as being the truth. Most nights she would cry herself to sleep in her tiny, windowless shack at the end of the property next to the outhouse and pig pens.

Therefore, it was understandable that going to school was something Sister Georgina's mother disliked, believing that other people also saw her as being no good. As a result, she had to be forced to go to school most days. Her caretakers insisted that she go, primarily because they were afraid to face the negative inquiries from the community if she did not. However, they had made it clear that her first priority was taking care of their household. Subsequently, her earliest memories were not playing with dolls, but rather, finding the easiest way to remove mango stains from clothes, and helping the pigs give birth. She did learn to read and write, but never unlearned the belief that she was ugly, useless, and would amount to nothing.

It was faith that sustained and nurtured Sister Georgina's mother during this difficult part of her life and had the affect of establishing her lifelong commitment to the church. She found great comfort reading and re-reading the healing words of her small tattered bible, as well as finding the strength to question the behavior of those around her. From an early age, the little voice inside her had let her know she was being abused and before she even knew what the word meant, was aware of her caretakers' hypocrisy. She learned to laugh to keep from crying and looked on in amazement as her caretakers behaved like the most faithful servants during Sunday service, but on arriving home, they would return to their brutish behaviors, making her life hell.

Sister Georgina's mother swore that she would be the opposite when she had her own family. She dreamed of being a wife and mother, creating a warm nurturing household where everyone knew just how much they were loved and cherished. She would spoil her children and could never see herself raising her voice or treating them badly. She would teach them the knowledge of her God, letting them know how He could sustain and give them the strength to survive difficult times. She would teach them not to be hypocrites, and to be true servants of the Lord. Therefore, it was with such unshakable faith that Sister Georgina's mother waited patiently, trusting wholeheartedly that the Lord would provide the means and opportunity for her escape.

She felt justified in her belief when it finally came in the form of a youth exchange trip to Washington, D.C. when she was eighteen. She wasn't supposed to travel with the group, but when one of the biological children of her family got sick, she was the reluctant replacement to ensure that the family's pre-ordered barrel stuffed with electrical goods, household trinkets, and foods were brought back to the island as scheduled. While there, she met a fellow Jamaican, who had been cleaning the hostel where they had been staying. They got talking and she had felt comfortable telling him her story. Fortunately, for her, he had become a U.S. citizen and suggested marriage as a viable option as opposed to returning to their homeland. They were married on the day she was due to return to Jamaica with the barrel. The young couple settled in the suburbs of Prince George's County, Maryland and had eight children (Sister Georgina being the second).

Her mother had never realized that the letters read by the Postmaster never said anything about the struggles or hardships those abroad faced. As she looked back, she realized it would not have made much difference as no one would have believed it. Listening to the letters gave her and everyone else hope, but it was only after she arrived in the United States herself that she understood. Her weekly letters back home deliberately addressed to 'Everyone' (and not her caretakers) joined those in reporting only the positives. She did not want to worry those she had left behind. Why mention that both she and her husband needed to work seven days a week, twelve to fifteen hours most days, doing two or three menial jobs between them, just to keep a roof over their heads and food in their children's mouths? So, yes, she shared her excitement about seeing the Capitol, The White House, and all the other iconic monuments every time she went downtown, but left out that she saw all of this on her way to clean as many toilets as possible.

Happily, her mother had found warmth hidden in the back streets of Glenarden, Maryland at a small African-American church. She had connected because it reflected the values and characteristics of her church home in Jamaica that she missed so much. The intimate church community had not changed over the years and made it their mission to offer a sense of belonging, as well as a reprieve from the stresses of daily life to all who attended. People walking by could easily overlook the presence of the church because of its inconspicuous appearance. Mrs. Pritchard, the church's secretary would be kept busy on a Sunday morning if one of the many invited guests actually showed up and she would have to give them directions (despite their expensive navigation systems or Mapquest printouts). The struggle to find the church was caused because it was two miles from the main road and its modest premises were hardly distinguishable from the other residential houses on the street. It was only by careful examination that a few renovations identified its stature as a church. A small, inoperable bell tower had been added and a wooden ramp had been erected adjacent to the front steps to accommodate the wheelchair of Brother Barnabus about ten years ago. Despite the passing of time, he continued to be the only person who had used it ever since. The front and the back yards had been cleared and converted into prime parking spaces, for about six cars and the church's old, but trusted transportation van. Arriving less than an hour before Sunday service meant skillfully finding parking on the street, avoiding driveways and the annoyance of the neighbors. Potential church members never came back after their painful experiences of trying to find the church and then having the added horror of finding parking.

On entering the church for the first time, most people were surprised by its strange layout and badly constructed interior. They were initially met by the male and female bathroom doors on either side of the entrance that led into a corridor that had been poorly divided with the Pastor's office on the left and an administration office to the right. Although, furnished with a small desk and two chairs, neither office could comfortably hold more than one person at a time. Conversations inside the room with the door closed could be heard in all its glorious details by those who happen to be walking down the hall. As a result, Mrs. Pritchard could always be found cleaning the entrance way whenever the Pastor had meetings in his office. The church's sanctuary accommodated just twelve pews, six on either side of the room. The back row had been used for years as a storage shelf for Bibles, hymn books, choir robes, and musical instruments. On unusually busy Sundays, these items would quickly be moved into storage bins to accommodate welcomed visitors. At the front of the church hall, was a slightly raised platform that housed the mandatory lectern, chairs for the Pastor and officers, a portable organ, musicians, and the five member choir. The Pulpit was flanked by two tall, overbearing vases displaying large bouquets of plastic flowers that was proudly washed and replaced every other Saturday.

The basement was the pride and joy of the church and it was where most members spent their time. Despite its minuscule features, the kitchen prepared mouthwatering soul food that assured a full cafeteria. As a result, the kitchen was busy six days a week, serving lunch for its elderly members who could make it to the church between 11:30am and 2:00pm during the week, and of course, Sunday brunch. If the elderly or sick members ordered ahead of time, their meals would be delivered by the Pastor or a student on vacation from university. The leftover food would then be divided between the staff or groups that were meeting that day. Everyone in the church would therefore hover around the cafeteria, making sure their presence indicated their intention to have whatever was available, as well as to avoid being in one of the three windowless basement meeting rooms.

On Sundays, having no other options, each of the basement rooms were reserved for use by the Sunday school classes. Although, everyone knew the church facilities were not ideal, the yellowing poster advertising the building fund with its oversized thermometer that never moved, meant talk of new church premises was always a permanent agenda item on the leadership's bi-weekly meetings.

Over the years, the church membership had remained steady at around seventy-five. Fortunately, only about thirty people showed up each week for Sunday service, otherwise the church would have definitely had a major problem trying to accommodate its entire membership all at once. As a regular most Sundays for nearly thirty years, Sister Georgina's mother, a thin built, quiet, reserved woman, sat in her pew at the back of the church, in-between the hymn books and choir robes. No one ever asked her why she appeared most comfortable sitting amongst the storage and even if they did, she probably didn't know why herself. If she had chosen to think about it, she most likely would have concluded that it reminded her of sitting quietly underneath the trees by the post office in Jamaica all those years ago. On a deeper examination, it may have also suggested that she had nothing of value to contribute to the church's affairs, preferring instead to be a passive observer. It may have also indicated that she had never shaken the habit of keeping away from people, believing as she did when she was a child that she was ugly and that the smell of the pigpen or outhouse still lingered on her despite the passing of time.

Whatever the case, Sister Georgina's mother subsequently limited her contributions to tithing, but made sure that her children were active in church life. Looking back, Sister Georgina remembered fondly the Sunday morning ritual that made sure everyone was fed, appropriately dressed, and out the door to arrive on time for the eleven o'clock service. To his credit, her father helped the process along with a sarcastic grin that did not hide his pure delight at the thought of being in the house alone for a couple of hours. As a non-believer, he accepted his wife's faith and thought it would be good for the children. Even after her death, he arranged for the church's secretary to collect them on her way to church until they were old enough to get there themselves. So, this Sunday morning routine for the majority of her childhood had unquestionably shaped her adult life in ways she could never have imagined.

Sister Georgina's faith had evolved slowly alongside her developmental milestones. In the beginning, it was from a sense of obligation, then, acceptance, and eventually, belief. As a child, she grew up surrounded by people giving testimonies all the time. She had simply copied their actions; when they knelt, she knelt, when they bowed, she bowed. The praise and positive reinforcement she received as a result, spurred on her mimicry. Together, with the church routine that seemed to be set in stone, she was provided with a great sense of permanence and order in her young life. She loved the seasonal events. Christmas was her favorite time of year, of course, with Harvest and Easter festivals being tied for second place. Running a close third, was the July 4th barbecue with its added bonus of fundraising activities to raise money for new church premises (and despite its reoccurring place on the church's calendar over the years, no one seemed to question what happened to the money when the new premises never materialized). At first, Sister Georgina loved participating- the face painting, the games, hook the fish was her forte, and as expected, sampling the vast array of food. But, as she got older, she embraced the added responsibility of running her own stall and eventually, the entire event.

Similarly, attending Sunday school began as a chore that had to be endured until she understood the meaning of the Bible stories and Proverbs. She enjoyed hearing about the mystical events of the Old Testament and being able to bring them to life in front of the church regardless of how badly the youth group had performed. Being a part of the church family made her feel safe. Seeing familiar faces every Sunday was a blessing and even though there was little contact with other members during the week, it was still comforting to know that she belonged.

Sister Georgina took pleasure in knowing the subtle nuances of the church membership and that her pew was reserved every Sunday. Everything about her church home made sense to her soul, from the passionate, but strained vocals of the choir, the calming poetry of the psalms that was read so poorly by an honored member, to the attention seeking, interfering, unscrupulous Pastor who loved to know the gossip on each member and kept the church's finances tightly under his lock and key. She felt they trusted and appreciated her growing leadership skills and talent at organizing. But, it was Sister Georgina's special talent for teaching that was spotted at an early age and fervently encouraged by both her biological and church families. She was watched with anticipation as she taught her dolls, unaware that her childish actions had secured her place as a future Sunday school teacher before turning the age of seven. Everyone just knew Sister Georgina was going to be a teacher and by the time she was twelve, she knew it as well.

However, first and foremost, serving her church family was her priority. She knew she could make a real difference in the church and unlike many who had come and gone over the years, she wanted to be one of the core people who ensured continuity for the church community. It had played such an important part in cementing her life in the faith, she wanted to do the same for the next generation of young leaders in the church. She was genuinely appreciative, but expectant of the honor when it was inevitably granted to her.

Being in leadership so early fueled Sister Georgina's confidence and she was comfortable standing in front of the Sunday school week after week. She relished being thought of so highly by the elders in her church and her mother, who she felt was watching from her heavenly vantage point. She soon earned a reputation for putting a modern spin on church doctrine. Sister Georgina's passion connected with the youth, providing them with a deeper level of understanding about scripture. It seemed to strengthen their resolve to lead more spiritual lives.

Unfortunately, Sister Georgina was not so welcomed when she stepped out into the wider community to teach the Good News to non-believers. The first couple of presentations, she remembered being ridiculed when she tried to talk about the wonders of sacrificing and abstinence. However, as the number of presentations to youth groups and schools increased, so did her oratory skills. It wasn't long before her confidence gave way to what some of her peers described as "arrogance," "self-righteousness," or "having a 'holier-than-thou' attitude." Ignoring such feedback, Sister Georgina didn't care what they called her. She knew the Truth and could not be shifted from it. She was definitely not going to pander to their ignorance. She was going to tell them the Truth whether they wanted to hear it or not. Saving souls was not pretty and certainly not for the faint of heart.

In order to stress the importance of her point, Sister Georgina adopted what she believed to be an outwardly manifestation of her faith. She wanted people to look at her and see a reflection of what it meant to be a Godly woman. She had never been described as being attractive; on the contrary, the polite amongst the church membership would use words such as "practical," "homebody," or "down to earth" to describe her physical attributes. Those who were not so polite described her as being "heavy," "big-boned," and "large." True, she loved her food, never missing one of Mrs. Cartwright's brunches but reasoned that her dresses (never trousers), devoid of color, pattern, or form worn with her flat shoes positively represented her virtuous attitude and that she was comfortable with her size twenty-six frame.

This outlook also influenced how she kept her hair and as a teenager made the decision to keep it as God intended. Therefore, Sister Georgina was never interested in the latest hair crazes, such as the Jerri curl or perms. Her natural hair was often divided into two large cornrows only being redone when the braids were barely indistinguishable from the new growth. On special occasions, she would make the effort and have it pressed and styled. Not being accustomed to the detailed intricacy of managing her own hair, the professional style would soon become evidence of her lack of self-care. Make-up was definitely not a consideration. A touch of Vaseline on her lips was the most she would do to enhance her external beauty (which was eventually replaced by lip balm when that became vogue). As natural as natural can be was her motto and she felt powerful as a result.

An example of Sister Georgina's powerful tough love approach was demonstrated at a youth club event. It was the Eighties and among her many titles, she was also a peer mentor. Feeling empowered by the popularity of Nancy Regan's signature catchphrase, Sister Georgina, without even asking her name, let alone anything about her circumstance, arrogantly told the sixteen-year-old who had come up to her after the presentation, *"you should have just said 'no.'"*

The Friday night youth event had been billed as an opportunity to talk openly about the stresses and pressures of life as a teenager. The organizers headlined the event with local peer mentors to avoid the accusation of being yet "another Christian event" to preach to the unconverted with the added incentives of free food and the opportunity to listen to the latest street music. Even with the innovative marketing efforts by the organizers, it was the usual suspects who turned up along with just a handful of inquisitive participants. The rows of chairs for the expected crowd was hurriedly turned into an intimate semi-circle. Similarly, the volunteers who had prepared the food sent for take-out containers to make sure nothing went to waste at the end of the evening.

Before taking their seats, participants were asked to anonymously write a topic for discussion on a note card with the recommendation it should be as controversial as possible to ensure a fiery discussion. The note cards were then placed in an envelope to be dramatically opened and pulled out one by one by the moderator during the evening. However, despite the promotional material, food, music, and friendly seating design giving the impression that an open discussion was welcomed, it quickly became evident that any hint of opposition to church doctrine would be suppressed. Consequently, with nothing diverting from the promoters desired path, the scheduled three hours flew by uneventfully and the youth filed out of the hall after collecting their pre-packed leftovers from the kitchen. Sister Georgina, one of the listed peer mentors, had regretted not having time to delve into her speech on the benefits of celibacy, but had reassured herself that there would be another opportunity soon. That opportunity arrived much sooner than she had anticipated when one of the unknown participants asked to pray with her as she was preparing to help with the cleanup.

"Of course," Sister Georgina replied instinctively. "Is there anything you would like to pray for?"

"Yes. I haven't told anybody, but I'm pregnant and scared. I don't know what to do," the girl replied with tears of relief streaming down her face.

Sister Georgina did not hide her immediate disgust. She shook her head from side to side and sighed deeply. With no empathy towards the girl's request for help, Sister Georgina told her, "you don't *look* pregnant. Are you sure?"

"Yes, I got the results from the doctor last week. He said I'm about six weeks," was the defensive reply.

"I'm sorry we did not get a chance to talk about this topic during the meeting, I would have liked the group to hear about the appalling statistics on teen pregnancies. You are now one of those numbers we're trying to avoid." Sister Georgina looked around the hall as if she was desperate to share this revelation with anyone who just happened to be nearby. But, as the other peer mentors were busy at the back of the hall cleaning up and putting away the chairs, she realized she had to deal with this emotionally charged situation herself. So, she took a deep breath, reminded herself that she had the Truth and that her words were sanctioned by the Lord. She would be the example of Christian mercy that her mother had taught her. She would counsel this young girl and help her see the error of her ways. Sister Georgina imagined she had an audience and launched into her prepared speech on celibacy:

"You have to strengthen your resolve. You should have kept yourself pure for your husband. Who would want to make a commitment to *you* now?" Sister Georgina asked harshly.

"I know, I know," was the timid teenager's response. She was ashamed of her predicament and seemed to expect the verbal attack and adopted the posture of a lamb awaiting its slaughter, lowering her head and fidgeting with the zipper on her hoodie.

"Watch my mouth... *NOOOOO...*" Sister Georgina said condescendingly. "Now, you've given away your most precious gift to some fool and you can never get it back. What are you going to do now that you are spoiled goods?" Sister Georgina asked, not realizing the pain her words were causing. On the contrary, she saw herself as being the bearer of God's Truth and it was her spiritual obligation to let this young girl know her failings. She knew others in her church family had described her as being *too rigid*, but she had reasoned there was no point in beating around the bush with important issues. It was what it was; a sin. So why sugar coat that? Besides, Sister Georgina would sleep well after such 'counseling' sessions where she would conclude that she had saved a non-believer. What more evidence was there that she was doing the work of the Lord?

"I don't know," was the trembling reply.

"A mutually faithful, monogamous relationship in the context of marriage will keep you safe, not only from an unwanted pregnancy, but from sexually transmitted diseases. I talk on this topic nearly every week at the youth group, why didn't you attend?"

"I don't know," was the response from the sixteen year old, accompanied by an uncomfortable shrug of her shoulders, never raising her eyes to meet Sister Georgina's scowling gaze.

By now, the young teenager had learned that there was no point in saying anything more to Sister Georgina and deeply regretted asking her to pray in the first place. The girl had wrongly assumed from her outward appearance that Sister Georgina would offer some much needed sympathy and understanding. The young girl decided to appease Sister Georgina instead by giving the obligatory head nod of acknowledgment of her wrongdoing and tried to hide the tears that fell freely down her face. But, because Sister Georgina was in full-stride, she continued unabatedly, and did not notice the young girl's demeanor becoming more and more distressed.

"I am so happy to wait for the Lord to bless me with a husband who will appreciate the value of my virginity," Sister Georgina said without pausing for breath, unaware she was continuing to pour salt on the wound of this girl trying to seek help.

She went on, "yes, of course it's difficult, we're human after all, but when we are strong, we become better servants of the Lord. God tests his faithful, he can't use you if you are weak. I've had no intention of casually giving some random man my most precious gift to be tossed away like garbage when I am no longer the flavor of the month. I feel so blessed to have the knowledge of God's Truth so young, and so should you. So, *why* would you lower yourself to be used as an instrument of stress relief for some Godless man to defile the act of lovemaking? You should remember the Lord always. He should be front and center of your thoughts so that when situations like this arise and you are tempted, you can brush them off. Remember, as a servant of the Lord you are always in obedience to his Truth. Your virginity is a gift to a future husband and it means he has no choice but to respect your commitment to the Lord and value and appreciate your worth. I have no intention of giving mine away." And trying to prove her point, she finally asked, "is the father going to take care of you?"

"No," the teen whispered ashamed.

Having not realized that she was not comforting her, Sister Georgina was unrelenting and continued sarcastically, "see, you can say 'no' when you want to." Interpreting the girl's cowering demeanor as testimony to the effectiveness of her counsel, Sister Georgina could no longer hide her pride at being disciplined in following God's word. Opportunities such as this fed her soul, making her feel superior, together, and in control. She rarely received positive feedback from others and had done such a good job of pretending that it did not bother her, both her church and family members assumed she didn't need it. As a result, she figuratively gave herself a self-congratulatory pat on her back. With her point proven, Sister Georgina made her pronouncement: "I think you should tell your parents and let them take the young man and his family to court to make sure he pays support for the child. He should not be allowed to get away without being responsible at all."

Sister Georgina felt proud of herself for not giving in to the urge to wag her finger at this young sinner, but the nodding of her head in disapproval seemed to have the same effect. Sister Georgina looked over the young girl's shoulder and saw that the hall was now empty of its guests. The other peer mentors who had finished cleaning up and stacking the chairs, annoyingly stood around in their coats, watching as one harassed mentor frantically searched his pockets and the surrounding area for the keys to lock the kitchen. Realizing that the keys were in her pocket, Sister Georgina knew she needed to go over and put him out of his misery. *Besides,* she thought to herself, *there is nothing else to say.* She just felt sorry for her. Her life was ruined and she did not hold out much hope for the child. As a believing youth, Sister Georgina saw her tough love approach as being necessary. Therefore, it was her responsibility to let this teenager know that she had sinned and needed to repent. It was up to her what she did next.

The girl mumbled something under her breath, which Sister Georgina chose to ignore by saying they were getting ready to close the hall. Even though her thoughts were on resolving the missing key situation, she did not forget the initial request for a prayer. She held the young girl's moist hands and quickly asked for guidance and strength to navigate the predicament she faced. She also thought it was appropriate to ask for forgiveness of her sin. The young girl seemed relieved when the brief prayer was finally over and was able to walk away making it clear that her burden had not been lifted.

So ungrateful, Sister Georgina thought as she sensed the rejection of her assistance. *I would rather die, than have a child out of wedlock,* Sister Georgina thought to herself. She knew it was not the Christian attitude to take, but she wanted to relish in the fact that her life was under control. Her life would be a testimony that God's way is the only way. But, being honest, she was also pleased when the young girl finally walked away. She turned her attention to the drama unfolding at the back of the room. As she joined the other youth leaders, her feelings about the young girl were quickly overshadowed by their relief at finding the keys and celebrating the evening's success.

It was not until Sister Georgina was tucked in bed that night did she allow herself to process the encounter with the teenager. *Would God be pleased with her representation of Him? Did she really help? Was there anything else that she could have said?* She allowed her self-evaluation to settle on the fact that she should have provided some literature on where the girl could go for additional support. Even though she was generally satisfied with her efforts, despite the passing of time, for some unknown reason she was never able to forget the incident. Ever so often, her thoughts would go back to the young, pregnant teen and she wondered what happened to her.

However, that night she consciously chose not to delve any deeper for fear of figuring out that her unease may possibly be rooted in jealousy. She had been blasé and casual when she described the benefits of being celibate to this teen, but in reality, it was personally becoming more and more of a challenge to manage her own growing sexual desires. Regardless of the end result of the young teen's actions, she had sex and Sister Georgina hadn't. She had found herself wondering what it would be like to be in the arms of someone and to have them touch her body lovingly. This teenager knew what it was like, so was Sister Georgina angry? Envious? She wasn't sure, but knew it made her realize that her physical needs were not being met. Thinking about her sexuality was doing her no good, so she quickly turned on the radio to drown out her rebellious thoughts and allowed the soothing gospel music to help her drift to sleep.

Her precautions did not stop the unconscious thoughts from recalling her feelings as a child when she relished the compliments of her elders when she covered her eyes or ears without being prompted when something inappropriate was being shown or discussed. Although she remained curious, from an early age, she had learned not to concern herself with such activities until she was lawfully married. She wholeheartedly respected the sense of mystery surrounding the unspeakable physical activities between a husband and wife, but as her knowledge of scripture grew, she was no longer satisfied with the conservative comments from the elders that there would be plenty of time to think about such things when she married. In fact, it created more of a problem since she had never seen her father show her mother any physical affection even though they had been married for nearly thirty years. Her siblings had once forced their father to kiss their mother on the cheek one Valentine's Day. This staged display of affection left a bitter taste in her mouth and she had vowed that things would be different when she was married.

At sixteen, she had accidentally come across some of her father's pornographic magazines. The shock had left her standing in disbelief for some time as she viewed the naked bodies sprawled over the pages, seemingly without any regret or shame. What was even more shocking was seeing the male genitals for the first time. She could not deny that it sparked a curiosity that meant she deliberately went back to review the material several times, before one of her brothers (who had also found its hiding place) had been caught by their father and he moved them to somewhere more secure. The offensive images resonated with Sister Georgina and replayed over and over in her mind for many years afterwards. She allowed herself to have a superficial intellectual discussion about the people in the magazine and how sad it was that they had displayed their bodies in such a degrading and ungodly manner. She had so many questions that she concluded it would be best to deliberately avoid the topic altogether and deny that she enjoyed seeing the bodies and the physical arousal she felt as a result.

At eighteen, she felt physically mature and ready to marry and experience the joys of an intimate relationship. However, she felt her limited knowledge was not enough to lay the foundation for a healthy sexual relationship. Up to that moment, her knowledge had been primarily deciphered from the fast forwarded inappropriate scenes on television. Her father had not given his permission for Sister Georgina and her siblings to attend the sex education classes offered by the school, reasoning that it would have been what her deceased mother would have wanted. Sister Georgina, having assumed the role vacated by her mother as her father never remarried, had agreed that the decision was the best one for her and her siblings. Even though Sister Georgina's formal education on these matters had been reduced to the school nurse informing her about her periods with the passing comment, "you can now have babies," her informal sex education was a different matter, altogether. While trying her best to present an image of disinterest, she would find herself groveling for snippets of information about the sexual exploits of her non-believing peers. Although she agreed that sex education should not be taught in school, she realized it was pitiful that her first glimpse of lovemaking was when she had hidden behind the couch as her father watched a documentary on the miracle of childbirth. It was the final straw because she had been left with so many questions and no one to ask. *It's the eighties, surely I should know the basics,* she reasoned to herself. Besides, she had read somewhere about problems that can be caused when there is a mismatch between a husband and a wife on the physical side of marriage. Therefore, she concluded that the little theoretical information she had, would not be sufficient to please her future husband.

Drawing on her faith as a guide and motivated to be the best future wife she could be, Sister Georgina decided to face her lack of sexual knowledge head on. Seeing mastery of her urges as a test, she was determined to pass with flying colors and show God that she truly was a shining example for others. By adopting her usual military approach to problem-solving, she felt she could objectively understand the process, especially why people make such a fuss about it, as well as how to handle the increasing sensations that choose to take up residence in certain intimate areas of her body. Her solution was to actively research the subject in "acceptable" Christian books, magazines, and videos. Her hard work paid off and just before her eighteenth birthday and graduating from high school, she completed her revolutionary curriculum on abstinence that glorified the Lord. When she made the original proposal to develop and deliver the classes, the Pastor and church elders immediately denied her request. She argued that without such theoretical knowledge it would drive young people into the life of non-believers simply out of curiosity. Her spirited argument about the need for young people to know the joys of Christian intimacy within the confines of a lawful relationship (and of course between a man and a woman) eventually won them over. It also secured her leadership role within her church home and the neighboring Christian community. After her curriculum was reviewed and cleared, she found herself with full classes on a regular basis. The Pastor soon forgot his initial objections and cemented her success by proudly proclaiming the idea as his own and offering her classes to other churches in the area for a nominal fee.

The positive feedback from the church community for Sister Georgina's efforts was rewarding, but the biggest relief was discovering that her sexual feelings were a normal aspect of human development. Her research made it clear that when married, such feelings should be encouraged and enjoyed. But, if single, the opposite applied and such feelings should be discouraged, as giving into the physical demands of the flesh was a clear sign of weakness. A single person's celibacy was a bold statement of their faith; a true sign of their commitment to God. Exercise, fasting, prayer, and keeping pure thoughts should keep such feelings in check and stop them from engaging in the ungodly practice of masturbation. For Sister Georgina, it meant she channeled her excess energies and frustrations into her schoolwork, Sunday school classes, presentations and workshops, and as a very last resort, exercise. She comforted herself with thoughts that God would be sending her husband soon as reward for her unquestioning submission.

When her fellow high school classmates began falling pregnant, became addicted to drugs, alcohol, and other negatives, it reinforced her view that the church's doctrine would keep her safe from harm. She comforted herself with the knowledge that God's way is The Way. No negotiation, no compromise. Sister Georgina had no doubts that when the time was right, she would be rewarded royally with a lawful loving relationship. This knowledge enabled her to be patient despite all the pressures from her non-believing peers, television, and movies that glorified the virtues of a Sodom and Gomorrah lifestyle. She would put up with the loneliness, the sexual frustrations, the sneers and taunts from those who didn't understand. She was not ashamed of her faith. On the contrary, she was proud and believed that her actions, no matter how small, would actually contribute to making the world a better place, as well as secure her place in the hereafter.

———— ～ ————

As Sister Georgina remained standing in the blue, plastic wadding pool shivering in her wet clothes and towels that were draped over her shoulders, she felt at peace. Her baptism was official entry into God's kingdom, so, yes, she was proud to be publicly declaring her faith. She wanted the world to know that she was a committed believer of Truth. She could make sense of the world she had been born into and escape a life of damnation in the hereafter. She did not have any desire to face the things she did not understand. Why should she? All she had to do was follow His will, without question or doubt. She would then be blessed with life and life in abundance. Wanting the moment to last forever, she was going to make the most of every second of the baptismal experience, so obviously she continued to refuse offers of help to change into dry clothes or make her way to the basement for Sunday brunch. So what the church hall was now emptied of its participants, and that the ushers were nearly finished cleaning up around her, stacking the bibles and hymn books on the last pew at back of the hall. She was happy, listening blissfully to the Pastor serenading the congregation as they ate their bunch and through her tears of joy, smiled and said a silent prayer of thanks.

37

The Righteous Sin

Chapter Two
Be Careful What You Wish For

As Sister Georgina climbed the few stairs to the stage to accept her degree and shake the hand of the university's President, she looked out at the audience. She could see hands waving frantically in the distance and the flashes of cameras as they took pictures with their telescopic lens. She really was pleased that the Pastor had gotten members of her church family to come and see her graduate. She had planned to organize a graduation celebration for herself, but knowing that only her aging father and possibly a couple of her siblings would attend, she had concluded it wasn't worth the trouble to mark the occasion. Plus, she definitely wanted to avoid advertising the fact that she didn't have many people in her corner. So, not caring how they managed to get more than the allocated amount of tickets or when they erupted with screams and shouts when her name was called, Sister Georgina was secretly delighted to be so publicly acknowledged. It made her feel special and normal after four years of being miserable, isolated and alone. However, as the audience had been asked to remain quiet until all the graduates had received their awards, she was embarrassed by their *ghetto* performance and planned to let them all know as soon as she got the chance at the formal luncheon afterwards.

Unknown to Sister Georgina, the Pastor's first few attempts to garner members for the trip had been met with general disinterest. Sister Georgina's reputation for having 'strange ways' meant most members did their best to avoid her when she was in town. Before she had gone off to college, interaction with Sister Georgina was usually limited to a polite kiss on the cheek or an energetic handshake after the Sunday morning service. So the thought of traveling miles in the church's uncomfortable and unreliable van to see her walk across the stage in her graduation regalia was not appealing, even to the most dedicated member. But, once the Pastor had ingeniously added the stop at the factory outlet shopping mall on Route 50, all seats were soon taken.

Sister Georgina quickly collected her diploma, smiled appreciatively for the camera, and then joined her fellow graduates in the reserved seats at the front of the auditorium. The jovial mood of her classmates in the row was accompanied by smiles, tears, and shouts of joy. Nothing could dampen their spirits today.

"Congratulations," the person sitting next to her said predictably as she took her seat. Sister Georgia had seen her around campus, but had never really engaged in a conversation until now. "Can you believe it? I can't. It's finally over, yeah!" The new graduate exclaimed as she waved her degree ecstatically in the air. Sister Georgina smiled charitably and returned the obligatory greetings.

"No more papers, no more professors, no more midterms or finals…but best of all, we can finally get on with the rest of our lives," she continued. "I've been waiting for this day to arrive ever since I started school," she laughed. "I am so glad it's finally here, but I have to admit, despite all the work, I did have a fucking good time!"

Sister Georgina drowned out the profanity, but agreed with the sentiments of what she said and nodded in agreement. After four years, she learned it wasn't worth stressing over the small stuff. Instead, she allowed herself to think about her own experiences and the life lessons she was taking away from her time as a student at Secus College.

There had been no doubt that Sister Georgina would graduate with honors from high school and go on to train as a teacher. It had been as predictable as the sun rising the next day. On paper, she was an exceptional student, achieving straight A's in all her subjects. But even with a 4.5 GPA, not one of the teachers would write her a letter of recommendation for her college applications. They felt she lacked the professional skills and would not be a suitable candidate for teacher training. Undeterred, Sister Georgina had circumvented the process by writing the recommendation herself and had the Pastor sign it. She knew they never liked her because she would constantly highlight their spelling and grammatical mistakes, demand references for their class lectures, or ask them to justify their use of outdated videos.

There was no doubt in her mind that the real reason no one wanted to provide a reference was the dossier she had sent to the board of education with copies to several local news stations at the end of her last semester. It included a summary report, spreadsheet, detailed descriptions of the infractions, pictures, and even personal statements from a few fellow students who did not know they were being recorded. Believing that she had a solid case, she named names; accusing teachers of pandering to students' reluctance to do the necessary academic work to graduate and the unethically circulated copies of exams with highlighted answers and cheat sheets around the lunchroom on a regular basis. She then personally accused the Principal of overlooking this grave issue because of her quest to achieve positive instructor evaluations and passing test scores to be in the running for the Administrator of the Year award, that had the added bonus of seeing the winner's compensation increased.

Sister Georgina had gone to the trouble of obtaining, directly from the board of education, an original copy of the twelfth grade curriculum and compared it to the "watered down" version that had been on display at her school for the few interested parents who chose to review it. She highlighted in her report where white-out had been used in the school's copy to omit classics texts, such as Shakespeare's _Hamlet_ and _Othello_, Toni Morrison's _The Bluest Eye_, and Richard Wright's _The Native Son_. She argued it was because the teachers did not know nor did they care to find out how they contributed to the body of knowledge in English Literature.

The clandestine statements from students had described their pre-calculus class where the teacher had shown pictures of his recent vacation to Europe, rather than preparing them for their finals. With their high school graduation a sure thing, her senior class had gotten used to just turning up at school and being given an A grade for their efforts. Sister Georgina felt humiliated, being the only one to prepare and complete mandated assignments and homework. Convinced that she was not motivated by anger, rather by the goal of raising teaching standards, she had taken it upon herself to complain, firstly, within the school, but after six weeks of inaction by the Principal, she wrote to the education board, and sent copies to the local newspapers and television stations to ensure a response. Like preaching to the unconverted, she knew she would make enemies, but Truth was Truth.

In her obsessive drive for justice, together with her youthfulness, she was totally oblivious to both the short and long-term consequences of her decision to shine the light on this wrong. The unwelcomed spotlight came at a cost for all. A few political groups heard about the story and used it to further their own agendas by holding press conferences on the lawn in front of the school. It wasn't long before students realized that waving annoyingly behind reporters on live television was no compensation for actually having to do the required work in order to graduate. For teachers, they had to face journalists and photographers who were more interested in searching for scandal in their personal lives, rather than the original story itself. The board of education faced the challenge of sorting out the community accolades for bending the rules of an oppressive educational system to give inner city students a chance at success, while at the same time, faced parental criticism for not preparing students for life in the real world. For Sister Georgina, it was the inevitable isolation. Everyone wanted her gone as soon as possible.

Always ready for the challenge, Sister Georgina walked around the school with her head held high. She would not be intimidated by the balled up bits of paper that were thrown at her during class or having to retreat to the staff lounge to avoid not having somewhere to sit during lunch. Therefore, in order to make the last few months of her school career tolerable for everyone, the Principal agreed that Sister Georgina could work from home and submit assignments by regular mail or via the new *facsimile machine*. On the odd occasions she had to go into school, she would be escorted everywhere by the guard for her own protection. She was extremely happy about this decision because it meant she did not have to get involved in any of the senior class activities, especially the dilemma of not having a prom date.

Without the drama of the last few months in high school, Sister Georgina turned her complete attention to choosing the right college to pursue her undergraduate degree. She knew she needed some independence, but didn't want to stray too far from the safety of both her biological and church families. Therefore, she quickly ruled out colleges outside of Maryland. She did however, want the challenge to experience life outside her traditional African-American and Christian comfort zones, so she ruled out historically black colleges as well as Christian schools. Attending such colleges, she rationalized, would be too easy. *The Lord tests his faithful*, she proclaimed, feeling secure in her racial identity and religious beliefs. Finalizing her college choices meant confronting this lack of experience of the non-believing and Caucasian dominated environments. 100 percent of her high school graduating class was African-American. Probably 85-95 percent of where she lived was African-American and the rest was made up of the Hispanic, African, or Caribbean communities. 99.9 percent of her church population had been African-American. The odd few white members of the congregation had somehow been connected to an African-American family. In all of her years at the church, she had never known a white visitor to wander in for Sunday service by chance (but neither had any other racial group for that matter, including her own). Trusting that an out-of-the-box college experience would ultimately help her be a more effective to her future students and church community, Sister Georgina rejected offers from large and more prestigious schools, along with their full scholarships, choosing instead to attend a small, private, liberal arts college on the other side of the Chesapeake Bay Bridge.

Like her church home, her university choice reflected the homely atmosphere she loved so much. The campus was small and intimate, with enrollment being capped at 1,500 students. The average tours for prospective students would last about an hour, only because many of the tour guides had perfected jokes and polite small talk that added on an extra thirty minutes. The library had a good relationship with the University of Maryland, primarily to give the private college some semblance of academic credibility, even though they were about three hours away from the College Park campus in good traffic. Unfortunately, students still had to wait weeks before their ordered books arrived via the interlibrary loan services.

The student lounge was functional, but limited to the same few organizers who planned events around their individual schedules. They seemed to have settled on offering movies every day of the week to have some sort of activity in the building. Sister Georgina's tour guide had joked that movie nights were a poor substitute for the lack of real entertainment on campus. But on seeing Sister Georgina's stern and confused response, the guide remained professional and recited the school's no tolerance policy for alcohol or drugs on campus. Sister Georgina had decided on this college because she felt the quiet and gentle composure of the school complemented her personality and work ethics. She wanted to stand out, but then again, she didn't. At Secus College, she did not have to worry about being lost in a sea of competing students. She could excel and make a name for herself, like she did with her abstinence classes. Another attraction was the college's "non-Christian-Christian" values. Depending on a prospective student's beliefs indicated on their application form, the admissions office would advise the tour guide to emphasize one way or the other. For Sister Georgina, the college provided the best of both worlds. She would be tested by being amongst non-believers on a predominately Caucasian campus, while having the security of being at a college with albeit, unspoken, Christian values and making the two hour trip back to her community if and when she needed cultural support.

On her bedroom wall, the college strategic planning notice board had become redundant. It had laid out her options in neat rows and clearly indicated why Secus College was the clear winner. However, what was omitted from the board was Sister's Georgina's belief that Secus College was the kind of school her future husband would also choose to attend. Like the obligatory missionary service for male members of the Mormon religion, Sister Georgina believed Secus College would be an ideal place for her future husband to develop positive life-long skills in a safe, nurturing environment. It was accessible to both the D.C. Metropolitan and Baltimore City African-American men. She reasoned that if they did not want to attend Howard, Morgan State, or the University of Maryland, they would find Secus a suitable alternative. He would be near home (because she knew he would have both family and community responsibilities and needed to be accessible). In addition, she felt that the campus would provide some level of independence, so he could develop decision making skills that would make him a better husband and father.

Filled with great anticipation and hope, Sister Georgina arrived on campus with high expectations. She left behind her dearly loved church community who had equally looked forward to the day when she would be sent off with a blessing from the Pastor. Despite her outward, *I'm over it* attitude in regards to her high school experience, inwardly, she was hurt and angry, desperately hoping that college life would be different. She wanted a fresh start; to leave behind unpleasant high school memories. Happy to be awarded valedictorian of her class, she knew it was because her academic work had warranted the prize, but also because the administration knew she would have filed a law suit if they didn't give her the honor. She couldn't hide her disappointment, when the Principal awarded the senior class prize, with its large monetary award to a student who barely made it to class each day. She felt insulted that her passion, hard work, and extra curricular contributions had been lost on them, but that was all behind her. She looked forward to life at Secus College and enjoyed being surrounded by like-minded students. They would help her grow to be the best representation of her Lord and Savior. She was excited and filled with hope as she set out to start her new life.

It wasn't long before she had settled into campus life, focusing on completing her coursework with good grades, retaining her virginity, and looking forward to marriage at the end of her four years. Sister Georgina knew she was a good student and was determined to let her peers and professors know this tidbit of information as quickly as possible. She would arrive to class on time, would do all the assigned readings, and would normally be the first to volunteer for the mandatory overhead projector presentations. She was always the last person in the library and her papers were handed in at least a week before they were due. Therefore, it was no shock when her grades consistently reflected her above average efforts. However, unlike her church family, who had tolerated her idiosyncrasies and overbearing attitude over the years, largely due to their sense of religious duty and respect for her deceased mother, her colleagues at Secus College felt no such obligation. They unanimously seemed to reach the same conclusion after their first encounter with Sister Georgina; she was someone to avoid.

Not wanting to leave anything to chance, Sister Georgina practiced her campus introductory speech in the mirror for months before the day finally arrived when she would put it into practice. She wanted any potential friend to know her academic and personal qualities so they could appreciate and value her commitment to following the word of the Lord.

"Hello, it's good to meet you. My name is Sister Georgina. Please feel free to use the Sister, it's just a term of endearment we use at my church and I would prefer it if you called me that as well. It's also a constant reminder for me that I am striving to be a good servant of the Lord. I am an Education major and plan to become a High School teacher. Most likely I will specialize in special education for my graduate program. I graduated valedictorian of my High School class where there were 1,443 students, so it was quite an honor. While at Secus I plan to make the Dean's list every year."

With this prepared introduction memorized, Sister Georgina felt she was making every effort to be sociable by being proactive and introducing herself to people she met around campus. She had carefully questioned her strategy, having realized that it was a contradiction, to want to be personally challenged by being in a non-Christian environment, and then go out of her way to avoid students who did not share her religious beliefs. However, she quickly rationalized that being upfront and honest was the best approach. Concluding it would be best to eliminate from her social group those students who did not recognize and agree with her Christian perspective. What she had not counted on was being eliminated from the social grouping of others. It didn't take long for her fellow students to realize that all her conversations consisted of reiterating her unwavering commitment to the Lord or that their unrighteous behaviors would lead them into eternal damnation, she soon found herself pretty isolated on campus.

With no-one to provide honest feedback, Sister Georgina did not realize how she came across to others. Together, with the fact that she had never prepared questions to ask someone about *their* interests meant she would unintentionally steer the conversation back to her agenda. As a teenager, she reasoned that as she had the Truth only needed to listen to others to interject that Truth. Why should she listen to what they had to say if she could see from their appearance, actions, and comments that it would be in opposition to the Truth? Why should she subject herself to such nonsense? The students at Secus however, did not consider it their business to provide such therapeutic feedback to Sister Georgina and chose, instead, to walk away whenever they saw her coming in their direction. Upset by not being able to make friends as she had hoped, she concluded it was their loss- not hers- and justified the lack of friends with the same argument that had gotten her through high school: *being a follower of the Lord is difficult and not many are chosen to walk this path*, comforting herself with the knowledge that she was blessed to know the Truth. With little else to focus on, Sister Georgina did what she did best and focused on her academic work. Unknown to her peers, her academic success kept her mind occupied and off any unwelcomed twinges or more importantly, thoughts of why her Lord and Savior had not yet provided the promised husband.

The hope of finding a husband at Secus College had faded on day one, when only fifteen African-American men joined the freshman class. None of them proved to have any potential as a husband, as they were either openly gay, interested only in white women, or were already in committed relationships. Contact with them was limited to the culturally expected head nod of acknowledgment when they passed each other on campus. Things did not get better over the years, with the same low numbers of brothers enrolling. She was really angry with herself for getting it so wrong. But putting on a brave face, she accepted the situation and decided to make the most of her experience at college.

She would leave with her degree in hand. She was young and had plenty of time. She trusted the Lord had a plan and would send her husband when the time was right.

It was living in the dorm that was most problematic for Sister Georgina, but fortunately, she requested and received a single room. She had argued that she did not want her prayer or fasting routines to disturb a roommate, but the real reason was to avoid being around any of their extra-curricular activities. She had deliberately discussed her school board complaint and the ensuing media frenzy while in the administration office, insinuating that she would make a similar complaint if her request was not granted. She need not have worried as the political correctness of the 1980s meant the college could not afford any adverse publicity that may deter the small number of minority students who chose to apply. So they were happy to assign her a single room with no additional cost.

On the supposedly "dry" campus, Sister Georgina's peers quickly began to live up to the reputation of being college students and got high on a multitude of illegal contraband, including alcohol. Sister Georgina had no idea where or how the students acquired them. She was grateful to shut her bedroom door and ignore such ungodly behaviors, but she could not ignore the noises coming from her neighbors who used their bedroom activities to pass their free time. She regularly saw doors with scarves and other contraptions to indicate that they should not be disturbed. As fast as possible, Sister Georgina would race down the hall to her room, and tried hard not to imagine what was going on behind the doors. Sister Georgina felt she had mastered various techniques for avoiding her sexual feelings and did not need to be reminded of them every time she went back to her room.

On the few occasions she allowed her sexual desires to come into her head, she would channel them into what she felt was a healthy place. When in the sanctuary of her dorm room, she would lie on her bed and dream of her husband, their extravagant white wedding, and blissful honeymoon. In her dreams, her husband would always be a well-dressed, articulate African-American man; Andrew Young or Jessie Jackson Jr. would somehow pop into her mind. He would tower over her with his physical height. He would be commanding, but of course, sensitive to her needs. When he would smile, she would have no choice but to melt both inwardly and outwardly. She would lower her eyes in submission. He would be successful in his chosen career and would have a good relationship with his peers, family, and colleagues. He would be emotionally secure in himself with the ability to communicate effectively what was going on for him. However, it would be his submission to God that made her the happiest. Because of that, she would happily submit to his authority. She was certainly not one of those feminist who wouldn't obey their husband. She would welcome his authority because it would be founded in God's wisdom. He would listen to her opinions and views, and would actively seek her counsel. But at the end of the day, he would make the decision that would be in the best interest of their family, this way she could feel secure knowing she could lean on him when she needed to. So there would be unwavering trust in their loving relationship. He would welcome her constructive criticisms and feedback. He would consider her emotional needs, allowing her to feel safe and comfortable sharing her most intimate secrets, knowing he wasn't going to throw it back in her face to humiliate her. He would hold her tightly and actively listen to her talk about her day over the dinner table without interruption, perhaps even gently touch her, making her feel so wanted and desired. Then, at the end of the day, he would expertly attend to her physical needs. In the words of Marvin Gaye's latest single, he would provide her with some much needed sexual healing.

Everyone who had made her life special would be at the wedding. It would be scheduled for about a month after her graduation and she would transform her beloved church home into the place where she would celebrate her marriage. Real, brightly colored flowers would line the aisle and alter, because she wanted to feel like she would be saying her vows in the Garden of Eden. She would hire a larger venue for the reception because there would be no room for a marquee in the church's small parking lot. Besides, the music would disturb the neighbors and she would not want to have any negativity around her to start her new life. The reception would be held at the nearby sports and learning complex. It was accessible for wheelchairs as well, so Brother Barnabus would not have to miss such a special occasion. The members would shower the happy couple with their best wishes and hopes for a good Christian marriage.

When Sister Georgina's thoughts went onto her wedding night, she could feel herself getting hot and bothered. Her husband would spread rose petals over the bed and after their prayers he would tell her how thankful he was to have her precious virginity. They would then consummate the marriage. He would encase her, making her feel like a precious jewel. He would kiss her passionately on her lips, cheeks, eyes, ears, neck, before slowly making his way down her body. He would take his time, as they would have a lifetime to explore. He would whisper ever so softly into her ear how much he appreciated her, her discipline, and patience. He would promise to take care of her for the rest of her life. The experience would be majestic, and her dreams would always end with her having multiple orgasms. She would come out of her day (and night) dreams not just hot and bothered, but confident that she would be blessed with such a husband and hoped that it would be very soon, so she could get on with the business of experiencing the joys of a sexual relationship in real life.

While she waited patiently for her husband to materialize, the food court, the main cafeteria, and local bakery offered Sister Georgina some refuge. Of course, the food was nothing like Mrs. Cartwright's soulful dishes at her church home, campus food was convenient, generic, and tasteless, but it served the purpose of providing her with much needed comfort. She could normally be found at one of the cafeterias several times a day, usually when it opened and just before they closed. This was because she could pile things onto her plate without too many folks commenting. It wasn't long before her meal plan was exhausted and she had to face the subsequent increase in her weight. She knew she ate because she was bored, lonely, and could give her increasing weight gain the blame for her husband-less status. When she was no longer able to fit comfortably into her clothes, she forced herself to remember that college life was not all about studying or eating. She would bite the bullet and make a conscious effort to address that aspect of her life on campus.

As there was safety in numbers, Sister Georgina decided to seek out and join a student Christian group. Besides, there was not much else on campus she felt particularly strongly about. But from the very first meeting of the SCG (Students for Christ Group), she knew it would be a challenge, as she was the only African-American member. But, by reminding herself that *God's Truth is universal* and that this was the experience she wanted when she had made her application, she strengthened her resolve by repeating that her presence would help them as well as herself. Besides, they could see she was definitely not an angry African-American woman, on the contrary, she always tried to see beyond color. She hadn't expected her position to be tested as soon as she walked into the very first meeting. Before even saying hello, one group member immediately felt it was important to share with her how she had supported a young 'colored' child during her last internship who had been crying.

"The little thing said 'I don't want to be black,'" the young SCG member said. "I truly understood how he felt and so I cried too. I wanted him to feel supported," she told Sister Georgina with pride. "You people have it so hard," she quipped, "and I wanted him to know that I understood and agreed with him," she added compassionately (in her mind) and touching her chest with both hands. This brought the image to Sister Georgina of a beauty pageant contestant trying to convince the audience that she truly cared about world peace. Knowing that racist views and hurtful things could be unintentional or just said out of ignorance, Sister Georgina bit her lip and remained silent. She struggled to hold onto the positive intentions of her colleague but instead, found her thoughts wandering about how she had messed up this young boy instead, by reinforcing the negative images he had of himself. Sister Georgina said a silent prayer and decided to address the issue the only way she knew how; to support her colleague and the rest of the SCG group by being a living example of the teaching of the Lord.

Sister Georgina responded to the group's politeness in kind even though she did not feel any sincerity behind their words. Being up for the challenge, she selflessly watered down her testimony as an African-

American woman on the assumption that some may misinterpret what she had to say. She wanted her spirit to be fed, and so decided to make the commitment to attend as often as she could. She valued being amongst people who wanted to talk about the Lord, and prayed that their faith would overcome their shortcomings. However, she never did decipher whether she was genuinely being welcomed as a new member or whether it was the group's excitement at finally getting ethnic support on their side.

In the little spare time she had, Sister Georgina helped organize and participated in the SCG's events to raise the profile of the Lord on campus. The skills she had developed as a youth leader proved beneficial and enabled the group to transform its image from being nerdy and prudish to popular and provocative. With Sister Georgina's creativity and eventual leadership in her Junior and Senior years, they went beyond the usual fundraising events. Sister Georgina pushed the envelope to make the Lord's presence real in their daily lives.

———————~———————

Now as she sat in the auditorium celebrating the end of her undergraduate years, Sister Georgina felt great pride and accomplished as she remembered the group's success, particularly the two most controversial activities during her tenure; the abortion debate and the "dress up in white day".

———————~———————

While researching her psychology paper, Sister Georgina first came across the work of Dr. Brenda Swanson, a leading pro-lifer. *There is no such thing as a coincidence in this….the Lord's world,* she said to herself. She was so excited after reading the article, that she had not waited to discuss her idea, let alone get the permission from the group, but went ahead and contacted Dr. Swanson with an invitation to participate in an academic debate. She knew she had a hot button topic on her hands and was confident that the other members would eventually see it too. She was right. By the time the author had replied, Sister Georgina had scheduled the date, advertised, and found a willing opponent. She was fortunate that Dr. Swanson had accepted the invitation.

The debate turned out to be high profile both on and off campus. The local newspaper wrote an article promoting the event and so, there was not an empty seat when the debate began. Sister Georgina and the others loved it. It was a fiery debate that Dr. Swanson clearly won. She had shaken her opponent to their core as she was a former pro-choice activist herself. She had a termination, believing it was her right as a woman to choose. However, immediately after the procedure, and the passing of many years, her feelings of regret did not diminish, rather they had intensified. It escalated to the point she began to share her experiences with anyone who would listen, leading her to speak out against abortions and joining the opposition as a result.

Dr. Swanson's opponent had not expected that their speaker could deflect most of their arguments because she had said them herself prior to her personal experience. What made the event even more memorable was the post-debate publicity had highlighted that the pro-choicers had disrupted scholarly activity and the right of free speech. Sister Georgina accepted the praise that was showered on the group by the wider university community. She had brought much needed publicity to the small college. But more important, was the thought that her actions may have stopped just one woman from having an abortion meant it had definitely been worth it. Despite the high praise for the work of the SCG, discord within the group was reaching fever pitch. The membership was all in agreement that Sister Georgina seemed to be taking an abrasive, dictatorial approach to leadership. However, whether through fear of being seen as racist or pure laziness, when it came time for their elections, Sister Georgina ran unopposed. As a result of the debate, recruitment was at an all-time high and so were the donations. Sister Georgina felt vindicated for her tough love approach.

There was no doubt about the impact of the 'dress up in white day' as the group celebrated their pride in being virgins. She had seconded the motion without hesitation when Shelly McCallum proposed the event, and was upset with herself for not coming up with the idea herself. Shelly told the group about a first year psychology student who had been humiliated by a couple of students in her class when she had told them of her virginity. She had left the class in tears and had been afraid to return. The young student had the confidence to report the matter to college administration, but they seemed to have played the issue down.

"How can we reach out to her and let her know she is not alone," Shelly asked innocently.

"Yes, you're right. How about a card and some flowers?" Another group member said.

"Perhaps a bigger gesture of support," Shelly pondered. "What if we all sit in her psychology class?" Shelly joked. "That would make everyone sit up and take notice." She paused and quickly followed her thoughts with, "we should all wear white as well! Because we can," she quipped.

On seeing the other group members light up at her suggestions, Sister Georgina shifted uncomfortably in her chair. She knew it was a good idea, but she wanted to deflect the accolades for Shelly.

"We need to pray about this," Sister Georgina replied sharply. "We need to be sure we are motivated by the right reasons." The thought of humiliating people was not a Christian thing to do, had crossed her mind. So, Sister Georgina eagerly led the group in prayer. Without pausing for reflection when she finished, Sister Georgina looked up and said boldly, "I think God would approve because we are motivated to celebrate his Truth. We can take a leaf out of the gay pride rallies and celebrate our virginity as something to be proud of."

The example of the 'N' word being turned positive by hip-hop artists and rappers had been the first thought that popped into her head, but she had settled on gay pride because she felt it would get the point across just as well and wouldn't make anyone feel uncomfortable. It also avoided the inevitable political discourse on the use of the 'N' word in any situation. The nods of agreement were quickly followed by a vote and the planning of the event went into full force. They agreed immediately on the theme (a wedding) and color (white, naturally, as the selling point was they could genuinely wear white on their wedding day). But they had to have several discussions about the type of dresses, as a traditional wedding dress was thought to be too elaborate for a college campus and for the male members of the group, the thought of wearing a white suit would be too flamboyant and they certainly did not want people to confuse their philosophy with that of the gay pride rallies. Besides, they would have to wear them all day to their classes. As a result, they agreed on simple white dresses for the women and white shirts and ties for the men. A search of local thrift stores had secured most of the required items, while others had them made, dyed, or purchased at regular price by the owner.

When the appointed day finally arrived, the twenty-two of the thirty-one SCG members met at 9:00 in the morning, already wearing their simple white outfits. They wanted to make the most of the entire day. They had agreed to take turns staffing their information table in the student lounge while others circled the campus several times handing out the SCG's promotional fliers, cookies (baked in the shape of a wedding couple), and fruit cake which was intended to serve as imitation wedding cakes. Sister Georgina loved the attention this event generated, so she walked around campus proud as a peacock. Despite the stares, whispers, and expected hurtful comments from some of their non-believing peers, she unquestionably felt a sense of superiority and smugness as she walked around the campus. She felt elated that she could celebrate her virginity so publicly and at every opportunity, shared the message of abstinence with anyone who would listen (whether they wanted to hear it or not). She was proud to be a living example of the Lord's teachings and had no regrets. She was pleased that the media coverage of the event was sympathetic to their cause and when she went back to her classes afterwards, she noticed that her peers looked at her differently. She concluded that they saw her as a force to be reckoned with and smiled as she remembered that day.

College life, however, was not all fun and games and the test that she had longed for before starting at Secus College finally occurred just before she was due to graduate. It came in the form of a dinner invitation from one of her professors. She assumed it was due to her academic abilities, but only after felt her participation in the SCG group had not gone unnoticed and more than likely was the primary reason for the invitation. On further evaluation, she believed that night deepened her faith as well as renewed her commitment to being a virgin, even though she found the experience extremely traumatic.

Her paper on the benefits of abstinence classes in public schools had received her mandatory A+. What was different on this occasion was that the professor had given her an opportunity to talk through her arguments when it had been returned. Previously, he would rush her out of his office, preferring to use his office hours for other tasks. She assumed he was genuinely interested in what she had to say, especially when the conversation moved from not just her academic work, but also her opinions of the news, campus life, and her faith. The invitation to his dinner party was an unexpected surprise when it came, but one she readily accepted. It was the first offer of its kind in the entire time she was a student at Secus.

She had a week to prepare and so, diligently searched the thrift stores to find something that would be suitable. Her weight of course was still a problem, but she felt the loose fitting dresses covered up the unsightly bulges around her stomach and thighs. As there was much preparation to do for the event, she decided to rent a car for the week. She had calculated that all the preparation warranted the extra expense. She would have to make the four hour roundtrip back to her hometown to have her hair and nails done. There were no local African-American hairdressers on this side of the Bay Bridge, so it would be easier to just drive home. Then there was the dinner party itself; she needed to get there and back. She had considered the possibility of meeting someone at the event who would graciously give her a ride home,but reasoned in the end, it would be better to be safe and have a car just in case.

"Sister Georgina, what are you doing here? Is school out on a holiday?"Sister Bee said when she spotted her coming out of the beauty salon. Before Sister Georgina could reply, her church sister was thinking about who she would call first to let them know Sister Georgina was back in town and that they needed to quickly get over to the church to straighten things up before she made her way there.

"Oh, hello Sister Bee! No, I've just come by to visit the beauty salon. One of my professors has invited me to dinner and I wanted to look nice," Sister Georgina stated.

"Really?!" Sister Bee was shocked and wanted more information. Getting Sister Georgina into a hair salon had been the topic of many unauthorized conversations over the years among the sisters. They really did want her to take more of an interest in her appearance. She had never taken anyone's advice before, perhaps it was because no one could come straight out and say it, so their hints and innuendos had been ignored. Sister Bee added this to her list of information she had to share with the others. By now, she was also so curious about this dinner invitation that had gotten Sister Georgina into a hair salon, she forgot about her fear of a potential tirade from Sister Georgina about being nosy and came right out and asked her, "is it a date?" She was now thinking about calling a meeting with the other church sisters to share this news.

"No, just the professor wanted to get together with me to talk about my paper. However, I do think some other dinner guests will be there." Sister Georgina was initially taken aback by the directness of Sister Bee, but valued the chance to talk about the dinner with someone. Being given the green light, Sister Bee jumped at the opportunity to question her more.

"If it is a dinner party, there will definitely be other guests, one may even be a special man, you never know, my sister. I definitely think you should be prepared. What are you planning to wear?"

Sister Georgina felt uncomfortable with such questioning. These were things she rarely (never) ever thought about and was embarrassed to let someone know that she had nothing special planned. Feeling cornered, she quickly stressed the professional nature of the function and therefore, felt there was no need to plan anything special. This did not stop Sister Bee from speculating about the other guests at the party and volunteered to help her.

"Just in case God chooses your husband to appear on this occasion," she prophesied. Sister Georgina did not want to admit it, but she was thankful for Sister Bee's practical words of support. The sister's excitement was contagious and forced Sister Georgina to acknowledge that she may be right. Her time at college had flown by so quickly, it had never occurred to her before now that she had never had a date.

On the drive back, she allowed herself to dream that her professor may see fit to invite an eligible suitor to sit opposite her at the dinner table.

Despite the time she took to get ready on the day of the dinner party, Sister Georgina was still one of the first to arrive, there were only a couple of cars in the driveway. So, she drove around the corner and continued her daydream, thankful she had rented the car. She sat motionless behind the wheel and allowed her imagination to run wild against her will. She smiled as she saw herself being greeted at the door with a warm welcoming smile and then ushered to sit at a beautifully laid table with an extravagant flower centerpiece. The handsome young African-American man in the seat next to her was able to call her by her name when he introduced himself, because it had been printed on a seating card in large, bold, italic, script lettering. After a four-course formal dinner that was served by impeccable staff, he would make it clear that their engaging conversation would continue long after the dinner party and into their future together.

It was about thirty minutes later when a couple more cars parked in the driveway that Sister Georgina, with a slight skip in her step, knocked hesitantly on the front door. When she was greeted at the door by the warm smile of the professor's wife, who seemed genuinely pleased to see her, she felt that her daydream was becoming reality.

"Welcome to our home! So happy you could join us. How was the drive over?" Without waiting for an answer, she continued, "make yourself at home," she said hurriedly and pointed to the large floor cushions and the buffet style dinner table. "Help yourself, and please don't feel obligated to wait for the others. The smaller table on the left is vegan and vegetarian foods, while the main table is for the meat lovers." And with that, she hurried back to the kitchen. The large cushions spread around the floor made her dreams of sitting at a formal dinner table, complete with china plates and wine glasses fade into the abyss.

She was definitely unprepared for the informality of the evening. She had never anticipated a scenario where she would be sitting uncomfortably on the floor. However, in an attempt to salvage the evening, she watched in anticipation as the other dinner guests entered through the front door. When the professor finally announced that everyone had arrived, she desperately tried to fight off the wave of depression that had immediately engulfed her. After all her preparations, the financial toll, and now the realization that there would be no suitable husband material in attendance, she did her best to hide her disappointment. To make matters worse, she was the only African-American there. A thin, Hispanic, young woman was the only other ethnic minority, but her purple and red hair, tattoos and piercings meant she was not going to look to her for support.

Having helped herself to the food from both tables (several times) to comfort herself, she decided to hold onto what she knew to be the Truth and through her sadness, engaged politely with the other guests. Sister Georgina struggled to make small talk about the weather, essay deadlines, and the up-coming graduation. So, she was pleased when one dinner guest, a junior, although clearly more mature than his academic year suggested, whose major was linguistics, offered her a glass of wine. She decided to take the initiative and make a statement about her faith in the hope she could gain some semblance of control, even if it was just a simple conversation.

"No thank you. I don't drink. It's against my religious beliefs. I think it's so important to always be in control of one's faculties and besides, the best high you can get is on the knowledge of God."

Much to Sister Georgina's amazement, the young man put the glass and bottle of wine back on the table and calmly replied, "tell me more. My name is Patrick, by the way." He extended his hand by way of a formal introduction. "I've seen you around campus a couple of times. You're a senior, right? Majoring in…umm…education?" Patrick had indeed noticed Sister Georgina and had looked forward to having a conversation with her when the opportunity eventually arose. His desire to travel the world had meant taking a couple of years off before starting his undergraduate program, much to his parent's disgust. After running out of money in the Australian outback, he had been forced to return home with the promise by his parents to fund the rest of his world trip after he completed his degree. Having been the recipient of kindness from countless strangers during his adventures abroad, he had learned the importance of being a friendly face. So aware of his responsibility to be proactive about challenging racial micro-aggressions, he intended to reach out to the limited number of students of color on campus to see what he could do to make their college experience a more positive one. He had observed Sister Georgina's sad demeanor every time he saw her from a distance and was looking forward to finally meeting her, hoping to brighten her day. Besides, by looking beyond her external appearance, he sensed she may be a great person to get to know.

"Yes and yes. My name is Sister Georgina. I'm a senior…looking forward to graduating in a couple of weeks and then beginning a career as a twelfth grade teacher."

Flattered by the invitation to share her views, but disappointed that he wasn't a potential partner (she had briefly given the thought some traction before quickly rejecting the idea having formed the opinion that he was not organizing his life properly due to his obvious maturity and still only being a junior) Sister Georgina was grateful for the attention. She returned the handshake before happily launching into the benefits of abstinence from alcohol.

"People would be much healthier…for a start, their thinking would be clearer, liver and heart functions would be better. Even lower their risks of cancers, and it would definitely decrease the burden on the nation's health care and criminal justice systems. People would be better off financially, making the economy better. You know, I could go on and on."

"Sounds like you would've agreed with prohibition," Patrick replied jokingly.

"Well, of course. Prohibition lasted about thirteen years, I think; a paradigm shift normally takes about fifteen. Perhaps if it had gone on for about twenty to twenty-five years it would've been different. Any real public change takes a while. And besides, the system of enforcement wasn't the best, as you know corruption was rampant. They also didn't do a good job teaching the virtues of abstinence. I am sure that would have made a big difference as well."

Realizing that she was serious, Patrick sought to clarify her reasoning, hoping desperately to be wrong about his growing suspicions about her closed-mindedness.

"So let me see…you think that what's good for you should be good for everyone else? To the extent you would enforce compliance?"

"If necessary, of course. We have seat belt laws, and the laws they're bringing in against smoking in public are definitely for the good of the community. Our society is dominated by things that ultimately serve the devil and putting laws in place to stop his progression should be mandatory. If I didn't know the Truth and was engaged in such ungodly behaviors, I would want someone to tell me and to force me to change."

"Okay…And what are you defining as the '*Truth*'?" Patrick replied nervously, saddened that his suspicious had been proven correct.

"The word of God of course, as outlined in the King James Bible," Sister Georgina said confidently with a smile. "There is only one Truth. If everyone followed His word, the world would be a much better place, filled with love and peace everywhere." Sister Georgina was so pleased to have an audience with someone who actually seemed interested in what she was saying after nearly four years at college. She allowed her excitement to get the better of her and launched predictably into sharing the joys of being a person of faith.

"Can't you imagine such a world? I am so glad the President and First Lady have openly acknowledged their belief in God and are seeking to bring in policies that can turn our nation into a truly God-fearing one. If he's true to his word, abortions will soon be a thing of the past, as should the ridiculous campaign to decriminalize homosexuality. So, the president is therefore absolutely right to be strict on immigration control. We definitely can't have non-believers, or worse still, foreigners, watering down the Truth. Just imagine, if they had their way, it would be like living in Sodom and Gomorrah."

As if she had just been given water after being in a desert for the past four years, she prattled on without pausing for breath, assuming that Patrick wanted to hear what she had to say.

"If you are ever in Prince George's County you must come to my church. Learning about the Truth will change your life. Sunday service starts promptly at 11:00am and the Pastor gives us inspirational guidance to get us through each week. While our bible classes are Wednesday at 7:30pm. It's at these classes we *analyze* the Truth. We get to explore the word of God and see how to apply it to our lives. If it's a bit far, you could come to our bible classes on campus at the Students for Christ group. Our next meeting is…Tuesday evening at 6:30pm. It would be great to see you there."

Patrick sighed, saddened that his honorable outreach had been met with such rigidity. He had heard enough and seeing no way to salvage the situation concluded that the best thing he could do was try and broaden her outlook. He hated being in this position and was angry with himself for opening the door for this particular conversation. But realizing that his sanity was the priority, he reasoned that it was time to shut the conversation down by deliberately being as provocative and controversial as possible. He knew his actions could be misconstrued, and it certainly was not his intention to embarrass or humiliate her, but if it got her to think differently in the long term, then his objectives would have been achieved.

"Okay, Okay," said Patrick as he rubbed both of his temples at the same time and frowning dramatically in a blatant display of disgust. "Now, I want you stay with me, Georgie," Patrick said as if he was talking to a kindergarten child. "I am going to be talking very fast and giving you a lot of information, let me know what you don't understand and when I have finished talking we can discuss it if you want. But, somehow I don't think you will want to… Anyway, no interruptions please. Now, are you ready?"

Sister Georgina shocked by the change in his demeanor, but sensing the condescending tone of his voice, nervously nodded her head in the affirmative.

"Okay then, here we go…" He then took a deep breath and began, education, as I am sure you know, should teach us the importance of being academically correct, as well as being receptive to new and different ideas and opinions. So, I hope you can understand that for some, *the Truth* is that the Bible is an Astrotheological literary hybrid. By the personification of what our early ancestors saw in the sky, they created myths and stories about their movements and relationships…

AKA the zodiac.

"The Egyptians documented this and it filtered down to other cultures around the world, and hence, they all share the same so called *biblical stories*. The virgin birth, the great flood, Moses, and so on... I believe there are about sixteen stories of "saviors" that were all born on December 25th, crucified, and resurrected, from all corners of the world, and documented, way, way, way before 0AD, such as Mithra in Persia 1200BC, Krishna in India 900BC, and Dionysus in Greece 500BC to name a few. But let me not digress, by the time it had filtered down to the Romans, they thought it would be a good idea to "historicalize" these mythical characters as a political tool of control.

"Constantine, the pagan leader at the time, in 225AD. No, no...I'm sorry, it was 325AD, a real sensible fellow. In the light of the growing Christian followers, he knew it would be in his political interest to adopt some of their beliefs to further his own agenda. He paid the travel expenses for several thousand priests to attend his conference in Nicea, to make sure they came up with a doctrine that legitimized and sanctioned the *Christ figure* AKA the personified Solar Deity, thereby, ensuring the continual dominance of the Roman Empire's pagan worldview, albeit, covertly.

"A case in point, did you know that the excessive food, drinking, drugging, sexual indulgences at Christmas can be traced right back to the Roman pagan week-long holiday of Saturnalia held December 17th - 25th. They even had carolers. Their tradition however, was to sing naked as they wandered around the streets! Shame they don't do that today. No...wait...I think some carolers still do! So, yes. Yes, indeed...every single bit of it...from the yule log, mistletoe, and tree... the whole kit and caboodle is pagan! As an academic, you should want to research this stuff for yourself. But, I digress. As history is written by the victors, their position was documented as historical facts and generally accepted without question. Still with me Georgie...?"

Seeing her horrified face, it was clear Patrick wasn't going to get a response any time soon, so he continued unabatedly. "Now, here's the good part, because of their political clout, that was now underpinned by a spiritual doctrine, '*THEIR*' way is promoted as being '*THE*' way.

And when backed by the threat and actual use of violence, surprise, surprise, it justified of some of the most brutal and oppressive practices and crimes against humanity, that has secured and perpetuated their continuing dominance to today.

"As a member of the African-American community, you should be well versed with the oppressive use of Christianity in the peculiar institution of slavery and its aftermath. But, as good old Siggie Freud theorized, the spiritual crutch of the general populace has led to their blind submission, excusing and defending such acts of unbelievable atrocity as simply being…*'God's will'*. So quoting the Bible as a measure of what is right and what is wrong is extremely problematic to me."

To the applause of a couple of dinner guests, Patrick poured himself a glass of wine which he sipped in a celebratory manner, knowing he had rendered Sister Georgina speechless. The intensity of the interaction meant an audience had gathered around them and were being thoroughly entertained by the one sided conversation, the increasingly distraught look on Sister Georgina's face, and her wilting body language. Although, Sister Georgina did not want to prove Patrick right, quickly admitted to herself that she had nothing to say. Never before having heard any of the arguments he presented, knew she had no scholarly footing on which to debate him. She briefly considered the race card, to respond to his arrogance as a white person questioning her awareness of African-American heritage. But, she also knew this wasn't worth pursuing as she had never studied her history, knowing it was too painful to think about, let alone research. As a result, all that was left was her emotions, which ranged from anger, disbelief, embarrassment, and confusion. She was therefore, thankful that an opportunist guest seized the gap in their conversation to ask about her role as president of the Students for Christ group. Turning her attention to respond to the questioner, she could now legitimately ignore Patrick and his elaborate nonsensical monologue, as well as how uncomfortable he had made her feel. She did not realize that it was a case of jumping out of the frying pan and into the fire.

As she outlined the goals of the SCG, she overheard one of the guests commenting that the Professor had been looking for some "feisty" dinner guests this time and got the first indication that something was wrong. When the professor's wife brought out the desserts to the buffet table, the conversation turned abruptly to sexual relationships and she knew for sure she had been set up. Initially, Sister Georgina did not run from the bombardment of criticism that was constantly thrown at her about her choice to be celibate (someone had commented on her outfit at the dress up in white day) by the mixed collections of gay, bisexual, and straight dinner guests. Instead she came out fighting. She tried to use the anger that had been building up inside her all evening to defend her position. It was her comfort zone, to intimidate, use a tone of voice that exuded confidence and of being self-assured. However, she had been left emotionally rattled by the events of the evening so far and her speech on the virtues of waiting was not greeted with the usual applause, but rather by snide comments. They found her Achille's heel and she could not deny the intimidation she felt as the other guests spoke in graphic details about the joys of sexual freedom and exploration.

"Wow, I thought you virgins were an oddity that had gone out with the dinosaurs."

"Have you ever thought about a three way?" One inquisitive diner asked directly.

"I am not sure what you mean," Sister Georgina naively replied.

"I mean, boy, boy, girl or girl, girl, boy, or even girl, girl, girl. Basically, whatever strikes your fancy. You don't even have to stop at threesome, it could be more," the diner continued graphically.

Sister Georgina had no response. She had just her theoretical knowledge of what happens with a regular couple, and so, had no notion of a threesome, foursome, or whatever. The whole thing boggled her mind and she was unable to hide her confusion. The diner seeing an opening to exploit her innocence and prove his point asked directly if she had lesbian fantasies. Sister Georgina was thankful for her dark skin because it hid her flushed face. She remembered her constant reviewing of her father's pornographic material she found as a child. Her face told the tale which was picked up immediately by the questioner who had every intention of milking the situation for all it was worth.

"What if I say, we were all meant to be bisexual? Our social conditioning has unquestionably programmed us to think that heterosexuality is the norm, but the evidence is overwhelming that our bodies react to other forms of sexual attraction. Our reaction to sexual exploration should not be interpreted as unacceptable, quite the opposite in fact, it should be embraced with open arms. There is no question it would make our communities more tolerable and understanding of difference. Don't you think it would provide you with a wider world view?" He preached.

"I'll gladly help by providing a physical demonstration," a female guest offered mockingly, but with a hint of authenticity as she smiled flirtatiously. Sister Georgina sat numb, not wanting to give any hint of acceptance to the offer.

Not letting up, the diners continued to talk openly about anal, bondage, and sadomasochism and it may well have been a foreign language to Sister Georgina. With the knowledge that 'winning the war sometimes means you have to lose a battle', she decided to no longer take their bait and just sit quietly, smile, and grin through coffee. By the end of the evening there was an agreement to disagree. Emotionally exhausted, she made her way to the rental car, and somehow found the strength to decide never to be in such a situation again. She rationalized that the other dinner guests had not been prepared to listen to what she had to say. They had come prepared for an argument and had enjoyed making it personal. She prided herself on having listened to their depravities and was pleased that she had faced the test she had wanted. She had come out of the experience knowing that, nothing, nothing, nothing was going to shake her from what she knew to be the Truth.

As was her norm, when she was tucked up in her bed, she processed some of the things that had been said. She hated the thought that she was so naïve about the most basic aspect of lovemaking. She certainly did not regret being celibate, but as tears rolled down her cheeks, she forced herself to face the reality that she had not had a date in the four years she had been at college. Sister Georgina could no longer avoid the fact that her bed was becoming a very painful place at the end of each night. She did not regret her decision to remain a virgin, but rather, it was her wish to already have her husband tucked up next to her.

She would have to keep waiting to experience some of the pleasures they talked about so vividly that evening. She addressed her questions quickly by placing it in the Lord's hands.

"How long must I wait Lord? How long? How long?" She pleaded before launching into an unorthodox prayer. "Know that I am your true servant. I have dedicated my life to you, let me experience the joys of what you have prescribed, know I am lonely and want to know what it feels like to be held and caressed. I trust you and will wait until you are ready to provide me with my husband. Amen."

She came up from her prayer strengthened in her faith. She accepted that when the time was right, the Lord would provide for her. He would not forsake such a committed servant. Through Him, all things are possible. She would not have to go out of her way to find a partner because the Lord would send one to her. When He did, she would be able to enjoy the passions and delights of a physical relationship for the rest of her life. So, until then, she would be patient. She hadn't believed all these years for nothing. She did briefly wonder why a potential suitor had never approached her in all the time she had attended college. Was it something about her? Had she kept herself so busy she had not seen him? She did not give this line of thought much energy, preferring to focus on feeling sorry for the direction-less guests and prayed for their deliverance from the negative consequences of such uninhibited behavior.

It was a couple of years after she graduated that she ran into one of the dinner guests. She felt a great sense of exoneration for her position when she was told about the many breakdowns in their relationships, a gambling addiction, a HIV, and several mental health diagnoses. She now had the satisfaction of knowing that following the Lord's road map meant avoidance of such pain. She was thankful to have the knowledge of Truth and had been saved from such heartaches. With a renewed sense of obligation to help others from such fates, it was one of those pivotal moments that energized Sister Georgina into teaching the values of her faith with renewed vigor.

After the infamous dinner and with her graduation fast approaching, the increased workload, teaching practice, and the silent racism of the SCG, meant she slowly began to prioritize, whenever funds allowed, making the commute back home to her father's house for Sunday service and brunch. Besides, she preferred the safety of the familiar (and of course, Mrs. Cartwright's tasty, well-seasoned food). Not that being with her biological and church family was any better than being on campus. She was well aware that many would deliberately avoid her, or just engage in polite conversation. But having grown used to the superficial conversations, she accepted it for what it was and would carry out her Christian duties regardless. She quickly reestablished herself in the church community and took back her leadership role. Her philosophy that kept her going was so simple, she wanted her love of Lord to shine and for as many people as possible to know the positive benefits of following the path of Truth He had prescribed. She wanted to be a positive role model of the Lord's Truth in action. With such a commitment, she was accepting that her undergraduate years were officially over and choose to welcome the life her Lord and Savior had planned for her.

As she watched her fellow graduates step down from the stage in their regalia, the voice of the young foul mouthed graduate sitting in the chair next to her came back into focus.

"...but on the other hand, China sounds interesting, but then again, I have always fancied Thailand. Anyway, how about you? What's next for you?"

Sister Georgina knew without hesitation that her main focus would be getting her life ready for a husband and children. With the Lord's guidance she would not have to suffer without a husband (or sex) for much longer.

68

Chapter Three
Outside the Box

Sister Georgina took her eyes off the television and looked over at her phone as it sat quietly on her side table. It was the third time in the last five minutes that she had looked at it. She was trying to break the habit of playing with her new Blackberry phone and had deliberately placed it away from her immediate reach. Unfortunately, doing so did not have the desired affect and she continued to obsess over possible email messages that may be flooding into her inbox. She reminded herself that there would have been the familiar ting, swish, or such noise to alert her if someone had tried to get in contact. Despite this tidbit of factual information, the desire to pick up the phone and check her messages did not diminish.

She believed in miracles and as crazy as it seemed, at the back of her mind, hoped that there would be a call or email message from an imaginary suitor. She had daydreamed on many occasions about such a call. He would call by accident looking for someone else. The sound of her sexy voice and their stimulating conversation would keep him talking. They would arrange to meet and their electric chemistry would mean the rest would be history. Marriage, children, a life filled with happiness... Sister Georgina's capacity to daydream had taken on a life of its own. However, the reality on this occasion, as all the others, was that her phone remained silent. She reluctantly looked back at the television and tried to fake an interest in the comedy show she was watching.

It was 7:30pm on Saturday night and she was dressed in her PJs flopped on her couch. To make matters worse, she had just demolished a large bag of Cheesy Puffs and was contemplating having the Ben & Jerry's Chunky Monkey ice cream she had been saving for an especially depressive evening. Her thirty-third birthday was fast approaching and she had earmarked it for that occasion. Deciding against the ice cream, she consoled herself by just licking her fingers to hide the evidence of her junk food addiction, even if it was only from herself. She hadn't felt like fixing herself something healthy to eat. Neither did she feel like ordering takeout, so whatever was in the cupboard had to suffice.

It was one of those rare evenings when there was nothing going on at the church. Everything was organized for Sunday service in the morning and she had nothing that urgently needed to be done to prepare for teaching her class at school on Monday. Sister Georgina had definitely earned a night off, as it was not often she had the luxury to just relax. But, the unusual downtime had the opposite effect and allowed her mind to think about things for years she had gone out of her way to avoid. By deliberately choosing to keep herself busy with a full schedule of events, she was grateful most nights to fall asleep immediately after saying her prayers. This strategy had kept any painful, depressing, and challenging thoughts at bay. But now, in the quietness of the evening, her mind decided to take full advantage of the space and force her to reflect on her own plight. Sister Georgina sat upright from her lounging position on the couch and sighed heavily because she realized she could no longer put off the inevitable. It was time for her to face the reality that was her life.

It had been fourteen years since she left Secus College and all the expectations for her life had so far eluded her. Time was slipping by way too quickly for her liking and she needed to make sense of what was going on. She nodded to herself and decided to take the bull by the horns. She never liked taking her cod liver oil capsules in the morning, but knowing it did her body good, especially in the winter, she swallowed it down. So, with the same attitude, Sister Georgina decided to hold her nose and force herself to dissect the current situation to process exactly what was going on in her life.

She got up from the couch and as she couldn't find the remote control, manually turned the sound down on the television. She then found a pen and a blank sheet of paper, having decided she should make notes. Wanting to ensure she gave her full attention to the task at hand, she sat, with difficulty, crossed legged on the floor with her back to the couch. She took a deep breath and then decided to write out what she understood to be the problem. She wrote at the top of the page in capital letters, rather than her usual script, 'NOT HAVING A HUSBAND'. She then decided to note the positives: eligible, professional, female. Her two academic degrees came next, then the fact that she owned her home and a car. She put the pen down and considered her list so far. To her, the list screamed stability, discipline, responsible. *These are values that any sensible husband should want from a wife. I've got so much to offer, why can't any man see that?* Her thoughts screamed their lack of understanding about the dilemma she faced and so answered her question with a question, "so why...why doesn't anyone want me?"

She took several deep breathes to calm herself down and remembered that she was trying to make sense of the situation. So to rise above her emotions, decided to treat it like an academic assignment she had in school and refocused on the task at hand. *An obedient and dedicated servant* was the next thing that she added to the list. She shook her head and smiled to herself, clearly pleased with this addition. As if to support her argument, she proudly listed her virginity as evidence of her submission. But taking advantage of the door that had now been opened for any thoughts to come in, her more painful ones seized the opportunity to rush from their hiding place in her sub-consciousness and into the forefront of her mind. Her virginity was not by choice. It had never been by choice. She had never had the opportunity to actually lose it.

She never wanted to face this fact, but it was the truth. Perhaps, the illusion of her virginity was a pious attempt to protect herself from the belief that she was unlovable. Whatever the case, it had been cute to talk about her virginity in her teens and twenties. It had underpinned her authority, giving her confidence to tell others just how wrong they were. But, now in her thirties, it just made people feel sorry for her and look at her with pity. Her once confident persona had been replaced by embarrassment and confusion. She found herself talking less and less about being a virgin, mainly because the tremors in her voice would have given away how she really felt. She could no longer hide the fact that she was confused by God's inactivity in her life. It felt as if He had forsaken her. She dramatically shook this thought from her mind. "Of course," she told herself, "that was not true." Regardless of the facts, she was not ashamed of being a virgin, but at this stage in her life, she wanted answers; answers that made sense to her soul.

Sister Georgia allowed the flicking screen on the television to come back into her focus. She stood and turned the sound back up and heard the canned laughter of the comedy program she had been pretending to watch. She wondered what would come on next and looked around desperately trying to find the remote or the TV guide magazine. But she paused, and stood still in the middle of her living room for a few seconds. She knew she was trying to avoid the thoughts that were lining up patiently outside the door of her consciousness waiting to be heard. She reluctantly turned the sound down on the television and returned to her seat on the floor. Immediately, the thought she had been running away from most of her adult life, was grateful to finally be given an audience and had every intention of making the most of its time in the spotlight. Based on the experience in her twenties, there was a real possibility…a very real possibility…that she could be in exactly the same position in another decade. Crudely translated, she would still be a virgin. The painful thought made her drop the pen she had been holding and watched it roll across her wooden floor until it was stopped by her slippers. She had never been the best housekeeper, but being so busy over the years she had begun to neglect basic chores. Picking up after herself became more and more difficult as it dawned on her that there was no one to see it. Preferring to think about the pen on the floor, her lack of housekeeping skills, or the Ben and Jerry's in her freezer, she knew she was avoiding the real dilemma.

"No, No, it could not all have been for nothing!" She silently screamed to herself as the tears began to slowly trickle down her face. "No!" She was defiant and ripped the paper on which she had written her list. Her Lord would never, never forsake her. Refusing to be defeated, she said aloud, "I just have to think outside the box," she convinced herself. However, another troublesome thought squeezed its way into her mind. *But, isn't that what I have been doing all these years?* She became totally confused and allowed her mind to review the last few years of her life.

———

In what now seemed like a heartbeat, she had applied and graduated with her Master's in Education. She had taken an accelerated program to get it out of the way as quickly as possible and had completed her certification in eighteen months. Sister Georgina didn't let onto anyone that the real reason she was in so much of a hurry to complete her program was so she did not have to worry about studying when she was married and had children. Her routine of studying and blocking out the distractions from meaningless activities and going nowhere conversations meant that on the surface, her life in her twenties looked as if it was on track. She had secured sponsorship for her Master's in Education, at the University of Maryland, College Park. She definitely did not have a strategic planning board this time to determine where she would complete her graduate program. Functionality determined her choice. She needed somewhere that was most convenient for her life and College Park was exit 23 on the Beltway, while hers was exit 20. She did not have to live on campus and could work full-time. With her busy schedule, it meant her graduate course was over as quickly as it began, as was the pre-requisite for her scholarship, two years of service in the Prince George's County Public School System.

She loved her job as a twelfth grade teacher, and later as a special education consultant. The youth faced enormous challenges with the constant stream of societal negatives being thrown at them twenty-four hours a day. She knew they were scared and desperate for guidance, but were intelligent enough to see through the nonsense being dished out to them in the guise of *formal education*. Her colleagues, most of whom lacked the courage to be creative in the classroom or to question the system where necessary, meant Sister Georgina embraced the need to be the voice of the youth. As a result, she was loved by her students and hated by her peers and the education board that had never forgotten the media fiasco when she was a high school student. Sister Georgina always confronted the moans and groans of her fellow teachers when they spoke so negatively about their students. To her, they needed to be reminded that no matter how obnoxious, rude, and out of control they were, teachers had the ethical responsibility of providing their students with the educational skills to enable them to navigate their future. Never being one to back away from the enormity of problems within the education system, Sister Georgina accepted it wholeheartedly and relished the opportunity to use her creative skills to motivate her students. As a result, students rarely cut her classes, much to the envy of her colleagues. She prided herself on finding different ways to actively engage the students in the process of learning, regardless of whether it was in line with departmental policy or not.

Unbeknownst to Sister Georgina, the education board kept a very close eye on her, secretly hoping that she would be out of compliance and they could finally have an excuse to give her a pink slip. One particular board member dreamed of the day he would call her into his office and say 'you're fired'. A couple of others wanted to have the added pleasure of seeing her stripped of her benefits and pension, while for others they wanted a media circus, so she could experience the same vicious scrutiny they had come under and have the last laugh in the end. They had nothing on her yet, despite the many years she had worked for them since leaving her graduate program. And due to her student's favorable test scores and positive evaluations, it meant she was technically untouchable. Despite their dislike for Sister Georgina, they were forced to promote her steadily over the years, until she refused an administrative position in order not to lose direct contact with her students. They decided to wait patiently for an opportunity to 'get her' and send a clear message to others to stay in line. What better way to intimidate the staff than through the missteps of one of the department's most revered whistleblowers.

Sister Georgina's success in the classroom, however, did not extend into her personal life. With every passing school year, her dreams began to diminish, as the large number of eligible male employees she anticipated would join the staff never materialized. Female teachers had always dominated the profession and in an effort by the education board to ensure gender diversity, they actively tried to recruit male teachers, especially African-American and Hispanic men. At the beginning of the recruitment campaign she had been hopeful. But as the years passed, like Secus College, the few who accepted positions had been unavailable. So, in an effort to continue to be hopeful, she put sticky notes all over her home to remind herself that the perfect life would be delivered if she stayed faithful.

However, being honest, she couldn't deny that cracks were beginning to appear in her façade and not wanting to face them, had preferred denial. *The Lord will provide,* she told herself on a daily basis. She would remain loyal and committed to the belief that her Lord and Savior would send her a husband. So what that she was in competition with other women for the few eligible African-American men in the area? So what that so many had been lost to the gay community, the religion of Islam, the drug culture, incarceration, or white women? She had nothing to fear. This was God's world, she just had to be patient. Her mother had summarized this concept with her Caribbean proverb, 'there is a moldy piece bit of bread for every moldy piece bit of cheese'. Sister Georgina printed it in large bold letters and placed it strategically on her fridge to keep her motivated.

In the meantime, life went on. The compensation from her teacher's job was not the best, but together with her savings, it was enough for her to purchase a small, single family home in Landover Hills, not far from her beloved church. She had decided on a home, rather than a condo or apartment because she wanted to comfortably accommodate a husband and first child if needed. Of course, she had not wanted to move from the home where she had lived all her life, but it was the final tie with her siblings that needed to be settled after their father had died. She had been completing her Master's program when he passed and although she had never admitted it to anyone, she was secretly happy. Not because he died, but because she could have her degree sent in the mail, avoiding the need to arrange yet another gathering where she would be forced to make small talk with her family. Most had moved on by now, with some siblings venturing further away. She received a post card from Alaska once and couldn't imagine why her younger brother would want to settle there. Another sibling had relocated to Atlanta. The rest had moved around the D.C. area. Sister Georgina was the only one who remained in Prince George's County and continued to live in the family home. But, when she finished her Masters and began to work full-time, she knew it was time to move on.

Spending over a year looking for a suitable property had left her feeling as if she had seen every home that was on sale in the area. Every other Saturday her realtor would show her at least a couple of houses, but either the bedrooms were too small, the kitchen was in need of a major upgrade, or there was no access to public transport and were subsequently rejected as a result. But once she saw the split level, three bedroom, two and half bathrooms, she had fallen in love. The home was on a quiet street, in an area of Landover Hills that the realtor had reported with pride was on the "up and up" and becoming gentrified (her only evidence being that her immediate neighbor and two of the other homes were owned by white people). Sister Georgina decided to buy the house, not because of the realtor's hard sell tactics, but because she could see herself raising a family in the home. From the moment she walked through the door, she saw herself sitting quietly in the library studying the bible while her children played safely in the yard with its spacious porch. She happily imagined creating her very own piece of heaven on earth.

Therefore, as a result of becoming a homeowner, working full-time in her teaching position, and together with her responsibilities as a church elder, she wondered where her twenties had gone. It felt as if she had just woken up one morning and ten years had gone by. But never in her worst nightmare, had she imagined that she would still be single and a virgin.

She remembered making the decision to "ask so she could receive." Her wish of wanting a husband and children never wavered over the years. As dating came first, she knew she had to push herself out of her comfort zone and be proactive about it. She would make the effort, and this meant starting with herself. She had never considered herself to be a beauty queen, but on the other hand, she was not an unattractive woman. Granted she was a few pounds overweight, never having lost the weight she gained as a freshman (the only weight watchers class she had attended, the instructor had told her she could do with losing about sixty pounds). She had been paying a gym membership for the past five years, but had only used it a couple of times in the first few weeks. She had read somewhere that she could eat whatever she wanted (in moderation of course) as long as she exercised to burn off the excess calories. She had never stopped the direct debit payments because every year, she convinced herself she would use the membership to lose weight. In line with this belief, Sister Georgina would always sign up for the latest fad diet at the beginning of each year. However, by February, the diet products had been relegated to the back of the cupboard. They were unable to compete with homemade macaroni cheese, Southern fried chicken, and collard greens cooked with the traditional smoked ham that Mrs. Cartwright served up most Sundays after service.

Even having the gym membership, Sister Georgina's busy schedule never seemed to allow her to get to the gym as often as she wanted, so she purchased a treadmill. Once it had been taken out of the box and set up by the installers, in what she had assigned as her future baby's room, it very quickly became a drying rack for her underwear. But, just having the treadmill made her feel as if she was making some sort of an effort. Similarly, she thought she was also making an effort when she would go to the beauty salon. Granted, it would only be for a special occasion; an anniversary party or some educational official coming to the school (and Sister Georgina felt the need to intimidate them by power dressing). However, even though she knew her stylist was an expert in his field, she would insist on having the same hair style every time. He would complain bitterly about her lack of trust in his skill, but as he wanted his customers to feel good when they left his salon, over the years he reluctantly accepted her peculiarity and had perfected the style she felt best suited her personality... two big braids.

Sister Georgina would leave the salon feeling on top of the world, believing that she didn't have to do anything to maintain the style until her next visit. So, the silk nightcap that never seemed to stay on her head at night despite the guarantee on the packaging, the wind, and her general rushing around left her hair with a signature messy look. She knew she could do something more with her hair if she wanted to, but it always seemed so much of a bother. Her students would sometimes make fun of her, telling her that she looked like a scarecrow, or that her Afro was going to eventually come back into fashion. She didn't care what they thought, she would never use chemicals, as the Lord would expect her to be satisfied with the hair texture He had given her. She would never consider dreadlocks because it was way too rebellious for her personality. Occasionally, she would have single braids, but as it was so expensive and she hated having to sit in the chair for hours at a time, it was something she did every two or three years.

Yes, she also knew she could pay a lot more attention to her dress, but couldn't see the point of spending money on fancy designer outfits that were going to be in vogue for one season only. She was definitely not as bad as the ninth grade science teacher who would proudly wear the same outfit every day of the school year. She remembered vivid discussion with her twelfth graders about when the teacher would wash her clothes, but as it turned out that she had simply bought five of the same outfit to cut down time in the morning having to think about what she would wear that day. Something she had learned from her idol, Albert Einstein.

Sister Georgina had a stock set of clothes she would mix and match, paying no attention to how they looked together. When accompanying one of the elders to the thrift store, she would search for nearly new items for herself. There was always plenty of wear still left in them. Her goal was to pay off her mortgage as soon as possible, and if she continued to be frugal, she would achieve her goal in a couple of years. She wanted her family to be in the best possible financial position, especially when they would be responsible for children. So Sister Georgina didn't care what others thought. Her intentions were honorable and she believed that her soulmate would be able to see through her weaknesses and recognize the exceptional qualities she would bring to a relationship of substance. Her future husband would not be put off by the fact she didn't have makeup or the latest fashion accessories. He would fall in love with her mind, her body, and see things as she saw them. So, as she entered her thirties, she felt that she had taken one step towards the Lord and was looking for the Lord to take two steps towards her.

With the personal changes she was making and advice from the various self-help books collected from nearby thrift stores, she set out with a high expectation and renewed vigor to achieve her goal. Sister Georgina began walking each day and was so proud to discover that she had lost weight, albeit, just a couple of pounds. She also changed her wardrobe. Nothing too drastic, but her dress length did come up a few inches above her ankle. Her makeup had evolved from the occasional lip balm, to a very light, brownish lipstick. An end of the school year gift certificte to a spa led to her first ever visit. Facials and massages were off the table (being touched so intimately by another woman made her uncomfortable), but she welcomed the manicure and pedicure. She loved being pampered and as a result, felt more attractive. She was hopeful that she was making a real transition. She needed this boost as she upped her tactics to find a mate. Realizing that her attitude also needed updating, she decided to open herself up to whomever the Lord sent. This meant she included the possibility of an African, Caribbean, Hispanic, or even a white man as a possible partner. She had never imagined anything other than an African-American man lying in bed besides her, but faced with the intense pain of loneliness, she was prepared to consider every option.

Her potential partner, had evolved as time had passed from the romantic picture she had created during her undergraduate years. Ideally, he would be a Denzel Washington, Morgan Freeman, or Samuel L. Jackson, although she did not tell anyone of this crush because of his unChristian behavior and use of foul language. They were role models of men who personified confidence, control, and sophistication, just like her *Mr. Right*. He would be accomplished in his field, but still would be able to make her laugh until she cried. He would do little things that would make her heart sing, like open the door, order her food, have intelligent conversation, or cuddle up at the end of his busy day and read from the Bible. She would be able to talk to him about any and everything without him feeling intimidated or defensive. And of course, he would be very, very athletic. She was not going to hide the fact from her husband that she would have a lot of time to catch up on, so he would have to perform his husbandly duties most nights.

She was looking for a 'good' man and the talk radio, magazine articles, her women's groups, and the water cooler discussions at work had worn the subject out. She knew she wasn't the only sister in this position, but other women were her competition. So when the church's single sisters would commiserate together, and talk about how to tackle their manless situations, Sister Georgina stayed on the sidelines. She resolved to stay firm in her belief that the Lord would provide for her.

She was by far the most conscientious believer, therefore, God would surely bless her with a husband before any of her church sisters. She would struggle on by herself just a little bit longer, but where to meet a good man was a problem for her as a very occasional trip to the mall was the extent of her social activities. Work and church were the only other places she went, and neither was known for its wide selection of eligible bachelors.

By chance, Sister Georgina had come across a magazine article on dating. She had been sitting in the dentist's office waiting to be seen for her six-month checkup. She had randomly picked up one of the courtesy gossip magazines off the coffee table to pass the time as she waited for her name to be called. As she aimlessly flicked through one, she was shocked to find the guidance she had been craving. Unlike the self-help books whose authors' bias could easily be identified, this simple article reviewed the changes in the world of dating as the millennium approached and had laid out action steps that the reader could take. She was so excited and believed that God directed her to find the article. She then did something she had never in a million years saw herself doing, but believing her actions to be divinely ordained, she discreetly tore the article out of the magazine, and folded it neatly before slipping it into her handbag. She resisted the urge to read it immediately and for the rest of the appointment, was on edge, fearing the dentist had discovered the theft and would demand the article back. But undiscovered, she went home and carefully spread the stolen article over her dining room table. She read and reread the article, highlighting key sentences and then committed herself to following its advice.

The first step, the article stated was to verbalize loudly her wish to date to friends and family. This would be a bold step by Sister Georgina as she had never had that kind of relationship with her siblings and had very few people she actually called friends. After their mother died, her siblings rarely spoke to each other about the depths of their loss and moved away from each other as soon as they were old enough. She had concluded it was an attempt to lessen the intensity of the pain they felt every time they saw each other and were reminded of their shared loss. After their father died, it, too, had compounded the pain and their already strained relationships suffered. Conversations dwindled to "how's work going?" or "how's your family?" The article made her realize that she had never confided in them about anything, especially something that made her feel so vulnerable. Besides, there were practical things to consider, although, everyone knew where to find her, most had long ago dropped her from their call and Christmas card lists.

Sister Georgina liked to convince herself that she stayed in contact with Belinda, a first cousin on her father's side. But if the truth were known, it was Belinda who stayed in touch with Sister Georgina. It was true that if Sister Georgina ever needed anyone to go to a school event or support a church function, she would ask Belinda. Over the years such occasions had become infrequent and she had little reason to call. So, it was up to her cousin to call and check in on her every so often and update her on family news. Belinda's philosophy was, 'you're family and so you should know.' This attitude, together with her never being at a loss of what to say, meant Sister Georgina could be passive in the conversation and fed with the information, expelling very little effort on her part. She liked her cousin very much for that.

So, despite being extremely uncomfortable, Sister Georgina decided to start with Belinda and ask the difficult question of if she knew any eligible men. It took weeks of stress, going over and over how the conversation with her cousin should play out. Just trying to build up the courage to ask her cousin for help was a struggle and meant she practiced at least twice a day, saying the sentence over and over again while pacing the floor as she did so. She paid close attention to the inflections in her voice and even recorded herself to check how it would sound. But when the stress of it all became too much, she tried to talk herself out of making the call. Unfortunately, as she believed that God was pushing her out of her comfort zone, she accepted that the call had to be made. So, she allocated 7:30pm on Friday night to make the call and was sitting by the phone at 7:22pm with a glass of water and prompts for the conversation written out on a note card in case she got nervous. She was happily surprised when at 7:26pm, the phone rang and she heard Belinda's chirpy voice on the other end. Belinda called to invite her to an upcoming barbecue, and as it turned out, it was the only call she actually had on the subject of dating. *It was God at work,* Sister Georgina muttered to herself.

"Hi, Geogie," Belinda greeted her. "How are you doing?" Belinda was the only one who had the confidence to address Sister Georgina so casually, but she had been calling her that since they were children, so Sister Georgina had overlooked the informality. Without waiting for a reply, knowing that Sister Georgina liked to listen, Belinda continued.

"Look, there's a barbecue next Saturday. Just a quiet thing to celebrate nephew Jose finally getting a job. He's been out of work since he left school three years ago and his parents were pulling their hair out. Finally, they said enough was enough and gave him a deadline. He went out the very next day and got a job with UPS! He started last week and actually said he liked it. They are so happy, they want to celebrate. It's going to be in Watkins Park, Mitchellville; the one that has the wonderful Christmas lights every year. I can give you directions if you need it. Exit 17 off the beltway is your best bet and following the signs to Six Flags. So, it should be nice. I hope the weather lasts. Do you think you will be able to come?"

"Not sure."

"Why not? It should be fun. They are hiring caters, the one from Island Hut, who I hear, makes some mean jerk chicken! Let me guess, it's because you don't have a date, isn't it?"

"It would be nice to go with someone," came the tense reply.

"I heard my brother, Bert, talk about some friend of his needing a date, so let me see what I can do." Belinda said it so matter-of-factly, she did not realize the effect this sentence had on Sister Georgina. Naturally, she did not hear the rest of Belinda's conversation about the updates on the family because she was too busy, firstly, saying a prayer of thanks to the Lord and then allowing her mind to jump straight onto wondering whether Cousin Bert's friend was marriage material.

She was well aware of Cousin's Bert's reputation within the family for being shady, always on the lookout for something for nothing. At family gatherings, he would predictably announce a get rich quick scheme that would put an end to everyone's money worries. All they had to do was invest a small amount of money. As nothing ever panned out, no one ever took any notice of his fanciful schemes. Helped along by alcohol, he would stagger around the family events annoyingly preaching that his efforts were disrespected and how we, as African-American people, didn't support each other. Despite her reservations, Sister Georgina's excitement outweighed her concerns about Bert's involvement.

When she sensed from Belinda's tone of voice that the one-sided conversation was coming to an end, she tried to prod for more details.

"Umm... so when will you speak with Bert?" Sister Georgina tried to ask nonchalantly.

"You know Bert. He's wheeling and dealing as usual. I will catch up with him at some point this week and let you know. Definitely before Saturday. Okay. Bye, now." Then the phone went silent.

Sister Georgina sat with the phone in her hand for another about five minutes before she eventually put it down. *This is what being in shock must feel like*, she told herself and smiled.

Although, the magazine article had made sense, Sister Georgina did not agree with the advice about keeping first date conversations to safe subjects, like favorite movies or places to visit. *Time stands still for no one, so why not get straight to the point*, she reasoned. She wanted to know right from the start if they were interested. She decided that "Are you looking for a wife?" would be her opening line; she wanted to sort out the wheat from the chaff.

Sister Georgina gave her apologies to everyone for not being able to participate in after school and church activities in the upcoming week. She could barely get through her classes. She chose, instead, to focus all her attention on what she would wear, how to have her hair, or would just rush home to patiently wait for the phone call from her cousin. It did not arrive until Thursday.

"I just heard from Bert, he's quite something..." Belinda was stopped in her tracks by Sister Georgina's surprising interruption.

"Is he coming on Saturday?"

"No, he can't make it. He has to work. He's a manager of a restaurant or something, but Bert says he's definitely interested in meeting you."

This was the news Sister Georgina wanted to hear. Her heart skipped a beat. It would be her first date, ever (a detail she kept quiet). She listened intently as her cousin, sensing that Sister Georgina did not want to hear anything else, told her all she knew about this mystery person.

"He is seriously looking for a wife, ready to settle down, I heard. Wants a big family and does not want to wait. Bert says he will call you as the guy will book a restaurant downtown and wants to know what kind of foods you like. Sounds like you're going on a date!"

It was a couple of agonizing days for Sister Georgina before Cousin Bert called her. Her agony however, disappeared completely when he confirmed the date and said that a table was booked at an expensive restaurant downtown. He also confirmed what she had already been told by Belinda, that her date was seriously looking for a wife. The information fueled her preparation efforts, warranting another week off from after school and church activities, a special trip to the hairdresser, as well as to the nail salon. She just knew it was going to be special and was not disappointed when her date, Ezra, was finally introduced to her.

Ezra was an African student from Uganda. He was about four years younger than Sister Georgina, so she had affectionately thought of him as her toy boy. Ezra was certainly not her dream man, not by a long shot, but he was decent enough. He had a job as a manager at a local family restaurant and was studying to be an accountant. Sister Georgina thought this was doable. He was taller than her, slim, and athletic. She overlooked his shiny jacket, ill-fitting trousers, and shoes that looked like they had never been shined. She liked his smile. He was definitely attractive to look at and felt what she believed to be a physical connection, or rather, a tingle in the lower regions of her body. He was a staunch Catholic, but she was willing to compromise because at least he had a relationship with God. When Sister Georgina sat down, she exhaled. She was actually on a date with an eligible man! God was blessing her. She said a silent prayer and smiled at the young man sitting opposite the beautifully laid dinner table.

Her cousin Bert had accompanied Sister Georgina to the restaurant and did the introductions before ordering himself take out, which was added to their bill as he hadn't ventured downtown for nothing, and then left the couple to get to know each other.

"I am glad he's finally leaving," Ezra said to Sister Georgina when Bert finally exited the building. He had a thick African accent, and Sister Georgina wondered what she could do about that. "Now, I can finally have some quality time with you," he continued and looked at her straight in the eyes.

Sister Georgina felt butterflies in her stomach. She smiled involuntarily. *Can this really be happening*, she found herself thinking. *Yes. Yes, it is and I think I can make it work,* she reassured herself.

"Thank you." She then took a deep breath before pulling out the list of questions she had written down so she didn't forget anything.

"Are you looking for a serious relationship," Sister Georgina began.

"No," Ezra replied with a big grin on his face. However, seeing Sister Georgina's shocked face, he quickly corrected himself. "Yes! Yes, I am," Ezra replied with a sense of desperation. "I was just joking." To lighten the mood after his failed attempt at humor, he tried to justify his position. "I like Bob Marley and he said that the worse thing a man can do is play with a woman's feelings. So go ahead and ask me all the questions you want."

A good answer. A very good answer, Sister Georgina thought.

"I believe in getting straight to the point also, Georgina. Is it okay to call you Georgina?"

In an effort to come across as being flexible, she nodded in agreement. From him, being called "Georgina" definitely made her sound *wifey* and she did all she could to not sound out her name with his last name in that moment.

"In my culture, I should be married by now with many, many children. My family back home is angry with me for not finding a wife. I have to settle down and soon!" His emphasis on 'soon' had unknowingly reassured her. She knew a real man would understand her reasoning. His answer made her feel like she never felt before. She took a deep breath and embraced the fact that her defenses were coming down. Although the butterflies in her stomach seemed to intensify the more she relaxed, despite the discomfort, she actually found herself enjoying the date. The waiter who cleared the table also took as trash the folded piece of paper on which she had written her questions. She hadn't scolded him. Instead, she realized that she would not need it after all.

Ezra definitely paid close attention to her and the things she said. She felt, for the first time, this may be it. She found him easy to talk to and to laugh at his jokes. Until they were told by the wait staff that they had to leave, they talked about their churches, commitment to walking in Truth, their jobs, and hobbies. When Sister Georgina looked around at the empty restaurant and the tables that had already been set for dinner service the following day, she felt like she was in a Lifetime romantic movie. She was so happy. Giggling like school children, they apologized to the wait staff and Ezra paid the bill in full. In an obvious attempt to impress her, he slowly counted out five single dollar bills, indicating he was leaving a *generous* tip. The waiter tried to hide his disgust and sarcastically stated that they should enjoy what was left of their evening. He held the chair for Sister Georgina to get up, making it obvious that he was not leaving until they left his table. Ezra then thoughtfully escorted Sister Georgina to McPherson Square metro station. When the moment arrived for him to leave, she realized she was nervous. It was clear; neither party wanted to overstep their boundaries and so, awkwardly hovered around each other, knowing that something intimate should occur, but not sure what.

"Well…umm…I really enjoyed this evening," Ezra said taking the lead.

"Yes, thank you so much, I had a wonderful time." Sister Georgina found herself smiling and lowering her eyes. Taking her eye movements to be an invitation to kiss her, Ezra leaned forward and kissed her gently on her right cheek. He then attempted an embrace, but as she was loaded down with her oversized handbag, doggie bag, and the coins for the Metro, it ended up just being a clumsy bump against each other. They both laughed it off and said goodbye.

As Sister Georgina went down the escalator, she could feel his eyes looking at her backside as she descended. She felt so *sexy*. Once on the platform and out of sight from her intended, she exhaled. This was the first time she remembered someone with romantic intentions getting so close to her. She relived the bump over and over and imagined it was in the confines of her bedroom. She was blown away with excitement and anticipation for what could happen and soon. She thought seriously about using her treadmill again. The possibility of losing her virginity, as God had ordained, felt imminent. So, by the time she got off the Orange line at New Carrollton station, where her car was parked, she realized she had not stopped smiling.

Just as she was getting into bed, her phone rang.

"Hello?" She answered hesitantly, wishing she had paid the phone company for the Caller ID upgrade.

"It's me, Ezra." He paused and waited for some indication whether his call would be welcomed or considered inappropriate.

"Oh! Hello! What…what a pleasant surprise!" Sister Georgina was pleased he had the confidence to call. It was good to hear his voice again, and she noticed that his African accent was becoming an endearing feature.

Encouraged by her response, Ezra asked about her journey home and plans for the next day, which somehow, led to them talking about whether the moon landing had actually taken place. Sister Georgina loved every minute of the late night conversation. After chatting for about thirty wonderful minutes, they prayed together before saying goodnight for a second time that evening.

"How about dinner at my restaurant this time? I want to show you off," Ezra said.

"Of course," was her emotional response.

The second date, as expected, was another magical experience for Sister Georgina. She had taken half the day off work to get ready. Having had her hair done, a mani-pedi, eyebrows plucked way too thin and sure it was lopsided, but with the glowing comments from Ezra, she felt beautiful and that it had all been worth it. She felt very special, indeed.

He had set aside the best table in his restaurant, a table in the corner, nearest the door to the kitchen, and told his wait staff to give her the royal treatment. As they wanted to impress the boss, the staff went out of their way to spoil her. She truly felt flattered. Although, it was frustrating that every so often Ezra was distracted to troubleshoot a problem in the kitchen or at the front desk, when he did have time to sit with her, it made her feel complete.

It was on their third date, that she had an uneasy feeling. *The Lion King* movie had just opened and her Pastor asked the congregation to see it because of its spiritual messages. Ezra had happily agreed to accompany her. When they got to the box office, he declared that he had forgotten his wallet and asked if she would mind paying. This was the first time he had asked her to pay for anything, so she happily obliged. She certainly didn't mind covering the ticket fees, but it had all seemed a bit staged. He then asked to borrow twenty dollars to buy their popcorn and drinks and pocketed the change. In that moment, Sister Georgina's image of Ezra being her knight in shining armor came crashing down.

Standing there at the kiosk, it wasn't the fact that he pocketed the money that made her feel so uncomfortable, it was the fact that he didn't talk to her about it. In an attempt to ignore her feelings about what had just happened and have a good time, she settled the issue by concluding it was a "cultural" or a "man" thing and he hadn't given her the change back publically because it would have made him feel less than a man. *There were a lot of people in the lobby*, Sister Georgina falsely remembered. No matter how hard she tried to push it aside, she felt uneasy as she lay in bed that night; something had shifted inside her heart. She decided she needed to talk to him about it. She wanted a marriage of open communication, no secrets. She said her prayers, confident that things would somehow work out for the best.

When Ezra greeted Sister Georgina with a broad smile, her heart fluttered. She had just pulled up outside his restaurant to pick him up for their date and was happy to find him standing outside waiting for her. She unlocked the car door and he got in. He gently took her hand from the steering wheel and kissed the back of it lovingly.

"How are you today my beauty?" He asked.

"I am doing well, thank you for asking. Are you excited about tonight?" Sister Georgina said.

"Yes, of course I am. I will be with you."

She reciprocated his smile and became even more excited about their evening together. She was treating him to a romantic dinner at a waterfront restaurant in Annapolis to celebrate their fourth date. She was hoping that today he would say something about having a life together and was grateful for that gesture as it confirmed her feelings of anticipation. She drove off with high expectations. Ezra affectionately touched her arm whenever they stopped at a red light, so she made sure not to take Route 50 to ensure they went through the maximum number of traffic lights. She talked about the happenings at her school and church and then made the fatal mistake of asking him how his day had been.

"I had a bad day, my dear. My professor says I cannot come to class without the required books. I do not know what to do because I don't get my check until next Friday."

"I am sorry to hear that. Is there anything I can do?" The words had come out of her mouth out of habit before she had a chance to think it through.

"Yes, can we go to my restaurant as we can eat for free and you can give me the money you were going to pay for the meal so I can use it for my school books?" Genuinely believing that this was a good idea, Ezra gave her one of his big broad smiles.

"How much are the books?" Sister Georgina asked out of curiosity.

"$500 should do it," Ezra replied without hesitation, believing he was about to receive the cash.

Sister Georgina smiled sweetly and told him that she needed to pray about it and would let him know the next day.

"Let's pray now," was the irritated retort. "God knows I really need these books now. I cannot get behind in my studies."

"When I mentioned that I would pray on it and let you know tomorrow, did you not understand what I said?" Sister Georgina used her classroom voice. "What you're doing now Ezra, is definitely not attractive. It feels as if you are trying to bully me." She was going to say her truth without apology.

Ezra pleaded that he would definitely pay her with his next pay check, but needed the books the next day otherwise he would not be allowed in class. Seeing he was not convincing Sister Georgina, he stated, "No, no, the money is really for my rent. My landlord will evict me tomorrow if I don't pay him something." Ezra said grasping for sympathy.

"That meant you lied to me." Ezra was confused by her response.

This is why men can never understand women, he thought. As he could not figure out a suitable response, he tried the diversionary tactic from Sister Georgina's insightful comment.

"$500 is not a lot of money and besides you know I will pay you back. Just come to my restaurant on Friday and it will be ready waiting for you," he said with a smile.

Seeing her tears, he knew he was in trouble. Despite being a few minutes from their destination, Sister Georgina turned the car around and this time took Route 50, homeward bound in silence. Thankfully, he did not live too far from her, off the Annapolis Road, so she dropped him off outside his gate. This time it was her turn to watch him slowly disappear from her rear view mirror as she drove away. His face was distraught, clearly indicating that he had no idea what had just happened.

Deciding she needed some more information about Ezra, called her cousin Belinda. She had not spoken to her since their last conversation, but by now, Belinda had gotten more information about Ezra from her brother. Despite her plans to pass the news onto Sister Georgina, she had gotten busy with other things, but a call initiated by Sister Georgina was serious, and decided to fill her in on what no one in the family had seen fit to tell her.

It really was Ezra's intention to marry her, but was going to pay Bert $3,000 when it was made official. Basically, he needed a green card to legalize his stay in the United States. He had been asking around for a while for someone to marry and Bert had offered Georgina. Ezra did not have any money, but Bert knowing how frugal Sister Georgina was with her money, told Ezra he should be able to get the money from her after they were married. Not taking Bert's advice and waiting until the after the wedding to ask Sister Georgina for money, he had miscalculated her.

Belinda also told Sister Georgina that Ezra had been using someone's social security card to work, which made sense, as everyone at his restaurant had been calling him Thomas. She then mentioned that he was never an accounting student taking classes at Prince George's Community College. After sharing pleasantries about the next family event, Sister Georgina, unemotionally, thanked her cousin for the information and said her goodnights. She had been considering giving him the money. She really did want to pray about it, but no longer could she ignore the uncomfortable feeling in her stomach. She reasoned to herself, that she still had time to meet someone else, get married and have children. It was early enoughin their relationship that she could let go and move on; for, no matter how she tried to make it work in her head, there really was no coming back from the information about Ezra. He was history.

Sister Georgina was so angry with Bert for the set up, she made it a point to not talk to him when she saw him at family functions. Burnt by the experience with Ezra, it took a couple of years and the loud ticking of her biological clock before she decided to try another dating tactic.

She was thankful for sticking to her principles and only allowing him to kiss her cheeks, but that didn't stop her from thinking about what he could have done if they had actually gotten to the bedroom.

Fueled by an unspoken desperation, Sister Georgina, undaunted, continued to step outside of her comfort zone. Being creative, she decided to lead the other single women in the church to organize a "Single's Night." They worked hard to promote the event, distributing flyers and posters around the local area and to neighborhood churches. The single women had been so hopeful on the first night, but after the third, it was agreed that it was a total failure. The group disbanded before the fourth event. The reasons were simple enough. The same female members attended each session without bringing a single male guest, which was a condition of entry. The only two male strangers who appeared at the second session were unanimously discounted by all as potential suitors because, one, at forty-five years old, had not worked for many years and was still living with his mother. He could provide no rational justification, except that he loved his mother. The other had no idea how many children he had fathered. No further explanation was needed by any of the sisters to discount him as a potential partner.

With the Single's Night fiasco a miserable failure, Sister Georgina, under the pretense of "being in leadership," decided to keep the single women positive by organizing a social group with the objective being to meet eligible suitors. This group was a bit more successful than the Single's Night, as they met monthly for about two years. But, this eventually fizzled out, as well. It was the philosophical differences this time that caused the group to disband. Several members wanted to be more creative in their attempts to meet brothers, which included attending a non-believing cruise down the Potomac and going to a bar in the exclusive Georgetown area of D.C. that had a night club attached. But, before the group split, they had been adventurous enough to attend a Christian speed-dating event. Sister Georgina had realized pretty quickly that five minutes was far too long to spend with some of the strange characters who attended. Plus, it was definitely not worth competing with the large number of women who happily took their seat the minute it was vacated by a previous dater.

It was a Christian internet dating site that proved to be her most successful venture into the world of dating. She could do this in the privacy of her home, which was ideal, since she could still present an image to the single church sisters that she still "had it together." At first, she had despised and ignored the media blitz about the growing popularity of online dating. However, as the lonely nights turned slowly from months to years, she knew she had to try something different. Despite her reservations about the impersonal nature of online dating, she overlooked them, believing that by taking one step forward, God would take two towards her. The subliminal manipulation of the advertisers finally got her to dive in and take advantage of their free introductions that was only offered that Labor Day weekend. She became hopeful that she may finally find her husband... online.

It was with excitement and anticipation that she assumed her inbox would be flooded with an endless supply of possible suitors once she pressed the *Submit* button on her profile. But, it was almost ten months before she got tired of the highs and lows that came from having her hopes dashed on such a regular basis. She loved the attention at the beginning of this adventure, turning on her computer and finding lots of emails from men on the site. She loved being in the surprising position of emailing several men at the same time. But one by one, they were eliminated as potential suitors for one reason or another.

Sister Georgina struck up a friendship with a gentleman named, Ronald. He was from South Carolina and she immediately warmed up to his welcoming southern charm. She had great hopes for this relationship. In his first few emails, he seemed keen and interested in pursuing a serious relationship. His words were so convincing and flattering, she felt as if she had been swept off her feet. He presented himself as considerate and understanding, and that was enough for Sister Georgina to lower her guard and give him her phone number. Ronald called and for several weeks they spoke at the end of each day. He had a wonderful voice and had a great sense of humor. She really felt that they had a connection. They both finally agreed that it was time to meet in person.

He asked Sister Georgina where she wanted to meet and she named the local Panera Bread café in Bowie; a reasonable distance from her house. Ronald was waiting for her as planned, but she was immediately disappointed because his picture was taken at least ten years ago and did not account for his graying hair and extensive belly fat, even though he could say the same about Sister Georgina. However, she felt she could overlook that misrepresentation and give him a chance. She purchased a cup of coffee for herself after she had given him ample opportunity to buy it for her, but when she returned to sit down, he suggested they go across the street to Starbucks instead as they had something that he wanted. She claimed it was not a problem and went with him, Panera coffee in hand.

Once they were inside, the pair sat down at a table again. Ronald did not buy a cup of coffee nor anything else, so Sister Georgina couldn't figure out why he wanted to move, especially when he could have easily offered to meet at Starbucks. She watched him as he sat uncomfortably on the edge of his chair. He then proceeded to say he was on a time limit and couldn't stay long. The meet and greet had lasted all of fifteen minutes. Sister Georgina said she didn't want to keep him from his appointment. Grateful for the exit, he promptly left. She threw her coffee away and had no idea what he thought of her. She found his behavior bizarre and was relieved when he never called or emailed her again.

Undeterred, she again had high hopes for Robert, some kind of computer programmer who was originally from Detroit. She did not understand until it was too late why he wanted to meet at the entrance of The Home Depot off exit 15 on the Beltway. She was instantly attracted to his boyish charm and his well-maintained muscular body that protruded proudly from beneath the stylish t-shirt he wore. She was even more impressed when he had introduced himself with a confident outstretched hand. She was, therefore, really looking forward to finally being able to sit down with him after he had picked up the tools he said he needed to purchase. Once in the store, Robert drifted off to search for a sales assistant and then disappeared down one of the aisles, never to be seen by Sister Georgina again. She left the store highly humiliated and embarrassed.

She was determined to be more vigilant next time, but this proved to not be the case and she became extremely angry with herself for not paying attention to the height listed on her next date's profile. When she arrived at the restaurant, Sister Georgina found out that he was about five inches shorter than her five foot, five inch frame. She went ahead with the date out of politeness and in the interest of giving him a fair chance. He seemed to sense that things were not going in his favor and tried flattery and bribery to elicit a second date. When neither produced the desired results, he decided on emotional blackmail and had burst into tears begging her to see him again. She politely told him goodbye after offering a tissue to dry his eyes and left. She was thankful she had parked a good distance from the restaurant, as she definitely did not want him to see her car out of fear he might stalk her.

The Christian nature of the dating site, apparently, did not deter the majority of her suitors who made it clear they were seeking sex without responsibility. As a result, she soon stopped meeting them for dinner and would arrange to have coffee instead. Eventually, that turned into just meeting for a 'hello' in parking lots. Realizing that she didn't need to waste any more of her time than was necessary, she decided to put an end to her cyber activities. The consistent disappointment led Sister Georgina to reluctantly form the opinion that dating was extremely stressful. Her heart simply could not take it anymore.

She never lost sight of her goal of marriage and kept fasting and praying. Although the church had many sisters who were in her same position, she chose to not confide in them. Over the years, she had watched most of them gossiping and seemingly enjoying the misery of others. So she certainly was not going to trust them with her innermost pain.

As was customary, she had no idea *how* to share her pain with others. She did not want anyone to think her faith was weakening. No, she would put her faith in the Lord. Only He knew the depth of her pain. When she weakened, she would *deal* with it. Outwardly, she would pretend that it was all under control, but in the safety of her home, she would cower in the fetal position under the sheets trying to hide from the pain coming from within. Or she would escape into the dream world of how her imaginary husband would lie next to her in bed and stare lovingly into her eyes.

When the pain became too intense, Sister Georgina did what she knew best and threw herself into helping others. Pretending she had it all together and avoiding the hypocrisy she felt, took the opportunity to tell the other sisters, who, unlike her did not hide their pain that God will deliver. In her attempt to "help" her single sisters, she decided to be proactive and formed a prayer circle. Its purpose was, of course, to pray for guidance and support from their Lord and Savior, but also, it sought to provide a venue for them to discuss solutions for the predicament they all found themselves. As a result, they came up with many different ideas on how to keep busy while they waited for the Lord to deliver their husbands.

With Valentine's Day quickly approaching, it was to be their first day of action. As Sister Georgina had done in college, she decided to have a reversal of the Valentine's Day theme. The sisters were to be proactive and give cards and flowers to each other. She valued the opportunity to be able to forget her own problems and was happy to rush over to one of the sister's homes after hearing that she had locked herself in the closet in an attempt to avoid the day. She had to be coaxed out with flowers and a card, for which the sister was truly grateful. They then prayed, sang hymns, and had tea together. However, at 11:30pm, Sister Georgina knew she had overstayed her welcome when the sister appeared in her pajamas, making it clear she was ready for bed. Unknown to the sister, Sister Georgina also wanted to avoid going back to an empty home, because there would be no one to help her through her pain.

Regardless of Sister Georgina's difficulties, it did not stop her from leading the prayer circle and coming up with many creative ways of keeping the ladies busy. She got the women to sign up for cooking classes and a women's football league. They volunteered their time to help at homeless shelters and food banks, all in addition to their regular duties at church. Sister Georgina had also found the opportunity to teach part-time at a local community center and help out at the county's election board. The sisters definitely enjoyed getting together to air their frustrations, but somehow, the conversation never got around to their sexual feelings and what to do about them. Sister Georgina thought about developing a class to address this and to keep them motivated, but let the idea go when she didn't know where to turn for material, but it was really because she feared that this time, she would not be able to hide her own frustrations. Whatever, she did though, she could no longer deny that her sexual feelings were becoming more and more prominent.

The mild romantic scenes on the made-for-TV movies had her mind wandering about the *how* and the *why*. So, she chose to deliberately not watch movies that even hinted at having sexual content, because more than likely, it would leave her sexually frustrated. And besides, watching them would not answer her questions of why the act was so appealing and the popular topic of many conversations. However, turning the channel was easy compared to her out of control biological reactions. In her twenties, her sexual energies were bearable because her busy lifestyle kept her occupied. But, with college over and work under control, her sexual urges began to bubble to the surface. It was slow at first, the odd twinge here and there. But she realized that things were changing when she would find herself day (and night) dreaming about what it would be liked to be kissed or made love to.

Now in her thirties, Sister Georgina was plagued by the desire to actually experience the event. She kept a close eye on her menstrual cycle and knew she was most sexually frustrated when she was ovulating and just before her period. So, twice a month she would be crawling the walls with frustration. This sparked solo investigations into what she could do to control her feelings. This ranged from going to the library and researching how Catholic nuns and priests managed, to fasting on a regular basis,as she had read somewhere that it would decrease the libido. But for her, it did nothing close to taking the edge off her feelings. She had also tried natural, herbal remedies, but she hadn't really given them a chance, often getting frustrated when they didn't work after the first two days of trying. The thought that it may take three to twelve months to kick in was definitely too long to wait.

Once, she was daring enough to log onto a website that sold sex toys. She had overheard one of the teachers at school talking about it and how it had been better than her husband, so one Saturday afternoon, she logged on. The first screen embarrassed her with its naked women surrounded by strange objects, creams, and pornographic DVDs. She had closed the site immediately, as she had no idea about what certain things were used for and had no idea where to start. After making herself a strong cup of black tea, she opened the site again. This time, however, she was determined to have a different attitude. She would be like Harry Potter when he explored Diagon Alley for the first time and wished she, too, had eight more eyes to be able to take in all of the strange and bizarre items on sale.

In an attempt to motivate one of her struggling readers, she had given him the option to choose his own books to earn extra credits. He had chosen the anti-Christian adventures of the young wizard and in good conscience, felt she could not turn around and tell him to choose another book. His enthusiasm for the story had drawn her in, as well. So, like Harry Potter, she tried to take in as much as she could, but unlike him could not make sense of the cryptic descriptions for each item that clearly assumed the reader had some idea how to use the product.

Sister Georgina had decided to play it safe and go for a traditional vibrator and clicked onto the section. She had no idea that there would be so many choices for imitation penises. She blocked out the shapeless blobs that included wires which were described as vibrators since she was not sure how they should be used. She honed in quickly on a black replica with three speeds so she would not have to drag the experience out longer than was necessary. The details claimed it had been molded from a real penis and took three AAA batteries that was included in the price. That was all she needed to know.

She grabbed her purse and tried not to think about the enormity of her decision to purchase such an unChristian-like object. When she was about to enter her shipping address, she paused. She thought about where she would hide it especially if she died and someone had to clear her house and found it. She would still be mortified. She also thought about the cold plastic penis entering into her and it didn't sound too appealing either. The price of nearly $100, which she thought was extortionate, pushed her over the edge and she put away her credit card. She logged off of the site for the final time, putting an end to her brief interlude into internet shopping for a vibrator.

Sister Georgina got up from her seat on the floor, not realizing just how uncomfortable it had become. She stretched her arms and legs in an effort to wake herself up and wondered what else she could be doing to find herself a husband. The television screen flickered and she noticed one of her favorite comedy shows was on. She sat back down and stared at the TV trying to find the motivation to watch it, clearly needing to escape the pressures of thinking about her forced abstinence. Despite making herself a strong cup of tea, she found it difficult to focus on the program and rather than channel surf, she surprised herself by turning off the television because it seemed like every station had a show about someone finding their soul mate. It added to her feelings of being unwanted and rejected and became too much to bear.

Surely, it isn't supposed to be like this, she wondered as the tears fell down her face. In the silence, the National Geographic show she had watched with another twelfth grade teacher earlier that week to determine its suitability for their classes, came to her mind. After reviewing the documentary about an indigenous tribe in the South Pacific, they both decided it was not appropriate. Concerned that parents and the Board of Education would object to the indigenous population shown so skimpily dressed had outweighed the benefits that the youngsters would learn about an alternative culture. With the passing of time, Sister Georgina, had learned to pick her battles and on this occasion, agreed with her colleague. The purpose of the video was to educate the students about how other cultures organized their social structures and the roles that individuals played. For Sister Georgina, the bigger picture was now her sanity. She needed to understand her role in the society in which she lived. She could no longer deny the pain of her loneliness; she felt like a fool that her commitment to Truth was overlooked and mocked by disbelievers. She had to face the question: *was her sacrifice all these years for nothing?*

Now, in the silence of her apartment, two of the women from the indigenous community were looking back at her from the television screen. The happy faces of these nameless women were shaking their heads in confusion and began talking about her.

"What is she doing?"

"She's crying," responded the other.

"She's been sitting in front of the television for a while, not moving... I think she may be sick," the first woman hypothesized.

"I think you're right. It might have something to do with the yellow dust on her hands and on her clothes?"

"Is it poisonous? Is she trying to kill herself? She looks so miserable," she inquired.

"Why doesn't someone come and help her?" asked the second.

"There doesn't seem to be anyone around. How strange. Does she not realize we are not supposed to be alone?"

They may not have television, telephones, or other modern technologies, but the women in the indigenous community could recognize that Sister Georgina was not *living*. The documentary narrator had described their community as "utopia" where everyone seemed to co-exist with their complementary roles. There was a woman for every man. The women could be as God intended, could raise their children, and have a societal sanctioned provider and protector. The idea that a solitary woman would be sitting alone on a Saturday night was alien to them. In the vision, Sister Georgina found herself holding up the plastic replica of a penis to show them. The women both stared at the object with intense curiosity. It was beyond absurd to them and they looked more confused than ever.

"I don't know what else to do," Sister Georgina said to the imaginary women.

"You must get a husband and have some children," the first indigenous woman replied matter-of-factly.

"I want to, but no one wants me," was Sister Georgina's pitiful response.

"This is not good, not good," came the reply from the woman on

the television.

As she and her fellow teacher had concluded that the indigenous society was less fortunate than theirs since it was *apparent* that the women were clearly oppressed, not given a voice in their society, was beneath the men of the village, and their heterosexuality was assumed, Sister Georgina could sense that they thought the same about her society. The sympathy on the faces of the imaginary women as they looked at her forced Sister Georgina to face the reality that she was no longer content with dreaming of what could be. Her life was passing by so quickly and she needed to force herself to keep going. She had nothing to lose. So, as she sat on the floor staring at the television screen in her pajamas with her sticky, yellow, cheesy fingers, she finally allowed herself to face her worse fears.

It had been creeping slowly into her mind and could no longer be pushed away; that she may die without experiencing the joys of married life. Sister Georgina had tried for years to avoid thinking about the pain of this reality, so she quickly shrugged the thought from her mind. Yes, things were bad, but after all these years, her commitment to the Lord could not be shaken. He will provide her with a husband. *She just knew it.* Her sacrifice would not be in vain. Sister Georgina got up with a renewed sense of purpose and headed to the bathroom to shower. She put on a clean robe and took her pain to the Lord.

Dear Lord, help me remain strong and steadfast during this difficult time. I am your servant. I am committed to your Truth and only your Truth. I was weak today, but I am thankful for your guidance and strength. I know you will help me through. I trust in your plan. Amen.

She slept soundly for the first time in months. She had absolute faith that her husband would soon come into her life.

Chapter Four
Making Lemonade

Organizing the Saturday afternoon social events for the elderly church members was always a fun thing for Sister Georgina. She loved seeing their smiling faces as they played games and interacted with each other. At the back of her mind, though, was her growing reputation of being able to assist with every church event because she didn't have a family of her own. She knew her fellow church members felt sorry for her, but she had gotten over the embarrassment. What else was she to do? The choice was simple; to help out or be at home in front of the television wallowing in her misery. She had chosen to keep busy.

———————◦———————

After her disastrous experience into the painful world of dating, Sister Georgina had gone back to school and started a PhD program in special education. She told those around her that it would further her career because it sounded so much better than the truth, which was to keep her mind off her increasing loneliness and sexual frustrations. But, instead she found herself arguing with the professors as she did when she was in high school. She would call them out on their poor presentation styles, lack of references, or irrelevant course material. They were constantly upset with her and strongly suggested that she visit the counseling center. Although, insulted by their insinuation that she needed mental health treatment, she had to accept that they may have had a point when she found herself struggling to get to class and to submit her assignments on time. Being honest with herself, she could not think of a reason to complete the course other than pure boredom.

That did not justify the time, effort, or financial expenditure it took to be successful, so she questioned her motivation. After getting over the fact that she may be perceived as a failure by her friends and family, she accepted the reality that she wasn't interested in obtaining the degree; her heart wasn't in it. Besides, working full-time in a demanding teaching position and studying at night, left little time to think about what she didn't have in her life. So, after nearly three years, she decided to let her academic course go. Her advisors did their best to talk her out of it, reasoning that she was doing so well and graciously allowed her a couple of months off without financial penalty to reconsider. Sister Georgina, fed up with studying, allowed herself to accept the fact that she could not muster up the energy nor the passion to continue and formally withdrew from the program.

With school now a memory and having nothing to replace it, she committed herself to working around the clock for her beloved church. She was a few months to her fortieth birthday and couldn't figure out where the time had gone. It seemed like only yesterday that she was baptized and now, here she was, twenty-one years later. Her life had not played out as she had expected. Oh, yes, she could pretend to others that everything was okay, when in reality, she was screaming on the inside, devastated that her life was slipping by right before her eyes.

Sister Georgina truly appreciated her church community. It was nice that they made sure no one sat in her pew on Sunday morning, to see their welcoming smiles, and be a part of their superficial conversations. Everyone seemed to love that she could prioritize their needs above hers, but just the same way she cared for others, she longed for someone to care for her. No one seemed to notice that what was going on for her was so much deeper. She knew it was because no one was interested enough to go there with her and she was extremely angry about it. *It wasn't fair.* She would give so much of herself each and every day and receive nothing in return. She could feel the tension within her beginning to boil. She did not know what the explosion would look or feel like, but she knew it would inevitably arrive. It never occurred to her that *she* could ask for help, despite being the one who prepared the church newsletter each week and privy to who needed the congregation's prayers. Her prayers at the beginning and end of the day would normally focus on the needs of others. She had drawn up a list she kept by her bedside and would diligently call each person's name to make sure the Lord heard her prayers. She had never entertained the thought that she needed to be on the prayer list herself or that she may deliberately be keeping busy to stop herself from thinking about her personal pain. With this reality check, Sister Georgina retreated back into her comfort zone, determining the best thing to do was to keep her head down and focus on getting through each day.

Sister Georgina didn't realize it, but her church family had indeed noticed her struggle. The regulars of the church had, for decades, overlooked her peculiarities primarily because she got things done. Her attention to detail, genuine commitment, and above average tithing contributions -much to the Pastor's delight- made Sister Georgina an invaluable member of the church. The Pastor was also particularly proud that the single sheet of paper they called their newsletter, had been transformed over the years into a six-page, glossy, color booklet with pictures and different fonts, dramatically outlining the happenings of the church. He especially liked his flattering picture that was a permanent feature on the front page.

Established church members put up with her reputation of being a difficult person to be around, however, over the last few years they began to notice that her harsh and condescending tone had increased. She was more irritable, moody, and seemed to get angry over petty and irrelevant things. But no one had been brave enough to talk to her about their concerns. She was notorious for her overzealous, and at times, sanctimonious attitude. They were afraid she would interpret their feedback as questioning her commitment to the Lord, so they chose, instead, to walk on eggshells whenever she was around for fear of feeling her wrath. Besides, they rationalized, she was in a position to do it, so why not let her get on with it? What they could not ignore was the decreasing attention she paid to her appearance. Never known for being a fashion icon, she had always been 'semi-acceptable'. But over time, her gradual decline meant she had become overtly messy and disheveled. Once she had kept her hair in cornrows so long, the new growth began to form dreadlocks. During the week, Sister Georgina's would dismiss thoughts about her clothes needing ironing, reasoning that 'it wasn't that bad'. And, besides, on Sunday, she would make some kind of effort for appearances sake.

Sister Canisa, a fairly new member of ten years, decided it was the Godly thing to do and mention something about it to her church sister. A steadfast sister, about fifteen years older than Sister Georgina who had her fair share of life stressors. Having had a child out of wedlock in her twenties, she knew first-hand what it felt like to be humiliated and ostracized by her fellow church sisters. Despite having stood her ground for several years, reluctantly decided to leave her church home when the relentless gossip and whispers finally took its toll. She went on to raise her son by herself and in spite of the difficulties, had no regrets.

Feeling a mix of pride and unease when her precious son enlisted in the ARMY, understood when she opened her front door six years later to an army chaplain and a commanding officer. She had her worse fears confirmed. After his funeral, she relocated from Medford, Massachusetts to where ever the pin landed on the map. It just so happened to be Glenarden, Prince George's County, Maryland and like Sister Georgina's mother, found her new church home to be a place where her soul could be comforted, while remaining distant and aloof. She remained in the background at most church functions, but was never afraid to speak up or take action when required by her faith to do so.

Sister Canisa saw an opening when Sister Georgina mentioned something about the housekeeping at the church. Using all her skills to be tactful, offered politely to help her with her personal laundry and housework. Immediately taking offense by the offer, in an attempt to cover up her embarrassment, Sister Georgina gathered enough composure to quote, "take the plank out of your own eye first," implying that Sister Canisa's help was not needed. The distraught sister apologized profusely but could see through her dramatic defense. She would not give up on a woman who she knew was in trouble and made it clear that she would be available when she was ready. Sister Georgina was secretly appreciative of Sister Canisa's offer and genuinely felt her love. She wanted to accept the help, but did not know how to get out from underneath the façade she had nurtured for years. How could she, now, after all this time, admit that she needed help? Although no one in her church family talked about it openly, everyone knew that she kept them at bay choosing instead to perfect an image of a competent person whose life was on track.

Once, during a storm, her power had gone out for a couple of days. She had spoken to Sister Canisa and a few others several times during the powerless days. She even went to help other members who had also lost power. Not once did she mention that she did not have power herself. Being in control was important for Sister Georgina. Vulnerability, in her mind, was an indication of weakness and someone without faith. Aware that she had developed a knack for hiding the depth of her pain, she never spoke about her sleepless nights, her junk food addiction, nor how she would cry uncontrollably into her pillow when the pain of loneliness became too much for her to bear.

The solution for Sister Georgina was, of course, to hold onto what she trusted the most; the notion that the Lord would deliver a husband. It was the mid-2000s and she now had some valuable life experience behind her. Despite everything that had happened to her, it was the belief in her Lord and Savior that made the world make sense. The Devil and his followers had a tight grip on the world, allowing the chaos and hatred to dominate, but for her, it made her faith even stronger. She was totally convinced that if people would believe the Truth, the world would definitely be a better place. It was like 'being a psychic' she once joked to one of the few new converts at the Wednesday night bible class.

"Knowing the Lord is like being able to see into the future," she smiled.

"I don't quite understand."

"Well, you know when you breathe, you inhale oxygen and exhale carbon dioxide," Sister Georgina explained, thinking she was still in her classroom of twelfth graders.

"I'm still not following."

"It's okay, let me explain. We breathe from the moment we are born to the last breath when we die. But every single breath we take flows throughout our body, giving every single cell the oxygen it needs. Our breath goes down our nostrils, through our lungs, and then into our bloodstream, pumped around the body by the heart through the big arteries first, and then to each of the capillaries... *Wow!* The process then removes the bad waste products. Because we do this so many times, we take the process for granted and never wonder about the marvel of it all.

"When I think about it, it tells me that there is order, structure, and purpose to the world we are living in. My God tells me that each breath I take is representative of my connection to the world I inhabit. So my smile can brighten someone's day and they, in turn, can smile at someone else, which can brighten their day, and so on and so on. We just have to *pay attention.*

"Just like each breath, my belief tells me that I am alive for a reason. If I decided to go where I wanted to go when I wanted to go, I would disrupt the entire process, no doubt, causing myself and others much harm. If the Lord is the originator of such order, then He deserves my total submission. My submission means that I want my contribution to make the life flow as He designed. Looking at what he has created, I know He knows exactly what he is doing."

Sister Georgina felt a bit like the Pastor. She was glad for the opportunity to testify to someone other than the church regulars, and besides, this new convert, had not yet heard of Sister Georgina's reputation. She inhaled deeply, feeling the joy of Truth reacting positively to the elaborate description.

At home that night, like most other nights, Sister Georgina reaffirmed her faith as she knelt by her bedside in submission to her Lord and Savior. She had meant every word she told the sister. Knowing the Lord gave meaning to her life. Despite the passing of time since her baptism, it had provided her with protection in the secular world. She knew there were so many people who did not understand, painfully reminding herself of the infamous dinner party at Secus College. She was humiliated because of her beliefs. But, knowing the devil has such a grip on this world, she believed that if the parents of the children she taught each day lived their faith as she did and exercised discipline, then her students would be so much better off. She witnessed their pain each day caused by the irresponsibility of fathers who felt no obligation to the children they seeded, or their mothers who had no idea how to put their children first. The secular world made crazy seem normal. It was her faith that kept her sane. She believed.

As she said her prayers, Sister Georgina found herself, revisiting her tried and tested 'aha' moment. Her faith told her to 'ask and it will be delivered' and even though she believed she had been asking all these years, she convinced herself she had been waiting; just expecting the Lord to deliver.

I need to demonstrate my faith, she rationalized. *I need to take one step towards him. And then, He WILL take two towards me...*

Sister Georgina took advantage of her renewed energy, got up from her knees, and found the notepad and pencil that laid on her bedside table. As she sat on her bed, she hesitated for a minute before writing, *'I wish to marry a man from within my church'.* She was trying to be different from her last attempt at defining what she wanted. This time she would be specific and could hold the Lord accountable if He did not deliver. It was scary to be so specific, but with the Lord, anything was possible. Her initial thought had been to require any potential suitor to actually be baptized into her church before she would give them any serious consideration. However, the fact that her church home rarely had new members, let alone someone who was marriage material, inevitably made Sister Georgina modify this criteria.

For as long as she could remember, most of the male members in her church were either too old or too young. The older male membership ranged in years from their late sixties to Mr. Bullman, who would be 93 on his next birthday. With the exception of Mr. Bullman, the majority had been in long-term relationships. She had a twinge of jealousy every time she helped the established couples in the church celebrate their decades together. In her mind, they had been blissfully happy every day of their married life. As for the younger male members, they seemed to leave the church as soon as puberty set in. If she pursued this as a viable option, she would be escorted off her job as a high school teacher by security with the possibility of imprisonment and a magazine exposé.

The choir director was single, but he was the *choir director*. No one openly ever said he was gay, but somehow everyone knew not to ask him why he didn't have a girlfriend or if he planned to marry. So, she conceded and decided to be more flexible, expecting potential suitors to attend, or at least be a regular visitor. This would be a real test of faith. She knew the ideal person she was looking for, so why should she settle for anything less? "The Lord will give me what I am asking for when the time is right," she stated out loud to reassure herself. She also believed that if she came across as being desperate or unhappy about the situation, it would reflect her lack of faith and that was certainly not going to happen. She would trust absolutely. It was going to happen.

Sister Georgina calculated that the Lord needed to deliver her husband very soon because at her age, she would need at least a year of courtship, then another year to get settled into married life, and yet another for a nine-month pregnancy. That did not leave much time for the Lord to do his thing, but she went to sleep that night more confident and secure in the knowledge that her Lord and Savior would give her what she wanted and soon.

Sister Georgina woke up the next morning excited in the belief that her husband's arrival was imminent. She looked around her bedroom, this time with the realization that it would be no place for her husband to reside, let alone come over for a visit. She called in sick. Her assistant at school had gotten used to such calls and had been asked by a member of the education board to record her increased number of absences. Unlike his colleagues, he had never forgotten about the goal of seeing Sister Georgina fired and had been keeping a watchful eye of her work performance over the years. This time however, Sister Georgina's sick day wasn't to sit depressed in her room watching afternoon television, it was to act as if her prayers had already been answered! This meant she had to take more care of her home. She immediately began to de-clutter on the firm belief that her husband-to-be would be coming by to pick her up for a date. She had gone into work sporadically, not wanting the distraction from cleaning her house and it was several weeks before she felt her home was presentable for guests.

The next task that presented itself was to deal with her appearance.

Unlike her last attempt at a makeover, this time she allowed herself to have the full spa treatment; hair, nails, feet, and eyebrows. Everyone at her school and church was astounded by her changes, and relieved she was pulling herself out of her depressed state and making changes for the better. Having addressed the external, Sister Georgina attended church this time with an air of expectation. The few new faces that had appeared at recent church functions were closely scrutinized for their potential as her future partner.

The first new face was Solomon. He was from Columbia, South America. He was a work colleague of Mr. Bilton, the church treasurer, and had recently arrived from his country. Sharing her mother's experience, Solomon had also found life in the United States as an immigrant extremely challenging. Mr. Bilton, in true Christian tradition had extended a hand in friendship and Solomon had jumped at it. Sister Georgina had seen him on several occasions at the church, but now had reason to examine his presence even more closely. At the end of Wednesday night Bible class, Sister Georgina didn't have time to waste and decided to get straight to the point.

"Oh, Sister G," a shocked Mr. Bilton said. Getting ready to leave, he had just bent over to pick up his things from the floor, when he looked up, there was Sister Georgina standing over him, invading his personal space. Despite falling backwards and holding his chest, Sister Georgina, without saying a word, made it clear she was not leaving without an introduction to his guest.

"The Pastor did not let us down again tonight, did he?" Mr. Bilton mumbled trying to make polite conversation. Ignoring his question, Sister Georgina went straight to what was on her mind.

"...And, who is this visitor?"

"Oh, yes," Mr. Bilton looked shocked that Sister Georgina did not want to engage their usual small talk. "This is Solomon. He's an intern at my office."

"Hello," Sister Georgina said, trying her best to be as enticing as possible. Solomon had witnessed her strange behavior and tried to figure out how to respond. Seeing she had Solomon's attention, Sister Georgina did not bother to wait for Mr. Bilton's formal introduction.

"So pleased to meet you," she said with an air of confidence. She was desperate to be in control of the tone of her voice and not give away any indication of her romantic interest.

"When does your internship end?" She asked, clearly not concerned with what or where he was studying. She just wanted to cut to the chase and figure out how long he planned to be around, whether he was the one the Lord was sending to her, and if he was worth her time in pursuing.

"My program ends next semester," the shy Solomon said.

"What about your family? Did they come with you?" Sister Georgina probed.

In the seconds before Solomon responded, her thoughts flowed straight onto how she would deal with the cultural differences. She knew little about the South American country and did not like the idea that she possibly had to learn another language. She did not want to be branded as being closed-minded to change, if that was what her Lord and Savior had in mind. But, now faced with the possibility of a South American husband, she definitely would need to gain some knowledge and understanding for a healthy marriage. She wondered how he would take to an occasional diet of microwave ready meals or hamburger and fries. Any husband, she assumed, of an exotic descent would prefer a home cooked meal, so she wondered if he would expect her to cook his cultural food every day. She also thought of how he would manage at church events. Would he be able to represent her effectively? As she stood in front of Solomon, with her mind racing with the questions, she could not avoid the one that had pushed its way to the forefront of her mind. *Would he want to engage in kinky sex?* She allowed her mind to wonder what it would be like making love to him. She hadn't given any thought to whether she found him to be attractive or not, she just jumped to whether he was husband material. *Would it mean doing things that she considered unacceptable?* Recalling the lasting impressions from the infamous dinner while an undergraduate, she knew that people experimented and wondered whether it would be his expectations. Was this the case in South America? Her church doctrine made it clear, that there would be no kinky or animalistic behavior. The act of making love was an expression of the spiritual bond between a husband and wife. Oral sex was therefore not a consideration, and the thought of anal sex was too horrendous to even consider as an option.

Before her thoughts could explore possible sadomasochism acts, Solomon told her, "No, they are still in Columbia," he responded nervously, totally unaware of the whirlwind courtship, engagement, marriage, and divorce that had taken place in Sister Georgina's mind.

"Well, thank you for coming. We appreciated your company at our Bible class this evening," Sister Georgina politely replied. As there was nothing else to say, she abruptly terminated the conversation and disappeared as inconspicuously as she had arrived. She did not want either of them to see her disappointment as her dreams of a marriage were dashed yet again. Sister Georgina quickly busied herself by stacking Bibles and hymn books that did not need to be stacked. Her hands began to shake involuntary and she felt her breathing increase. *It was just the disappointment,* she surmised. Mr. Bilton knew something was wrong as Sister Georgina seemed to be acting strangely, but chose not to say anything because he did not want her to snap at him again.

Little did Sister Georgina know, Solomon was referring to his parents and siblings when he spoke about his family. He was single and available. He had worked as an accountant in his little village in Columbia and his hard work and diligence had caught the attention of the head office in Washington D.C. He had been offered an internship with the possibility of employment on completion. He was of course excited, not just because of the career opportunity, but more-so, for social reasons. He knew from a very early age that he was attracted to large, 'take control' women. He felt it would complement his shy, subservient personality. In his village where the norm was well-proportioned women, he knew if he had spoken openly about his preference he most likely would have been frowned upon. So, he secretly indulged his fetish by watching American movies about big, beautiful women and imagined being gently enclosed and enveloped by their soft mounds of flesh.

When he arrived in the U.S. and had settled into the internship program and residence, he fervently began the search for his ideal woman. He had welcomed the friendship of Mr. Bilton and was pleased to attend his church. He had immediately spotted Sister Georgina and found her attractive, but had no idea how to approach her. He thought that she was interested in him when she initially came to introduce herself, but after she rushed away so quickly, assumed that she was not interested. It was a couple of months later that Sister Georgina heard the announcement that Solomon had proposed to one of the other single church sisters. She was at least two sizes bigger than Sister Georgina. She had smiled out of politeness, but it was not enough to contain her anger and jealously. She went home and cried for hours.

Sister Georgina then considered Owen. He was from Guyana, also a country in South America. However, as it was once part the British Empire, it was considered one of the Caribbean countries, so she knew the language barrier would not be an issue. As a direct descendant of an immigrant, she was embarrassed that she knew so little about her mother's island community and its culture. But, the same thoughts she had about Solomon, resurfaced and forced her to speculate about Owen's sexual appetite. He was not a regular visitor to the church, and when he did attend, her efforts to make eye contact were not reciprocated. So the only information she had been able to obtain from the Pastor was his home country. Sister Georgina reluctantly gave up on Owen as a potential suitor, but was proud of herself for being open-minded and willing to go ahead with the possibility of marrying him, albeit in her mind only. The thought that there was no chemistry between Owen and herself never crossed her mind. Regardless of the circumstances, Sister Georgina she was determined to make it work.

When it came to Brian, Sister Georgina had no intention of making lemonade. He had actually made his intentions known ever since his family joined the church about three years ago. Brian Kennedy and his family had relocated from Oklahoma, although the family was originally from Alabama. They were used to moving around the country due to the military background of Mr. Kennedy and as Brian got older, they were thankful never to be in one place for too long. Much to the relief of Sister Georgina and all the other single church sisters, the family would only attend Sunday service about once every six weeks. They did not come to bible classes and rarely participated in church activities. But as they faithfully paid their tithes, the Pastor considered them to be dutiful members who needed to be welcomed as such whenever they did arrive.

Brian, an only child, had a very close relationship with his parents. They had struggled to conceive and only after several difficult miscarriages and still births, he surprised everyone by being born a healthy bundle of joy. As their miracle baby, his parents had vowed to protect and keep him safe from the horrors of the outside world. They made it their business to oversee everything that entered into his environment, as well as decide upon his major life decisions. Because of this, Brian never had the opportunity to discover things for himself and incorrectly assumed that non-family members should also be there to take care of him.

He had attended Prince George's Community College, eventually obtaining his Associate's degree in Information Technology. He then held a position at the local computer store, fixing laptops. His proficiency at his job, as well as his impressive patience for handling difficult customers was noted by his bosses. This meant that they consistently overlooked the many complaints from female customers about his sexually inappropriate behaviors. Staring at their breasts, or holding onto their receipts longer than necessary were the most common feedback. Never having a girlfriend, Brian was desperate to right this situation with every female he met. His father realized *the talk* about women when he was twenty-four came way too late. He could only watch in horror from a distant as he was regularly cursed at and publicly humiliated by women who rejected his sexually explicit offers to "make their toes curl." Still attempting to shelter their son, his parents were thankful that the women at the small church in Glenarden were at least gentler in their rejection.

Brian had spied Sister Georgina, as well as the other single sisters, when his family joined the church when he was about twenty-eight. He expected when he entered into the personal space of a female that they would immediately be grateful for his interest and ask him out on a date. He was genuinely confused when nothing materialized as expected. Convinced that there was nothing wrong with his approach, he saw no reason to change it. Therefore, whenever his family came to Sunday service, he could literally be seen running from one single sister to the next, in the hope that one would eventually take the bait. When he turned thirty and his dating technique had been proven to be ineffective, his parents approached the Pastor. They were looking for a "good girl" to take care of their son, someone who would be kind and understanding. The Pastor immediately thought of Sister Georgina knowing that they shared so much in common. Mostly the fact that they were both known to be virgins and were desperate. It was April at the time and he told Brian's parents to expect a June wedding.

"Come in, come in, my dear," the Pastor said excitedly as he waved a sweaty and flustered Sister Georgina into his office. She had received his frantic call about meeting immediately and had rearranged her schedule to turn up two hours later.

"What is it Pastor? I have been worried ever since I got your call!"

"I can't talk about such things on the phone, but I think you will agree with me when I tell you, that this is wonderful, wonderful news"

"Please, just tell me. All this suspense is unnecessary"

"I have received a proposal of marriage for you! Isn't that great?"

"What?!" Despite her shock at the announcement, she found herself exhaling in relief and saying a quick prayer of thanks. She smiled to herself, extremely flattered by the unexpected announcement. The man of her dreams knew her better than she knew herself. This was the best proposal she could receive. Her mystery man knew her well enough to "come correct." She allowed the joy of receiving the proposal to sink in, as images of her ideal man rushed into her consciousness. It was followed quickly by her Garden of Eden wedding before settling on the wedding night. She immediately thought about being naked on the bed with her husband standing over her ready to consummate their marriage. She was shaken abruptly from her daydream when her handbag fell off her lap and onto the floor with a loud crash.

"It's okay, my dear. You can be excited! After all, you have been waiting so long for this moment to arrive," the Pastor said noticing her embarrassed, flushed face.

The act of picking up her bag from the floor brought her back to reality. She bit her tongue and reminded herself that she was sitting in the Pastor's office, with Mrs. Pritchard most likely on the other side of the door. She then realized that she hadn't asked the most important question.

"Who is he?"

"You know him. He has been a member here forever. He is a good young man. He has a good job, well educated, has very, very good parents. I think you will both be very happy together."

The Pastor still deliberately omitted his name, being fully aware of Brian's reputation amongst the single sisters. Instead, he continued to stress his positive qualities.

"He is ready to marry immediately and he wants to have children straight away. And... umm...buy a marital home. He's been waiting for the right woman." Finding it difficult to think about the positive qualities of such a union, the Pastor's hesitations aroused Sister Georgina's suspicions.

"Who is he?" Sister Georgina shrieked. She had no time to think about the niceties of her behavior.

"Brian Kennedy. His family....."

Before the Pastor had finished saying his name, the romantic images of her wedding night had been replaced by the horrific image of Brian's five foot six inch, underweight frame... (Brian tried to disguise his frame, unsuccessfully, with oversized clothes and glasses, and his light brown skin was always covered with severe acne and no one could recall a time when his face was not infected) ...standing with one hand on the men's restroom door and his other on his crotch with a creepy smile, singing Michael Jackson's, "The Way You Make Me Feel" as the women walked past him to get to the church's exit. Never did Sister Georgina imagine that she would turn down a marriage proposal, but on this occasion, she had no choice. Being unable to handle the rejection, the Kennedy family left to join the mega church on Route 214, hoping there would be someone to take them up on their offer.

As a result of this experience, Sister Georgina allowed herself to be more creative in her thinking about a partner. She wondered if the

Lord would send her a Hispanic or white man. She had never dreamt lying next to someone with a different skin color. She had never given it serious thought before now. Not that it was an issue, but it's just that she had never considered it as a real possibility. But now, at her age, she was open to any available option. God may test her and she would be up for the challenge. She would be willing to learn Spanish, she loved Mexican food, and considered it would be fun to learn how to cook their traditional dishes. She paused to consider how she would feel at Sunday service with her Hispanic or white man beside her. Would they truly be able to understand her, or would their understanding be as shallow as her colleagues in the Student for Christ Group when she was at Secus College? Would she be able to tell if they liked her for who she was or because of the color of her skin? A large Hispanic family had once descended on their little church to support the visiting Pastor, but as they never came back, she resigned herself that this option had little hope of materializing.

Her newly found openness meant she stretched her mind to consider someone who had a criminal background. Yes, she would consider a reformed drug dealer, a petty thief, or even a burglar. She heard the voice in her head challenge her to think about such crimes as rape or the molestation of children. She avoided answering the question and moved onto considering if he had been unemployed and reasoned he would have to justify why and what he had been doing with his time. More than likely, they would have children. This was never an ideal situation for her, but she would consider it as long as he could show he was taking care of them and his responsibilities as a father. Despite her philosophical discussion with herself, she knew it boiled down to the simple fact that if they had a penis, were between the ages of eighteen and seventy, she would consider them. *God doesn't discriminate*, she reasoned, *and neither will I.*

However, her bottom line was non-negotiable, and that was his submission to the Lord. Memories of her non-believing father and the confusion it had caused in her household meant she was determined to hold out. But, on the rare occasion she allowed the truth of her situation to surface, she reluctantly concluded that the gift of her virginity, its significance, and her sacrifice would be lost on someone who was not committed to the Lord.

That night, while she knelt to say her prayers, Sister Georgina faced her desperation by reflecting on her behavior. Learning from the many self-help books she read, she questioned herself on what she could have done differently.

No, she defensively concluded. Getting to the point was better for her psyche. She had no time to waste. Her next thought was a surprise and definitely not something she had anticipated to come into her head. At school last week, she had called Child Protective Services as one of the students had reported that she was being sexually abused at home. Sister Georgina, a mandated reporter, knew she should not investigate the incident herself. But she couldn't help it. She wanted to know more about the student's horrific experience. She kept pressing the bewildered student for more and more details. Of course, the incident was abhorrent, but she still wanted to know. Sister Georgina was angry with herself for her behavior; knowing she had probed for sexual details as a voyeur. She knew she had a problem, but where could she turn for help? She saw no point in going to a non-believer; they would not understand the healing power of the Lord. She resolved to be more diligent in her fasting and prayers. *It will be okay,* she tried to reassure herself, rocking back and forth. She had to resolve this sooner rather than later, but she did not know how much longer she could hold out. *The Lord and Savior will never abandon you.*

As she held Mrs. Peterson's hands steady on number eighty-eighty and called *BINGO* on her behalf, the only possible conclusion she reached was to be more steadfast in her prayers. Sister Georgina decided that she would make her demands of her God more forceful. She would challenge Him to prove His power. She wanted a husband so badly and would channel her feelings of desperation into her faith. On her days off, she would spend them in total prayer and fasting. Her prayers would be longer and more emotional to the extent when she arose from her knees she would be wet with perspiration. From now on, she would demand of her God that He answer her prayers. He would listen to her. She would beg and bargain with Him until He answered. Sister Georgina's confidence returned as she walked with Mrs. Peterson to collect her prize. God would answer her prayers. She would begin as soon as she got home, and unlike her failed diets year after year, this commitment she would see through to the end. The direction of her life depended on it, and she just knew He would make it happen.

Chapter Five
At Last

Sister Georgina remained on the floor, but had just turned around to sit with her back to the side of the bed. Even after twenty minutes of consistent praying, the only thing she could think of saying was *thank you* and if she was not sore from kneeling for so long, she would have continued for another thirty minutes, at least, as she hadn't tired of saying it. Despite the late hour, she did not want to get into bed, as sleeping was the furthest thing from her mind. She was way too excited. Her prayers had finally been answered. There was no doubt in her mind. Her Lord had given her exactly what she asked for; a husband who she had met in her beloved church. She exhaled deeply and thought to herself, *what a difference twenty-four hours can make.* So, in the dim light of her bedside lamp, she reflected for the umpteenth time on the life-changing events of the day.

As Sister Georgina got ready for Sunday service, she felt an unusual wave of anticipation in the air. It was different and made her feel her ring finger. This feeling had come over her a couple of times recently, but today, it was stronger. She paused and allowed herself to be present in the moment. She enjoyed the warm glow of how it made her feel and concluded it was because she would soon be sharing the word of the Lord with her students. She found herself smiling and finished getting ready for church.

In the middle of Sunday school, one of the teachers complained about a child who would not stop crying. Sister Georgina made the unusual decision to return the child to its mother in the main service. She normally would have given the child one-on-one attention in the hope that they would settle down and then rejoin their Sunday school class, avoiding the need to disturb the parent. But this time, even when the child stopped crying, she did not deviate from her plan to return the child. Sister Georgina walked to the back of the church, hoping no one would be too disturbed by her actions. She politely waited at the back of the hall by the Pastor's office for a suitable break in the service. She surveyed the congregation for the parent and spotted them in the third row. It was at that time, her heart skipped a beat. The Pastor had just gotten to the part where he was introducing visitors and a man in the fourth row stood up. Something bubbled unexpectedly in her stomach. *She just knew this was it.*

She went into action and took note of everything she could. He was standing next to Mrs. Gilchrist, an established member of the church, perhaps he was a relative of hers. He was about six-foot two or three inches, wearing a reasonable suit. He had short, graying hair, possibly late fifties or early sixties, and presented as being professional. Shaking, Sister Georgina turned and rushed back to Sunday school. She delivered the child back to his class where he promptly started to cry again. This time, Sister Georgina gave her regular response, "he will settle down shortly."

Who was he and where had he been? I know he is the one.

If Sister Georgina knew his last name she would have been sounding it out. She was confident that he would be her husband. "The Lord truly does answered prayers," she said to herself as she sat down to develop a plan of attack. She could not remember the last time she felt this buzz of excitement. She sent word to the other teachers to end classes a couple of minutes early to ensure that she could go back into the main hall before the end of service. She had to make sure she did not miss an introduction. She didn't realize that her jittery action had prompted one of the teachers to ask if anything was wrong. As soon as she had the chance, she flew back upstairs and proceeded to accidentally, on purpose, maneuver herself for the predictable introduction before any of the other single sisters spied him also. Sister Georgina surprised herself by her deliberate actions and quickly justified them as stepping out in faith. She seemed to be operating on automatic pilot. *It's God's will,* she comforted herself. *He has made it happen!* It was now her turn to do all she could to help the process along.

Standing anxiously by the entry door, she was brought back to reality by another member of the congregation who had tracked her down to talk about the upcoming youth service. She halfheartedly engaged in the conversation as she desperately kept her eye on her husband-to-be. She saw from the corner of her eye that Mrs. Gilchrist and her husband were meandering slowly towards where she was standing. Mrs. Gilchrist was busy introducing other members to him and engaging in what looked like trivial small talk. Unbeknownst to them, Sister Georgina was becoming more and more agitated that they were taking so long to get to her. She strategically allowed the one-way conversation with the church member to continue, because she wanted to ensure she was not by herself when they finally got to her. She had no idea what the conversation was about nor did she care at this point. She was only picking up a few words here and there, but her company didn't seem to mind her responses of nods and the occasional mumble of agreement. She muttered a silent prayer to calm herself. Her heart was beating faster and sweat was beginning to make her hands moist. In the next moment she heard the words she had been waiting for.

"Excuse me, I don't mean to interrupt." It was Mrs. Gilchrist and her husband. Sister Georgina unconsciously made her companion aware that they were no longer required and there would not be a response to her question that was left hanging in midair because she hadn't heard it in the first place.

With a very broad smile on her face, Mrs. Gilchrist announced, "This is my brother from another mother," she said with a laugh, clearly having told this joke many times. "He has finally decided to grace me with a visit." Without pausing for breath, she announced that she had been asking him for years, but that this was the first time he decided to come.

"I do feel guilty because if it wasn't for his business meeting in DuPont Circle tomorrow, I don't think he would have come up to see me at all!"

"Welcome!" Sister Georgina heard herself say and hoped that it had not given away any of her thoughts of marriage. She discretely wiped her hand on her skirt before outstretching it towards him, hoping that it was not too sweaty. He took his time to respond to the request for a handshake. She processed this hesitancy quickly as a positive sign of a good Christian, for a Christian man would not shake women's so freely. His verbal response also seemed a bit strained. Again, she justified this was because he had met so many people this morning and maybe exhausted. She also knew his sister was hard work.

Sister Georgina turned her body so he had her full attention. She was pleased with what she was seeing. He did not have a ring on his finger and he was presentable. He was definitely a good height, which was how it should be. He did have a bit of a belly, but that was negligible. She smiled and hoped that he didn't pick up on her intentions, but Mrs. Gilchrist did and followed through by asking if she would mind taking her guest downstairs for brunch. She nodded her agreement and Mrs. Gilchrist smiled and said she would follow them shortly. Sister Georgina knew what the extra pat on her hand meant when she left them and was grateful for the opportunity that was being presented.

On her way downstairs, other members of the congregation without prompting seemed to get the unspoken message and not come anywhere near the newly formed couple. Like a lioness after her prey, Sister Georgina went for the jugular. She asked him if he enjoyed the service and continued to make small talk, emphasizing future events at the church. By the time they were in the line for brunch, she had pulled out of him that his name was Otis Jeters and he worked as a risk assessor for a national insurance firm for about twenty-five years. His meeting tomorrow would be over by four and later that evening he would be flying back to Pittsburgh from Ronald Regan Airport. It had been tough to get this little bit of information out of him and she noticed that he had not asked any questions about her. Communication was definitely not a strong point for him, but these were things she could work on when they were married. In the mean time, she would remedy this by fixing him a plate in hopes that this gesture would impress him. She was thankful that Sister Olivia had been on cooking detail this week, but wished it was Mrs. Cartwright who reluctantly gave up her kitchen duties having suffered from a stroke a couple of years ago. Sister Olivia's food should be good enough to tempt this visitor to come back, if not for Sister Georgina, but at least the food. Guests were provided with a free lunch on their first visit. If this hadn't been the case she would have covered the cost.

Yes, she was desperate, Sister Georgina reflected, but like a gambler with their last dollar, she felt she had nothing to lose. She settled him at the lunch table with his plate before returning to get her own. She saw no visible signs from him that he noticed she had prioritized his needs above hers. If he had, it would have warranted some thanks and appreciation, highlighting that he actually cared. Sister Georgina, slightly disappointed, decided to persevere. He seemed okay, but even at this stage, it was definitely hard trying to engage him.

By the time Sister Georgina joined him at the table, Mrs. Gilchrist was not far behind. They were both a bit disappointed when he was already halfway through with his meal, not waiting for either of them. Mrs. Gilchrist tried to cover up her embarrassment about her brother's lack of etiquette by talking non-stop about his strengths. Sister Georgina on the other hand, had dealt with the issue by telling herself, it didn't really matter and that she needed to focus on the more important concern: *that an eligible man was sitting across from her at the lunch table in her beloved church.* So, she decided to make the most of the situation and tuned in very carefully to Mrs. Gilchrist's comments about her half-brother. As a result, she learned that Otis had an important role in his company and that he still found time to care for his mother back in Greensboro, North Carolina, where the family was originally from. Mrs. Gilchrist's non-stop conversation had previously been an annoyance to Sister Georgina, but on this occasion, she welcomed the information she was sharing.

When the lunchroom was beginning to empty and their interaction was forced to come to an end, Sister Georgina was desperately trying to think of how she could bring the conversation to exchanging contact details. It came as a complete surprise when Otis, announced quietly that he wanted to attend a lecture that evening at a community center downtown and asked if they would like to go with him. His half-sister dutifully declined the offer allowing Sister Georgina's voice to tremble as she accepted and gave him her number. She was floored. Picking up on no verbal or non-verbal cues, despite her efforts to make this happen, it had seemingly come out of the blue. Nothing he said indicated that he was interested in her in that way, but now was not the time to quibble about what she had or had not missed. She was very grateful and without knowing what the lecture would be about, happily agreed.

Otis called Sister Georgina about 5:00pm to remind her that he would be around to pick her up at 6:30pm that evening. She thanked him as calmly as she could and said she would see him then. *Men are really unaware of the affect they have on women*, she thought to herself. When she left the church at 1:30pm, she rushed straight over to Prince George's Mall. She actually bought a more flattering dress with shoes to match. She wasn't able to find a suitable handbag, otherwise she would have bought that as well. It was too important of an occasion to rely on her wardrobe that was filled with thrift store finds. She wanted to make sure she looked her best.

She then had her nails done to match the color of her new dress and shoes. She was thinking about the possibility of having her hair done as well, but realized that she did not have the time. Even on a good day, the process would be a minimum of three hours. She used her limited hairdressing skills to put the final touches to her makeover. Bursting with excitement, Sister Georgina did something she never thought she would do. Having spent years nurturing an image of being able to 'wait until the Lord provided,' she picked up the phone and called Sister Canisa. She did not have time to think deeply about the fact she had never asked anyone over before nor how it would be perceived. She had no time to worry about such matters. She needed a second opinion about her outfit and hair, as well as someone to pray with her, but most importantly to be a chaperone. She saw Sister Canisa as being genuine. And even though she had rejected her previous offers of help with her housework, Sister Georgina secretly valued the gesture and had never forgotten. She knew Sister Canisa had not been put off by her brash temperament that kept most people at bay and saw her as someone she could trust. Sister Canisa, on the other hand, was confused by the surprise invitation and had to ask several times for the caller to repeat their name, before she finally accepted that it was Sister Georgina. She agreed, primarily out of religious obligations, but also out of curiosity as no one had ever seen the inside of Sister Georgina's home. Sister Georgina was grateful for her support and felt confident; this was the Lord answering her prayers. She was so glad she spent the previous weeks cleaning the house. She was proud to be able to open her home to the sister and soon her husband-to-be.

Bursting with excitement, Sister Georgina met Sister Canisa at the door, and immediately asked for feedback on her presentation. Startled and confused, Sister Canisa quickly realized what was happening and allowed herself to offer Sister Georgina the emotional support she was seeking. Since the failure of the 'get out and about social group,' the sisters had never really gotten together again to support their practical and emotional needs. Sister Georgina had been reluctant to start anything new, realizing that her heart could not take any more, and eventually the sisters stopped asking her for new ideas on what to do about their 'manless' situation. Together, with everyone's busy work and family commitments, they somehow got into a routine of seeing each other only at church on Sunday. So, although greatly taken aback by Sister Georgina's unusual display of emotion, she smiled warmly, realizing that the most supportive thing she could do was to keep quiet and allow her to enjoy the unusual event of preparing for her date. Sister Georgina was ready 30 minutes before Otis was due to arrive and so spent the time praying with Sister Canisa.

Otis did not apologize when he arrived late. He mumbled something about not being familiar with the GPS system in his rental car and had gotten lost. She did think to herself that he could have called to say he was running late, but what mattered was that he had arrived.

She was not going to let anything spoil her date, least of all, the thirty minutes that she had been on her knees praying with her sister with such passion because she believed that he had changed his mind.

When they were finally leaving her home, she turned and waved good-bye to her sister who had agreed to stay until she got back. She was thankful for her sacrifice, as she would be there to hear the news immediately on her return, but more importantly, because it would send her date the message that she would not be entertaining any untoward requests. After all this time, she wanted to enjoy all the steps of an official courtship. In her world, no one dates for the sake of dating; it meant marriage. She allowed herself to be nervously excited.

Otis opened the car door for her without being encouraged. This sparked her, as it was a first sign that this actually was a date. Naturally, she thanked him and got into the car delicately, not wanting to be caught out like some actresses had been photographed by the paparazzi. She just wished she had lost more weight. She could not read anything about his personality from the state of the rental car. She noticed a McDonald's wrapper on the floor, a sure sign of his bachelor status and chose to indulge herself with images of sending him off on business trips with a lunch box of home cooked meals stuffed with love notes. Sister Georgina, again, initiated the conversation and finally asked about the evening's lecture. The topic was on attracting more African-American men to the church. It was music to her ears. She felt her pulsing ring finger and smiled. Her stomach fluttered and she discreetly bowed her head in order to give thanks.

The light from her bedside lamp blinked and reminded her that she would need to change the bulb soon. Sister Georgina smiled as it was a task she would delegate to Otis. She looked around her bedroom from her vantage point on the floor and started thinking about the things she needed to do in her bedroom to make it comfortable for her husband. She knew her life was about to change and was more than ready.

Chapter Six
Can't See the Forest for the Trees

The nurse listened intently as Sister Georgina joyfully shared the arrangements for her up-coming wedding the following weekend. She held her arm out eagerly for the nurse to take her blood pressure before continuing her one-sided conversation about the details of her big day.

"It's definitely not the wedding of my dreams. I originally planned an elaborate one for about two hundred and fifty people, but as I am going to be forty at the end of the month, I wanted to be married before I was officially over the hill! So, the wedding next Saturday will be a *really* small and intimate wedding... about thirty people total."

Despite her best efforts, to emphasize the word 'really,' '*wedding*' was the one that came across loud and clear. The nurse was desperately trying to hurry the procedures along so she could get Sister Georgina out of her exam room and on her way as quickly as possible. Her bored composure was lost on Sister Georgina as nothing was going to contain her excitement. The day she had waited for all her adult life was just a few days away and there was still so much to do. Although, Sister Georgina had taken a humorous approach, she really had no idea how she was going to tell the excluded church members that they were not invited.

"I think they will understand. Plus, we can always plan a large reception party at some point," she explained, again with no real concern whether the nurse was actually listening or not.

"This wedding is just so we can get on with the business of being married. We're not getting any younger," she smiled, hoping the nurse would understand her feeble attempt at an X-rated joke. She did not respond, so Sister Georgina continued eagerly, sharing that her fiancé was sixty-two years old and she saw age as just a number, dismissing the twenty-three year difference as being insignificant. She chose instead to show off that he was established in his career and surprisingly, had no baggage. "Can you believe it?" Sister Georgina exclaimed happily. "No baby mama drama! The Lord certainly knew what he was doing when He sent Otis to me. I'm not sure how I would have handled that."

Sister Georgina knew she was behaving like a bridezilla, but she truly felt as if she was the only woman in the world getting married. She wanted to relish every minute of the process. After all, she did wait so long. "We both share the same love of God and once we agreed to date, we knew the relationship would be serious. I think three months is long enough to know whether or not you want to be with someone." Desperately trying to justify her position and hide the fact that during that three month time period, they had a total of five official dates. "He was married before. It lasted about two years. But that was when he was in his early twenties, so it was a while ago."

In an effort to stress his charitable and loving nature, Sister Georgina spilled the juicy details, obtained from Mrs. Gilchrest, of course, that his young wife had embezzled money from her employers. He had done the honorable thing and kept her out of jail by agreeing to pay off the debts. It took him about twenty years, but he did it.

"Can you believe he did that? I mean…the marriage ended shortly after he found out, but he continued to pay off the debt. It took him *years*! I think that was such a Godly thing to do. I also understand why he's been on his own ever since. Then, he met me!" Sister Georgina laughed.

Hardly pausing for breath, she told the nurse that her fiancé - she loved saying that word- had put in for a transfer to the Washington D.C. branch of his office. They were waiting for it to come through. However, not wanting to delay the wedding, he would commute to Maryland every weekend. Sister Georgina tried to not let the nurse know that this wasn't an ideal situation for her, but as soon as the decision to marry had been made, there was no real reason to wait. Her home was okay for both of them. He could sell or rent out his town-house in Pittsburgh when his transfer came through.

As if trying to justify her choice, Sister Georgina launched into the fact that he didn't smoke, drink, nor do drugs. He also didn't gamble or have any debts that she knew about. This was so wonderful. Words could hardly express her gratitude to God for sending her such an ideal man. She then proudly launched into talking about his charity work at his church and in the community. He was a mentor for African-American boys and sat on the board of his housing association.

"He's politically aware and when he can, volunteers for the local democratic campaign." This was something she had been impressed by from their first date. "And to top it all off…"Sister Georgina wanted to make sure the nurse understood the quality of man she was going to marry, "…he even takes time out to care for his elderly mother in Greensboro, North Carolina. And you know what they say – how a man treats his mother is how he will treat his wife."

She continued on, sharing the important news with the nurse that he organizes his mother's household; making sure her lawn was cut and that the care staff was top notch. Sister Georgina concluded her love story by saying his acceptance of the Lord as his personal savior was what made her finally accept his proposal.

The nurse seized the pause in conversation to ask Sister Georgina to open her mouth so she could take her temperature. She was pleased it also had the added benefit of stopping her from talking, if only for a few minutes. The silence forced Sister Georgina to think about what she had just said. Listening to herself, she knew she was painting a glorious picture of her soon-to-be-husband. But she hoped, as if by some miracle, that if she continued to talk about his strengths she could forget about the things that were unsettling in the relationship and that they would somehow just disappear.

Otis was presentable as a husband and she knew she would be a fool to turn down his proposal. With her fortieth birthday looming, she reasoned that this was her first, and possibly, her last opportunity to make her dreams of having a husband and children a reality. She didn't have time to worry about whether she loved him or not or even if he truly loved her. When she allowed herself to think about the lack of romance in her relationship, she had faith that they would grow to love each other. She had to make it work. So when Otis asked for her hand in marriage, it came as no real surprise, as Sister Georgina believed she had orchestrated the entire event from behind the scenes. She had left nothing to chance.

From the start she had transformed herself into the equivalent of a delicious entrée, complete with two sides, dessert, and a freshly made ice tea. With the help of Mrs. Gilchrist, she ensured he was practically starved to make it extremely difficult for him to resist the meal she had prepared. All he had to do was eat. And as any good parent would do for their weaning child, Sister Georgina would have cut up his meal into small pieces and fed it to him, if needed.

When he returned to Pittsburgh after that first business trip to Washington D.C., he had been bombarded with requests to return to Maryland for one event or another by his half-sister and Sister Georgina. He consistently refused, explaining that he was pretty settled in Pittsburgh and was not interested in having a relationship with anyone. But Mrs. Gilchrist passionately argued for him to change his mind.

"I know we don't know each other that well, but we are still family and I really do have your best interest at heart. I really do think you should you should jump at the chance of being in a relationship with Sister Georgina. She is such a kind and loving person. Can you believe she has spent all of her life in the church, I don't think you could find another righteous woman. You've been stuck in Pittsburgh all by yourself – it's about time you have a wife. What would Daddy say if he was still here? I know he would be saying the same thing. You can't be an island all by yourself. You are fortunate that you've been in good health, but what's going to happen when you get older? I guarantee that there will come a time when you need some help.

"Yes, I know Sister Georgina has issues, but don't we all? You're getting up in age and which of your family members will be giving up their lives to come and take care of you? Sister Georgina would have your best interest at heart, as well as be company for you as you get older. It isn't too late for you to have children; I hear Sister Georgina really wants to have children. You could even adopt, an older child, perhaps. Why don't you want to have a good woman by your side? You know she can help you get out of your shell and communicate more. And besides...." Mrs. Cartwright had every intention of nagging him until he agreed.

Sadly, it wasn't the spirited and reasoned argument presented by his half-sister or Sister Georgina's careful orchestrated efforts that eventually wore him down; it was his long held philosophical belief that if it was being offered and it benefited him, he should take it. He had a hard life and the only thing that made sense to him was making sure he got what was due to him. He didn't actually like Sister Georgina, in fact, he was actually turned off by her personality as well as her physical body. He really had no interest in getting to know her, but at his age, he reasoned that beggars could not be choosers and marrying her would likely be in his best interest long-term. Besides, he had nothing to lose. On the contrary, he could be patient and nothing about his lifestyle had to change. He enjoyed the attention that she lavished on him and valued the fact that she did not expect anything from him in return. Even if she did, he had no intention of reciprocating. His sister's comments made him think more deeply about his future and when his friends also supported the same sentiments, decided to bow to public opinion. His proposal wasn't anything out of the ordinary, just over dinner at the local steakhouse. He mumbled something about making their relationship legal and Sister Georgina instantly knew what he meant. A waiter offered to take their picture and they posed for a staged kiss on the cheek while it was taken.

With the thermometer still in her mouth, Sister Georgina allowed her mind to continue to wander while the nurse was busy preparing the EKG.

Sister Georgina felt secure that Otis didn't seem interested in other women, or men for that matter, and was pretty confident that if someone called and told her that he was having an affair, she would know they were lying. She had done her homework. The background check she paid for came back clean, apart from some unpaid parking tickets. She had discretely asked Mrs. Gilchrist for more details about him, but since she had last seen him twenty-five years ago, she knew very little about him, except that he was a quiet, gentle person and that everyone knew better than to ask him any personal questions. She had even tried to get more information about Otis from her half-sister (his sister from another father), but she also did not have any real information to add. But what his half-sister had chosen to not share with Mrs. Gilchrist and Sister Georgina was that she had never seen nor heard about him being with another woman since he split with his wife nearly thirty years ago. Along with the rest of the family, she wondered what he had been doing all these years to relieve his "manly urges."

Single mindedly, Sister Georgina was happy with the sparse report on his temperament, interpreting it to mean that like her, he was disciplined and had been saving himself for the "one." Now, with their upcoming public declaration of his love for her, she should feel happy to be that *one*. But she wasn't. On the rare occasions she allowed the voice within to be heard, she knew that he didn't make her feel as if she were "the one." She got the impression that it was never about her; that she could have been Sister Susie, Beatrice, or Betty as their conversation so far had been generic. She never knew how he felt about anything, she had no idea what would make him smile, what music he liked, or how he felt about her. The only confirmation she had received to date was when someone Otis knew had passed them on the street, and he smiled at them. Otis nodded his head in approval in response to the non-verbal gesture. She had sensed that this simple signal meant he liked having a woman by his side, perhaps because it gave him the appearance of respectability or it stopped suspicious speculations about why he wanted to be on his own all the time. Something just wasn't right. She did not feel like pressing the matter with Mrs. Gilchrist, even though she deduced from her tone of voice that she knew more than she was letting on. Besides, she had no interest in exploring this or anything else that had the potential to make her think differently about her engagement. She tried consciously to focus on the positive aspects of this special time in her life, but there was no way she could avoid the thoughts that were slowly shining a light onto things that had began to unsettle her.

On their first date, Sister Georgina watched him discreetly during the lecture from the corner of her eye. Not just because she wanted to reassure herself that this was real, but because it also gave her insight on his personality and character. She watched him as he read the pamphlets and newsletters carefully that were handed to them at the door as opposed to talking with her. She watched as he interacted with the other participants who attended, again, paying little attention to her. He had gotten himself a drink and snacks and never offered to get her anything. She said nothing as he toyed with his phone and she hid her annoyance when he chatted causally to someone he had just met about the Steelers football game earlier that day. It made her jealous that the extent of their conversation that evening had been mild.

"I thought the lecture was very interesting. They raised some good points, but I am not sure how they are going to put it into practice."

Although Sister Georgina had an opinion, he didn't wait for her answer. She quickly picked up that no response was needed. She figured that he had simply forgotten what it meant to have a woman by his side, or that he was shy. Whatever the case, she reminded herself that the priority was to be a good submissive wife. She resolved to sit quietly by his side. Things would work out; it *was* God's plan after all.

But even at this early stage, it had given Sister Georgina a feeling of unease. Yes, the wedding was rushed and there had been so much to do. However, Otis never offered to help, practically nor financially. Sister Georgina got the impression that since the wedding was something she wanted, she could deal with it. Otis stuck rigidly to his weekday plans of working in Pittsburgh yet, he had never extended an invitation for Sister Georgina to visit and she never asked. His weekend routine was always the same. Maryland two weekends a month, one weekend in Greensboro to spend with his mother, and the other weekend he stayed in Pittsburgh to attend to his duties. During the week, she could expect a call only on Wednesdays at 9pm. The call would end by 9:02pm. The conversation was always business-like and cold. If she called him, she had to have a legitimate reason. To call, "just to say *I love you*" or to talk for the sake of talking seemed to be the furthest thing from his mind. Sister Georgina longed for the calls late into the night or first thing in the morning by her husband-to-be. When her various attempts to keep him on the phone failed, she replaced her negative thoughts believing it was force of habit or that he lacked the minutes on his cell phone plan. *No big deal*, she decided.

She was especially worried when she was never able to receive some much needed tender, loving care from him. She had a really tough week as one of her students had a serious asthma attack in her classroom. He had been rushed to the hospital and even though he survived, everyone was shaken by the incident. She had offered students and colleagues emotional support and was drained as a result. So, she was happy it was Otis' weekend to visit and looked forward to receiving some of his attention.

Otis was staying with his sister, so she waited patiently for him to call Friday night to let her know he had arrived in Maryland. The call came after 9:00pm and before Sister Georgina could say hello, Otis mentioned that he had made good time on the interstate and had gotten to his sister's house a couple of hours ago. He had dinner and was going to bed because he arranged for a round of golf in the morning. She said okay and was ready to tell him about her week, when she heard the phone go silent on the other end. She dismissed her disappointment and comforted herself with the thought that they would have a date later tomorrow night.

After his game, he spent the afternoon at the club and by the time he got back he called saying he was too tired to go out. He met her at church the following day, but there was no time to speak with him then, and immediately after brunch, he left for Pittsburgh.

Unfortunately, Sister Georgina's biggest disappointment came on their final date before the wedding. They were eating at the same local steak house where he had proposed. She told Otis it would be their quality time. She wanted it to be a very special occasion, primarily to build up excitement for the wedding itself. But really, she wanted feedback about how he felt about her. She had been upfront that this would be the time when they would exchange wedding gifts. She knew she was looking for some kind of romantic acknowledgment from him. She planned something truly special and had it planned since they had gotten engaged. She wanted him to know from the gift how much she valued their commitment. She had wrapped a set of keys to her fully paid off home accompanied by the deed reflecting that his name had been added. She was so excited to give it to him. Materially, she knew it was worth thousands of dollars, but it didn't matter as she would be spending the rest of her life with him. What was hers was now his.

"Well, what do you think?" She probed.

"It's okay," he said casually, as he haphazardly replaced the deed and set of house keys back into the gift box. He then returned to pouring A1 sauce over his half-eaten steak.

"This is my special gift to you, just to let you know how I am looking forward to our life together," Sister Georgina pleaded for some kind of recognition.

Not looking up from his meal, he grunted and continued eating.

"Do you have a gift for me?" Sister Georgina prodded expectedly.

"Can you pass me the dessert menu? It's by the sugar," said Otis, clearly ignoring her question.

He had nothing for her and seemed genuinely confused that it was an expectation that he should buy her something. It hurt. It took all her strength to keep calm, because he accepted her gift as if she had given him a pair of socks that had been purchased from the dollar store. She said a silent prayer under her breath to calm herself and hoped that it would also hold back her tears. She tried to think differently about the situation and decided that she should be grateful. He was giving her the gift she has wanted all her life. She would have the privilege of wearing his name. But, no matter how she tried to comfort herself, she did not feel like a bride-to-be. The fact that she finally arrived at this point was truly a miracle. She would never forget her years of torment as a single person. She would, therefore, have faith that walking with the Lord, their prayers as a couple and a commitment to their vows would mean that any problem they encountered could be overcome. It was literally days before they would became man and wife. *Everything will be alright once we're married,* she reassured herself.

As the nurse took off the monitors, Sister Georgina felt it appropriate to change the topic of conversation and returned to her questions about trying for a baby immediately after her wedding. After all, that was the reason she came for the checkup in the first place. She proudly mentioned to the nurse that her husband-to-be was definitely on the same page regarding the intimate side of their relationship. He was old school, Sister Georgina stressed. "He finds overt displays of affection disrespectful to women. He's so considerate. The young boys today could learn a thing or two from such behavior."

She smiled at the nurse and was beginning to start a debate about the lack of social morals in today's society and paused to take a breath. The nurse took advantage of the moment and calmly shared that she had also married an older man, but the marriage ended after a couple of years because they could not connect on a personal level and it had been too frustrating for her. This brief comment made Sister Georgina pause for thought, as she wasn't quite sure what she meant. Rather than ask for further explanation, she offered her condolences at the break up of their marriage before returning to think about her own situation.

She had been genuinely pleased that Otis wanted to be celibate before the wedding. She had prided herself on her virginity for so long, so of course was pleased that it would be respected. But, she was a disappointed when he had made no attempts to touch her during their three-month, five official dates courtship. This piece of information she would not be sharing with the nurse. She had no indication that he even found her remotely attractive. Therefore, they had not required the services of the planned chaperon. So the extent of their pre-wedding intimacy was when he had accidentally bumped into her when they were exiting the movie theatre. He had apologized immediately, and made sure he kept his distance from her in the future. Sister Georgina quickly concluded she was happy to wait until they married to develop that side of their relationship. She knew that after the wedding, things would be different. *She just knew it.* What mattered was that after years of sacrifice, she was about to be intimate with a man who would spiritually, and legally, be her husband.

It wasn't until she left the Clinic, that Sister Georgina wondered what personal reasons the nurse had meant. She regretted that she had not followed up on the conversation. What the nurse said in passing had stuck a cord with her, and she had a sense of unease about the physical and emotional side of their relationship. But, on the drive home, she felt that her union was orchestrated by her Lord and Savior and so, she would put aside her fears. She turned her thoughts to her mini pre-wedding gathering. She was definitely not having a bachelorette party, just a few of the other church sisters were coming over to celebrate and pray with her. She arrived at her house minutes later to find so many of them milling around her home taking advantage of the opportunity by looking at the contents of her freezer, closets and her bathroom cabinets. It was so exciting. Her home had never been so full.

The wedding reception, as well as the pre-wedding gathering was being held at her house. Both would be very simple affairs. Besides being married at the church and having the Pastor officiate, nothing from her original plans had survived. The rushed nature of the wedding meant that her spectacular flower arrangements had become two big bunches of flowers that would replace the plastic ones flanking the pulpit. She would have flower petals sprinkled down the aisle by two of her young nieces, who she had met for the first time at the rehearsal. Thankfully, the parking situation had been resolved by informing guests that they would park outside her home and along the neighboring streets, then they would be shuttled back and forth in the church's van. She estimated that it should take two trips for her thirty guests to travel the short distance.

The furniture in both her living and dining rooms were temporarily relocated to the yard and had been covered with plastic to protect it from the elements. Chairs had been borrowed from the church's cafeteria and circled the two rooms. The space next to the fireplace where the television had been was replaced by a folding table covered by a beautiful white lace tablecloth that had been set aside to receive wedding gifts. Next to it was two hand-decorated chairs that were waiting patiently for the special couple to occupy. At the other end of the room was another folding table, covered with a plain, white, plastic tablecloth and was allocated for the small buffet. Sister Olivia had done her best with a limited menu, space, and numbers, so she settled on just serving finger foods. The church sisters put up white, paper decorations they had made themselves throughout the open plan floor and halfway up the stairs leading to the bedroom.

Yes, Sister Georgina was disappointed to compromise so much on her dream, once in a lifetime wedding, as it was a far cry from the "Garden of Eden" she originally wanted. But at this stage, she was just thankful that there would be a wedding. She told her church family that on their first anniversary they would have a more formal wedding reception. This small wedding was primarily to get the formalities out of the way, and most knew what she meant and completely understood.

Sister Georgina was shooed upstairs with the instructions to get ready by her church sisters as they continued to fuss over the wedding decorations. She only had time to grab a chicken leg and a napkin before obeying their orders. As she sat on her bed, dreaming of what was to come, she paused to take in the moment. She wanted to remember these last few days of bliss and the intensity of the joy she was currently feeling. She was so thankful that God had finally answered her prayers.

Chapter Seven
The Calm Before the Storm

With tears streaming down her face, Sister Georgina sat in the parking lot of the Giant supermarket near her house transfixed to the radio. She often caught Michael Baisden's controversial talk show on her way home from work, but since the topics they covered were not normally dealt with in a substantive manner, she preferred the straight news programming offering by NPR. But today, the talk show host had exceeded himself, as he was covering the subject of being married and celibate. It was not a subject often discussed, so she was grateful that it was being given some airtime. She felt compelled to sit and listen to the program with her groceries wilting in the trunk of her car. As expected, the coverage of the topic was way too brief for her liking and the voices of the affected was overshadowed by commercial interruptions, musical interludes, and jokes. But what did come through the speakers resonated painfully with Sister Georgina, especially when one woman spoke passionately about the agonizing torture of lying next to her husband night after night. The lady shared how she secretly wanted him to touch her, but she knew nothing would happen if he did. Her sense of frustration was devastating. Sister Georgina could identify with that experience all too well, the only difference being that when her husband was home, he would be lying in the room next door. Her tears fell uncontrollably at her reality.

It had been three years since their wedding and she was still a virgin. She hadn't told anyone of her predicament. How could she explain it? What words could she use to express what she was going through?

How would she describe the embarrassment, the humiliation, the desperation, the rejection she felt all the time? Onlookers would find it hard to believe. *She* found it hard to believe. With the words of the talk show fading into the background, she tried to make sense of the last three years of her marriage and how she had arrived at such a point of despair.

～

The newly wedded couple had been driven in the church van to Sister Georgina's house a couple of hours later than they had been expected. The Pastor had, of course, gone over time with tales of his own wedding, his journey to the church that day, and reiterating the blessing that was marriage. Both Sister Olivia and Sister Georgina were equally devastated by the delay. Despite her best efforts, Sister Olivia had been unable to keep the chicken wings and drumsticks from drying out. Knowing that it would be unacceptable to serve, she rushed to several soul food restaurants to try and get some replacements, but had been unsuccessful. She was then forced to go to the local warehouse store, having to pay their membership fee to join as she had forgotten the church's card and purchased their pre-cooked offerings. For Sister Georgina, when the Pastor said the words, "you are now husband and wife," it took all her strength not to grab Otis' hand and drag him out of the church, telling the guests "thank you for coming" as she sped by them and then rushing home to finally experience the joys of making love.

Even though she was bursting with anticipation, she reminded herself that she had waited for so long, a few more hours wouldn't hurt. Besides, she wanted to enjoy feeling beautiful. Her wedding dress was a gift from her church sisters and she enjoyed the process of choosing it and seeing it hanging up in her room as she dreamt of the day she would wear it. It had been worth waiting for, as she loved the experience of floating down the aisle in the arms of her older brother who was standing in for their deceased father. Her nieces had done an excellent job as flower girls, but the youngest stole everyone's heart as she desperately tried to pick up the petals thrown on the ground by her sister. When Sister Georgina heard the wedding march, her tears automatically began to flow. Her brother's smile reassured her and she gratefully took his arm and proudly walked down the aisle to start her new life. Otis had politely kissed her on the cheek when the Pastor said, "you may now kiss the bride." She convinced herself that it was because he was shy and was determined to not get upset by the lack of affection at the altar. During their reception, she did notice he kept away from her and despite sitting next to each other, there were no physical displays of affection. Therefore, it proved to be extremely difficult for Sister Georgina to concentrate on polite conversations as she circulated among the guests. But, she did not have much to worry about because as the soon as the speeches were over, most guests' disappointment over the poor quality of food, as well as *sensing* that they needed to leave, gave their congratulations to the couple and left. So, by 7:00pm, the newlyweds had the house to themselves.

With their prayers over, there was nothing else to do but venture upstairs to the bedroom. It was at this point she finally slowed down, and playing with her wedding ring, finally allowed her nervousness to come through. *What would it be like? Would it hurt? Would he be gentle?* She became flustered as she walked up the stairs, tripping on the hem of her simple, white gown. She smiled to herself and exhaled. She stood meekly outside her bedroom door, in anticipation that her knight would open it and symbolically invite her into their new life together. She wanted everything to be perfect so God would be pleased.

What she did not expect, was her new husband to stop outside the spare bedroom door and say that he had a long day. Making it clear he was not expecting an answer, he went inside and shut the door behind him. Earlier that day, she had shown him the spare room as a place where he could get ready in peace. He had placed his small overnight case in the corner and hung his suit in the closet. Sister Georgina had smiled to herself as she watched him neatly lay the newspaper he had in his hands and his reading glasses on the night stand. She remembered how happy she felt knowing that in a couple of hours, they would be placed on the other side of *her* bed. Now, she wondered whether her simple gesture of civility had given him the impression that this was to be *his* room. With her thoughts racing between whether she should knock on the door, barge in, or do nothing, the light under the door turned off. In shock, Sister Georgina remained standing in the dark corridor with the wilting bouquet in her hands.

She had no idea how much time had passed before she realized that she was cold. The furnace had been programmed to turn itself off at midnight. But she was left sitting in the same place she stood when Otis had gone to sleep. She did not care; her mind needed a logical answer to this strange turn of events.

"Did he really…*really*? But we're married. We are supposed to make love. He's supposed to make me feel special," she whispered into the darkness as if someone was there to converse with her. With her tears hardening on her face, Sister Georgina decided it was time to go to her room. With her head held down, she wondered how she could look anyone in their eyes. Although she did not have a close relationship with her church sisters, she knew they would be watching her closely to get some hint about how she enjoyed her wedding night. How was she going to hide her feelings of humiliation, embarrassment, and anger about what had *not* happened? She got herself ready for bed while silently crying hysterically. She then prayed for guidance before dressing in her new imitation Victoria Secret lingerie, just in case her husband decided he wanted to join her late that night.

As she stared at the ceiling, she continued her prayers. This time, apologizing to the Lord for everything she had ever done wrong throughout her life. Nothing had prepared her for the intense rejection she now felt. *What could I have done to be treated this way? Did I do anything to upset him? Why does he not want to touch me?*

She forced herself to see the positives and refused to be ungrateful. She was married before her fortieth birthday, her husband was lying in the next room, and tomorrow would be another day. She decided to entertain this thought before finally falling asleep.

There was no denying that from her wedding night onwards, she knew something was drastically wrong. She hadn't pushed the issue about consummating the marriage and gracefully hid her disappointment. She did not want him to think of her as one of those nagging women. So while she remained paralyzingly confused, her husband seemed pretty content and pottered about the house when he was there, as if nothing was wrong.

Immediately following the wedding, they had quickly gotten into a routine. Otis had kept to his schedule of coming to Maryland just twice a month. There had been no more talk of a transfer to the D.C. office, so the only thing that changed was that Otis stayed with Sister Georgina instead of Mrs. Gilchrist. He would arrive on Friday night about 7pm and settle into the spare room before having the meal that Sister Georgina lovingly prepared. He would then watch television or read the paper before retiring to bed. Normally, he would have things he wanted to do on Saturday, like play golf or go downtown to some event or another. On a rare occasion, he would suggest a trip or activity that they could do together, but it was usually something only he wanted to do. Sister Georgina made a suggestion once or twice, but for whatever reason, it never happened and she never suggested anything again. Sunday, of course, was reserved for church. They would attend the 11am service and then he would leave directly after brunch.

The stresses and strains of her marriage became bearable when she was able to stand next to Otis at Sunday service twice a month. She was grateful that he had stood up in the eyes of the Lord and married her. She loved the respect that the title '*Mrs. Jeters*' had given her. The ring on her finger made her feel accepted into the society, but once church was over and Otis was on his way back to Pittsburgh, the illusion she had created always came crashing down.

Sister Georgina made the decision to be the dutiful wife and hold fast to her vows. Her loving actions would make him appreciate her. But while she waited for his metamorphosis into the man of her dreams, there was no doubt that the stress was taking its toll on her. This fact was brought home so unmistakably when Sister Georgina nearly had a major accident on the Beltway as she drove home one evening. A truck she was traveling behind accidentally dropped part of its load while traveling at 65 miles an hour. She had to swerve sharply to avoid the mattress in the middle of the fast lane. Badly shaken, she was again thankful that it was one of Otis' weekends. So she pulled off the Beltway and called him for help. Surprisingly, he answered the call. Most times, she would be forced to leave a message clearly stating why she was calling. Irritated by the intrusion into his game time, he couldn't understand why she was so upset. After hearing her story, he implied that her nerves couldn't be *that* bad if she could safely park and make a call to him. Annoyed, he told her to wait until she calmed down and then drive herself home. He then told her not to disturb him again as the Steelers were winning. It was a couple of hours before she could muster up the strength to continue her journey. When she finally arrived home, still shaken by the experience, tried to relay the incident to him desperately seeking some kind of comfort. He remained cold and indifferent, not addressing the incident at all, but instead, asked what would be for dinner.

She could no longer deny that her needs were not being met in the marriage. She needed some emotional connection, but none was forthcoming. She replayed hopeful stories of difficult marriages that had been turned around. She remembered a sister had given a testimony revealing that her husband had once held a gun to her head. He had threatened to blow her brains all over their new couch. She did not call the police, but instead prayed and fasted and eventually her husband repented, begging for her forgiveness. She told Sister Georgina with pride that after the incident he had become the husband that she knew he could be. Spurred on by such stories, Sister Georgina decided to remain hopeful. She did not want to make him uncomfortable, so she never mentioned her pain. Instead, she focused on making the most of the two weekends he was in town. She enjoyed looking after his practical needs. She liked preparing his meals, setting the table, and making sure everything looked good. She interpreted his silence around the table was because he loved the meal she had made for him so he wanted to savor it. She made sure his lunch was packed and his clothes were washed and ironed, ready for him as he departed for Pittsburgh.

Her marriage was God's will and she wasn't going to give up on it. So, as she did in her single days, Sister Georgina turned to the books to understand and find creative ideas to turn her marriage around. One book on how to spice up your marriage, suggested a romantic night to surprise the man of the house. The "devil is in the details," the very un-Christian book suggested and went on to tell the story about someone from the South who knew their partner's favorite dish was a traditional peach cobbler. "Anticipation is a great aphrodisiac," the author pronounced, explaining that she told her partner at least a week before that she was going to make his favorite dish. Every day, she reminded him that she would be making this peach cobbler to wet his appetite. She would then discuss the specifics to excite all his senses. She had soft music playing, sprayed perfume, and hinted to the reader that she had nothing on under her apron. When the appointed time arrived, she served him his dinner as usual and then instructed him, seductively, to go into the bedroom to await his dessert. She then wrote excitedly about how she had surprised him by drizzling the peach cobbler all over her chest. Her husband, initially shocked by her actions, immediately reacted positively to the adult activity. Naturally, the author was pleased with the result. Duly inspired, Sister Georgina was confident that this time her actions would provoke the same response for her, as well.

When the designated Friday evening came around, giddy with anticipation, Sister Georgina waited patiently for him to arrive. She had made his favorite meal and told him she would be making a red velvet cake with cream cheese for dessert. She sent a reminder note via email with the menu to get him excited because she did not have his address in Pittsburgh. She paid great attention to the details, having set the table with the special tablecloth, lit scented candles, turned the radio from its permanent gospel music station to an R&B one to guarantee that some baby-making music would be playing in the background. Sister Georgina even made an effort with her appearance and stepped it up by dressing in a strapless maxi dress that was one of her honeymoon outfits that she never had a chance to wear. She convinced herself, that he will get the message loud and clear that tonight is the night.

Otis arrived at his usual time and as soon as Sister Georgina heard his car in the driveway, she rushed to greet him by the front door.

"Hi, how was your week?" She mumbled, unable to hide the nervousness in her voice.

"Are you not cold in that outfit?" The first comment out of Otis' mouth implied annoyance with her. He slammed his car door, giving her the impression that his week had not been okay or that the traffic on Interstate 95 had taken its toll on him.

Embarrassed, she hurried back into the house after gathering all her strength to say she had cooked his favorite meal as promised and that he should make himself comfortable at the table. From her vantage point in the kitchen, she could see Otis put his bags down by the side of the stairs and make his way to the dining room table. However, on his way to his seat, he blew out the candles that had been strategically placed around the living room to tempt his sense of smell, mumbling something about how it would affect his allergies. He then turned the radio to the sports channel so he could hear the results of the football game. Before she came out of the kitchen with trembling hands, Sister Georgina dished out his food on the regular plates and not the ones designated for special occasions. She put on the unattractive house coat that had been hanging on the back of the kitchen door and sat in silence with him as he ate his meal. She had concluded that if she placed the red velvet cake on her breasts, as the author had suggested, she would face the humiliation of him telling her to wash it off before he returned to reading the paper or listening to sports radio.

It was about two years into the marriage when another chapter of the 'spice up your marriage' book had challenged her to be more daring and to do something that she had never ever done before. Sister Georgina was more than conscious of the fact that Otis had never asked to see her body and resolved to force the issue by standing in front of him in all her glory. The book described a scene from a Hollywood movie where the heroine had seductively stepped out of the shower and the leading man was compelled to hand her a towel. The encounter had been so romantic and inevitably led to the two becoming one. She knew that no one, apart from her doctors, had seen her naked since her mother's untimely death, so it was going to take all her courage. But knowing that her options at this stage were limited, she was willing to do what was necessary to make her marriage work.

When Otis came home as expected, this time she was already upstairs in the hall bathroom that had been designated as *his* since she had the on-suite in the master bedroom. Hearing him at the bottom of the stairs, she turned on the shower and with the door wide open, waited for him to walk past. She did not know how she misjudged his steps, but when she heard him walking around his room, she knew she had missed the opportunity to exercise this plan. She wasn't sure what happened, whether the noise from the shower had distracted her or that he had simply run pass the open door. Whatever it was, it was yet another plan that had fallen by the wayside. As each of her plans failed, she could feel her anxiety building. Her hands would tremble and sweat, she would unconsciously rock back and forth as she tried to make sense of the thoughts that raced around her mind. *Am I ugly? Am I not good enough? Does my husband really not want me?* She didn't know what to think anymore, but knew that it wasn't supposed to be like this.

The two weekends a month that Otis came down to visit meant time flew by and before she realized, three years had passed. Nothing had changed during that time. She had continued to present an image of being happy and grateful that she had a husband in her life, albeit, in name only. Their conversations when they did speak would focus on safe topics such as the weather, her school schedule, household business, or how his mother was doing even though Sister Georgina had never been invited to meet her. She had, of course, done her best during this time to entice, cajole, but mostly beg him to give her the attention she craved. At first, he was polite and would say he had a big meeting in the morning, or that he was tired and needed at least eight full hours of sleep. But, then, he shifted and accused her of nagging and suggested that it was her who had the problem. He would make cruel and sarcastic comments about her appearance, like waving his hand by his open mouth when she had walked past, implying that she had bad breath or that the cream she put on her face was evidence that she was making herself unattractive and hence, she was not a good wife. She had no idea why he would say such cruel and unkind things to her. She could make no sense of it because in her mind she had done nothing except try to love him. Sister Georgina soon felt like Ingrid Berman in the Oscar winning movie, <u>Gaslight</u>. Like the main character, her husband tried to convince her that she was going insane in order to steal her jewels. Sister Georgina had no physical jewels, but felt her husband was employing the same strategy to convince her that nothing was wrong with their marriage and that it was all in her imagination.

On the many occasions she tried to discuss their marriage, he shut her down and seemed to punish her by missing a couple of his weekend visits. As a result, she didn't feel that she was able to talk with him about anything. She could sense that he wasn't really interested in what she had to say anyway. He never asked her about her life, her interests, or how her week had gone. He would get the people and places she talked about mixed up no matter how many times she told him. She felt he was aloof, distant, and not invested in their relationship at all.

At forty-three, she recognized that her biological clock was nearing its midnight hour and she did not want to accept that the hot flashes she began to have were signaling the onset of perimenopause. Being pushed by desperation, she repeated the mantra that with the Lord anything was possible, and tried to not give up hope. Sister Georgina wanted two children; a boy and girl would be ideal. But at this late stage, she would be happy with just one. And of course, she wanted to raise them in a two parent household. Therefore, she reasoned that if they worked together, they could still achieve their goals. With the Lord, it was never too late.

She tried to focus on his positive qualities. He was a gentle and kind man. She cared about his wellbeing, she was happy to support him. But after he left one Sunday afternoon, she looked up from the dishes she had been washing in the kitchen and realized that she had washed the same plate for two hours. She had to face the truth of her situation. Having had a wedding ceremony, a ring on her finger, a framed marriage certificate hanging on the wall, and received both legal and public recognition, it all seemed to mean nothing. She was lonelier than when she was single. The trappings of marriage could not hide the reality that without the physical and emotional intimacy, she technically wasn't married at all. It had taken a while for Sister Georgina to reluctantly reach this conclusion and the journey to get there had been a very long and complex one.

With all the drama associated with her marriage, added to the mix was the problem she faced on a theological level. She believed her submission to God was directly tied to having a successful marriage. The love she demonstrated towards her husband was indicative of the love she demonstrated to her Lord and Savior. She had come from the school of thought that claimed love is something that grows between the couple over time as they live together as man and wife. Love was about commitment, sacrifice, trust, compromise, and hard work. If she gave up on her marriage, she would be risking her salvation. But standing at the kitchen sink, she could no longer ignore the reality that her marriage was nothing but a sham. The plate that she had been washing for hours, symbolically fell from her hands and shattered into thousands of small pieces on the tiled floor.

It was the Pastor's powerful sermon the previous week on the importance of 'speaking up' that gave her the confidence to insist on confronting the issue head on. So as Otis watched television one Saturday evening, Sister Georgina thought it was time to broach the subject. She made him a cup of hot chocolate and sat next to him and asked gently, in her sweet voice that would have made the married sisters proud, if they could have a quick chat.

"Um?" Otis responded, making it clear he had no idea what she was talking about.

"Are you happy?"

As if knowing where the conversation was heading, immediately he went into shut down mode. "I haven't given it much thought. The game will be on in a moment..."

Sister Georgina knew there were no games scheduled that day. His body language made it clear that he wanted to get back to watching television, undisturbed. She decided to be strategic, but direct, and asked a general question.

"What kind of physical relationship would you like?"

"Please, not now," he said, seemingly puzzled that she would even ask such a thing.

"Well, we haven't consummated the marriage and I was wondering…." Before she could finish her sentence, Otis picked up his newspaper in defiance and made it clear he was no longer willing to talk. Shocked but undeterred by his response, Sister Georgina persisted. She knew better than to get caught up in a conversation that went nowhere as it certainly would not achieve her goal of having sex.

She took a deep breath and again in her sweet voice, she bravely asked if he would like to go upstairs to the bedroom trying to use language not to humiliate or offend. This opening only allowed her husband to tell her he was okay and returned his attention quickly to his newspaper. Finding her courage, Sister Georgina pulled the newspaper away from his face and reached over to kiss him. But before her lips could touch his face, he turned away and she ended up kissing his cheek. The kiss brought back memories of her father and mother on that infamous Valentine's Day. The emotionless expression of affection was a neon sign that things were not as they should be.

Perhaps, it was the tension in air or the sad disposition of Sister Georgina, but Otis surprisingly took control of the conversation while he flipped through the television channels.

"Look, I know I told you, my urologist…" he mumbled reluctantly.

Knowing he never told her anything of the sort, knew he needed to say something to stop the conversation, as well as put an end to her pathetic efforts to get him to engage in some sort of sexual activity. It meant his statement teetered on the edge of the truth.

He had enjoyed a very good sex life as a young man. Once he discovered the joys of sexual intercourse, he made it his mission to obtain as much as he could. He often thought back to his teenage years when he and his friends would compete to see how many women they could sleep with in one night. His own record had been five. They had simply walked up and down the main street on a busy Saturday night and smiled at the attractive women who passed them by. They would shout flattering words and then wait to see who took the bait. As one of his friends had a car in the alley, they would take turns with a strict time limit of fifteen minutes per catch. He remembered fondly how they would peer through the steamy windows to check on each other's love making techniques. Then there was the time when he had juggled at least four women at the same time and laughed when they fought viciously about who should get him as the prize when they eventually found out about each other. He laughed even harder when he rejected all of them when the entertainment value had worn off, because their catty behavior was definitely not what he was looking for in a girlfriend.

As he got older and actually began to hear what more and more women said to him about not satisfying their sexual needs when he ejaculated, he genuinely didn't understand why they would get even more upset when he reminded them that 'they should get theirs'. He hated the fact that their complaints ruined his orgasmic high and deliberately decided to seek out younger and younger women in the hope that they would not know any better. This strategy soon backfired as rather than be the receptacle for his sperm like he wanted, the women demanded he be a fatherly figure, which of course, he had no interest in becoming. He then called upon the services of prostitutes, but hated paying for it. He believed that they were to be grateful that he was willing to make love to them, and if the presence of their pimp was not obvious on the conclusion of his business, he would try to persuade them to give him their services for free.

Surprisingly, he had gotten some insight into his own behavior when the Jeffery Dalmer news story broke. The cannibal wanted his sexual partners to only do his bidding and ate their bodies to get rid of them. Otis sympathized with him because that was exactly what he wanted as well. Unlike Jeffrey, he wouldn't ingest his partners, but rather, chose to leave them instead. Although it had taken him years to figure out, he was pleased to finally understand that his sexual preference was basically to have someone please him. In fact, it was a turn off for him to even think about his partner's needs. As far as he was concerned, it had always been and would always be a one way street for him. And like Jeffrey, Otis found that isolating himself was the best way to keep his secrets hidden.

As a young man, he took pride in keeping his body in good shape and spent hours in the gym. He had dreams of being a world famous bodybuilder like Arnold Schwarzenegger, so he had no hesitation in taking the steroids on sale in the locker room. He liked the way it made him look and feel. Despite his dedication to the sport, he was unrepentant when he was dismissed from competition after competition for his steroid use. It was decades before the long-term consequences of his overuse showed itself. His shrinking testicles and enlarged breasts, coupled with his desire to avoid physical and emotional intimacy, meant the need for massages with happy endings dwindled to nothing. He began to see the truth in the old saying about 'wearing out your penis in your youth'. He became content with pleasuring himself and relished in the fact that no one had to see his body.

He celebrated being celibate because it came without the annoyance of being responsible for someone else's feelings and it was free. Therefore, like how a person unable to read finds ways of hiding their illiteracy, he, too, learned ways to manage his sexual preference. His occasional trips to the urologist were not to explore his options about reversing the symptoms of his steroid use, but rather, simply an annual checkup, much to his doctor's frustration. Unlike some of his peers who seemed to relish the thought of controlling women with sex, he now found joy in the opposite. He liked presenting himself as an eligible bachelor and seeing women salivate at the thought of having their social and biological needs met by him. He had gotten most of the things he wanted from such women and knew very well that he had no intention of giving them anything return. He settled on Sister Georgina simply because at that time in his life, he had grown tired of the endless parade of desperate women. He felt that Sister Georgina would take care of him without expecting anything in return, but now, he considered her demands were beginning outweigh all the other women put together. This was definitely not what he had signed up for.

"What? You never told me…" Sister Georgina shouted and could feel herself getting ready to explode. Taking control, she took a deep breath to calm herself. She really wanted to hear what he had to say. So, remembering to speak in her sweet voice she said, "is everything alright? Is there anything I can do? Go ahead, I am sorry to interrupt."

Otis strategically revealed that he had gone to his urologist to have a few things checked out. He claimed that it should be nothing to worry about. He had been given the okay, but he still wanted to take it easy. He was lying, but why stop now...

"My father died of prostate cancer and so did a good friend of mine. My friend knew he was having issues but wasn't able to do anything about it because he didn't have health insurance. I went to visit him a couple of times in hospital before he eventually died. He looked *terrible*," Otis stated assertively. Sister Georgina had never known him to be a conversationalist, but in this instant, he chimed on with ease, trying hard to avoid the conversation that Sister Georgina so desperately wanted to have. But he saw her stunned face and hurriedly got back to the issue at hand.

"At my age, I just need to be careful," he announced.

Sister Georgina had the confirmation that his sudden openness and personal revelation had more to do with diverting the conversation away from their lack of sexual activity.

"I am so sorry to hear that," Sister Georgina said emphasizing her sweet voice, hoping to contain her anger and sarcasm. "Is there anything I can do?"

"No," Otis said definitively, hoping that it would put an end to this and all future conversations like this once and for all. "I will let you know when things are okay," he offered. He held out his hand to seal the agreement and she felt compelled to ask why a handshake and not a kiss.

"Don't make such a big deal about it," Otis responded annoyed. But realizing his oversight and didn't have any real defense, he felt obligated to kiss her on the cheek. Sister Georgina felt like her uncle had kissed her. Having run out of things to say, he returned his glance to the television screen.

Despite her best efforts to ignore her feelings and accept her husband's position, Sister Georgina was taken aback by his outright selfishness and wished he had told her before the wedding. But she knew that it wouldn't have made much difference to her ultimate decision to marry him. She needed to keep the conversation going in the hopes that it would somehow come around to her desires.

"But, what about me, Otis? I have needs," she mumbled. She glanced over at her husband; his eyes were turning red and he was frozen in anger. She could see he was ready to explode. She had pushed him to his limit without realizing it. She said goodnight and left him to flip aimlessly through the television channels.

After this attempt, fearful of upsetting him, she decided it was best to not say anything more about the state of their marriage. As the months turned into years, Sister Georgina continued to care for him as she had been doing and kept her intense unhappiness to herself. She put on a brave face and continued to hide the fact that her marriage was not normal. Many nights she would lie in her bed trying to figure out how to make sense of her predicament. With no real solution, she would end up just covering her head with the sheets in a feeble attempt to stop the pain of her intrusive thoughts. But she was not going to give up so easily. Her biological clock said time was an issue, so she would make *something* happen.

———————— ⌇ ————————

There was no doubt that what was being described by the talk radio host as a consequence of being "backed-up" made sense to her. She was definitely experiencing mood swings, she was irritable, and her behavior was erratic. So as Sister Georgia sat in the car, she knew she was in trouble. She was not sure what her next steps should be; perhaps she needed to communicate better or not be so demanding. She would try to accept Otis for who he is and not pressure him to do things that he clearly did not want to do. Sister Georgina resolved to keep trying, seeing no other option. But knowing that her Lord and Savior was by her side, knew her prayers would be answered. Sister Georgina checked her face for tear stains in the rear view mirror and then slowly drove home, determined to make her marriage work. However, this time she would play dirty.

157

The Righteous Sin

Chapter Eight
The Best Laid Plans of Mice and Men

Although the honeymoon suite was certainly stunning, the most attractive part of the room for Sister Georgina was the cold, tiled floor next to the toilet. She knew she would have to come out of the bathroom eventually, but now was not the time. She really needed the space to think, to process what had just happened. But no matter which way she looked at it, the surprise birthday trip to the Eastern Shore was officially a disaster. Her mind was racing. Perhaps she should pray. No, not next to the toilet, that would be too disrespectful. Maybe the Lord was testing her. She knew the Lord tests his faithful with the things that they love the most, but this seemed downright cruel. *What was she to learn from such an experience? Were her expectations too high? How had this happened?* The humiliation she felt was unbearable. Sister Georgina could not fathom how her emotions had gone from one extreme to another in a matter of minutes. She had been so hopeful when she woke up that morning, and now, here she was, cowering on the bathroom floor of the honeymoon suite shocked by the intensity of her absolute rage. The only thing she was sure about was that this was her very last attempt to try and seduce her husband.

———————— ~ ————————

She had been planning and preparing for this surprise trip for months. They had never gone on a honeymoon, in fact, they had never been anywhere overnight together, so Sister Georgina figured that an overnight break together might be what they needed to finally end her celibacy. They would be forced to share a bed. The thought had her in a spin just thinking about his warm body *finally* lying next to her. Otis's sixty-seventh birthday was just around the corner and she figured that she should make it a surprise birthday present. Sister Georgina secretly wished the roles were reversed and it was Otis who was doing the planning to treat *her* to a romantic trip away for some tender, loving care. But pushing her concerns away, she replaced them with planning how to execute his birthday surprise.

First on her list was an appointment to see her gynecologist. They were happy to give Sister Georgina information about conception after forty, despite the fact that she was extremely well informed about her biological functionalities.

"Because of your age, it's going to be particularly difficult for you to conceive. You should tell your husband you want more sex. Every day, preferably! That will definitely increase your chances." The doctor laughed causally in response to her question about getting pregnant.

Sister Georgina could hardly contain herself and gritted her teeth as she replied, trying not to show the pain of her situation. How could she tell the doctor that she needed to catch up on nearly twenty-five years of missed lovemaking? She hid her anger and remained silent, because she had an objective and becoming emotional would not help her case. She smiled passively at the doctor instead, feigning helplessness.

"Thank you, Doctor. I know it's my fault that I've left it too late, but is there anything I can *do?* Is there anything I can *take* to increase my chances of becoming pregnant?" She added a tremble in her voice for dramatic effect. Sister Georgina was well aware that she did not have to *act*, as it was all she could do to hold down the tension that has built up inside her for the past forty years. With nowhere for it to go, she felt herself tethering on the edge.

"You can increase your chances by having an affair as well!" The doctor suggested with a broad smile, indicating it was a joke. Sister Georgina didn't laugh. Of course, an affair was out of the question for Sister Georgina. She hadn't spent a lifetime professing her faith to blatantly disobey one of the key principles she fought so hard to uphold. *Thou shalt not commit adultery.* But of course, she had never faced this as a possibility, so technically it was not even worth considering as an option. Unintentionally, she rolled her eyes, indicating her annoyance at the Doctor's insensitivity.

For the first time in the examination room, the doctor realized that something was wrong, but with so many patients waiting, she had no time to explore. She immediately went into *physician mode* and continued. "Well let me just say…it is possible to conceive and have a healthy baby after forty. But it is much more difficult. Those celebrities you see on television have the finances and support to make it look so easy. After 44, it is more difficult to conceive and carry a pregnancy to term. And you should know that there may be serious health complications, so I would think very seriously about it before you proceed. Did you know your blood pressure is slightly elevated? I would like you to come back in to have it more thoroughly checked out. Do you have any severe headaches?"

On seeing Sister Georgina's face, she knew no further explanation of the dangers of a pregnancy at her age was required, nor was she interested in hearing more about her elevated blood pressure. However, the doctor sensed that there was a need to apologize and continue with the formal medical assessment.

"I am sorry for being so flippant, but it was my way of saying increasing your lovemaking, especially around the time you are ovulating, will definitely help your chances to conceive. I understand you still have your cycle?"

"Yes," Sister Georgina said hesitantly, trying to maintain her helpless persona and chose not to mention that it had become more infrequent the past few years. "I really want to have children and it may be my last chance. My husband is much older than me, but with some encouragement…maybe…" Sister Georgina's voice trailed off in anticipation that the Doctor would know what she meant.

"You know I am not supposed to give you such a prescription but…" She smiled warmly, "I have some samples that your husband might like," hoping that the sample would avoid another medical complaint. "If you're serious about children, I think we should make an office appointment for you to discuss your options, okay?" And with that she left the examination room. Returning shortly to give her the sample packet of the new infamous 'blue pill,' Sister Georgina smiled. *Mission accomplished,* she thought to herself. The packet in her hands was confirmation that God was on her side. For the first time in a long time, she felt some of her pain subside. She had actually not just been *heard,* but also *understood* and provided with practical support. Sister Georgina was hopeful.

When she got home, she immediately consulted the calendar. She would be ovulating around the time of his birthday and so planned the trip around those dates. She was thankful that she could disguise her true motives, all the while, giving him the impression that it would be all about him. Realizing that Otis was not the only one who may need help sexually, she knew that she also needed some help- and lots of it. After years of begging and being consistently rejected, any sexual feeling she had left would need a crow bar to get out. So she welcomed the help and thought about her brief excursion into the sex toy website when she was single. She logged back onto the site and this time, not thinking about the price, put in an order for some female warming creams to help her get in the mood.

A hiccup in her plans came when she was looking at the Viagra tablets, which she had done as often as she could since getting them from the doctor. She had come home from school during her lunch break to check on them and dream about the possibilities, as well as congratulate herself for a plan well executed. She plotted how she was going to give it to her husband without him noticing. The coffee she was drinking, slipped from her hands and spilled all over the table. Instantly, the sample packet of Viagra was covered in the warm, brown liquid which seeped under the plastic casing with ease. By the time she got a paper towel and attempted to dry the pills, it was clear; they were soggy and useless. She screamed out loud, knowing that no one would hear her.

Once she calmed herself down, she decided to resolve the problem as swiftly as the coffee had caused the damage. She remembered that the sex website offered Viagra for sale. But she questioned whether or not it would be the real thing. She had no idea, but would give it a go anyway. Sister Georgina faced her computer and clicked on the bookmark icon for the website. She quickly found the wonder drug and put in an order. Over the next few days, she enjoyed tracking its progress as it meandered across the country, making its way to her mailbox. She wanted to be home when the package arrived just in case, her husband had unexpectedly arrived to collect it. The parcel, in its plain brown packaging with no identifying marks, arrived as expected and she opened it excitedly. She knew something was wrong when she looked into the box and saw the small blue circular pills labeled "Vigra" and not the expected "*Viagra*." She went back to look at the webpage, and sure enough, it was not a mistake. Just the advertising wizards manipulating people like her who desperately wanted to get hold of the tablets without having a prescription. She was annoyed that she had been conned. Not losing her military attitude, she quickly thought of a plan B. She wasn't giving up so easily.

She decided she would ask the Pastor if he knew anyone she could ask for a sample. She would say that she was putting together a project and needed it for the display board. Yes, it would be a small lie, but the cause was a good one, so she would neglect to tell him about the personal nature of her project. It seemed like a plausible suggestion, so she made the phone call before she went back to work.

The Pastor was able to deal very quickly with Sister Georgina's request on her next *extended* lunch hour, of which her secretary had made another note for submission to the Board of Education. The Pastor immediately offered her one of the many sample packages his urologist had given him. And despite not asking, Sister Georgina had to suffer the Pastor's defensive comments about him not needing any help in *that* department and kept his wife very satisfied. But as a woman on a mission, Sister Georgina refused to be side tracked as her next challenge was figuring out a way of getting her husband to take it without noticing. So in her spare time, she watched as many crime shows as possible, hoping to pick up some tips on how to give someone poison.

The next practical task was to organize the birthday trip and fortunately, this sort of fell into her hands by way of compensation for an error on the part of the hotel. Sister Georgina had stayed at the Hilton while attending a teacher training conference in San Antonio, Texas.

Sister Georgina had been pleased to get away from her strange home situation and attend the four day conference. It was a wonderful trip. She didn't realize how much she needed the break. Not realizing that most of the conference saw her poolside and visiting the Alamo, instead of being at the presentation on the effective use of textbook sharing and incentives in the classroom. Sister Georgina wasn't going to worry about anything; she was going to enjoy the time off. She was confident that her colleague who did attend had taken good notes as she had to do a presentation for her colleagues when she returned to Maryland. Her colleague did share the conference notes with her, but also with her secretary, whose notations on Sister Georgina's digressions for the Board of Education had nearly filled her report book.

When she got back to her hotel room on the third day, after sitting by the pool and missing the morning presentations, yet again, Sister Georgina noticed that her door was opened. She thought nothing of it, assuming it was being cleaned and went in. Another guest was in the room unpacking his things and putting them neatly into the drawers. She surprised the guest, a short fellow, and the label on his luggage indicated he was from the Middle East. He looked up and was clearly angry about the intrusion.

"I am so sorry. I think you have made a mistake," Sister Georgina quickly stated to justify her intrusion as she stood there in the hotel robe.

"I think *you're* mistaken," he responded. "This is my room; room 2145." She went immediately for her room key folder, and it stated clearly, *Room 2145.*

"I think we need to speak with the front desk." She looked around for her things and realized they had been removed. She called down to the concierge and asked immediately for the manager. He took some time before he called her back, so she spent a few uncomfortable minutes watching the Middle Eastern gentleman continue to unpack his things.

"I am so sorry, Mrs. Jeters. We cannot apologize enough. Your things were removed from the room on the belief that it had been vacated. A conference administrator had reported that you were not at the required sessions. It is an error on our part. Please come down to the front deck and we will sort this out."

"Thank you, I am on my way," she said into the telephone and left the Middle Eastern gentleman to his unpacking.

By way of compensation, she spent her final day in an upgraded suite and was given an offer for a free a weekend stay at a Hilton Hotel of her choice. Sister Georgina was so pleased and was very happy that the mix up occurred because it allowed her to begin planning for her husband's surprise trip almost immediately. She spent the flight back home thinking about where she would redeem her voucher. She decided on a hotel in Maryland because she didn't want to drive too far. She wanted to make sure they wouldn't be too tired when they arrived, so a five-hour trip to New York would definitely be out of the question. She also didn't want to alert too much suspicion, so Pennsylvania and West Virginia were off the table as well. However, the Hilton in Eastern Shore would definitely work. It was about ninety minutes away in good traffic. The hotel had a beautiful golf course so Otis would be able to enjoy a couple of rounds if he wanted to. But if she had her way, there was going to be no chance of any activities except what she had planned. She booked the weekend and then turned her concentration to getting him there.

Sister Georgina was aware that Otis had been dropping hints every so often about the problems he was having at his office. He told her how much he disliked his boss because of his micromanagement of the team. Despite his years of experience, he was being treated like a junior member of the staff. He knew he could do better and felt it was time he branched out on his own; he just needed the capital to do so. After the wedding, Sister Georgina had found out that Otis did not own his townhouse in Pittsburgh and had been renting it, so the only money he had to invest was the equity in her home. With her blemish free credit history, there would be no problem securing a loan and he would be on his way to self-employment and financial freedom. The house- *her* house, was paid off in full because of her frugal spending and had the capital he needed. Yes, she had signed over half the house to him as a wedding gift, but now he wanted her agreement and signature to use the equity to fund his business.

It would be difficult for a while, but with their faith, the Lord would make the business a success. She figured everything would be okay and that he would be able to repay the loan very quickly so it would be as if they never borrowed the money in the first place. The best advertisement, he said, would come from word of mouth and he had been sowing the seeds now for years. He had built up a good customer base and reputation, so he felt he could do well. Sister Georgina sat quietly at the dining table and listened carefully while Otis laid out his plan of action. This was the most she heard him talk about his work in all the time they had been together so she gave him her full attention. At the end of his sales pitch, she said she would pray about it and sleep on it before making a final decision. But she could see from Otis' demeanor and attitude that, her agreement was already a foregone conclusion and gave her a smile as he bid her goodnight. Sister Georgina watched him as he went up the stairs, looking like someone who had just unloaded a burden they had been carrying for a while.

As she lay awake that night, the thought came into her mind for the first time whether he had just married her for the money. $300,000 was no small amount. They had been married for nearly five years and she felt sure she would have picked up on something like that before now. She reminded herself that she had caught Ezra's ill intentions, but her mind added that it could have been because he was so blatant about wanting money from her. However, Otis could be much more patient and ruthless in his pursuit of money. *The wedding had been beautiful,* Sister Georgina reminisced. "No," she unwittingly said out loud and hoped she had not disturbed her husband in the room next door. She got up and went downstairs to the lounge; put on the simulated propane fire, not for the warmth, but to look at the flames as they danced around. It helped her think. She sat on the couch and watched the artificial flames as she processed her thoughts.

How dare Otis put you in this position? The first thought pushed its way into her consciousness. *He has* never *been a husband to you,* they continued. She tried to push the negative thoughts to the back of her mind and replace them with positive ones. But, somehow, her mind did not cooperate, and as if given permission, her mind was soon flooded with things she had not wanted to think about. Otis was not a husband, had never been a husband. He never even tried to meet any of her emotional, financial, or physical needs. He never listened to her; they were strangers living under the same roof. She wondered if he even knew her name. Sister Georgina had never asked him for money and he had never offered her any. They could barely manage a superficial conversation about the weather or traffic. He only spends two weekends a month with her and never deviated from his routine.

Rationalizing that she was being ungrateful, Sister Georgina thanked her Savior for answering her prayers and sending Otis to her. She could never forget what she had suffered before he came into her life. He was with her every other weekend and stood by her side in church when he was there. Pleased with having come up with some positives, *any* positives, she returned to thinking about his request. If she signed over the equity, they would have nothing left. There would be nothing left for a rainy day, let alone, a baby fund. They would need the equity while she was pregnant and unable tho work because of her high risk age.

But the reality that she wasn't pregnant set in. The reality was that African-American men had it hard in this society. It is difficult for them sometimes to get the respect they deserve. As a good wife, she should want to lift him up as her husband and as a member of her community. If he had this dream for a lifetime, then perhaps he is right to want his wife to share his dream and support him. Her faith dictated that she should be obedient to him. *He was her guide on earth*, the voice through which her Savior spoke to her came through. No matter the sacrifice, Sister Georgina felt that a wife should support her husband, regardless. They were a team so his dream was her dream. If that included remortgaging her home to provide the funds he needed for his risk management business, then it was her duty as a loyal and supportive wife to sign over her investment to enable him to plan for their future. She had to trust him then perhaps he would trust her. She believed in him. What finally made it easy for her to make the decision was the fact that by agreeing to his request, she could demand just about anything from him in return. What she needed from the marriage, to her, was priceless; a baby and to rightfully experience the process of getting there.

The following morning, she told Otis that she would be happy to support him. Otis smiled and said something about being a "tortoise" and "patience having paid off." He shook her hand enthusiastically to cement the deal. She was particularly upset by this unemotional gesture, but remained calm. She reminded herself that he was not used to intimacy and had not done it intentionally. His unusual communication with her and the gesture of connectivity made her feel that their relationship could be more than roommates. Otis thought that his error may have jeopardized his request, so he apologized immediately and tried to cover up his thoughtlessness by saying it was a business agreement. Sister Georgina reminded him that they were still husband and wife regardless of any business deal and forced Otis into feeling obligated to kiss her. He scornfully pecked her left cheek before rushing off to make an appointment with a bank manager. Sister Georgina didn't say anything at the time, but she was reminded of the memory of her father kissing her mother on that Valentine's Day when she was a child.

Despite all her efforts, she could not avoid the fact that her marriage lacked the emotional connection she craved. But this was a start, even if money was involved. So ever since the agreement was made and the check was deposited, Otis kept himself busy setting up his business while Sister Georgina put the finishing touches on her plan to lose her virginity and get pregnant. A couple of days before the big day arrived, she packed a small bag for both of them and snuck it out to the car without him noticing.

When the day arrived, she could barely contain her excitement. She was happy and full of hope, so began the day by thanking the Lord for Otis' sixty-seven years. She then showered him with so much unconditional love, he hardly knew what to make of it all. Sister Georgina served him his favorite, fully-cooked breakfast in bed; eggs sunny side up with salt and pepper, just as he liked them. She then fixed him a bath with scented oils, much to his disgust, but she didn't care. She liked the smell and it would help her get in the mood. By now, he was getting a bit suspicious of her actions and asked leading questions about her motives, hoping that she would not ask for sex. Having anticipated his suspicions, she quickly reassured him that it wasn't every day he turned sixty-seven and her motive was just to love him. He smiled directly at her, and she thought to herself, that the self-development book was right; in order to receive love, she had to give love. They finally had a connection. She felt a familiar twinge in the lower regions of her body and was excited about the possibilities. After laying out his clothes, she left him alone to get ready. She told him she was taking him to the cinema and then to dinner to celebrate.

They left for the 'movie' about 2pm, as she had timed the trip so they would arrive at the hotel right when it was time to check-in. She distracted him by talking about the movie and how excited she was to see it also. But when they drove pass the exit for the theatre, he inquired about where they were going. Enjoying the deception, Sister Georgina continued the ruse by saying she just wanted to go quickly to a store. Otis knew that something was up when they got to the toll booth at the Bay Bridge. Sister Georgina could feel excitement building. Otis on the other hand, in an attempt to avoid dealing with the intensely pleasurable experience, chose not to engage Sister Georgina and ask questions about what was happening or where they were going, rather he pretended to fall asleep. Sister Georgina was not going to let that upset her, so she put on her favorite gospel CD and sang along the whole way to Cambridge. She woke him up when they drove into the hotel's impressive entrance.

"Oh, I wish you had told me ahead of time. I need to be reachable if someone from the office needs to get a hold of me," he said. There was no 'thank you, what a wonderful surprise,' or 'how thoughtful.'

Unfazed, Sister Georgina responded, "I am sure they can manage without you for a day, and I am pretty sure the hotel has email. Today is your birthday and we're going to celebrate in style," Sister Georgina said gleefully, not wanting to acknowledge the worried look on his face nor her motives behind the overnight trip.

"Congratulations on your marriage! Here is your room key and please enjoy you stay with us," the receptionist said. Because she did not have to pay for the room, Sister Georgina had upgraded to the honeymoon suite. When they opened the door to their room, she was pleasantly surprised. The room was massive. It had a separate bedroom, with a king size bed and en-suite with a Jacuzzi. In addition, it had an open lounge with the proper dining and seating areas. They had two televisions, as well as a small bar area and a magnificent view of the Chesapeake. This was the first time they would sleep in the same room. *He cannot get out of this*, Sister Georgina smiled to herself.

"What should we do first? It's your birthday, you decide," Sister Georgina said to her husband.

"Well, we can explore Cambridge and then have dinner," he angrily retorted.

"Sounds like a plan!" Sister Georgina had a broad smile on her face. She changed her clothes into what she thought was more flattering for her figure and took time to make a special effort with her hair. Otis never commented on how she looked voluntarily, so prompting the issue when she stepped out of the bathroom, she asked, "…and how do I look?" He replied that she should not look for compliments as they wouldn't be a compliment. She felt he was gunning for an argument. But, surprise, surprise! She wasn't biting; not today.

She noticed that he seemed fearful so she tried to calm his fears by continuing to be as loving and gentle as possible. They were then off to explore Cambridge. There was not much to see in the small town. The Wal-Mart Superstore seemed to dominate, but other than that they went and visited a small strip mall, which by chance had a movie theater. Otis asked if he could see the movie they originally discussed and Sister Georgina was happy to accommodate his wishes. But after a brief discussion, they both realized that if they saw the movie they would eat much later than they wanted. So, the pair headed back to the hotel. Its seafood restaurant had a great reputation for its crab cakes which were Sister Georgina's favorite. But tonight, she had another motive for ordering the crab cakes. Sister Georgina had been thinking all day about how to get Otis to take the Viagra tablet without him noticing. She knew what she was planning was probably illegal, but at this point, she didn't really care. What would the police charge her with? Trying to get her husband to have an illegal erection? She had already crushed the tablet and put its contents into a piece of foil like she had seen on the crime shows, ready to be sprinkled into his food or drink. But her dilemma was caused because it had to be something he would eat or drink in its entirety.

When they arrived at the restaurant, Sister Georgina asked for a booth in the corner to be as far away from prying eyes as possible. The waiter brought the menu and told them about the night's specials. Sister Georgina didn't need to look at the menu because she already knew what she was going to order and so felt Otis was taking an extraordinarily long time looking over the menu. She didn't know what to say to him if she was discovered. Otis finally looked up and announced that he had decided on the steak and would save some room for dessert since they had red velvet cake with cream cheese frosting available. Sister Georgina smiled remembering one of her attempts to seduce her husband and sat up in her seat. She reminded him that it was a fish restaurant and he should take advantage of the fresh local seafood that was on special that evening since there were several good steak houses near their home. She gently suggested that he choose something else, but insisted that he should definitely treat himself to the dessert. Otis nodded in agreement and decided on the trout. She was pleased because the cream cheese frosting more than likely would have an extra ingredient.

They were pleasantly surprised to see non-alcoholic wine being offered on the wine list and took advantage by ordering a bottle. Sister Georgina, seeing an opportunity, jokingly asked the waiter to bring the red instead of the white, saying she preferred the red. Changing her mind about the cream cheese, felt it would be a better option to put the crushed tablet into the faux red wine reasoning that it would have been seen through the glass. The waiter brought the red as requested and poured them each a glass. Otis took a sip and declared it was such a nice change to see a restaurant accommodate non-drinkers.

It wasn't long before he decided to go to the bathroom and Sister Georgina seized the opportunity to empty the contents of the foil packet into his glass and said a prayer while she did it. When he returned, they had a pleasant dinner conversation and talked about their plans for the next day. Otis decided to take advantage of the golf course and would be up early. Sister Georgina says she would sleep in late and then walk around the town again. She watched in delight as he took sip after sip until his glass was empty. She spent the rest of the evening trying to flirt as much as possible to get in the mood for the inevitable.

After dessert and coffee, they made their way slowly back to honeymoon suite. Sister Georgina was energized by her accomplishment and went straight to the bathroom to get herself ready while Otis made himself comfortable in front of the television. Sister Georgina paced herself. She wanted to give the medication time to get into his system and would give him about thirty minutes. She came out of the bathroom in her Victoria Secret nightgown, pleased that she would finally get some use out of it and sat on the bed with Otis. He was engrossed in a documentary on the food channel; something he normally would have never watched. Looking at the clock, she used her sweet voice to ask if he was ready for bed.

"Come and join me," she invited.

"I just want to see the end of this program. It's pretty interesting."

Sister Georgina was slightly annoyed, but remained calm. "Of course, take your time," she chimed and got comfortable in the bed. After another fifteen minutes had passed, she called him again and his response was that the program would be over at the top of the hour. Sister Georgina decided to use the extra ten minutes to sneak into the bathroom and use the cream she had purchased from the website and rushed back to the bed. Checking the clock, she realized that the warming tingles had worn off after about fifteen minutes. This meant Otis was watching another program. She had to remain hopeful and excited, so she thought about sexual images that resembled what she had seen in her father's pornographic magazine all those years ago in a feeble attempt to excite herself. When she looked up, she was so pleased to see Otis shuffling towards her and inside her head she screamed with delight. *Finally! It's going to happen!* Although she knew it was probably inappropriate, she closed her eyes and lowered her head and said a prayer of thanks because this is the moment she had been waiting for all of her adult life.

When she opened her eyes and lifted her head she saw Otis sitting uncomfortably at the end of the bed. He clearly knew what she expected. She patted the bed before pulling back the sheets on his side, making it clear that the invitation would not be ignored. She smiled, but her nervousness meant it was seen by Otis as an uncomfortable grin.

"What would you like me to do for you?" She said, trying to be as enticing as possible. "How about a cuddle?"

Progress, Sister Georgina thought as Otis stood up. There was no escaping; she had him trapped. She said another word of thanks and happily held her arms open. Otis reluctantly laid down next to her, strategically avoiding her embrace. What she just said made him feel better as he did not have to think about pleasing her. He made no effort to touch or caress her, but Sister Georgina was not discouraged. Instead, her heart sang with joy. She stroked his arms gently, and then his back, in the hope that something would begin to move in the right direction. She could finally feel a slight tingling in her body and was pleased she could get excited without artificial help. She spoke quietly to reassure him, sensing that he was uncomfortable. She said it was okay and that she would be gentle. But as her excitement got the best of her, she stopped touching his body and lifted up her gown and placed his hand between her legs.

That was the final straw as far as Otis was concerned. He wanted nothing to do with her grotesque, elephant sized body. He definitely could not muster the enthusiasm to even think about penetrating her. Noticing that he moved his hand away from her vagina, she changed her approach and decided to continue to touch him all over his body, and made a bold move for his penis. But before she could get to it, he held her hand, making it clear she should go no further. It was off limits.

She became desperate and opened her legs to make it clear what she expected. She forgot about tending to his needs and her embarrassment and allowed her desperation to dominate. It was going to happen if it was the last thing she did. She touched herself to try and keep up her sexual excitement which was now diminishing by the second. Otis told her to hold on and he would be back in a minute and went off to the bathroom. She felt a bit awkward laying on the bed with her legs wide open as if she was in her gynecologist's office waiting for her annual pap smear. She wasn't going to move; this was the furthest she had gotten so she wasn't going to pass on the opportunity.

After what felt like hours, Otis finally emerged from the bathroom and laid down in the bed with his back towards her. Sister Georgina was confused, but continued to lay there with her legs open. Otis made himself comfortable by fluffing up his pillow and giving a loud yawn before returning to his position with his back towards her.

After a minute or so, she said with a quivering voice, "I'm still waiting."

"Why?" Otis half-heartedly responded confused at her statement.

"I thought we were going to make love," she said clearly distressed. She was not going to give him any way out. She was done being nice.

"Ahhh…Well…" Her husband searched desperately for an answer. With no options left, he used the tried and true tactic of denial. "What gave you that impression?" He asked, fiending a slight yawn. "I am tired and going to sleep. Besides, I'm not in the mood."

"Oh, *really*? You're tired? You didn't seem *tired* when you were watching that fucking TV or stuffing your face with dessert! Do you think I would be laying here with my legs wide open catching flies for the sake of it?" Sister Georgina broke down. She never knew she had it in her to be so rude, but it felt good to get it off her chest. This had gone on for too long and she was going to get to the bottom of it once and for all.

"What happened?!" She took a sharp glance at Otis, then, it clicked. He had gone to the bathroom to masturbate. His precious sperm were now swimming down the sewage pipes. Sister Georgina thought of all the years she held on so dearly to her virginity; she remembered the lonely nights she suffered; she remembered being humiliated and laughed at; she remembered their first date and how he had kept her waiting without an apology. She thought about how he had not offered to pay for anything for their wedding. She remembered his lack of affection at the altar. Then, she remembered their wedding night. Oh, yes. She remembered every single second of the wedding night. She recalled trying to please her husband over the years they had been together and how nothing worked. She remembered signing over her home. She remembered the Viagra. She remembered lying on the bed with her legs wide open, waiting like a fool to be fucked by her husband after all of her sacrifices. She thought about the child she had hoped to conceive tonight. She remembered the feeling of humiliation and the embarrassment he caused her hundreds of times. Now, all her hopes and dreams were following his sperm through the sewer. That was the pin that finally burst her bubble. Sister Georgina snapped and could no longer contain her anger.

"Tell me you didn't. Tell me you *fucking* didn't!" She yelled at him with scornful eyes. "You fucking piece of shit. How could you? After all I have done for you? You fucker! You motherfucking bastard! Why did you marry me? Why the *fuck* did you marry me? Eh? Eh?" The Jamaican accent she picked up from her parents as a child that never escaped her in public, found its way out of her mouth as she began hitting him, punching him, and trying to scratch his face. It was as if she was possessed by the Devil. Otis was in shock and did his best to protect himself, but he did not retaliate.

"Why? What the hell is wrong with you? Why can't you fucking talk about it? Why don't you open your damn mouth and tell me what the fuck is going on with you? Don't you have an ounce of decency or some fucking consideration for me to tell me what the fuck is going on? Do you think I signed up for *this* shit?" She sucked her teeth and pointed her hands towards him confused and frustrated.

Otis was speechless. Never in his wildest imagination had he expected this behavior from the meek Christian woman he had married. At this point, they were face-to-face. He sat bewildered as he watched her transform into something unrecognizable. Sister Georgina, offended by his lack of response, decided to give him something to really think about. She shook her right hand a couple of times before taking all the force she could muster to slap him across his face as hard as she could. Her hand tingled when she moved it from his skin and she could see the deep impression it left on his face.

Otis still did not respond to her outburst. It fueled her anger to keep going. This time, she did not coordinate any of her actions and began to scream loudly while punching and kicking him wherever her arms and legs landed. She paused to allow reason and logic to take over for a moment and realized that she wanted Otis to know the depth of her pain. She decided to channel all her anger towards his penis. He wasn't using it to give her any pleasure anyway, so she might as well give it something to remember her by. As if telepathically communicated, Otis knew what she was thinking and instinctively used both hands to protect what was left of his manhood. She quickly looked around the room and saw a heavy table lamp and reasoned that it could do the most damage. She snatched the wire out of the electrical socket, picked it up, and screamed loudly as she rushed towards Otis' penis.

As she passed the large mirror that graced the wall above the desk, Sister Georgina saw a reflection of herself. Her eyes were wide open, while her signature messy hair made her look wild and out of control. It was possessed stranger who looked back at her. She dropped the lamp to the floor and stood still for a few seconds, staring at herself in the mirror before turning and locking herself in the bathroom. It wasn't long before she heard an official knock on the door and hotel security asking if everything was okay. Otis muttered that all was fine and apologized about the noise. He had never hit a woman before and had no intention of starting now. But he had no more patience for Sister Georgina and her intensifying demands. It was time for him to start making alternative plans.

As Sister Georgina cowered in the corner next to the toilet bowl, Otis plotted his next move. Embarrassed, confused, and angry, she had no intention of coming out for a while. She didn't know what to ask the Lord for; guidance, perhaps? The devil had gotten a hold of her. Whatever the case, there was no going back from what just happened.

Chapter Nine
Like Expensive Wine

For as far back as she could remember, this was the first night that she had not knelt by her bedside in prayer at the end of the day. How could she after what had just happened? Her emotions were all over the place and she had no idea how to make sense of them. On the one hand, she felt angry, ashamed, and mortified by her weakness. She was truly disappointed in herself that after all this time, she had given away her most precious gift so easily. But on the other hand, she felt satisfied, relieved, and dare she say it…even *energized* and filled with life. As she thought about the events of the day, she knew her life would never be the same again. But the one thing she knew for sure was that she wanted more.

Sister Georgina sat on her porch as she drifted off to sleep with her book lying on the floor next to her. It was Saturday night, the weather was beautifully calm, and it was too early in the season for mosquitoes. She had a wonderfully, relaxing afternoon, but now, having awakened, her mind had surprised her with thoughts of being ravished, truly and completely. After the disaster of the honeymoon trip, she accepted that her sexless and emotionless marriage was her fate. Divorce was never an option, so she decided to live in hope that God would somehow intervene and miraculously turn her marriage into something more substantial. Otis, for whatever reason, remained unwilling to discuss the issue, and continued his routine of being oblivious to her needs. So, Sister Georgina was surprised that after all these years, her unwanted urges had resurfaced. She worked extremely hard over time to ignore, avoid, and deny their very existence. When her cycle finally stopped and biological children were no longer a viable option, Sister Georgina went back to her OBGYN and had been brave enough to ask for something to reduce her libido. Sadly, the treatment didn't work and instead made her irritable, miserable, and moody. Sister Georgina decided again to try fasting, but it also did not produce the desired results.

What had worked successfully for many years, and particularly now, was for her to keep busy and to not allow such thoughts to take root. So as she had previously done when her involuntary sexual thoughts surfaced, they were quickly replaced by more serious topics, such as the church trip to the botanical gardens or organizing their movie night. But tonight, there was no avoiding the rush of excitement at the intensity of her thoughts. She was thankful she was alone.

Before her nap, she had spoken to her husband in name only. It was his weekend to visit his mother in North Carolina. He had driven and would maybe pop in on his way back to Pittsburgh. The truth was, he had only ever stopped in Maryland *once* and that was because he had forgotten something; not because he had missed her. Regardless, he was at least five glorious hours away. Perhaps it was the knowledge that she was alone, that had given energy to these thoughts that wouldn't be dismissed so easily. She felt the unwelcomed sensations in the lower regions of her body as her erotic thoughts spread quickly. She reluctantly and unenthusiastically decided to address the problem with her fingers.

Due to her *experience*, over the years she reinterpreted her views on masturbation. She knew it was something she should not do, but as it was the total extent of her sexual activity, reasoned that getting it over and done with quickly was the better option, and far better than having thoughts of murdering her husband. It was never her favorite activity, and definitely something she did rarely and begrudgingly. Embarrassed at first by her weakness, she was soon lost in the moment, liking how it felt despite her attempts to deny her feelings.

She was brought back to reality with a jolt when the lawn chair became far too uncomfortable for her activities. She couldn't remember removing her underwear or how her summer dress was now over her waist. Nonetheless, she halfheartedly accepted the added excitement this brought and continued to amuse herself in the evening light. As she glanced upwards over the fence towards her neighbor's house, she thought she saw the curtains move. She wasn't certain, but decided instantly to take her activities inside the house. She was so embarrassed, she cursed at herself for having let her guard down. The bedroom window next door had a perfect view of her porch. As a Sunday school teacher, she could not be caught in such a situation, so she promptly collected her book and went inside to her library. She ensured that the curtains were fully closed before turning the dial on the radio from its regular gospel station to the R&B one. She *definitely* could not have the Lord's music playing in the background while she finished what she had started.

It was the Quiet Storm on WHUR 96.3 and Barry White was playing. She melted as she settled into her recliner. She decided to swiftly fulfill her human urges and then get ready for the Saturday night movie on television. It was a repeat, but provided a plausible excuse for not suffering the indignity of wallowing in her sexual dissatisfaction for too long.

Since her horrific experience in the hotel with Otis, she had kept her promise and never tried to seduce him again. She had chosen to simply ignore his existence and they had once again fallen into a pattern devoid of marital intimacy. Scared of her now exposed propensity to violence, she decided to return to her life in the church and cope with her unsatisfactory situation as best she could.

She gently, but hurriedly touched her body in a feeble attempt to build up some semblance of context for the release of her frustrations. Her brief glance at the bedroom window next door meant she found herself thinking intimately about its male resident. She knew very little about him, as he was hardly ever home due to his job as some sort of international contractor. She had nodded at him a few times over the fence as he was cutting his grass, or tending to his flowerbed. He was attractive enough, but she hadn't really given him much thought.

One day last summer she had seen him shirtless and in a pair of rugged jean shorts as he washed his car. She greeted him with a smile as she parked her car in the driveway and said jokingly that he should do hers as well. Surprisingly, the next day, she discovered that her car had also been cleaned and assumed it had been him. It was such a kind gesture, but she never caught up with him to thank him. Now, she found herself daydreaming about him and gave herself permission to fantasize about how he would pleasure her, bringing her to a mind-blowing climax. For years she had only thought about her husband fulfilling her sexual needs, so it was a shock to have a stranger infiltrate her daydream. But in the bigger scheme of things, it gave her the appearance of some variety, but it didn't really matter because her fingers could never replace the real thing.

Barry White's sensuous proclamations sped the process along and soon nature's body lotion made her fingers warm and sticky. Her activities provided minor relief. She sighed, saddened at the predicament she found herself, but before her anger could take root she heard the doorbell ring. She wasn't expecting anyone and as curiosity got the best of her, without replacing her underwear, or wiping her hands she went to peek out of the window. She made a crack in the curtains and saw the middle-aged, white man from next door. He had a smile on his face that made it clear he was not interested in the overgrown tree branches on his side of the fence, but rather her fingers in its current state. Last summer he had responded to an unspoken need of hers with his gracious act of kindness, and now he seemed prepared to display such gallantry again, but this time on a much more personal level.

Sister Georgina heard her breathing intensify as she stood in shock behind the curtains. She hoped he had not seen them move. She needed some time to think, to process, to get a plan of action together. This was unchartered waters. His mischievous smile was unquestionably appealing and despite her inexperience in these matters, she knew what would be inevitable if she opened the door. Painfully aware of her vulnerability and that her resistance was at an all-time low, she faced the reality of her situation. She proudly declared her virginity for all of her adult life. She eagerly looked forward to catching up when she finally married a few weeks before her fortieth birthday, having done everything *correct* according to her faith. Nothing, however, had prepared her for the loneliness and torture of being in a marriage without physical or emotional intimacy. So the thought that her fingers would be redundant, even for a night, was therefore, very appealing indeed. Her stomach turned as such thoughts quickly gathered momentum. Perhaps, she would finally know what all the fuss was about after all this time. She could keep a secret; who would know? *God would.* She physically shook the intrusive thoughts immediately from her mind and reminded herself that the devil works in many ways and she was having none of it. Besides, he was white, she had put on so much weight, and her house was in such a mess she couldn't possibly entertain. She bowed her head to seek solace in her faith as she had done so many times before.

Dear Lord, you know I am your servant, and have dedicated my life to serving your Truth. You know the sacrifices I have made, the humiliation I have suffered. You know I believe in your majesty, that all things are possible through you and only you. So, do not forsake me now. I am on my knees Lord, humbling myself, no…no…begging you to give me the strength to resist this temptation. You know I want nothing more than to please you, to be your true servant, but this test, this test, which the Devil has presented me with…has weakened me like no other. I need you now…NOW. Help me to resist, to overcome, and to glorify your name.

Sister Georgina stopped rocking back and forth, took several deep breaths, and then wiped the sweat from her forehead that had been building over the last few minutes. As she paused, a sense of calmness came over her. She sighed knowingly.

Thank you, my Lord. I have absolute trust; that whatever happens, it is because it is meant to happen. I place my life in your hands. Amen.

Sister Georgina slowly got up from her knees with her head still lowered. She knew her resolve to defeat the devil and his wicked temptation had failed miserably. But being brutally honest, she knew that before crouching to her knees. Her genuine pride at resisting all these years had long since given way to superficial gestures that had perpetuated the illusion of her continual belief. She knew she was a hypocrite, simply worn down by trying to keep up appearances of being this *good Christian woman*; the embodiment of purity and virtue. But now, she was no longer prepared to fight this battle. She wanted to know what it felt like and did not want to die without knowing. She was prepared for the consequences, even if it meant eternity in Hell. No longer would she allow any grandiose attempts to convince herself otherwise to hide the fact that she wanted it to happen. ...And it seemed like her Lord and Savior knew it, too.

This resolution brought a welcomed sigh of relief for Sister Georgina. So, when the knock at the door came the second time, she took another deep breath, paused slightly, and allowed her hand to unlock the door. Her head remained tilted slightly downwards and with no words spoken, her gentleman caller entered her home. She appreciated his initiative as he delicately lifted her head and held her cheeks passionately with both his hands. He kissed her firmly on the lips. She could no longer accept that the experience was not welcomed and the way her body was reacting, it was long overdue. She had reconciled her dilemma by simply accepting that God truly does answer prayers, even those that have been unspoken and denied. *Dear Lord*, she whispered under her breath, *thank you.*

Sister Georgina was overwhelmed by the care and tenderness he was showing her even though he had only been in her home for a few minutes. It was a strange sensation to be so tenderly caressed. She could feel her body reacting in ways she had never experienced. Already, the feelings were too intense for her; she decided to employ the same tactics she did as a child when the Ferris wheel at the local fair became too intense. She blocked her mind and switched off her feelings. She was numb as she moved into the corner of the room a short distance from the curtains. Her neighbor seemed to sense her withdrawal so he slowed down. He turned off the overhead lights, leaving just the glow of the small table lamp.

Unaware of the power of his words, he whispered softly, "it will be alright," not once, but several times. Her defenses crumbled. The ecstasy she felt when Luther sang those same words came flooding back and her body felt obligated to respond accordingly. She surprised herself by reaching out to the stranger with open arms and he joined her in the corner. He put his fingers on her lips, and she knew not to say anything. She gladly submitted to his authority. He started with her hands, perhaps because he sensed where they had already been. He showed no hesitancy or disgust as he sucked her fingers one at a time. He had taken his time, and with each gesture, he transmitted the message to her that she was wanted, desired, and deserving.

"Oh, you feel good," he moaned.

This can't be happening, she thought, but relished the opportunity to touch his face, his neck, and his chest. She was too afraid to venture anywhere else. He could see that she was still a bit nervous and whispered the words she had longed to hear.

"I want you to enjoy yourself. I want you to feel good. I think you're beautiful, special and unique." He touched her gently around the neck, and then made his way down her body. The sensations rippled down her back. He then made his way up her arms; stopping thoughtfully to whisper how beautiful he thought she was. He continued to relax her by kissing and caressing her neck. This experience sent shudders through her body. She did not know that she could *feel* so much. She felt savored like expensive wine. He seemed intent on using all of his senses to enhance the experience and clearly wanted her to do the same. He sensed that she was feeling overwhelmed and again slowed his touches even more. Each kiss was planted gently and with purpose. She was discovering erotic zones she never knew she had. She relished the fact that he knew what he was doing and seemed fixated on her pleasure.

She had no resistance when he lifted her sundress over her head and left her standing naked in front of him. She was surprised when he stood back and with just the light from the table lamp, he admired her body. Her cellulite, flabby bits, and sagging breasts didn't seem to matter. His eyes spoke volumes as they showed his approval. She didn't feel exposed or humiliated, rather, she felt valued and appreciated. She knew she could escape from the corner if she truly wanted to, but chose instead to watch as he began to undress, but stopped when he reached his underwear. She was unsure of why, but did not have much time to ponder the reasons. Instead, she became excited as he joined her again in the corner and held her tightly. It was still early in the evening and there was no need to rush. His hug was warming and sensual and she savored feeling his breath caress her neck. She liked being in the corner encased by his broad, strong arms. She felt safe and nurtured. All the while, he made it known that he was there for her and only wanted to make her feel good. Together, with the atmospheric sounds of the R&B station playing its baby-making music through the speakers, the auditory, psychological, and physical combination made it so difficult to resist.

In order to avoid the intensity of her feelings and take the onus off of her, she stretched out to touch him. She wanted to be in her comfort zone; to be caring for someone else and not for herself. To have someone make it blatantly clear that they wanted to accommodate *her* was unnatural in her world. As if reading her mind, the man realized that her motives were to avoid the pleasure he was so happy to give her. He rejected her subtleties and held her close. He repeated his earlier statement, sternly, but sensuously, that all he was there to do was to give her pleasure. It was all too much for her to take in.

She slid down the wall until she was fully seated on the floor. She decided to painfully remember the torture of her research class, rather than the fairground experience to avoid the intensity of her feelings. She vividly recalled the uncomfortable lecture chairs, the frayed posters on the walls, and scuffed floors she had contributed to in an attempt to relieve her boredom. But now, the memory of the lecture hall proved to be a wonderful escape. His kisses to her navel brought her back to the situation at hand. He was lifting her off the floor, despite her weight, and led her to the armchair. The last person who occupied the armchair was the Pastor who had blessed the group that met to plan the trip to the botanical gardens. Now, it was being used to accomplish the crime of infidelity.

He sat her down and then got on his knees in front of her. He parted her legs, verbalizing his delight. He could tell she was uncomfortable at being on display, but chose to continue as her breathing intensified. She enjoyed being told how in awe he was of her and what he planned to do. She flinched and moaned as he sucked, sometimes hard, then gentle, then hard again. He then devoured her, as he wanted her to feel his energy, his passion, and his desire. He was proud of her screams, it was addictive, empowering and he wanted to hear more.

Sister Georgina felt her tears building; she had never experienced such pleasure. She finally understood why people would go on and on about it. She could see the sweat glistening on her skin. She had gotten lost in the experience and was ready when her neighbor lifted her out of the chair and placed her on the floor. It was cold, but just had the effect of cooling her down a bit. He made her feel good. He had been selfless in his approach, but now all she wanted to do was give him a little bit of the pleasure he made her feel. She wasn't sure *what* to do, so she explored his body with her hands. She rubbed his back gently, she kissed him behind his ears, rubbed his arms, and she got a reaction in his voice that told her he liked what she did. She did it some more and soon he was moaning in delight. This pleased her so much. Sister Georgina paused as her partner for the night got up to retrieve his trousers. He had come prepared. Like Casanova, he wanted her to feel completely relaxed and not have to worry about pregnancy or sexually transmitted diseases.

The pause in the activities gave Sister Georgina a moment to reflect. She was in her living room about to finally lose her virginity to a man she barely knew apart from a few nods across the garden fence. Her mind raced through all the reasons why she should not go through with the inevitable: the embarrassment she would feel in the morning, how could she face herself, her friends, the church community. But such thoughts were replaced very quickly by the thought of him entering her and she shivered in anticipation. He had done a good job in preparing her for the act, as he had made her feel so loved and cared for in the short time they were together. Her mind then raced to making the floor more comfortable for both of them and remembered the sleeping bag behind the sofa. As she readied the floor, she felt her sweat on her body and put on the ceiling fan. She was ready for a long night of passion.

Sister Georgina welcomed him back with a smile that spoke volumes. No longer was the fairground or research class a required distraction any more, as her mind was firmly concentrating on the sensations she was feeling. She lay back and allowed him to enter her. She thought about her hymen, but felt that after all these years, she must have broken it during her day to day activities. She did feel some pain as he attempted to go deeper and deeper into her, but it soon changed from pain to pleasure with every stroke as he entered and reentered her. The sensation was soon replaced by a small unrecognizable feeling. It soon increased, making her pant ever so lightly until she didn't seem to have any control over what was happening to her body and was forced to just to go with the flow. The domino effect culminated in hearing herself scream followed by an explosion which released a wave of fluid. When she opened her eyes she saw his face and was highly embarrassed at having made so much noise, but it was immediately replaced by joy when she saw her neighbor smiling broadly with delight.

"Shall we do it again?" He asked her invitingly.

Sister Georgina nodded the affirmative.

———————— ～ ————————

No matter how she tried, she could not make sense of the events of the day. She had been left confused, unsure of which way to turn next. She was angry with herself for letting the encounter happen, but then again she was not. She was disappointed in not being able to resist the temptation, but at the same time, happy to have acquiesced because it made her feel alive. '*Marvin Gaye certainly knew what he was talking about,*' she smiled to herself before falling asleep…

Satisfied.

Chapter Ten
The Storm

"Tell me what to do!" Sister Georgina pleaded as tears streamed down her face. "Tell me what to do! Please, tell me what to do," she repeated. "How do I please the Lord?!" She screamed and the sisters of the church's national and regional leadership teams continued to hold her down, and debated whether to call the authorities or not. With no guidance forthcoming, Sister Georgina's mind raced erratically from the surety and safety she once felt to the uncertainty and confusion she now was experiencing. *How could this have happened? How could she be so stupid? She knew true happiness,* she argued with herself. *But God didn't answer her prayers…but he did, didn't he? He would have? …Wouldn't He? Was her faith real? Did her counsel to those people all these years count for nothing? Or did her counsel send them straight into the hands of the devil?* Sister Georgina heard a piercing scream and wondered who would do such a thing in a public place, not realizing that it was her.

It took about thirty minutes before the church sisters were finally able to get Sister Georgina off of the floor and safely back into her hotel room. Her gut-wrenching scream was a call to action and they immediately went into overdrive and formed a circle around her. They prayed over her while a couple sang some calming hymns. They had tried to hide the disturbance by clapping and singing loudly as they escorted her back to her room. Staff and the other hotel guests kept away from them, hoping to avoid the proclamations of their faith. They were extremely thankful that the incident was not reported; they could definitely do without the negative publicity for their various churches.

Many of them hoped and prayed that all Sister Georgina needed was some rest.

They had no idea that in her mind she was battling with the disconnect between the intense happiness she felt during her baptism, to the humiliation she now experienced. She saw her entire life as a mockery. She no longer felt the confidence or the surety of anything, and with each step, she doubted herself. How could she have thrown it away for a moment of weakness? She felt her life was worthless. What was the point? She had lost everything. Her life was a lie. The humiliation she felt was unbearable. She was a fraud; a hypocrite. This was something she had never conceived, expected, nor prepared for. She was lost, confused, and directionless. She no longer had answers and didn't know where to turn. She was filled with anger, resentment, and disappointment. She had sacrificed her dreams, her needs, and her desires and no longer knew why. She suffered and now her world was crashing down around her. She didn't want to get off the floor. She knew she was being ungrateful. She knew that there were others who were suffering far worse than she was- death, war, poverty, disabilities... Theirs were much bigger problems than hers. She was supposed to be grateful for the blessings she did have in her life. She could see, she could walk, talk, and hear. But at this moment, she didn't care. Her reserves were depleted and she didn't know where to go to fill herself back up.

She needed to ask for help. It was *her* turn, but no one seemed to be able to assist. She would no longer contain her feelings of resentment and hostility. She just wanted to put an end to her suffering. The Lord would forgive her, for He knew how she suffered. Sister Deborah volunteered to sit with Sister Georgina while she rested.

Despite this unusual venture, Sister Deborah, the regional chair, believed that Sister Georgina should be hospitalized, but her request to call the Prince George's crisis response team had been outvoted. Not wanting anything to reflect badly on her facilitation skills, the opposition had been led by Sister Brenda, the national committee chair and principal coordinator of the women's conference. She had led the workshop on finding marital bliss in which Sister Georgina had finally snapped. Feeling guilty for the un-Christian behavior of her fellow sisters, Sister Deborah wanted at least to offer a supportive listening ear.

"Tell me, my dear, what's happened that has made you react this way?" She asked as she stroked Sister Georgina gently on her arm as she laid on the bed in the fetal position.

Sister Georgina had exhausted herself as a result of her behavior in the hotel reception. But, with Sister Deborah's calming voice it gave her some refuge and she was receptive to the question. However, she was not yet ready to say anything to someone she did not know, so used the opportunity to allow her mind to wander.

———◞◟———

The sound of a door slamming woke Sister Georgina. She immediately felt the breeze of the cool evening air. She shivered as her summer dress was no defense against the elements of the night. The security light on the side of the house was on and meant she could see her contorted body in her lawn chair. She could also see that the porch door was wide open and could hear her husband shouting about the front door being unlocked and the dangerous situation she put herself in.

"Sorry," she heard herself shout towards the door. "I think I've been asleep since this afternoon. My body probably needed the rest," she defended herself.

Her husband followed up his statement by saying, "you know, I want you to be safe. You are my world and I don't want anything to happen to you." Sister Georgina instantly smiled and felt loved. "I brought you your favorite for dinner," he continued. "The crab cakes at Joe's were sold out, but I told them it was for you and they made it right then. They were not going to have their favorite customer going without. It didn't take them long to whip them up. I'll heat them up for you, then I'll be back to relax with you on the porch."

Sister Georgina could track his movement inside the house. She heard him make his way into the kitchen via the library to the downstairs bathroom.

"I hope you're hungry," her husband said coming out onto the porch with a wonderfully arranged tray of all her favorite snacks accompanied by a single, red rose in a small vase. "Oh. I forgot the hot sauce," he said thoughtfully and was on his feet rushing towards the kitchen before Sister Georgina could say anything.

She allowed her mind to process the strange sensations she was feeling. Gradually, her mind began to remember. "No!" Sister Georgina exclaimed, "no, it couldn't be real," she said out loud without realizing it.

"What was that?" Otis questioned her inaudible statement from inside the house.

"It's nothing," she responded. "I was just remembering my dream I had this afternoon."

"Sounds interesting! Tell me all about it when I come out," he chipped.

When he was out of view, she lifted up her dress and touched herself. She wasn't wearing any underwear.

"NO… NO…NO! It was a dream, it was a dream," she repeated as she shook her head at herself.

The sound of a door slamming woke Sister Georgina.

"It's 3:00 in the morning, isn't it time you came inside?" She heard her husband instructed angrily from inside the house.

She was back in the lawn chair on the porch. This time, as she picked up her book, glanced at the bedroom window of the house next door. She couldn't be sure, but she thought she saw the curtains move discreetly. Questions raced through her head that seemed to challenge the very fabric of her being. Then, like an uninvited guest, the truth would burst through into her dreams. She immediately felt horrified as she found herself remembering. The white man from next door would have *never* come over, and if he did, she *never* would have let him in. She would *never* sleep with anyone outside the sanctity of marriage. Her marriage had its issues. *Didn't it?* She was puzzled. She paused. Her husband was the model of a husband; he was thoughtful, considerate, and loving. She couldn't want anything more from a life partner. But something didn't feel right. She just didn't know what.

The sound of a door slamming woke Sister Georgina and this time she knew... Her dreams were always the same since the night *it* happened. It was as if she was stuck in a world of deja vu. She would transport herself back to that evening, retelling the story with the hopes of a different ending. Desperate, she even gave her husband a central role in the reenactment, casting him as her knight in shining armor, coming home in time to rescue her before the fateful event occurred. If he didn't come home, she would lift her dress to find that she was not wearing any underwear. Or she would glance up at the bedroom window of the house next door and see the smiling face of the neighbor.

No matter how hard she tried, she could not hide from the truth. The evidence of her night of passion had been captured in the slight blood stains on the sleeping bag behind the couch. She cried hysterically as she hand-washed it as retribution for her sin. But even when it had been cleaned, *she still knew*. The devil won. When she wasn't sleeping, she had bouts of uncontrollable crying. She called in sick or left work early as she could no longer concentrate on her duties. She preferred to sit for hours in prayer asking for forgiveness, rocking back and forth. To make matters worse, she had to face the fact that she actually enjoyed committing her sin so much. She had tried to deny it, but she remembered her orgasms so clearly and how much pleasure she experienced.

Regardless of the reasons, for Sister Georgina, her infidelity was unforgivable. Her marriage hadn't been *that* bad. She remembered Otis standing next to her in church and how wonderful it made her feel. But, then, she had to face the fact that she had spoiled it all by being unfaithful. It wasn't a small, insignificant sin; it was one of *the* sins and she needed to be punished. She planned to confess to her husband, but for some reason, he had not come home for his bi-weekly weekend visits. He had called and said he was busy with work, then the calls stopped coming. She had no idea how long it had been since she last saw him.

How was she supposed to reconcile with her thoughts that it should not happen again, when she so desperately wanted it to happen? She craved so badly to be touched lovingly, passionately, and so intensely. *She needed more.* Initially, after the event, she found herself trying to coordinate her return home at the same time as her neighbor for an 'accidental-on-purpose' meeting in the front yard. However, when she saw the mailman pass his house several days in a row without leaving any mail, she knew he was not there. She never felt so torn in wanting someone, while at the same time not wanting to want them.

With no signs of her neighbor after two weeks had gone by, the feeling of being used began to take on a life of its own. She had spoken theoretically about it in her abstinence classes when she was a peer mentor, but now, she was experiencing the reality. It was so much worse. She had been used and thrown away like a piece of trash. She found that she would go to the window several times an hour and even got up during the night to check to see if he had come home. It wasn't long before she knew the time his security lights had been programmed to turn on and off. But as each day that went by, she found herself becoming angry and frustrated.

She stopped counting the days that she was missing school and just assumed that she had enough sick days to cover her absences. She had never been one to miss work in the early days of her career and even had gained a reputation for not using her sick days. But praying for forgiveness, worrying all day, and being up all night to check her neighbor's lights had taken its toll on her physically and emotionally. Sister Georgina found going to school more and more difficult. She had called in on a regular basis, so she was expecting the certified letter from the Board of Education. At least she should be able to formally arrange an official leave of absence to properly get herself together. She looked forward to the meeting that had been scheduled for the following week.

Sister Georgina did not know that this was the moment the chair of the Board of Education had been waiting for most of his professional career. One of the teachers who had been publicly humiliated during the media frenzy when she was a high school student was his mother. Even though her fifteen minutes of fame was long over, he watched her read and re-read the negative newspaper articles about her lack of teaching skills over and over again. Granted, what the articles had reported was true, but not being able to deal with criticism well, she personalized it and isolated herself as a result. His mother had stopped going to class, and despite the employee assistant counseling that had been offered, she was unable to go back to teaching. She even found playing in the park with her boys difficult through fear she would be stalked by the paparazzi. Although it had taken a couple of years for her to shake the depression, her son had concluded that her sparkle was gone and would never return. She left her teaching career, and despite her monumental student debts, went to work at the local supermarket. Her oldest son blamed Sister Georgina totally for her demise.

In order to not be too far from his mother, he decided not to attend the college of his dreams in New York to study art. Instead, he went to Montgomery Community College and then on to the University of Maryland, coming home every day, missing all of the usual rites of passage for college students. He had been pleased to just graduate after six years of college since all the family stresses and heavy financial burden had taken its toll on him. But unlike his mother, he chose to maneuver himself into a position to throw out the criticism. He soon became preoccupied with gaining power at all costs, which many attributed to a Napoleon complex due to his short stature. When he landed an internship at the Education Department, he knew he wanted to work there and through careful political maneuvering, nurtured a career in this field.

He developed a management style that his subordinates hated, but his bosses loved. He quickly earned the nickname of the "TD" (Tasmanian Devil), because he would go into a school, and rush around, upturning routines and structures seemingly, without rhyme or reason. And before the dust settled, he would be moving on.

The net effort of his job usually resulted in poor services for the children or in school closures, which most of the staff that was left behind soon realized, was the ultimate objective. Everyone soon realized that watching people beg for their jobs as he gave them their pink slips, was his most favorite thing to do. As soon as he was in a leadership position, he began to monitor Sister Georgina's career from a distance. He also studied the official records of the media fiasco and had systematically been collecting evidence along the way. So, it was with great pleasure that he read the most recent report submitted by Sister Georgina's secretary.

"Thank you so much for coming in today, Mrs. Jeters. We see things have not been going so well for you," said TD. He had looked forward to this meeting and wanted to make the most of the occasion. When Sister Georgina entered the room and held out her hand, TD made a point of not shaking it. Instead, he just pointed to the seat at the far end of the conference table, while he sat at the other end with two very nervous staff members from Human Resources.

She knew her appearance was not what it should be and had tried before she left the house to make an effort. She touched her hair in the hope that it would miraculously become the salon style she imagined.

"Yes, I have been struggling. That's why I went to my doctor and completed the FLMA form. I spoke with her yesterday and she said the documents had already been sent as required. Was there something else I needed to do?"

"I will ask the questions, Mrs. Jeters," TD scowled.

Relishing every second, he slowly took his reading glasses out of its case and placed it strategically onto the edge of his nose. He then leisurely perused the report on the table in front of him, licking his finger to ease the task of turning each page, as well as to add dramatic effect to this mundane activity. Sister Georgina looked on bewildered, as did the two representatives from HR. TD feigned a cough that echoed through the room, breaking the uncomfortable silence. He then lowered his head to stare menacingly at Sister Georgina over the top of his glasses.

"I want you to know that we are considering pressing charges."

"For what?" Sister Georgina's voice trembled.

"Like I said before, Mrs. Jeters, *I* will ask the questions. Now. Let me see…shall we start with fraud?"

"*WHAT?*"

"Isn't that another question, Mrs. Jeters. It's hard to believe that *you* have been teaching all these years and seem to be having so much difficulty following orders," TD grinned, condescendingly. "Ah, yes…

the department paid for you to attend the conference in San Antonio, Texas, didn't we? And from the conference records, I see you did not attend scheduled workshops as required. That means we paid for you to have a vacation? I understand the weather was nice at that time; did you get a chance to get some sun, Mrs. Jeters? So, the flight... accommodations... food, and miscellaneous sundries... I think it will all add up to quite a few dollars, don't you think? I wonder what the tax payers would say?"

Being unable to hide his real motives, he continued with an air of suspense. "What about the papers, Mrs. Jeters? How do you think it would look on the front pages of the local newspapers? Any ideas, Mrs. Jeters? You *do* have some firsthand experience with getting stories to the press, don't you? '*Children suffer as teacher takes paid vacation*'..." He grinned ecstatically. "Or...what about... '*teacher takes a class poolside*'?" Catchy, don't you think? Those titles would sell a lot of papers, I'm sure of it. I should have been a journalist, it's fun to come up with these titles." He laughed at his own jokes, even though no one else in the room thought they were funny.

Sister Georgina looked on stunned. She tried to make sense of what was happening.

"And, by our calculation, you have been sneaking off for *years*, having extended lunches, shortened work days, and not submitting leave slips as required." TD smiled, clearly loving his role as judge, jury, and executioner.

"I don't understand..."a shocked Sister Georgina explained.

"You're a thief, Mrs. Jeters! What's there to understand? You've deliberately taken taxpayers' money under false pretenses!"

"But, I am an excellent teacher. My work over the years has been impeccable"

"Do you think we care about your reputation?" TD stopped himself from reminding her about what she had done to his mother. His slip into emotionality meant he better get to the point quickly before he exposed himself. "We have prepared a letter of resignation, which if you sign it now, we will not press charges. But, if you don't, trust me, Mrs. Jeters, my next call will be to the State Attorney."

One of the HR staff members got up and made the long walk to her at the other end of the table. He held out a pen and the letter, clearly with the expectation that she would sign without even reading it. Shocked and confused, Sister Georgina's eyes welled up as she tried to make out the scrambled words on the paper.

"I have rights," she mumbled. "I don't have to sign anything," she choked in-between her sobs.

"Yes, I am sure you do, but, here and now, Mrs. Jeters... just sign it so I can go get my lunch. I believe its turkey today. A nice healthy option," smiling, he looked at the HR staff for validation.

Although, she could barely read the letter through her tears, she made out that she was giving up her rights to her pension and benefits so the Board of Education would not prosecute her for repayment of all the money paid out to her inappropriately. There would be no recourse and her signature would be final. Beaten down by the events of the previous weeks, she felt the devil was taking his revenge. She deserved to be punished. But her *career...her livelihood*? She signed the paper, got up, and left the room in silence, leaving behind an ecstatic administrator.

She knew her marriage was a sham, but with no one else to turn to, she called Otis' cell phone number. His phone was dead. She realized that it had been a while since she heard from him. It had to have been a couple of months at least; perhaps even longer. He told her one excuse after another, and then, he just stopped calling. She had been glad for the additional space to giving herself more time to prepare for her 'I was unfaithful' confession speech. Sister Georgina had been hands off in his business venture even though she had sponsored it, assuming he wanted it that way. She never pressed for anything else. He had never invited her to visit the office once it had been set up nor to his home in Pittsburgh, and she had never asked. When she decided to call his office, it would be the first time. She was desperate to talk to someone about what had just happened. She remembered his lack of concern when she was shaken up over her near miss on the Beltway, but today was another day. She was hopeful that he would offer her some kind words of support about losing her job and the awful experience with the education official.

"Hello, can I speak with Mr. Jeters? I am Mrs. Jeters," Sister Georgina wanted to give the impression to the person answering the phone that she expected to be put through to him without a problem.

"I am sorry, no one by that name works here," was the response that came through the phone. "You must have the wrong number."

Sister Georgina read the number out loud and the voice on the other end confirmed it was correct, but their answer was the same as before. Getting desperate, she described her husband. The person at the phone sensed her anguish and calmly repeated what she had said, making it apparent that she was genuinely sorry she couldn't help her.

Sister Georgina called Mrs. Gilchrist. She had never gone into details with her about the state of her marriage and Mrs. Gilchrist had gotten into the habit of not asking. She knew when her half-brother refused to change his work schedule or relocate to Maryland, that the marriage would never work, but chose not to discuss that with Sister Georgina.

"I am sorry to call you, but your brother's cell phone has been cut off and I need to get hold of him," Sister Georgina said as soon as she heard someone pick up the phone before any of the usual pleasantries.

"He's in Canada. Didn't you know?"

"What's he doing there?" The bewildered Sister Georgina asked.

"I'm not quite sure," Mrs. Gilchrist replied, but the stress in Sister Georgina's voice made her continue. "The only reason I found that out is because, *his* sister called me angry about the state of their mother in North Carolina. It turns out that he had taken most of the money from the sale of her house and left her at the mercy of social services. He made some sort of bad investment in a body building competition... you know, the promotion, sponsorship, or something... Anyways, he was hoping it would bring him millions. I'm not sure what happened, but his sister is trying to find out. His side of the family thinks that he has run off to Canada because he lost all her money. I thought he was a saint to have taken care of her all these years, but it turns out he would only go down to Carolina to collect her pension. They also..."

Sister Georgina had never hung up on anyone before, but as there is always a first time for everything, she hung up on Mrs. Gilchrist. She didn't feel up to telling her the story or trying to figure it all out. She retreated to her bed and it was a week before she spoke with anyone else.

When the doorbell rang, like Pavlov and his dogs, her mind immediately leaped to the return of her next door neighbor. She jumped out of bed, rushed around the bedroom searching for the housecoat which she felt was the sexiest. She then ran to the bathroom, brushed her hair and rinsed her mouth in a feeble attempt to make herself look as presentable as possible under the circumstances. She was truly disappointed when she opened the front door to find the mailman on the other side. He gave her the regular mail and then an electronic box to sign for a certified letter and left without saying a word.

On top of her mail was a postcard from Dubai. She dropped the certified letter, along with the rest of her mail, on the floor. She just stared at the picture of the famous World Island Resort for several minutes before building the courage to turn it over and read the words on the back.

"Had a great time the other night, hope you did too. Thanks, again. On contract for a while. Not sure of end date, poss. 18 months. Take care."

Her hands trembled as she read the postcard's message over and over again. *Had she read it correctly?* She needed to read it again, and then again. Extremely disappointed, Sister Georgina was beyond tears. Her gentleman caller would not be returning anytime soon. She didn't bother picking up the other mail that had fallen, as she was too exhausted from the deep shame and humiliation that had suddenly engulfed her. Devoid of feelings and having no idea how to handle the situation, Sister Georgina decided to crawl back into bed and hide from the world. In the safety of her cocoon, her emotions went from one extreme to another. Yes, she wanted more sex, but it was a sin and she needed to repent. She remembered the book she read in her youth about sex being encouraged for married people and not if you are single. She was married, but didn't have sex with her husband. How did it relate to her? What was she to do? All her problem solving skills seemed to escape her. Nothing seemed to make sense to her anymore except staying in bed under her covers.

It was another couple of weeks before she decided to leave the house. The back of her cupboard was now empty of plain rice, noodles, and other non-perishables. She forced herself to get up to get more food. She went through her clothes pile on the floor and put on whatever was the least smelly. It took her a while to locate her purse because of the growing mess, but once she found it, she made her way to the front door.

She vaguely remembered signing for the certified letter she stepped on, but decided to pick it up and finally open it. After reading the first few words, this time it was her turn to fall to the floor. The letter confirmed the sale of her property and the new owners were due to take possession in thirty days. Because she had not opened the letter until now, the thirty days had dwindled to five.

She picked up the phone and dialed the number at the top of the letter.

"How can we help you?" The person said politely at the other end of the phone. She was pleased to have gotten a live person and not an automated phone system.

"It's about…" she could not even bring herself to say her address.

"You can just give me the reference number at the top of the page," the perceptive person replied.

Sister Georgina rattled off the number and was put through to the short sale department.

"I received this letter and it says something about my house being sold?"

"Yes…and? What is it that you want to know?" The male voice said abruptly.

"How did this happen? It's *my* house. I *live* here," Sister Georgina mumbled.

"I really don't have time to go through this, but let me see…ah…. umm, yes. This deal has been in the works for about a year now. It's a shame really, especially when our slogan says, '*we buy your house in fourteen days,'"* he laughed. "It's been one of our longest, I don't know why. I would have to read the file more closely to let you know what happened and I don't have time to do that at the moment. What I can tell you is that your husband…"

The rest of what he said was a blur to Sister Georgina. She picked up on the conversation when he was letting her know that the house changed hands five months ago.

"Ahh…I see something here about the second mortgage being changed to a sale. And you've been paying rent on it until the new owners took possession. Ummm…Is there anything else you need to know? Oh, wait…I see here... the new owners say they don't mind that you leave stuff in the house. They will get rid of it for you. They plan to renovate before they move in." On receiving no reply, the male voice at the end of the line assumed he had answered Sister Georgina's question and with nothing more to say, put the phone down.

Sister Georgina called Mrs. Gilchrist, not having time to be embarrassed about hanging up on her before. And as before, she overlooked the usual salutations and asked, "has your brother ever stolen anything?"

"Yes, I told you. Remember when he was married before? He embezzled money from his employers and he worked for years making restitution to keep from going to prison. His first wife was so upset, that's why she left him. I told you before you married him. Why, what's happened?"

Sister Georgina searched her mind, trying to remember the story Mrs. Gilchrist had told her all those years ago. Had she convinced herself that it was *his wife* who embezzled the money? She wished she had invested the extra $25 for a more detailed background check on Otis, rather than the bargain one she opted for. Perhaps, if she had done so she would have gotten the information about his previous charges. And again, not wanting to talk about her humiliation, she hung up on Mrs. Gilchrist for a second time.

By now, the light under the curtains indicated that it was night. Sister Georgina had obviously been sitting in the same spot for hours with the phone in her hands, oblivious to its dead battery. The need to go to the bathroom, as well as hunger pains did not deter her from picking herself up off the floor and making her way back to her bedroom and the sanctity of her bed covers. Before she reached her bed, she thought to check her savings account. When she last looked at it, she had nearly $65,000 saved. She turned to the drawer of her bedside table where she kept her bank book. The last entry showed a balance of $10; just enough to keep the account open and not receive notification from the bank that the account was closed.

She remembered they had gone to the bank on one of their rare outings together, months and months ago. She was pleased when he had offered to go to the teller on her behalf and didn't think twice about it when he told her the teller had made a mistake on the withdrawal slip. He had her write it out several times before she got it right. From the withdrawals in her savings book, she could see he had just added zeros to her original number. *Now she knew.* He had not physically hit her when she lashed out at him so violently at the hotel, but his patience had definitely paid off. Otis had truly gotten his revenge and she knew what it felt like to be slapped in the face. Hard.

She thought of calling Sister Canisa or even the Pastor, but had second thoughts. *What was there left to say?* She was a sinner and needed to be punished. She retreated back to her bed. This time, she was able to ignore her hunger pains. She saw no reason for getting out of bed…*ever.* It took another few of days of not eating, not sleeping, and not cleaning herself, before she realized that she needed help and had to make a phone call. She decided to call the Pastor in hopes that he could make sense of her current situation and offer her a solution.

"Hello, my beloved Sister! How are you doing? Did you catch up on your school work yet?"

Sister Georgina had forgotten that she had told everyone at Church she was behind in her work for school and was taking a bit of a break from her church duties. But before she had a chance to respond, he continued, "I was looking at the building fund the other day and I think we do need another fundraiser. I don't think we can wait until the 4th of July barbecue. I put it on the leadership agenda, but just wanted to let you know before the meeting. Will you be able to attend next week? Did I tell you that the van is in desperate need of repair yet again? When I picked up Brother Barnabas for Sunday service, we nearly broke down on the Beltway! He was pretty shaken up and said he was going to take Metro Access next time so he would not have to go through the stress of wondering whether we are going to make it to our destination or not. Can you arrange for the mechanic to come by to look at it? I know you have a good rapport with him. You always seem to be able to get him to give you a good price. I remembered when I tried it once, and I think he doubled the price!"

He paused for breath before launching into the sermon he delivered last Sunday remembering she had missed it. Sister Georgina, although tempted to put the phone down on him as well, resisted the urge and took advantage of the gap in his conversation to say humbly, "Pastor, I need help." Sister Georgina stated softly.

"What was that?

"I am having some marital problems," Sister Georgina decided that this problem will be first, and would, more than likely, lead up to her other, more pressing problems.

"I figured that when you came and asked for those pills. You hang in there, my Sister. Things get better, trust. Anything is possible with God by your side." He had no intention of getting involved with her marital problems and continued to talk about his own problems. "When my wife and I were having issues, we also sought counsel. We both found it very useful to have a neutral party to mediate. Would you like their number?"

Picking up on her unusual tone of voice, he sensed that something was genuinely *wrong* with Sister Georgina. He could tell that she needed to talk and knew it was beyond his capabilities. He wanted to avoid the conversation he knew was coming, but before he could come up with an excuse, she said, "I was never married, Pastor."

"As I officiated your wedding, I can *assure* that you were married, my dear. The wedding was legally binding according to the law of the land, as well as in the eyes of God. I wouldn't dream of cutting any corners with your wedding, my dear."

"But, technically, we've *never* been married Pastor," she persisted.

"I don't think my husband actually likes me."

"Be patient. Things take time to cook to perfection. It's been seven years, I think, since you've been married. You still have a long way to go to catch up with me and the first lady! You've so much to learn about each other. I hope you play games and have fun with each other... that really does help. I told this couple the same thing the other day and they were shocked! I don't think they played since they were children. Getting to know each other is hard work. But persevere; it's worth it in the end."

As if forcing him to do his job, and despite her reservations, she pressed on, desperate for some clarification on her situation, "I think he has left me. And, he sold my house and took all of my money." The pause at the other end of the phone let her know that the Pastor was truly out of his depths.

After all the years he had been preaching, the Pastor had convinced himself that he was doing an excellent job of ministering to his flock. But now, in the twilight of his life, he was forced to face something he had been hiding from everyone, including himself, for all these years; he was a fraud. He remembered his time in amateur drama classes and how he had found it so easy to follow a script and improvise whenever possible. He followed the same method in the ministry and it worked; giving him and his family a very comfortable lifestyle. But as the problem Sister Georgina faced was *off-script,* he did not know what to say to her. He knew she was a sister who had devoted her entire life to service to the Lord and had genuinely wanted to do everything that her faith dictated. But now? What could he say that would offer her some comfort or relief? He had no idea.

"Let's put it in the Lord's hands. Let's pray, my sister." Without any further hesitation, the Pastor prayed with her and she remembered why, despite his faults, he had remained her Pastor all these years. Although comforted, she wished she had also told him about her grave sin and losing her job.

"I hope you still plan on going next week. You will be surrounded by beautiful sisters, who I am sure, will offer you support in your hour of need, my dear." The Pastor was reminding her about the church's national women's conference that was scheduled for next week in Arlington, Virginia. Sister Georgina usually went to represent their church.

"I will let you know." With the conversation clearly at an end, Sister Georgina added, "please don't tell anyone, Pastor. I am not ready to share this news."

Despite his reservations, the Pastor replied that he was speaking from his home as she had called after ten o'clock and Mrs. Pritchard was not hovering outside his office. She had no need to fear. He would keep her confidence until she was ready to share the news with others. "But, my sister, I want you to know that others would want to support you, if you just let them," he added.

She knew he was right, but did not feel strong enough yet. But, the next day, she attempted to call Sister Canisa, but was forced to leave a message as she did not answer.

The email that was delivered to her inbox in the morning was another reminder of the upcoming women's conference. Her memories of previous conferences had been positive, and she usually came away with a real sense of sisterhood, as well as information about how to run a loving home. She felt that it was another confirmation she should go and made the decision to check into the hotel early and would stay there until the end of the conference. If the letter and phone call about her house being sold were true, she did not want to be around to see others take it from her. Perhaps, at the conference she would get some much needed support or even some ideas about how to manage the traumatic situation she found herself in. She felt a sense of hopefulness and began to feel joyful.

The conference had boasted relevant workshops for both married and single women. Sister Georgina's expectations for a resolution to her problems were high. She didn't know where else to turn any more. The conference was her last resort. None of the sisters from her church home decided to come as it was in Virginia. They either considered it as being too far to travel, did not have the time to be away from work or their family, or simply planned to rely on the information Sister Georgina usually shared. Being husbandless, jobless, and homeless and at a loss of what to do, Sister Georgina really had no excuse not to attend.

Maybe, she didn't see it before, but with each passing workshop, Sister Georgina's hopes began to fade. Most of the sisters smiled and were pleasant enough, but none went beyond the superficial. No one seemed to recognize the intensity of her pain. Even if they did, they must have preferred to ignore it. Sister Georgina sat by herself most of the time and shared a polite 'hello' when required. At first, she did not want to let anyone suspect that she was in pain. But, as she sat in each session, her thoughts began to wonder about where she was going to live and how she would survive. She thought about her mother's death and how different her life would have turned out if she had survived.

Her pain intensified. She attended all the classes specifically designed for married women only. The first session covered things a woman could do to pique her husband's interest. Basic topics on the agenda were cooking and family health, but the class on how to keep the excitement in the marriage had the most impact on the audience. Sister Georgina attended four of five sessions and left without being able to ask her one, burning question: *but what if your husband doesn't want you?* She had cried consistently through them all. A couple of the sisters saw her tears, but had chosen to not say anything. Sister Georgina hid her pain, not wanting to make anyone feel uncomfortable, so she would sniffle and make it seem as if she suffered from allergies rather than from tears of intense pain.

By the last session, she could no longer contain her emotions. The conference was coming to a close and she had no idea what she was going to do next. Where would she go? She got angry. So what she didn't know any sisters at the conference? They were not behaving as sisters. She was in deep trouble, supposedly, surrounded by women who shared her faith and no one could see her. It was the final ninety minute session, when her tears flowed freely down her face. None of the sisters, *not one*, had approached her to ask what was wrong. At the end of the session, feeling like she had no choice, she made her way to the presenter's table. She found the strength to ask her question, but was sweetly, yet abruptly, dismissed. This was the straw that broke the camel's back.

Sister Deborah suspected that Sister Brenda's motives were not solely based on Sister Georgina's best interest, as she had led the workshop where she was first found crying, hysterically. It was clear that Sister Georgina had tired herself out from her unexpected eruption of emotions.

As she lay on her hotel bed, she heard Sister Deborah say lovingly, while stroking her hair and reciting passages from the bible, "oh, my beloved sister, I can see you're in a lot of pain. Tell me what's going on. Tell me how I can help... It's okay, my sister, *please* tell me... I will listen."

Sister Georgina believed her offer was genuine, and at last, felt God's presence. She had never met the sister, although they had spoken over the phone a couple of times in relation to some event or another. She was based in the Midwest; Tulsa, Oklahoma she thought she said during the ice breaker event.

"Is it that bad? Are you feeling like you don't want to go on anymore?" Sister Deborah could remain calm in moments of intense pressure as she had seen her fair share of tornadoes and hurricanes. Having raised her family in Middle America's homeland, she learned the value of a calming voice when they were huddled closely in basements as the storm passed over. A medical doctor by profession, she had no regrets about giving it all up to concentrate on being married to her childhood sweetheart and caring full-time for her three children. Grown, and now out on their own, Sister Deborah decided to fill her days with helping others, in an attempt to share the love and joy she had in her life.

"Is it that bad? Are you feeling like you don't want to go on anymore?" Sister Deborah repeated her question, quietly, but sternly, expecting a response. Sister Georgina would never admit this to anyone, but she was ready to meet her Lord and Savior. So, she nodded and heard Sister Deborah make a phone call.

When the crisis response team arrived, they asked her the same question and she gave them the same answer. They asked her if she had a plan. Not quite knowing how to answer it, mumbled something about carbon monoxide. Then they turned their attention to Sister Deborah. Before she knew it, her bags were being packed and she was being led from the hotel by members of the crisis team. She didn't care at this point. She had been worn down. Nothing made sense to her any more.

Chapter Eleven
Being the Change

"You look like you had a rough night."

What a horrible comment, and this person doesn't even know me, thought Sister Georgina. If she had a choice, she would have turned around immediately and walked back out the door. But, since one of the rules of the treatment center was to attend daily therapy sessions, Sister Georgina reluctantly stood by the door and made sure her face indicated her disapproval.

With a smile on her face, Dr. P. said, "I know you don't want to be here, but you are, so let's make it work for the both of us."

The doctor's response was lost on Sister Georgina. Granted, it was *true* that she had a rough night and most of the events of the evening had become a blur. She vaguely remembered waking up and struggling to open her eyes. They were so swollen from crying so much. But, as she slowly became conscious of her surroundings and the gray, pictureless walls of the square, windowless room came into focus, the painful memories of the night before came flooding back. She looked to her right and saw a small, empty bed opposite her. If she stretched out her arms she could touch it if she wanted. She didn't. It had been made neatly with a worn, gray blanket with white stripes. It looked so *institutional.* However, before she could concentrate on that, she was distracted by the stench coming from her own blanket. The reality of where she was became clearer with each breath she took, as the strong smell of urine, cigarette smoke, and human excretion, forced her to think about the many, many residents who had contributed to the blanket's condition.

How could this have happened? How could she have fallen so low? This was not supposed to happen to her. She was a good servant to Truth. But as soon as that thought entered her head, her sin, her grave sin, bubbled to the surface and she began to cry.

Sister Georgina reluctantly took a deep breath and sat upright on the bed. She wanted to blow her nose, but had nothing to wipe it. She chose instead to sniff uncomfortably, not wanting to contribute anything else to the blanket. Next to each bed were two narrow cupboards. She opened the one nearest her and found her bag. Sister Georgina was speechless. She never felt so *loved.* It had been packed neatly and with a great deal of care. Included things she didn't know she had, such as the packet of tissues that was placed on top of her clothes, as if the person who packed it knew they would be needed first. She was thankful that Sister Deborah stayed with her, holding her hand, that she reminded her of the positives in her life, and prayed with her until she had been signed into the mental health residential facility.

As Sister Georgina considered whether her next move should be to get out of bed or to go back to sleep, the door opened and a young, energetic, African-American woman bounced into the room.

"How are you feeling this morning, Mrs. Jeters?" She joyfully inquired.

"As to be expected," Sister Georgina replied sadly.

"Well, we have a lot planned for you today," the woman continued. "After breakfast, you will have your first group session, then some exercise, household chores, and then you'll start individual sessions with Dr. P. Her name is Patsy, but everyone just calls her P."

Sister Georgina didn't show any emotion, so the young woman appropriately addressed her unspoken concerns. "You will be amazed how quickly time passes. In case you have forgotten, we met last night when you came in. My name is Roxanne and my role here is to support you. I'll give you a moment to get ready. The bathroom is the second door on the right, and then I will be back to take you to the kitchen for breakfast."

And with that, Roxanne bounced out of the room. Sister Georgina's well organized scheduled meant she had little time to think about her life outside the walls of the facility. However, walking into Dr. P's office that afternoon, she knew she would have to face the confused mess that was her life.

Sister Georgina decided to avoid eye contact with the doctor. She was angry that this so-called *professional* could take such an insensitive attitude when meeting a patient for the first time. Besides, whatever the hell she was offering, Sister Georgina didn't need it. Being in "treatment," "therapy," "counseling," or whatever they wanted to call it, was a sign of weakness as far as she was concerned. Rather than get herself even more riled up, Sister Georgina remembered the scene from the Denzel Washington movie <u>Antwone Fischer</u>. He had been forced to see a psychiatrist, but had chosen not to say anything during his sessions. Sister Georgina decided she would do the same. She sat down dramatically in the chair that had awkwardly been placed in the middle of the room. Embarrassingly, she fell backwards, not expecting it to be so soft and comfortable. She struggled to sit upright on the edge of the chair to try and present a stern posture, but it's comfort made it a real challenge.

"It's okay if you chose not to talk we could just listen to some music instead. Would you prefer that?"

"Yes," came her unconscious response, forgetting already her decision not to say anything.

"Well, let's see, I have Luther, umm….some more Luther, and yes…even more Luther," Dr. P laughed. "If you hadn't figured it out by now, I like Luther Vandross. When he sings *A House is Not a Home* I get goosebumps, despite the fact that I've been listening to the same song for the past twenty years! It can never get old for me. But, then... I can say the same about *Superstar.* They are both equally my favorites. I have even told my daughter to make sure he's played at my funeral."

And without waiting for a response, the doctor got up from her desk, walked over to the bookshelf and connected her phone to speakers. The sounds of Luther's soulful voice soon filled her office.

She returned to her desk and busied herself with paperwork, ignoring Sister Georgina as she still struggled to sit upright on the edge of the chair.

"*Luther's* fine," said Sister Georgina sarcastically. It was only after a few bars of the song that she realized it brought back memories of being with her neighbor. The anger, shame, and confusion she felt at the time came flooding back, but she was unaware she channeled them into her present. *How disrespectful of this* doctor *to not have the decency to wait for her reply, and* secondly, *what a morbid conversation to have with her daughter.* She exaggerated her discomfort by standing up several times to supposedly smooth out the edge of the chair she was sitting on. But the doctor did not take the bait and continued her work, undisturbed.

Sister Georgina decided to take in her new environment as the sounds of Luther's hypnotic vocals continued to fill the room. The focal point of the office was the very large bay window. It was framed dramatically by red and black velvet curtains accentuated by its historic tassels. She agreed that they were appropriate for the mid-18th century building. Underneath, just as suitable, was a customized curved window seat. She *almost* wished she was talking to the doctor so could ask to sit by the window as the handmade thick and fluffy flowered cushion on top of the seat looked so inviting.

The bay window had been clearly designed to show off the facility's beautifully manicured green lawns that looked to be about three acres. It had a few sculpted bushes and pruned trees. One very large tree dominated the grounds with its solid trunk and majestic outstretched branches. Benches had been discretely placed around a small water fountain for residents to enjoy. A wooden fence indicated the end of the property, but the green fields continued. However, the neighboring unmanicured land was more beautiful, due to its use for grazing by two horses. It was such a calming sight and she could understand why the doctor would not want anything to block this soothing view. The horses were of course, oblivious to their importance to Sister Georgina at this moment and continued about their business peacefully.

Sister Georgina then turned her attention to the inside of the room. The doctor sat at her large, heavy, antique desk with its fancy carvings. She assumed the piece, along with its matching bookshelf and side table, were chosen to go with the historical period of the facility. But the furniture placement was odd, leading Sister Georgina to conclude that the view from the window should not be blocked at all costs. The doctor's desk was placed against the wall and meant its uniqueness was hidden and she had her back to anyone who sat in the chairs. She could however, see people as they walked past her door when it was opened.

The two soft and extremely comfortable untherapeutic armchairs in the middle of the room would have been more at home in a hotel lobby, placed in front of their grand wood-burning fireplace. She imagined the hotel guests curling up with a cup of hot chocolate and a good book. The chairs had been placed on a beautifully patterned red and black, circular, oriental rug and positioned strategically across from each other to invite conversation. She concluded the rug was not a handmade original because of the presence of many well-established coffee cup rings, discoloration, and scuff marks.

The office walls were decorated with framed pictures of smiling people, animals playing happily, and beautiful nature scenes. One wall had been reserved for her numerous academic degrees and licenses to practice. The matching antique bookshelf and side table were crowded with her travel memorabilia and photographs of her family, relatives, and friends. Noticeably, one shelf was dedicated solely to a plaque which said *'tomorrow's belongs to no one'*, which Sister Georgina concluded was also a bit morbid. Sister Georgina's first instinct about the doctor being insensitive had been confirmed.

Distracted from her tour of the office by Dr. P's unflattering attempt to sing-along with Luther, it was a clear indication that her presence in the room had been forgotten. This time she coughed even louder and finally got the Doctor's attention.

"Sorry, was I that bad?" Dr. P said, not embarrassed at all.

"Yes, of course. It was painful listening to you. And why after so many years of listening to the same song do you still not know the words?"

"Who says I should know the words?" Came the unexpected response. Realizing that she had broken her vow of silence after only five minutes, Sister Georgina continued. "For someone who is supposedly *trained* to make someone feel at ease and to help, I don't think you are doing a good job. Do I need to put in a complaint to your licensing board about your indifference? I know someone should complain about you flaunting your happiness everywhere I look." She pointed angrily at the personal pictures on the bookshelf. "… Don't you think people like me who are *depressed*, unhappy, and *forced* to be in a "mental institution" find that insensitive?" There was no reason to beat about the bush, Sister Georgina rationalized.

"So let me see, because *you're* depressed, I have to be also?" She paused, and then said calmly, "Let's start over. I know you don't want to be here, but it's clear you have a lot to say. And believe it or not, I actually want to hear it."

Giving Sister Georgina her full attention, she got up from her desk, turned the music off, and made herself comfortable by curling up in the chair with her notepad and pen placed discretely on her lap. She sat looking at Sister Georgina with expectation.

"I'm not sure what you want me to say."

"You can say anything you want, it's your time."

As with Sister Deborah, Sister Georgina had no intention of spilling her guts to a complete stranger, but it was difficult to resist such an invitation. She decided to talk about the picture window as a deliberate act of defiance…or avoidance; she wasn't sure which. "Okay, let's talk about…the wonderful view from the window."

"Why thank you. It's one of the reasons I *love* coming to work. On the negative side, it can be *too* relaxing and sometimes I get so carried away looking at those two beautiful horses, I actually forget I have so many reports to write."

"Why aren't all the rooms as nice as this?"

"You have a point; I know you're in a small room."

"Very *small*," Sister Georgina said stressing the word 'small'.

"I think your room was originally used as a laundry closet. There are no windows, right?" Sister Georgina nodded. "Like most things nowadays, they're trying to maximize on any available space and squeeze as many folks into the place as possible in order to be financially viable."

Seizing the opportunity of being in conversation, Dr. P diverted the chat back to its original purpose and asked, "What do you want from our time together?"

"I have no idea, I don't believe in therapy."

"You want to know something?" Dr. P whispered, "*neither do I.*"

"How can you say that? You sit here everyday making judgments about people... about whether they're sane or not. You *must* believe in what you're doing."

"Do you think the education system actually prepares our youth for the future?" She asked, answering the question with a question.

"Now, don't you get me started!" Sister Georgina laughed. "You have no idea about how bad..." She stopped speaking as she looked up and saw Dr. P nodding in agreement.

"My point exactly. So, how about we just relax, chat, and see where we go? Will that work for you?"

Realizing that she had agreed to open up, Sister Georgina nervously nodded her agreement. Dr. P continued on in an effort to reassure her. "Listen; don't think for one minute that you'll find me at the local supermarket gossiping about your business. I can lose my license for that, and after all the time and money I've spent getting them, rest assured, I won't make that mistake. I have to legally take notes, but definitely will not be writing down everything you say... just key phrases to let me know your progress and also to prove that I actually did something. But, to be honest, when you leave my office and I finish writing up my notes, that's gonna be the last time I think about your situation until we meet again. Why? Because, I have my own problems to think about," Dr. P said laughing.

"But, whatever the case, the formality of the process should not stop you from getting what you need. That doesn't mean you have to spill your guts and tell me your life story, it just means you're getting what you need. So, if we spend our time together just looking out of the window and watching those magnificent horses over there, that's perfectly fine by me. Or, if you prefer, you can just listen to me rattle on and on without you saying a word. That's fine, too.

"The goal is for you to get something from these sessions and because I am not *you*, I can't tell you what that should look or feel like. I have no idea what will work for you. My goal is just to be me and hope that's enough to help you better understand yourself. So, although we have to comply with the strange, convoluted, and in some cases, downright oppressive rules and regulations of the system, we can still make the most of our time together.

"Here, I've tried to create the feeling of being with my girlfriend… 'cause when I have a problem, being able to kick off my shoes, curl up into a comfy chair and talk until I feel relieved, and then have her to tell me what I can do differently, makes me feel appreciated. And by being able to reflect, I normally have an understanding of what I can do next. Good strategy, right? Oh, by the way, before I forget, I have a tendency of being pretty direct and straight to the point… is that okay? There's no beating about the bush with me. I've kinda forgotten because I've been this way for such a long time. So many people have told me that I can come across as being quite tactless sometimes. If I do that, and it is upsetting to you, *please*, you've got my permission to tell me. I don't mean to make you feel uncomfortable, challenged, or defensive; it's just that I'm trying to make sure I understand what you're saying."

Having assumed that Sister Georgina's bemused demeanor meant she required further clarification, the doctor rattled on. "*For years*, I talked about wanting to lose weight, but I would insist on ordering take-out most nights, siting in front of the television, and just vegetating. When I got on the scale, I would be so upset. Then, I'd consistently complain to my friends about not being able to lose weight despite the various diets I was on. It was my best friend who got up in my face telling me what a liar I was. Of course, I was upset and hurt by the things she had to say, but I knew she loved me and I trusted her. So her words forced me to look at my behavior and I asked myself: *did I actually believe what I was saying?* In other words, did my words match my behaviors? It didn't. That's when I decided to do something about it. I had to be in alignment. My words had to match what I was doing, so that meant changing my eating and exercise habits, not some of the time, but *all* of the time."

As she paused, Dr. P smiled and continued, "I hope you get used to me telling my stories…I try to give real life examples to illustrate a point. My example just means, this is a process, and you have to be willing to do the emotional work, not just give the impression you want to do the work."

"Emotional work?" Sister Georgina asked, inquisitively.

Dr. P nodded approvingly of the question. "Uh huh...If what we discuss makes sense to you or quiets that voice inside of you... You know, the one that tells you not to do something, then you do it anyway, and when stuff happens you ask yourself, '*why didn't I listen to that voice?*' If our conversations make sense to that voice, apply it into your life, if it doesn't, simply throw it away."

The doctor was in full stride and continued on with her explanation. "Let me say it another way…I know you're familiar with physical therapy. Sister Georgina nodded. "Well, if someone has a sports injury, they would have a course of physical therapy. Depending on the injury, of course, it may start with…let's say, three times a week. The therapist would work on the injury, which may be extremely painful at first, but after doing exercises at home as the weeks go by, the pain should decrease, as well as the amount of weekly sessions. What was once three times a week, becomes two, then one, and then once every two weeks, etc. The process can be over a long period of time; weeks, months, years, depending on the injury.

"I describe mental therapy the same way. For some, it can be immediate, it can take days or weeks, while for others, it can be years. We have to identify what's causing the pain, and then face it by seeing it for what it is. We can then work the muscles; consequently, the pain decreases and hopefully dissipates, with the intention of leaving you free to make your life what you want it to be. And just like physical therapy, if you ignore it, the pain may get worse.

"We live in a society where we're not generally encouraged to do this emotional work, so most of us ignore it, deny it, or run away from addressing it. I had this guy once, he came to a 5:00pm session, and by 5:10pm, he said he needed to go. It was all too much for him. I think I just asked him whether he wanted to remain married since he had cheated on his wife for years. There is no doubt about it, we live in a society where a lot of people ignore their *stuff* with the hope that it will somehow magically disappear or they feel like they've somehow managed to escape being affected. We all have stuff to work on, so you're in good company.

"The goal is to be able to push through the pain and to figure out what's causing it. This underlying stuff is hard, but as far as I am concerned, it's definitely worth it. And I am under no illusion that the mental health system we have at the moment is pretty...*messed up.* Trust me when I say, I could happily use another word to describe it. It's hard when the process is determined by negative images, inadequate training, lack of effective supervision, limited support, and *insurance companies.* Oh...that reminds me, I understand your insurance runs out in thirty days?"

"Yes," Sister Georgina said remembering the piece of paper she had been forced to sign by TD. She became upset by the thought of not being able to have healthcare, earn a living, or have a means to support herself. The realization of the importance of the piece of paper she signed was just being to sink in. "They mentioned something like that to me when I was admitted last night."

"So, as I said before, let's make the best of the time we have together for tomorrow is promised to no one." And with that, she opened her notebook indicating that the session had officially begun.

As Roxanne had told her when she first arrived, her time at the facility seemed to fly by. She could never get used to the coldness of the institution, no matter how much they tried to dress it up. She hated her bedroom, hated the food, and hated some of the staff and other residents. But she was truly appreciative that she did not have to share her tiny room with anyone and loved being n the grounds, feeding the horses, and sitting peacefully by the water fountain. However, she was most grateful that she was not alone and having to face her problems by herself. Although it was not her intention, during their time together, she found herself telling Dr. P about her life, her college and teaching experiences, and her love life that had culminated in her so-called *"marriage."* She also shared with her the *sin* which she believed was the catalyst for her breakdown. The doctor listened intently and interjected, challenged and sought clarification as appropriate. Their sessions seemed to merge into one very long conversation that had left her seeing things differently. By the time Sister Georgina was discharged, she actually felt ready to finally face *herself.*

"Do you feel like you have been an actor in your own life?"

"Wow…acting, in my own life…I am not sure what you mean," Sister Georgina said hesitantly.

"From what you've told me, it sounds like you've been trying to follow a script in living your life that has been written by someone else."

"I have never thought of it that way. But since the script has been determined by my Lord and Savior, I have been more than happy to follow it," Sister Georgina stated confidently.

"But, are you following the script? Or, like me saying I wanted to lose weight, but was just giving the appearance of trying to follow it, when in actuality, my actions were saying the opposite… Gandhi is quoted as saying *'your actions indicate your priorities'*…"

"Now you're upsetting me… are you saying I am a *hypocrite*?"

"Remember, I'm not here to tell you what to think or what to believe. My job is just to give you things to think about."

"Okay, okay… I was following Truth. It felt so right."

"If you were born in a remote village in Afghanistan, it would feel *'right'* to not learn to read or write, you would willingly stay inside all day, every day, in order not to bring shame on your family. And if you hear about women who transgressed, you most likely, would be out in the streets to participate in their stoning. Or, if you were born in North Korea, it would feel 'normal' to choose one of twenty-eight haircuts permitted by the government, it would feel 'right' to sacrifice your family members to ensure the political regime was maintained, and even worship the Supreme Leader as if he were God."

"You're making me think too much. I was born in the U.S. and have a hard time relating to such examples," said Sister Georgina, conveniently forgetting her desire to teach the twelfth grade class about the indigenous tribe in the South Pacific.

"Sister Georgina, you are an educated woman, which you paid a great deal of money for the privilege of obtaining. It is your fundamental human right to be able to think what you want to. As Aristotle says, *the mark of an educated person is to be able to hold an idea without having to accept it.* There's no need to get emotional or defensive, I'm just asking you to think on a deeper level; go beyond the superficial to just ask yourself...if you believed, like those women who just happened to be born in Afghanistan or in North Korea and believed as they were told to believe?"

"I did," she responded begrudgingly.

"Well, just because you were born in the U.S., it doesn't mean the same isn't true. You may have internalized beliefs that could be just as ridiculous. But how would you know unless you questioned or critically analyzed the belief?"

"But my faith makes sense to my soul."

"I am not saying that it doesn't. I am just reflecting what I'm hearing. So let me rephrase…have you asked yourself the question, *did you actually walk in faith?*"

"Well, of course I did…I was virgin until…" Sister Georgina abruptly stopped her flow of thought mid-sentence.

"Okay, let's dissect this a little. As I said before, it doesn't matter to me when you lost your virginity. And the truth is, I really don't care. But from what you just said, it sounds like you see it as some kind of measure of your faith…to wear as a badge of honor?"

"No, No…I truly believed that it's God's will," Sister Georgina looked guilty. Dr. P pressed on.

"Did holding onto your virginity make you feel superior to other people?" Looking even more guilty, she remembered how she felt walking around Secus College campus dressed in white. "Or did you use it as an excuse to hide behind and/or to keep people away from you?" She knew all too well that she had pushed people away with her holier-than-thou attitude, to the extent they did not want to be around her.

"Stop, stop! You're giving me too much to think about."

"Sorry. I know I get excited sometimes…let me slow down. Tell me about the state of your bedroom? Is it clean? Organized? Are you one of those women who can only sleep on one side of their bed because there are clothes and junk on the other side? Or how do you take of care you? Do you care about the foods you put in your body? Do you exercise? In other words do you neglect your responsibilities to care for yourself?"

Sister Georgina nodded. Memories of sitting in front of the television eating cheesy puffs or an entire carton of ice cream flooded into her consciousness. Her unused treadmill and gym membership were also not far behind.

"All I am saying, by using your criteria, such things also indicate the level of someone's faith." Seeing Sister Georgina's discomfort, Dr. P added, "there are no right or wrong answers. It's just your understanding of them that counts."

Although, she had said nothing out loud, Sister Georgina's horrified face made it clear that she understood. She remained silent, upset by being forced to think on a deeper level, but knew it was what she needed.

"Does that mean I've been paying lip service to what I professed to believe?"

"Well, it looks like it."

"Okay, Dr. P, you've made your point. I never really had time to get to the gym and besides, why should I take care of myself if there was no one there to see me?"

"But *you* were. Think about it…when you don't take care of yourself, what does that say about how you view yourself? That you're not worth it? That, you don't deserve to be cared for, even by your own self? You do see how that doesn't make any sense?"

Looking perplexed, Sister Georgina nodded and then asked, "could it be that I was looking for…umm…or …waiting for someone to….care for me?"

"Could be…I don't know. But would you even recognize if someone cared for you, if your measure of caring for yourself was so low?

Sister Georgina nodded in agreement. If she had been brutally honest with herself, she knew from the moment she met Otis that he didn't care about her. He never even asked her what her name was. She had allowed herself to be used and abused. She had chosen not to see it because of her sense of desperation. He had offered her nothing but crumbs and she had been willing to accept it.

"But if I didn't marry Otis, I may never have married."

"You see what I mean about your faith? How would you have known that you wouldn't? You seemed to be so busy looking for crumbs, you may have missed an opportunity to have the entire cake."

Seeing Sister Georgina's sullen face and her intensified breathing, in a more calming and relaxing tone of voice Dr. P said, "take a deep breath…and again. One more." When she could see that Sister Georgina's anxiety level had decreased, she continued. "Now, I want you to rise above your emotion and focus on trying to understand on a deeper, more substantive level. It's a bit like peeling the layers of an onion to see what's there. We may not even come up with any answers, but let's see what's there anyway. Our goal is to look at something for what it *is*, rather than what we would like it to be. Listen, we make choices in our lives, from the simple ones of whether we have tea or coffee, to the big decisions of whether we marry someone or not. If you're unaware that you have a choice, you can be living your life on automatic pilot, making choices not because you want to, but just because you think you ought to."

With this revelation, Sister Georgina's mind raced, "I am thinking…I stayed at Secus College because I thought I was supposed to. I could have left and gone somewhere else. I had four miserable years there."

"That's exactly right…why did you stay?"

"Because I didn't think I should move. I thought I needed to stay. I had made the decision…it would have messed up my transcript and people would have thought I wasn't stable."

"So, because you thought that other people would think badly of you, you stayed somewhere for four years where you didn't want to be? That's what I mean by accepting crumbs. Even if you didn't want to leave, you could also have chosen to engage in activities that brought you pleasure. But this isn't a *'coulda, woulda, shoulda'* situation. It's about learning about our patterns of behaviors and if we don't like it, we can change it. As far as I am concerned, life seems to be flying by so quickly, or as my plaque over there says, *'when we don't know if we will survive tomorrow, the question we need to ask ourselves is why put off being happy?'* Why put off telling someone that you love them or that you appreciate them; why not use the time we have to engage in behaviors that create the reality that you want?"

By now, Sister Georgina, was reflecting on her life without much prompting from Dr. P. "…I could have cleaned up and taken better care of myself, I could have done a lot more. I just dreamed of things, but it was always for *'someday in the future'* and that day never came. My God… it feels like I've wasted my life."

"Hang on, hang on…let's not run before we can walk. Who said anything about wasting your life? That's not what this is about. Everything you have done so far has made you who you are; a unique individual. No one else in the world has had your experiences. I don't know about you, but I think it is absolutely fascinating that I am so unique. We all know that our fingerprints are our distinguishing feature, but so are our experiences. That makes me realize that I can make choices that can define my uniqueness. I don't have to fit into a box that has been pre-designed for me. Of course, in our society, being unique comes with a consequence. If I want to go on vacation to the Bahamas, it means I have to save up the money. That means making the choice to not go out on Saturday night or to not go to the coffee shop for a latte on my way to work. The choices we make every single minute of the day create our reality."

Seeing Sister Georgina's perplexed face, Dr. P continued, "from what you shared with me, 99.9 percent of your thoughts were on what you didn't have and therefore, you unknowingly created a reality that matched that. You didn't have a sex life, for example, and that's exactly what you got; no sex!"

"No...I have to challenge you Doctor. I did think about it. I dreamed about it all the time," shouted Sister Georgina defensively.

"I am sure you did, *just dream*. The question I am exploring was whether you actually *believed* that you could have it in reality. If you did, your actions would indicate that. So, did you actually think that you would have a healthy sex life? Or did you just think about the wedding night?"

Not stopping to think, Sister Georgina continued, "but I didn't know Otis was going to treat me so badly."

"I hope this doesn't sound too harsh...but is how Otis treated you the real problem? Or is it *you*? Isn't the question you need to ask, *'why did you allow Otis to treat you in that way?'* From what you've told me, I am suggesting that from the very start, you knew that he didn't meet your needs. When you first met him and he didn't even ask you anything about yourself...what did that tell you? You also said he struggled to have a conversation with you...what did *that* tell you? He never made you feel special...what did that *tell you*?

"It was you, Sister Georgina, who tried to make the relationship into something it was not. So, it's horrible what he did to you, but you have to be a big girl and accept responsibility for allowing him into your life. He could only treat you the way you allowed yourself to be treated. You could have not taken him up on his offer that first day... you could have left him the day after you were married and got the married annulled. The entire drama around this supposed *'relationship'* has stopped you from focusing on what would truly make you happy. So, the next question we need to ask ourselves is, *'where did the idea come from that you should settle for crumbs?'*

"How old were you when your mother died? And when after that had someone hugged or kissed you, told you that you were very special, or actually listened to you?"

Dr. P stopped her list of examples when she saw that Sister Georgina's eyes had filled with water. She pointed to the box of tissues on the floor next to the chair. Sister Georgina took one and wiped the tears that were now falling freely down her face.

"It sounds like you have never grieved your mother's death."

Although, it raised some painful memories, Sister Georgina walked Dr. P through her youthful recollections of her mother's passing and the implication of her loss on her life to date. Dr. P then asked the question of whether she thought her mother was really a positive role model.

"How dare you?! What do you mean my mother wasn't a positive role model? Of course she was! She was a wonderful example of a believing woman."

"Why don't you ask me why I would ask such a question? Remember, you neither have to agree or disagree. It's my job to ask questions to make you think and reflect."

"Okay…what makes you ask such a question? Especially when I've already told you my mother was nothing but a pillar of Christian virtues."

"I hope you don't mind if I use my own example. Although I hoped my career choice was my own, in the context of my life, it was kind of *'pre-ordained'*. My mother, like yours was a caretaker, and spent her entire life taking care of others, and she did so at the expense of herself. Did you know there are some scholars that actually say most descendants of slaves were bred to be nothing but caretakers at the expense of themselves? Anyway, guess what my siblings and I learned to emulate! Yes…*caring for others at the expense of ourselves.*

"If any relationship is to be harmonious, it should be one in which there is give and take. A relationship that is just *give* is out of balance. A relationship that just takes is also out of balance. So by our mother's example, of predominately just giving, it may have become our norm, our comfort zone, to just be givers. Therefore, if someone gives unconditionally to us, most likely, we would find it uncomfortable and seek out relationships in which we are the givers. We would then proceed to spend hours and hours blaming the other person for treating us so badly. I am doing my best to work on my own negative behavioral patterns, so I totally understand just how difficult it can be. It is definitely a work in progress.

Anyway, Otis sounds like he was a taker and you sound like a giver, so if you met anyone else, and his name was Robert, Keshawn, or Greg, there is a strong possibility that you would end up in exactly the same position you are now. For you to actually find the joy you are looking for in a relationship means you have to receive, as well as give. So what does this all mean? Well, I think like you, I loved my mother, and yes, I know she did the very best she could but… and it's hard for me to say this as well, but the example she set for me and my siblings was how not to love ourselves."

"Really?" Sister Georgina amazed at the doctor's self-disclosure.

"Now, I like telling my stories, but know I am sharing them for a reason. So, tell me, what are you hearing me say?"

"That because my mother was raised in a physically and emotionally abusive home, she accepted a marriage where there was no affection or intimacy, which she accepted as her 'lot' in life. This may have taught me not to expect any love or affection, teaching me that life was meant to be a struggle; to just dream, rather than believe life could be different. Her choosing to sit at the back of the church in the pew that was set aside for storage could mean she was willing to accept crumbs. She struggled all her short life and didn't expect anything different. You know, I've never known her to relax or do things she actually enjoyed. She sacrificed everything for us. She never liked it when we wanted to do anything for her. I know we made her happy; I know she loved telling us her back home stories. But, now it's out in the open…it pails in comparison to the bigger picture of things.

"The best example I can think of is my mother's cutlery. She had purchased them from the pennies that were left over after the bills had been paid. It took her years to save up. When it arrived, she loved it. However, she put it up in a very special place, only to be taken down and used at Thanksgiving and Christmas dinners. It came in a presentation box and once the holidays were over, it was packed up and put back in its case to be taken out the following year. When she died, someone who never realized just how prized the cutlery was just threw it out. I know I was a young girl, but I still suffer from nightmares, remembering that cutlery set lying on top of that trash pile waiting to be taken away and dumped. I wish we had used it every day."

"Keep going. What do you think that has meant for your life?"

"…I think…I think …it's taught me that special things are for special occasions."

"And if love is special…"

"…then it should only be for special occasions." Sister Georgina remembered painfully how she would wait for Otis's meaningless weekend visits. "I think she also taught me how not to love myself." She continued hesitantly.

"Remember, we're not trying to put anyone down, and were certainly not blaming your mother. But think about this…if your parents taught you that two plus two equaled five, what would you believe? If it was reinforced by uncles, aunts, and other members of your extended family, what would you believe? What if they told you that same thing at elementary school, high school, college, even at graduate school, what are you likely to believe? Added to the mix, is the community, scholars… imagine everyone saying two plus two equals five. What would you believe?"

"That two plus two equals five."

"Exactly…if we are not encouraged to question, to reason, to critically think, it's totally understandable that you would just accept that two plus two equals five without question. So let's apply this analogy to your life. Your mother's caretakers told her she was nothing, the environment reflected that belief as well. If she believed she was nothing, was worthless, and that life is a struggle and she accepted that belief, then it is entirely reasonable that her behaviors reflected that belief as well. You, Sister Georgina, being raised in such an environment, were more than likely going to pick up that belief system. You may then choose experiences to reinforce that belief. I think the biblical saying is, *'as a man thinketh…so is he.'*"

"Oh…wow…this is all so deep."

"…Let's go even deeper…if your faith tells you that you are created of God…then you should believe that you are special, unique, created for a purpose, and that you have a unique gift you have been given to share with the world. You should believe that nothing is impossible…rather, see it as being reality…what does the bible say about having the faith of a mustard seed? That it can move mountains! Take that beautiful tree in the yard. Although, it's hard to believe, but it was once a seed, and if you believe as you say you do, if God can do that for a tree, what makes you think he can't do that for you? Take your 'sin' for example. I don't think you would ever be reflecting on what you really want from this life, if you didn't have that experience. And if that experience helps you to be a better you, then I say the experience was a necessary one."

Sister Georgina's mind was racing. As much as she liked the sexual act, the truth was, for her, it needed to be in the confines of a monogamous relationship. By listening to her inner voice, she now knew she did not have to compromise on that. She had spent so much time obsessing and being consumed with fitting into a stereotypical image of what a Christian woman should be, she forgot that being in submission to do His will, meant exactly that. And if she was interpreting that little voice inside her to be His voice, then she had no choice but to pay attention to it. She needed to be pro-active about finding out what He wanted her to do with the gift that was her life. The joy she was looking for could be found in doing what she felt she was put on this earth to do. It wasn't about talking, rather it was about doing.

Sister Georgina had not shared with Dr. P the young teen she had 'counseled' at the youth mentoring program in the eighties. She had mumbled something under her breath and at the time, Sister

Georgina had made out as if she hadn't heard what she said, but now she remembered. The young girl had mumbled that it was her father. Her father was the father of her child. She had not known what to say and so, pretended that she didn't hear. She remembered her words with embarrassment to this young girl and now knew, she had not been helpful at all. She was judgmental and dismissive. Most likely, that young girl had been raped as her grandmother had been.

She had been so desperate to give, *to help*, according to her comfort zone, she had not paid attention to receiving what this incident had to offer her. She 'gave' without question. She had not listened because she felt she had nothing to learn from her and that she had all the answers. She had been more interested in having an audience and being right, she ignored the young girl's pain. She had felt uneasy at the time, and over the years, wondered why her mind kept going back to that young girl. Now she knew. If she had only responded truthfully, and had not been too busy giving her pronouncements... If she had been humbled when she realized that she did not have all the answers, she could have taken something from that experience. She could have questioned her own behavior, her own attitude, her own concept of 'helping'. This may have changed the entire direction of her life.

Dr. P kept talking and had not realized that Sister Georgina's mind had wandered, so she was flustered when she interrupted her flow and demanded to know, "is it too late to change?"

"It's never too late to make a change."

"This really is work, isn't it?! My brain hurts. I now see why they say ignorance is bliss! It's so much easier just to act in my own life using someone else's script. It seems I've been going about my day-to-day activities as if in a trance, not really thinking about the choices I make or that I can change the outcome."

"And what is it that your faith tells you? That you're special, right? And if you truly believed that, then your actions should reflect that belief. That's what I mean about being in alignment." Then she added, using her serious voice, "what will you do differently when you leave here, Sister Georgina?"

Without hesitating, she responded, "to realize that if I want to truly serve the Lord, then I need to accept the God within and strive to be the best me that I can be."

No words were needed as Sister Georgina hugged Sister Deborah and Sister Canisa in a loving embrace in the middle of the parking lot. She had never initiated a hug before and never knew she had it in her to express her love and affection so openly. But the fact that she did, made her realize she could do things differently. That's what she wanted to do when she saw their smiling faces coming towards her. That was what she needed to do to break the habit of always thinking about what other people would say, and then lastly, she needed to take action. So she did.

The women were shocked to find themselves being greeted by a very *different* Sister Georgina than the one who had entered the facility. All three of the women remained in the embrace for a few minutes. Sister Georgina knew she was going to be okay. As she got into the car, she was actually excited about her future. She lowered her head and gave thanks for the experience of being in the residential facility. It had shifted her outlook on life from negative to positive, in just thirty days. It had made her realize the value of her life. She felt that the Lord had watched over her and provided her with this experience to strengthen her.

Chapter Twelve
The Third Baptism

Eager to share the excitement with the other children, the little girl wriggled free from Sister Georgina's arms and jumped to the ground. The children screamed and danced with delight as the rain began to fall, letting the 'inswas', or flying ants, know it was time to vacate their underground homes and cover the skies. Sister Georgina could barely see the children who were inches away from her, as hundreds and thousands of insects flapped their wings in unison. The school caretaker put on the lights of his truck to see just how many he was catching in his nets. He intended to pluck off their wings and sell them by the pound to the highest bidder. He told Sister Georgina that they tasted like nuts and was a traditional Zambian delicacy, but she would take his word for it, as she was definitely not going to try it herself.

"It's like this every year," Ayesha said with a smile. Her fellow teacher stood by her side in the bare, dusty school yard in the middle of the remote village in the Eastern Province of Zambia. They both treasured the magical moment of hearing the children's happy screams as they jumped up and down, waving their arms around in the pouring rain, in the warmth of the early evening light witnessing this annual miracle of nature. Sister Georgina reveled in the intense joy she felt at that moment. She was amazed at how much her life had changed.

Although, the Pastor had agreed to not say anything about Sister Georgina's problems, he had not agreed to not ask someone to call and check on her. It had been a few days after the Women's conference had ended when he realized he hadn't received his usual call from her updating him on how the conference had gone and to review the information to report in the church's newsletter. He tried to leave a message on her home phone to no avail and her cell phone kept going straight to voicemail. Now, well over eighty years old, the Pastor struggled to make sense of the new technology and never got the hang of leaving voicemail messages. In any other circumstance, he would have waited until one of his grandchildren visited and asked them to make the call, but as the days passed by with no word, his concern increased. In an attempt to be discreet, he decided to leave a cryptic message for Sister Canisa.

"Hello…hello…Sister Canisa, is that you…? How do I know its recording? Do I just keep talking? Now, I am not supposed to say anything, and all I can say is that it is nothing to worry about. So it's not urgent, just when you find the time. I think it would be a good idea if you check on Sister Georgina. She may tell you that she is okay, but I think you should still check on her. And of course let me know if you find out anything. And do not accept *no* for an answer. I have to go…I think Mrs. Pritchard is listening on the other side of the door."

On hearing the Pastor's message, as well as the solemn message Sister Georgina had left on her own voicemail, meant Sister Canisa immediately followed up. She also became extremely concerned when both her home and cell phone went unanswered. She had even gone to her house several times, but with no sign of life, she realized no one was there. But she persevered, and every so often would try to get in contact with Sister Georgina and kept calling. It was nearly a week before the phone was answered by a strange woman.

Unaware of the politics at Sister Georgina's small church in Glenarden and with no one at the Women's conference from her home church, Sister Deborah had no idea who to contact. She had returned to Tulsa, Oklahoma with the things Sister Georgina was not allowed to take into the facility, which included her cell phone. The batteries had long since died and she could not find her phone charger. As the phone was in desperate need of an upgrade, Sister Deborah had to special order one, as no store seemed to stock accessories for outdated models. As soon as it arrived, she plugged it in to charge and it rang almost immediately. Sister Deborah instantly brought Sister Canisa up-to-date and both women decided to work together to support Sister Georgina in her hour of need.

Sister Canisa's first step had been to go once again to Sister Georgina's home, but this time she would go inside to collect more clothes for her stay in the residential facility. She found the spare key that had been taped underneath the now discolored ornamental garden frog that Sister Georgina had picked up on a weekend trip to Williamsburg. As the back door was the nearest, she went there to let herself in but was stopped in her tracks after seeing the door ajar and hearing voices coming from inside the house. She immediately rummaged through her bag and got her phone out ready to dial 911, but as curiosity got the better of her, she decided to peek through the window first. She saw three well-dressed strangers standing around pointing at the walls and the very large architectural blueprint spread out over the dining room table. Realizing that they clearly had no interest in Sister Georgina's not very valuable material possessions, she felt safe to walk inside but held tightly onto her phone just in case.

They were just as shocked to see her, and like Sister Canisa, they quickly determined that there was no need to call the police. The purchasers happily updated Sister Canisa about their recent acquisition and boasted about their expected large profit margin once the renovation was complete. Sister Canisa chose to listen intently without saying much, clearly having the objective of learning as much as she could about the sale of the property. Soon, everyone was chatting like old friends over black coffee and saltine crackers, the only thing edible in Sister Georgina's cupboard. She found the purchasers extremely agreeable, and was pleased when they said they had no problem with her taking more of Sister Georgina's things as they were still waiting for their building permits to come through before they could start work. She would just need to call them to arrange a time. Sister Canisa readily agreed and was given the purchasers' business cards with their handwritten cell phone numbers on the back. Sister Canisa left after collecting some of Sister Georgina's clothes, but rather than go straight to the mental health facility, she decided to go to her job.

Unknown to the purchasers- and well before the popularity of selfies, Sister Canisa had several pictures of herself on her cubicle walls, posing with several ex-presidents and other high profile political dignitaries that were past and current customers of the law firm where she worked. Since arriving in the area, Sister Canisa had earned a stellar reputation as a legal secretary at one of the top law firms in downtown Washington, D.C. From their office, the staff never had to battle the 4th of July crowds as they had a barbecue and watched the fireworks from the privacy of their rooftop terrace.

Thanks to the lengthy delay by the permit office and the efficiency of the Beckly and Beckly law firm, it wasn't long before the purchasers of Sister Georgina's home were served with a *cease and desist* order before any demolition or renovation work had started. The first application to the court was to hold the matter until Sister Georgina became available. The purchasers, naturally appealed this ruling, citing their loss of money with each passing day, however, they were informed that this position did not constitute a legal argument. The case was subsequently adjourned until Sister Georgina could handle the matter, whenever that would be. While Sister Georgina was released after thirty days, her newly acquired lawyers advised her to provide the court with medical documentation that stated she was not in a position at the time to argue the case before a judge. The months of additional delay to the legal proceeding allowed more time for Sister Georgina to recuperate, much to the purchasers' disgust. In the mean time, Sister Georgina accepted, with gratitude, Sister Canisa's offer of a place to stay while she figured out what she was going to do.

Not wanting to lose the benefits of what she had learned at the residential facility, Sister Georgina decided to focus on being comfortable in her own skin. Yes, she was totally aware that it was going to be something she would have to work on for the rest of her life, but as she had already spent nearly fifty years disliking herself, she was definitely ready to try the opposite. She decided to start by simply looking at herself in the mirror. She had always hated her reflection and had mastered the art of quickly looking at herself in the mirror before rushing off to do other things. She had never cared about how her hair looked or the condition of her skin. She had eaten things that made her feel comforted and hadn't given a second thought to the effect it would have on her body. But, now, things were going to change.

She initially gave herself the task of looking at her naked body in all its glorious details for just one minute. She failed miserably the first time, having only managed to do so for three or four seconds before her eyes looked away in disgust. With this reaction, she realized that she did not want to see her dull skin with its dark marks and blemishes, her broad nose, unflattering cheeks, yellowing teeth, nor the rolls of unsightly fat that made her body shapeless. However, unlike her previous attempts to change herself, this time she questioned… *'If she didn't even want to look at herself, what were the subliminal messages she was giving herself and to other people?'* 'That she was unlovable?' Or, 'was she assuming that other people also did not want to look at her?'

It was a hard challenge, but with her mind made up, she was determined to persevere. Each day, she was able to look at herself in the mirror for a few seconds longer than the day before. By sticking to her challenge, the days soon turned into weeks and the weeks into months and she got to know each mark and blemish. She began to value how they all contributed to making her so unique. When she saw herself smile in the mirror, she didn't need anyone to tell her that the smile was better than her usual frown. She had smiled, then frowned, then smiled. The energy that radiated from her was different when she smiled. She also realized that she didn't need anyone else to validate what she already knew to be true, although it was nice to hear from other people that her smile made her beauty shine. She then consciously made the choice to smile more and became aware of the things, events, and people that made her smile. Soon, it made her smile to speak about herself and others, not in the harsh condescending manner she used to, but this time, in a way that was gentle and loving.

Her toughest challenge, by far, was trying to change her predominately negative thoughts to positive ones. First, she had to accept that they were mostly negative and the journal she kept for several weeks had proved, beyond a reasonable doubt, that she had a well-established pattern of negative thinking that dominated her daily thoughts. She had never realized that her most common thoughts were, *'it's not going to work out,' 'I can't,' 'I've tried that already and it didn't work', or 'it's never going to happen.'* She reflected back on her single days and the thousands and thousands of hours she had thought so negatively about herself and her circumstances. Even though she was afraid, Sister Georgina decided to dig deeper in her quest for self-discovery.

She was thankful to be able to have the occasional pep talk with Dr. P. She was nervous to call her the first time, as she was no longer a patient and knew that she would not get paid. But Sister Georgina pushed past her fear and followed her instincts. She could literally hear Dr. P laughing on the other end of the phone as she reminded her how she felt about the mental health system. She was glad that Sister Georgina made the call and explained that she was fulfilling her life's purpose by helping people change, if that's what they wanted to do. She then told her that she was the type of therapist portrayed by the Denzel Washington character in the <u>Antwone Fisher</u> movie. Like him, she was prepared to be creative and do whatever it takes to help someone navigate their feelings, even if it meant having them over for dinner. Sister Georgina laughed as she remembered how she had thought about the same movie and had missed its positive message altogether. Dr. P was often busy, but would set aside at least twenty minutes most weeks to speak with her and whenever her scheduled allowed, they would meet at a local cafe. Sister Georgina would normally have a list of questions she wanted to ask Dr. P and truly valued having someone in her corner to help her explore her most pressing issues.

"What would be the purpose of me just paying lip service to all the things I've wanted in my life; a husband, children?" She demanded of Dr. P one Saturday afternoon. Oblivious to the busyness of the coffee shop, the two women continued their intense conversation.

"What makes you think I have all the answers?" Dr. P responded coldly, but clearly challenged Sister Georgina to go beyond her comfort zone. Sister Georgina hated Dr. P at this moment, but didn't get defensive or angry, instead she remembered that she was giving her the gift of her time and was there because she genuinely cared about her. She therefore focused on what Dr. P was trying to communicate.

"Okay, I know you want to empower me, and break the pattern I have of always looking to another human being to figure things out for me. It's just so much easier if someone could just tell me. Besides, you have all this knowledge, why wouldn't I just ask you?"

"Because, for one, I *don't* have all the answers. I'm trying to figure this shit out myself. Secondly, it would give you someone to blame if things didn't work out the way you wanted it to. And third, by giving me the responsibility to figure things out for you takes away your power…and therein, could possibly lie the problem?" Dr. P said. "Why don't you play detective? Ask yourself how it benefit you to pay lip service to saying you wanted a husband and children." And with that, she drank the cold remnants at the bottom of her coffee mug, picked up her bag and said, "see you next time." Then she left with a mischievous smile on her face.

As always, Dr. P would pique her curiosity and so she would gladly do the homework. Sister Georgina wrote the question down on a fresh page in her notebook: *'had she paid lip service to what she had wanted in her life?'* As she completed her chores during the weeks that followed, she thought about the question over and over. The first answer that popped into her mind was that she had not been aware, and therefore, could not be blamed for the outcome. But, assuming that Dr. P would not accept this as a valid response, she decided to go further. She kept asking herself how would it benefit her to believe that she was not worthy and that she was unlovable? An answer came when she least expected it. While in line to collect her dry cleaning, she had overheard someone say how they loved their dress, but hated having to get it professionally cleaned all the time. They had now paid more for the cleaning than they had for the actual dress. The comments somehow made Sister Georgina think about consequences. She then remembered during her high school days, learning about the law of cause and effect. Then, she applied the concept to her current dilemma. If she believed that she was unlovable, the consequences of such a belief would be actions which reflected that belief. The fact that she had trouble looking at herself in the mirror was an obvious example of cause and effect in action.

Together, with the data she collected about her negative thinking patterns, she reasoned, that regardless of what she said out of her mouth or in her daily prayers, her dominant actions indicated that she actually believed she was unlovable. Could she then have unconsciously made choices in her life that reflected that she was unlovable? By marrying someone who she knew didn't even like her, was a clear example of cause and effect in action. Therefore, the benefit of such a belief would allow her to continue to believe that she actually was unlovable and unworthy... To experience the alternative, she would have to accept that she actually was lovable and worthy.

Out of habit, or whether it was a conscious choice to avoid thinking about herself as being lovable, Sister Georgina focused instead on exploring what would make her believe such a thing about herself. From previous conversations with Dr. P, she knew it could have been from her mother or a shared cultural history of oppression that made being unlovable her norm. She then thought about how difficult it had been for her to accept help or to receive; from her church, her biological family, and even the neighbor when they had sex. Never learning to love herself, she concluded was because she had no positive examples of how to when she was growing up as a child, and as an adult.

Reflecting on her childhood, Sister Georgina thought about how she had mimicked the adults she observed while growing up. When she did so, she would be positively rewarded with their words and nods of approval. She smiled to herself as she remembered vividly how the church elders would vet the books before she would be allowed to read them, fearing it would corrupt her young mind. She had welcomed their intervention, and like the church's yearly calendar of events, it was something that was set in stone. It had provided her with a sense of security and safety. With no other form of positive feedback in her young life, she understood why she conformed, without questioning, to the only reality that was being presented to her. Hence, she would avoid questioning or challenging the status quo. Having also picked up along the way the notion that no one seemed to like people who went against what was considered normal and that it was far better to just go along.

Sister Georgina decided to go even further and asked herself more tough questions, such as; *did being raised in such an environment teach her how to not question or think? Had she learned that conformity was love?* She reflected on her obsessive drive for academic success. *Had she been trying to do the right thing? Or was she trying to prove how much she could conform in order to get people to love her, to recognize her, to validate her?* Was that why she had tried to get her teachers and peers to conform at high school? At college? And in her professional career?

In an effort to find answers to her questions, Sister Georgina hit the books. She found herself reading more and more, wanting to discover as much as possible about the external and internal world in which she inhabited. The Aristotle statement Dr. P had quoted came back to her, again and again. Learning did not mean she did not believe, on the contrary, it should have the effect of strengthening her faith. And if it did not, she had to be open to wherever the knowledge would take her. With the benefit of hindsight, Sister Georgina laughed at her naiveté, and reflected with embarrassment at her youthful pronouncements about *'knowing the Truth'* with such certainty. To know that you know nothing as Socrates said, meant Sister Georgina had to accept just how little she did know. This wasn't hard for her to acknowledge because when she thought she had found answers to her many questions, thousands more would appear that also needed to be answered.

No longer confined by the belief that there was only one way to think, she gave herself permission to go on a roller coaster ride into the world of research that took her from one extreme position to another and she was enjoying every minute of it. For no longer were ideas set in concrete like it was when she was growing up. If it helped her make sense of the world she lived in, she would go to wherever the knowledge would take her. She was no longer afraid.

Reading feverishly about anything that interested her, meant the librarians at the local library would call her whenever a new book came in on something that they thought she would find intriguing. At the top of the list were books on her cultural heritage. It had always been too painful for her to even think about her African-American history, and besides, she had never wanted anyone to think she was associated with the radical members of her community. However, she surprised herself when she found they provided possible answers to her current reality. For like severed limbs and accidental deaths, African-Americans and those in the diaspora, were causalities of a war that had been started centuries before her arrival into this world. It meant that her negative self-image and 'man-less' situation was therefore, not personal, even though it felt so very, very personal.

Another topic of interest that kept her reading well into the night and eventually gave her permission to forgive herself, was the knowledge that she was living in a world filled with a strange twisted notion of sex and sexuality. Not the sexual act that creates energy that can literally move mountains, but rather, the one that sees both parties 'trying to get theirs'; devoid of emotional investment or responsibility, reducing the process to simply masturbating on each other. So although her brief, but memorable, experience with her neighbor had made her feel wanted, having enjoyed his touches, gentleness, and intimacy, she knew she had held back. She didn't give herself to him completely. She had obsessed and idolized about having a husband, sex, and the sexual relationship, more than likely, so she could fit into society's constructed image of what constituted *normal*.

Sister Georgina had talked to herself about wanting things to be different, and even though she had changed some things external-ly, she had never changed how she thought about issues. From the choices she made and her actions, the things she did on a daily basis, unknowingly reflected what she was really thinking. Simply, *more of the same.* With this revelation, she began to see how her "pity party" attitude over the years could have held her captive. Paying lip service to what she had wanted in her life and expecting it to magically ma-terialize in front of her, required no effort by her, whatsoever. She thought about the wonderful ice skaters or the outstanding gymnasts she enjoyed watching during the Olympics. They made their craft look so easy, making the audience forget about their years of prac-tice, dedication, and sacrifices. Their actions spoke loudly about the consequences that they wanted to accomplish.

It was time for action. Sister Georgina decided to begin her journey by becoming aware of the things she did on a day-to-day basis. *Why did she decide to wear the clothes she did in the morning? How did they make her feel about herself? Why did she never learn to do her hair? What would be the consequence of her choice?* Sister Georgina reflected on her personal presentation over the years. Did she unconsciously choose her clothes to say *keep away from me?* Or did she wear her hair to give the message *'I can't be bothered?'* Why did she expect men to be telepathic and see her good intentions with-out giving them any evidence of it? The questions to herself became tougher... *'if she believed that she was in submission to her Lord and Savior, then why did she not take care of the gift that was her physical body?'* Her latest visit to the doctor confirmed that she was border-line diabetic. The chickens were coming home to roost after all the damage she had done to her body over the years of abuse and neglect.

Perhaps, she was now beginning to understand what Dr. P was trying to tell her; that, the uniqueness of every person means know-ing that they have a right to interpret things as they see them, that loving yourself means trusting your own voice. If Dr. P had told her what to think, most likely, she would have accepted it without ques-tion. She would then be perpetuating the pattern of relinquishing her power to someone else. She had spent years expecting others to make changes, had cajoled and bullied them, had manipulated them by guilt, shame, or appealing to their basic humanity, but the results would always be the same; it was expecting them to be the ones who made the changes. And unknowingly, she put them into a position of power. Now, she realized that it was *she* who needed to make the changes and accept the consequences, whatever they would be.

With this realization, Sister Georgina understood why she may have given up her power and allowed others to think for her. It was scary to be in control and take responsibility for the choices she made in her life. But actually thinking like her Lord and Savior would awaken the power within her. It just meant accepting, trusting, knowing, and believing that God resided within her. She would then know she had the ability to change her reality and would recognize just how powerful she was. Simply by changing how she thought about herself and the world she lived in, she could create a new reality.

Instead of hoping for the change to occur outwardly, this time as Gandhi had said, she was going to be the change she wanted to see in the world, by simply changing herself. Sister Georgina's uniqueness was soon reflected back at her when she did her mirror exercises. She had to accept that she was unique and didn't have to be like anyone else because she couldn't be like anyone else; she could only be herself. So she began to love her nose, through which she could inhale and exhale, love her cheeks which shaped her face and would show off her broad smile, with all her own teeth. She was soon extremely grateful for the body in which she lived and had no choice but to do right by it.

Now, knowing and accepting her uniqueness meant she could focus on what was right for her. Looking back, when she was searching for a husband, their character, their integrity, what they stood for, was the furthest thing from her mind. Now, knowing she is worthy, knew she had a right to a relationship that brought both parties real joy; passion and love; one where give and take would be distributed equally. She could show her partner who she really was, by being vulnerable; expressing her likes and dislikes without fear they would leave her if she did. If it was not forthcoming, and it meant being single, well, so be it. She would use her creative energy to be the best person she could be, living her life to the fullest, with or without a husband.

With the knowledge she was gaining, Sister Georgina was determined to apply what worked to her life. She began to trust her instincts by finally listening to her inner voice. She knew it had always been speaking to her, but had chosen not to listen to it or did so when it was too late. Would it make a difference? She didn't know, but decided that she would pay attention to find out if it did.

With this new outlook, Sister Georgina organized a comedy event at the church. She wanted to laugh, to be surrounded by people who focused on the joy that life offered, rather than its misery. It went really well, and soon it became a regular event with non-members attending, as well. Another surprising consequence of her shift in outlook was her interactions with her biological and church families. It seemed to be more sincere- more genuine. She had been the talk of the church when she first came home from the residential facility and was aware that Belinda had been in touch with every single family member far and wide to share the news of her mental breakdown and hospitalization. Some folks were sympathetic, other oblivious, while others would whisper under their breath when she entered the room. She could literally feel their negative energy when in their presence. Sister Georgina decided to use the opportunity to apply what she had learned and realized that she didn't have to take this personally, knowing that most were operating out of ignorance of their own humanity. As a result, she changed her previous defensive behaviors and did not put them down with her 'holier-than-thou' attitude, instead, she applied the golden rule, by being respectful and knowing 'they were entitled to think whatever they liked.' Because what was good for her, was also good for others.

She soon realized that the people around her could also *feel* the shift in her attitude and responded differently towards her. No longer hesitant of her wrath nor condemning attitude, she made it comfortable for those around her to say what was actually on their mind by simply sharing her thoughts, tactfully of course. By seeking to just be herself, she was consciously creating a new reality, one in which she was able to feel the genuine love and care of others. This thinking freed her to focus on falling in love with herself and thereby, falling in love with other members of the human family. And soon, there was no doubt in her mind…it felt good; really good.

"Who knew?" She smiled knowingly to herself.

The other thing she felt compelled to do was start an empowerment group. She billed it as a '*getting to know yourself group*'. She had posted it on the bulletin board and in the church's newsletter for several weeks before she got even one response. But happy to have another person to talk to about all the things she was learning, they decided to meet every other Monday at 6:30pm in one of the windowless basement rooms at the church. Not realizing that others could see the changes they were making in their lives, unknowingly, became a walking advertisement for the group. It wasn't long before two other members signed up and the bi-weekly meeting became weekly. When interest grew, they decided to meet again on Thursday night, as well as on Saturday morning. Before she knew it the group numbers had increased to ten dedicated individuals. They debated questions like '*what does it really mean to fall in love with themselves?*' '*What did the famous quote* 'know thy self' *really mean?*' '*Does knowing themselves really mean knowing God?*'

Like recovering addicts, they nurtured an environment where they could challenge each other, question their actions and the mindless habits that had been formed during their childhood. Sister Georgina was happy to receive the accolades when Dr. P came to speak to their little group. She had been grateful for her ongoing friendship and care. She was understanding and supportive when her colleagues found Dr. P's approach to be intense and challenging. But by trusting the process, they were soon proud when their hard work was rewarded when they were able to recognize and accept their own worth.

In line with this new outlook, Sister Georgina now made regular trips to the hairdresser and spa, allowing her positive inner attitude to spill over into her outward appearance. Her hairstylist was so happy, he could hardly contain his excitement. She was now willing to try new styles, this time her changes would not be a variation of her previous so-called *traditional values*, but rather experiential, trial and error, and paying attention to how it made her feel. She would explore and analyze how she felt, whether it was based on her previous mindset, how it benefited her, or how others would perceive her. Not driven by what they would think of her, but being aware of her responsibility and connection to others meant she had to be thoughtful about how she presented herself to the world. She had never put much thought into her clothes, but change meant she would leave alone the dark colors and try pinks, reds, and yellows instead to share the inner joy she felt. But she wasn't sure whether it was the bright colors or the crystals she carried around to protect her from the invisible *junk* in the air that enhanced her general well-being. Whatever it was, she was so thankful she was feeling better.

Caring about what she put into her mind, she canceled her cable subscription and was happy for her television to become a monitor for her to watch empowering YouTube videos and podcasts from her computer. She wanted to feed her mind with positive information. Sister Georgina had also committed to maintaining the exercise routine she established while in the residential facility. It soon became her regular routine to go to the local organic supermarket after her morning run. She continued to get up at the crack of dawn to jog around the local park near Sister Canisa's home. Just knowing that the cells of her body completely regenerate every seven years, and with some cells changing even more frequently, she knew she had the ability to choose how they regenerated. She made sure she was having a balanced diet, cutting back on the junk foods, and ensured she took her vitamin C and multi-vitamins, because she was determined she would reflect the epitome of self-care. Her high blood pressure soon diminished, much to the shock of her doctor.

As much as she liked saving money, she also realized she had done so at the expense of her health and general well-being. How she felt also had a lot to do with what she had been putting into her body. Yes, she liked her freshly baked sweet treats from the local bakery, and never did she think the day would come when she would find herself walking past a bakery, with its straight from the oven pastries displayed so prominently in the window. But her research into what she was putting into her mouth made her smile and think about the 'wolf in sheep's clothing' that was the delicious powdered sugared covered jelly doughnuts and the damage it would do to the temple that was her body. She thought back to the wonderful foods that Mrs. Cartwright had prepared for brunch, not realizing that they were perpetuating a diet that contributed to their ongoing health concerns.

She realized that she needed to leave the nameless, chemically laden, genetically modified, Frankenstein foods alone. She deserved better than that and simply buying less, but the best of what was on sale, ideally, following a vegan diet of colorful, local, fresh, organic fruits and vegetables, she would be taking care of her body as her Lord and Savior had intended. She soon craved fresh organic vegetables and fruits that she loved to juice. She missed her hamburgers and fries and definitely hadn't wanted to replace them with kale and chia seeds. Who cared that it had taken a good six months to break her addiction to the fried chicken served at the local soul food place, near her church. She remembered placing her order several times, forgetting she had decided to give it up. It was only her resolve to break the habit and not give in to temptation that saw her apologize to the staff for the inconvenience and walk out of the store. The evidence of how her body felt and looked was enough to keep her motivated and on track. Knowing that it was never too late to change, she was grateful to have been given the gift of her physical body and had made up her mind to treat it well from this point on. It had taken a few months before her taste buds became accustomed to the change, but the more she persevered, the more positively her body responded and soon it craved the healthier option.

It was one of those moments that Sister Georgina was craving her favorite passion fruit, pineapple, and mango smoothie. She decided to follow her instincts and make an evening trip to the organic wholefood store. Sister Canisa told her she would take her by car to the supermarket if she waited an hour or so for her to complete an assignment. But as the little voice inside her told her to go as she had planned. Sister Georgina decided to leave and take the short bus trip to the store. As she rarely traveled on the bus, she was like a schoolgirl valuing the new experience, looking around with fascination at the maps, advertisements, and people who got on and off the bus. Despite her efforts to pay attention to what was going on around her, she did not notice the person trying to get her attention until they were in her personal space.

"Georgina."

The school secretary was the last person she wanted to see or talk to. She knew she was only doing her job, but it still hurt when she found out that it was her who had given TD all the ammunition he needed to have her fired from the job she felt she was born to do. She was angry and wanted to curse her out, but took a deep breath instead and gave her a nod of acknowledgment. She really had nothing to say to her.

"I am sorry about what happened. It was a shock to us all and we miss you. How are you? How are you doing?" Her former secretary insisted on saying.

"Oh…I am fine" She replied trying to remain as pleasant as possible. "Thank you. I appreciate your kind words. Please let everyone know I miss them all too."

"TD is a real monster. Do you know he held a special staff meeting after hours to let us all know you were fired? We know he did it to throw his weight around and make us all feel scared. Morale is so low, it's hard for anyone to get excited about the work we do. You know he got a promotion; he's now in Baltimore at some top job. I cannot believe the damage he is doing and everyone is too afraid to say or do anything to stop him."

Sister Georgina was having trouble concentrating; she really didn't want to hear about him. Her mind wandered a little and then was brought back to the conversation when she heard the secretary say, "…and he said after what you did to his mother, you deserved everything you got."

"What was that?"

"I said, he told the principal that his mother was never the same after what happened when you were at high school, remember? When you got the media involved... One of the teachers was his mother. He has been after you for years. He approached me..."

"Wait, you mean to say he has been planning this for years?"

"Yes...he is very vindictive."

Sister Georgina was thankful she had listened to the voice within. She was thankful she had traveled on the bus that evening and she was extremely thankful her secretary had seen her and had this conversation with her. She was thankful she had control of her anger and not cursed her out. She was thankful to have listened to the information she shared. She was glad to take her contact details and knew she would be making another appointment with her lawyers in the morning.

It was nearly three years before both cases finally went to court, and despite the associated stresses, they were both settled surprisingly quickly. Before the judge could hear the case to rescind the sale of Sister Georgina's house due to criminal fraud, the lawyers of Beckly and Beckly had brokered a deal. As a legal strategy, the lawyers knew the purchasers would be financially out of their depth and amidst threats of one court order after another; they were actively encouraged to write the sale off as a loss, and transfer the deed back into the sole name of Sister Georgina. As she would bear the cost of this and other associative administrative fees, they should settle for the nominal sum of $250. They did.

For the second case, *Mrs. Georgina Jeters v. the Board of Education*, saw all the interns at the Beckly and Beckly office excited at the thought of being given the opportunity to present this case in court. The senior partners felt it was an open and shut case, and therefore, they trusted that even the interns could win.

In addition to the secretary's statement, they had received several hundred letters of support for Sister Georgina and against TD. After sifting through the anonymous letters from the signed ones, and then the relevant from the TD haters, they found one signed by the two human resources staff members who were with TD on the day he had fired Sister Georgina. They were both prepared to testify that after Sister Georgina had left the room, TD had boasted that he had "avenged his mother's nemesis" and had told them what happened. They had not believed him and searched the archives for evidence in the education records. They had also discovered that the secret and unauthorized documentation of Sister Georgina's performance and attendance over the years had in fact violated her rights, as it had not been conducted in accordance to the department's standard operating procedures.

As a result of the requirement to disclose, the Board of Education's lawyers decided to settle much to the annoyance of the Beckly and Beckly interns. Sister Georgina received a letter of apology, reinstatement of her job with full benefits, pension, along with a settlement of $365,000 for lost wages and distress caused. She refused calls from the Beckly and Beckly interns to seek additional compensation. After the case, the local newspaper reported on her win, as well as the leadership shakeup at the Education Department that had resulted in the dismissal of an "up and coming administrator."

Although the newspaper article had been brief, it had somehow caught the attention of one of Otis's golfing buddies. They had given him a call and of course had mentioned details of her financial settlement. It wasn't long before Otis was calling, having obtained Sister Georgina's new cell phone number from Mrs. Gilchrist.

"Hello, this is Otis."

"Who is this?" Sister Georgina said, genuinely not recognizing his voice.

"It's Otis. How are you doing?" He tried to be as upbeat as he could.

Shocked to hear his voice at the other end of her phone, she demanded to know how he had gotten her number. In the seconds, it took for her to realize that she already knew the answer. Since being awarded her settlement she had to change her number several times. People she had only known briefly or who were complete strangers had somehow found the courage to call her to ask for money. But she had understood why and had not taken it personally. She took a deep breath and knowing she had nothing to say to him, smiled before putting the phone down and then proceeded to block his number from her phone.

Mrs. Gilchrist petitioned on his behalf for several months afterwards about how he wished to speak to her and wanted to let her know that he had changed. He was working on promoting a new body building project and thought she would be interested in sponsoring the event. Sister Georgina had simply told her that she had no wish to speak to him and resolved the matter by giving her Dr. P's card for Otis to contact for private counseling sessions. When she heard he had taken up the offer and was seeing Dr. P, her first thoughts were that he was doing it to get her to talk to him, but then she trusted the process. He was on his life's journey and whatever he took from the experience would help him.

She was proud of herself and how she had handled Otis. She had already given him too much of her precious time and energy over the years. It had been hard to accept that he did not have her best interest at heart, but knowing that she had given him permission to treat her in that way was surprisingly freeing. She could make choices and was pleased to be choosing the ones that uplifted her soul. She had been surprised that the phone call from Otis hadn't affected her as much as she had expected and concluded that she was *'doing her emotional work'*. She was truly proud of herself.

Sister Georgina had relied on the generosity of others while waiting for her cases to get to court, and rather than be embarrassed or ashamed, she had chosen to embrace the experience. It forced her to be humble, to receive, and be accepting of the love from others. The leadership team at her beloved church had agreed to divert some of the church's building fund to provide Sister Georgina with a small stipend. It covered her rent and basics until she found work. So as uncomfortable as it was to receive help, she embraced it, recalling what Dr. P had said about the give and take of the universe. She realized that she was not so lonely, for by showing herself for who she was, had allowed others to accept her. She had been surprised by the willingness of so many of the members, to reach out and to offer her their support. Sister Canisa said she was welcomed to stay in her guest bedroom for as long as she wanted. She had accepted the offer and valued the opportunity to unlearn her mother's unintentional negative behavior patterns and receive.

It had been about a year before she found a part-time job at a three person non-profit agency that provided research on education. It wasn't ideal, but it was peaceful and Sister Georgina was content. She was soon addicted to a drama free life, by choosing experiences that enriched her. She was determined that in seven years, her entire life would be renewed, physically, mentally and spiritually. She would ensure that there was balance in her life. And it was not long before her exercises and healthy eating regimes meant glowing skin and a loss of nearly sixty pounds.

When the court cases were both behind her, she was able to make some major decisions. By allowing herself to listen to the voice within, Sister Georgina realized that she did not want to move back into her home, nor return to work. She therefore, declined the position, choosing instead to take an early severance package. She also put her home up for sale, sold most of her furniture, and gave the rest away. Sister Georgina reasoned that she hadn't needed most of her things in house for years, so she could let go and move on. She reflected on how she had once valued and sacrificed for the material things her life. Seeing herself as 'no longer being of the world', she was no longer going to allow the acquisition of material possessions to have the power to enslave her life. She was choosing to finally *live*.

The last thing the law firm did for Sister Georgina was organize her divorce. As both parties agreed, it was settled quickly and harmoniously. The interns made sure that Sister Georgina and Otis were kept apart when they came into the law offices to sign the papers. And with an agreement to keep him out of jail, the interns arranged for Otis to repay the money he had stolen from Sister Georgina's saving account, and that he received none of her settlement or profits from the sale of her home. They were sorry at the Beckly and Beckly office when her case was finally closed.

It was just a tattered advertisement posted on the office's notice board, and she was surprised it caught her attention. She had never thought about traveling abroad, but a position to do what she loved- fighting for educational injustices around the world was too attractive an offer. Her resume screamed *'I fight injustices'*. After updating a detailed resume and having several intensive interviews, she received notification of her start date as expected. The red tape, training, and paperwork meant it was almost a year before she was ready to leave to go on her first assignment. She was happy to discover it was to her mother's home country of Jamaica. She was kept busy on her trip with work related activities, but still found time to take a drive to her mother's village and visited what remained of the decaying post office, the large wooded sign post, and the majestic trees that still shaded the area.

Her next posting was more challenging, as it was a remote village in the outskirts of Petauke, in Eastern Province of Zambia, Central Africa. But on her fifty-fifth birthday, Sister Georgina found herself on a dilapidated bus heading from Lusaka, the capital, for the eight hour journey. She was proud of herself for changing her entire life. Realizing that these last few years she had been so busy getting to know herself and doing things that she loved, she had almost forgotten how she had spent years wishing her life away, sitting aimlessly in front of the television eating cheesy puffs and ice cream. Yes, she would have liked to have children; yes, she would have liked to have a husband, but she put it in God's hands and had moved on with her life. The painful bumps of the many potholes along the way eventually took its toll on the bus and it broke down several times. It was repaired by both the passengers, as well as the drivers. The adventure of it all, accompanied by the warm, loving nature of the sun meant it was exhausting, but smiling, Sister Georgina got off the bus twelve hours later. She was happy.

Despite the bus delay of nearly four hours and the lateness of the hour, the bus station was as busy as ever. After collecting her dust covered bags from the top of the bus, she was unsure of which direction to go. Sister Georgina stood looking confused and made her foreign status obvious to the many independent sellers who descended on her with their bags of peanuts, fruits, and other items she didn't want. She was quickly rescued by a young woman who had a warm welcoming smile and had been waving a hand-made sign, torn from a brown cardboard box which read, *"As-salamu alaykum (welcome) Mrs. Jeters."* She had kept her married name simply because she hadn't gotten around to changing it, despite being granted her divorce decree. The woman quickly introduced herself as, *Ayesha* and told Sister Georgina that she was one of the teachers already in place at the school she would be attending.

"Hello! Thank you for waiting. The bus delay was so long, I didn't expect you to wait all this time for me," Sister Georgina said struggling with her bag.

"Why wouldn't I wait? I got the message that you were on the bus, so of course I waited..?" Ayesha responded with curiosity.

"It's just that in the U.S., I probably would have had to take a taxi cab," said Sister Georgina.

"Well, not here...so welcome to Africa! Let me introduce myself, my name is Ayesha," and held out her hand for her to shake.

"Thank you, it is good to be here. My name is Sister Georgina."

"Did your mother name you Sister Georgina?" Ayesha innocently inquired.

"No, it is really just to remind me that I am a sister to everyone," Sister Georgina regurgitated her usual response to the question.

"But, we are *all* brothers and sisters to each other. Do people not know that in the States?"

Sister Georgina had never faced this issue before and was rendered silent for a few minutes. She then responded, having processed it through the new outlook she had to life. Simply, if it made sense, she would embrace new knowledge and in this instance she responded in a way that surprised even herself.

"No, most don't and need reminding, but by living it means I don't need the label. Call me Georgina," she smiled.

"Okay, Georgina, I will take you to my home and settle you in before we go to the main office for your work details." With the introductions out of the way, Ayesha went to pick up Georgina's luggage at the same time as Georgina. Their hands touched and both women laughed out loud as it indicated that they were both thinking the same thing. They took it as a sign of their forthcoming friendship. Taking one handle each they continued to laugh as they made their way out of the bustling bus station.

Ayesha was a Muslim teacher from Tunisia. She had been accepted into the same educational program as Georgina and had come to Zambia with her husband and two small children. She had been at the school for about a year and had been assigned to orient Georgina into life in the remote African village. It wasn't long before they were enjoying each other's friendship. After work most evenings, the women would play with Ayesha's three and five year old children until they went to bed. They would then enjoy the evening sitting by the bonfire in their backyard, talking late into the night. She valued the companionship; it was different and it felt genuine. Georgina was determined to be herself. It felt strange, because for so long, she had been trying to be something she was not. Now, she felt she could just be herself, at last; and she now had someone who accepted her on those terms. She was also made sure that the relationship was reciprocal; one in which there was both give *and* take.

The women had many conversations about their respective faiths, and decided to focus on the commonalities: the joy, peace, and happiness it brought them, rather than the differences. From this point of view, the women found they had more in common than they realized. Georgina remembered, in horror, how she thought scornfully of anyone who did not share her particular belief. The emotive image Dr. P used of women in a remote village in Afghanistan voluntarily participating in a stoning of a woman who had dared to leave her home, forced her to think that she could have been one of those narrow-minded women inflicting such a punishment on another human being. With this image etched into the front of her mind, she decided to be open, not just to new experiences, but to knowledge that takes her out of her comfort zone.

Nothing resonated as Truth to her as the knowledge of God as described in the Bible. Yes, she could imagine the early ancestors trying to make sense of what they were seeing in the physical world. And yes, she could see how they could come up with myths and stories to rationalize the world they found themselves. Those myths and stories did survive centuries and appeared in differing cultures. She reasoned it could be because they were designed to capture deeper truths that expanded human consciousness, provided divine truths, or wise counsel. *Did that do for them what the Bible did for her?* As far as she was concerned, those, and other sacred texts could provide insight into a person's unique role in the universe and how each person has the ability to decipher a meaning for themselves, and permission to create the world that they want. So, even though her belief had told her that she also had these innate abilities, she had chosen to ignore it and focused on the superficiality of her Christian faith. She had been so caught up in the stresses of daily life, she missed its key point: *the application.* If she truly believed, then she would not have been so afraid of thinking she was not good enough, of being judged negatively, or knowing that she was actually part of a magnificent universe, alive for a unique purpose.

Knowing that the biblical stories could be copied from Egyptian texts, did not mean it could not inspire her. On the contrary, it could make sense if the stories were written at a time when very few people could read, and had been designed to illustrate a point on a subconscious level. What mattered the most was not the outwardly trappings of the faith, but rather, its application. If she believed, then what does it matter if someone has another perspective? If for her, the individuality of a snowflake or the organs in the body indicates God is real, it should also tell her that each person has a different purpose or experience for a reason. It was her responsibility to trust that God knew why. So when Ayesha invited Georgina to the Mosque, she went and actually enjoyed the experience, although she found sitting on the floor for the entire ninety minute service difficult. She loved the fact that Ayesha accompanied her as she searched for a church home while she was in the Northern Province. They talked for hours about their submission to God and how they could be better servants of God. They would fast, cook, and (what Sister Georgina loved the most) shared the care of the children together.

Due to their busy work schedules, it was a while before Georgina finally met Ayesha's husband. As a contractor, his work meant he was usually away for weeks at a time. However, when they did, he unexpectedly made her heart skip a beat. After what had now become a typical evening, with the children fed, bathed, and put to bed, Ayesha and Georgina were sitting by the fire pit talking as usual.

"*As-salamu alaykum*, my beloved wife," he said excitedly as soon as he walked through the door into the yard. He rushed over to her and hugged so lovingly before planting a long intimate kiss on her lips. "I missed you today and thought about you nonstop. Did I tell you that you are my world?"

"Yes," said Ayesha returning the smile with a twinkle in her eyes. "Yes, you've told me every day for the past six years we have been married."

Georgina thought that public displays of affection in her faith was something that was frowned upon, and found herself wishing they practiced it because she felt jealous and wished she was being greeted like that.

Picking up on her presence, he turned his attention to her, "*As-salamu alaykum*. You must be the famous Georgina I have heard so much about. I am Yousef; she must have told you about me. I want to thank you for caring for my wife. She is not so alone when I am gone for weeks at a time. I appreciate you being such good company for her. I apologize for my overt display of affection, it is not something I would normally do in public, but I just have to let her know that I was happy to see her. I do not want to make you feel uncomfortable. You are a welcomed guest in my home."

As if he had read her mind, Georgina felt uncomfortable. He epitomized the phrase, *tall, dark, and handsome*. He stood a regal six foot four, and with his intelligence, confidence, and emotionally secure personality, he presented as a commanding force. She instantly felt safe and secure in his presence. She was surprised by the resurfacing of long forgotten feelings within her. She was embarrassed and tried to hide her attraction to her friend's husband. It had not gone unnoticed by Ayesha.

"Let me get you some dinner. We exchanged recipes and I tried Georgina's vegan casserole tonight. The children loved it. You sit and chat with Georgina," Ayesha demanded of her husband.

"Certainly not, my beloved wife, I love you caring for me, but let me care for you too. You continue to sit and enjoy the fire with your friend and I will join you with my dinner shortly," and with that he was off back into the kitchen.

Georgina held her head down in an attempt to hide her shame because she had no idea what to say to her friend.

"You like him, don't you?" Ayesha broke the ice.

"Yes, he seems like a really nice man."

"Yes he is, a very Godly man. I fell in love with him after I heard him say the call to prayer. He is striving to live the words of Allah, not just go through the motion. He truly does make me feel like a queen. A lot of his brothers in the Mosque tell him that I should be beaten and be made to feel like his servant, but his interpretation of the Quran says the opposite. He believes in treating me and the children like gifts from God. And we have a wonderful life together. I am very happy."

When he came back from the kitchen with his meal, the conversation turned to his work trip, family updates, and plans for the coming week. As it was getting late, Ayesha then demanded that Yousef take Georgina home.

"My wife, you know it will be my pleasure to walk her home."

Georgina's residence wasn't far, just a couple of houses away, but to get there meant traveling along a dark, narrow, dirt road so it was always safer to be escorted.

"What made you travel to this remote village in Zambia?" Yousef asked

"I didn't really have a choice. They just told me where to come and here I am," Georgina said.

"Would you have gone where they told you if it was…let's say the Ukraine?" He said with a smile.

"No, I don't think so. I have never thought about Ukraine."

"There, you see? You *are* thinking about what you do," Yousef prodded.

"Well, now that you mentioned it, I did tell the head office I wanted to go somewhere warm and tropical. They had a section on the form that indicated priorities, I choose the commonwealth. I had a wonderful time in Jamaica, not so long ago," said Georgina, not realizing that she was speaking so easily with a complete stranger.

"What made you enjoy you time there so much?" Yousef inquired.

"Well, I had a wonderful host. After we finished our official duties, she took me to the places that was off limits to regular tourists. Of course, we did some of the key tourist things like going to Dunn's River Falls and visiting the home of Bob Marley. But, I felt like a real local when we visited some of the places I had heard so much about from my mother when I was a little girl." Georgina did not realize how nice it was to have a conversation with a man who seemed genuinely interested in what she had to say.

The small flashlight that Georgina had in her hand suddenly went out and they were left in darkness. Yousef heard her gasp and quickly sought to reassure her, "we have become so dependent on modern technologies that we forget that we managed pretty well since the beginning of time without it! Just stop a minute…" Yousef said as he stopped in the middle of the quiet dirt track and looked up at the moon. "It is possible to see being guided by the moon, or for you to develop your senses to note the things around you." His confidence made something inside her flutter.

"Come, let's try it," he presented her with an unexpected challenge, but one that was difficult for her to resist."

"Okay…"

Yousef expertly led the way to her home. He pointed out shrubs and large rocks to avoid. She surprised herself when she spotted a moving creature in front of them, unsure of whether it was a snake or a lizard. It didn't make any difference as she was getting ready to scream, but Yousef shooed it away before any noise was able to come out of her mouth. She closed her mouth and tried to not let Yousef know that butterflies suddenly fluttered uncontrollably in her stomach. She found it difficult to say anything else except a quiet *goodnight* when he left her safely at her door.

The short walk home with Yousef by her side caused Georgina to toss and turn most of the night for the first time in years. She found herself thinking about sex. By getting on with the business of living, it had somehow kept her sexual feelings in check. Now, they had unexpectedly returned and she had to face what it meant. She really liked him, and found herself dreaming about being greeted in the same way he had greeted his wife. She imagined being made loved to by him with the missing ingredient that would make her willing to give herself completely to him.

"But she is a good friend and I need to stop this nonsense," Georgina said to herself. "I will *not* jeopardize my friendship, it means too much to me." With that, Georgina decided to turn to prayer for strength to overcome her feelings for Yousef every time she felt such thoughts or feelings arise.

Ayesha and Georgina continued to nurture their relationship, and Georgina made a point of always trying to be away whenever she knew Yousef would be around. Ayesha noticed her distance from her husband and would tease her about it. But, rather than be upset or jealous, Ayesha seemed genuinely pleased by Georgina's attraction to her husband and had told her so on several occasions. She had even told her that Yousef liked her too. Georgina couldn't believe they were having such a conversation and had put it down to cultural differences.

Over the eighteen months they were together in Zambia after both women extended their contract on two separate occasions, they had many more relaxing nights by the fire pit, going on safari trips, traveling around the country, as well as crossing the border into Zimbabwe, Botswana, and Malawi. They were having such fun and did not want to think about their time together coming to an end. Both women were devastated when their requests for yet another extension of their contract was denied. They were told it was finally time for them to leave.

Georgina had returned to the United States several times for the holidays while she worked in Zambia. She had loved spending time with Sisters Canisa and Deborah, and enjoyed catching up with Dr. P. She volunteered at the mental hospital whenever she was available and had made a large donation to cover the costs for people who did not have insurance. She gave some money to the church to repay their stipend from when she was unemployed, but most of her donation went towards the building of a small library inside the church. She included the stipulations that there would be no restrictions on the type of books, periodicals, or access on the computers. And despite the Pastor's insistence, they would not be using the same contractor that did the renovations on the old church.

She was brought up-to-date by Mrs. Gilchrist about the lovely funeral services they had for Brother Barnabus and Mrs. Cartwright. And desperate to share the gossip about her half-brother, Mrs. Gilchrist mentioned to Georgina that Otis had been doing really well in counseling. Georgina smiled and repeated to her what she had told her on many previous occasions: that she didn't care to know as she had no interest in what he was doing. She was thankful for the experience and had moved on with her life. She wished him nothing but the best and was choosing to use her precious time and energy on things that would enrich her life. She had forgiven him. She planned to enjoy the experiences that God had in store for her.

With the thought of relocation looming, she tried not to think about leaving. Not because she didn't want to be there, but because she would miss Ayesha, the children, and of course, Yousef; although she admitted this to no one. Her mind had gone back to them every time she traveled to the U.S. and could not wait to get back and catch up on all the things she had missed. The first time she had returned from her visit home, the children jumped into her arms. She remembered feeling their love as their arms wrapped tightly around her neck. They held onto her so tightly for fear she would leave them again. She loved them and wanted to see them grow up. The thought that she would have to leave them for good was devastating.

As the days drew nearer and nearer for their contracts to end, Georgina was becoming more and more depressed, while Ayesha and her family seemed more and more excited. The family had all been fasting, but did not invite her to participate, which was unusual. She tried to comfort herself, reminding herself that everything happens for a reason and to trust in God's plan. But, her emotions got the better of her a week before they were scheduled to leave. Georgina tried to talk to Ayesha about their final days together. No longer afraid, she took the initiative to share her heartfelt comments about how she liked to spend their last week together. But when her comments were met with a warm, but non-committal smile, Georgina exploded.

"How can you be so calm? I'm so upset that I'm leaving. I will miss you all so much. I am not sure how I will cope. I will miss seeing the children everyday. I want you to let me know everything that happens as they go through school. I want them to write to me and let me know about their homework. I want to hear about their exploits around the world. I also want our sisterhood to continue. You haven't even asked for my contact details in the U.S. Do you not want to contact me after we leave next week? It hurts to even think about what's going to happen when I get home."

Ayesha got up and rushed over to the lunch room door. She quickly glanced up and down the hallway to make sure no one was loitering around and could overhear their conversation. She then shut the door. Her actions made Georgina nervous about the pending conversation and sat upright in her chair expecting the worse.

"We break our fast tomorrow and then we were going to tell you. But you must not tell Yousef that I told you. He is supposed to ask you first, but I can see your pain and I must put you out of your misery."

"What are you talking about?"

"We are fasting because we wanted to make sure that what we were going to ask you is God's will. I don't need another day to know it is the right thing to do."

"Tell me…what?"

"My husband and I would love for you to join us in marriage. How do you feel about being my sister-wife?" Ayesha said beaming with joy.

Speechless, Georgina slipped from her chair and had to be steadied by Ayesha.

"I don't understand…what do you mean?"

"Yousef and I have been talking about taking a second wife ever since we've been married, but never found someone suitable before. We have spent this time thinking and praying about our decision to ask you. Yousef plans to propose tomorrow, if you accept, we can plan after that where we go and what we do. I think it is so exciting!"

"I don't know what to say…I definitely need a minute. I'm glad you've told me. I really do need some time to think. Please, can you take my class in yours? I can't concentrate after hearing this."

"Of course," said Ayesha. "This is a lot to take in, I know, but think carefully. We all love you and want you to be a part of our family."

Georgina stumbled out of the lunchroom and into the yard. She had to find somewhere quiet and once off the school grounds, she wandered aimlessly down what was considered by the locals to be their main road. The orange colored, dirt road was covered in twigs and branches, rocks and stones, making it difficult to navigate in her flip flops. But having left in such a hurry, she forgot about her walking shoes. She passed a group of chickens and goats that stared suspiciously at her, clearly annoyed by the intrusion into their domain. The sounds of birds chirping in the distance was interrupted by a rooster calling, despite the time of day. A person on a bicycle rode by and then a child on their way home. They had both nodded and given her the traditional greeting and she responded in kind, as they went by. She passed several traditional roundaval houses with their intricate thatched roofs, outdoor kitchen (an area set aside for a fire pit) and outhouses (a fence that had been put around a hole in the ground). As she kept walking, her sightings of the houses became less and less.

Not realizing how far she had walked, she soon became aware of the vast open landscape that appeared to stretch beyond the horizon. She found a large flat rock by the side of the road near a watering troth. It clearly had been designed to accommodate the human care-taker, while the livestock drank their water. It was an ideal spot for looking out into the wilderness. And although, some traffic passed by- a cow, followed about forty-five minutes later by a donkey and cart, she had not been disturbed. The picture perfect view of the Savannah allowed Georgina to take in the majesty of the environment. She allowed it to wash over her as she sat in shock trying to take in the news she had just received from Ayesha.

Never in her wildest dreams would she have imagined an offer such as this. An interfaith, polygamist marriage is unthinkable. The thought of Yousef having sex with Ayesha and then coming to her bed to sleep with her... it was just awful. The thought of introducing her husband and his first wife to her church family in Glenarden sent shivers up her spine. What an abomination in the sight of God. She needed to say *thank you, but no thanks*. But, then, she stopped herself. She had come too far to return to the rigidity of her previous mindset. Her mind went back to the night of the infamous dinner party when she had been confronted by Patrick. At the time she had quickly dismissed his words as being absurd and ridiculous, but now, that painful conversation reminded her to stop and think about things differently.

Could her purpose be to marry and become a second wife? Or could her purpose be to show that it is possible to be happy and single? After all, she knew she was a talented teacher and by her example, she could teach people that the sexual relationship is truly sacred, necessary for strong marriages, strong families, and strong communities. And if the arguments of some scholars are to be believed, her example, or *sacrifice*, would contribute to a paradigm shift that could relegate the current status quo, obsolete. Georgina was excited by the prospect of being part of such a movement and allowed her thoughts to explore the possibilities. *Would she be based in the U.S., Africa, Europe, or elsewhere?* She had no idea. But by accepting that she was valuable and worthy, she knew she could choose a path because it was what *she* wanted and not because it was expected or demanded. It definitely did not have to look or feel like something that has been established by someone else. No one else on the planet had the same experiences she did, so why should she try and measure up to someone else's standard when she could just be herself?

Whether she chose to marry or not, it would be her responsibility to trust that the decision would be the right one for her. So, after all this time, she was thankful for the experience of her sin. Georgina knew that for most of her life, she had willingly given others the ability to tell her what to think and to make decisions for her. But, looking back, her sin forced her to rethink her life; something she never would have done, otherwise. It had unknowingly been the catalyst to a journey of self-discovery, for her to think, to question, to reason for *herself.* She decided to put that belief into practice and decided to begin with the decision now before her.

There was no doubt, that she loved Yousef, Ayesha, and the children and had felt part of the family since she arrived. But just as quickly, the thought came into her head that Yousef and Ayesha had been praying and fasting over this decision for the past couple of weeks. They believed it was God's will that they ask her. *Was their God her God? Was He trying to tell her something?* She had watched them practice their faith over the past eighteen months they have been together. Yousef was truly a God-fearing man and there was no question in her mind that he was striving to practice what he preached. And it was a very attractive feature, indeed. He was family-focused and made his wife and children feel so safe, so loved. She had watched him playing, reading, and engaging so thoughtfully with his children. It was a joy to see, but what made him think that it was possible to overlook their religious differences? She may have strong disagreements with his faith, but would she be able to overlook them as they had done and believe that it was possible to have a happy marriage? She didn't know.

Out of all the thoughts that raced around her mind, the one that stood out the most was the question of *if she did join him in marriage, would she feel loved?* Georgina knew Yousef would definitely not be offering her crumbs. Georgina loved Ayesha as a sister and the thought of having her as a sister-wife was not difficult. She briefly allowed her thoughts to linger on the possibility of a family dinner around the table. She imagined Yousef coming home, kissing Ayesha and then her. In fact, if she was honest, it was a wonderful thought. She also could not deny the immense pleasure she would have by being a mother to Ayesha's and Yousef's two beautiful children. Experiencing the joy of watching them grow, being a significant part of their lives; she had found it to be priceless. She imagined herself thirty years down the road and having them caring for her in her hour of need and it brought a smile to her face. The benefits of the invitation could, therefore, not be dismissed too lightly.

Despite her decision, she wanted to ensure that she was starting out into whatever journey she decided on with a new outlook. She needed to be renewed, revitalized, and reborn. She walked over to the trough and blessed the water by saying a simple prayer. She then dipped her hands into it and sprinkled it onto herself. She visualized the cascade of water flowing all over her body and imagined herself being thoroughly soaked, cleansed, and refreshed. She then imagined all the negativity falling away from her and felt herself letting go and embracing the new. She smiled at the thought of her two previous baptisms. She then took the scarf from her head and laid it on the ground in an attempt to protect herself from the ants and other crawling insects that could bite terribly. She then kneeled on it and bowed her head in submission and allowed herself to hear her thoughts. *Would she find the love that she was looking for in a relationship with Yousef, Ayesha, and their children, or would she find herself by being happy and single; perhaps, empowering many others along the way?* She had no idea of the answer, but knew what she had to do.

"Dear Lord, you know I am your servant, and have dedicated my life to serving your Truth; that will never change. I believe in your majesty, even more now, than I did before and I know that all things are possible through you and only you. I am on my knees, Lord, humbling myself, asking for your guidance. You know I want nothing more than to please you, to be your true servant, to walk in your path and to glorify your name. "

Before standing up and preparing herself to return to the remote village's school, she paused and took several deep breaths before slowly opening her eyes. She looked out into the seemingly endless Savannah and a sense of peace came over her. Kneeling quietly by the side of the road, as if a light switch had suddenly been turned on, *she knew.* She smiled knowingly, awakened to her connection to world before her, from the small insignificant biting insects that crawled around her feet to the Creator of it all. No longer an observer, or following a script designed by others, she recognized and accepted that she was an integral part of the majesty that lay in front of her.

"Thank you, my Lord. I have absolute trust that whatever happens, it is because it is meant to happen. I place my life in your hands. Amen."

She had reconciled her dilemma by simply accepting that God truly does answer prayers, even those that have been unspoken and denied.

"Dear Lord," she whispered under her breath, *"thank you."*

Acknowledgements

I will always be eternally grateful to everyone who has helped me complete this part of my life's journey. For having unquestionable faith in my abilities, for being understanding, supportive, and sending positive vibes across the airwaves even when I did not call or write. Knowing you were in my life, kept me going to completion of this book. I am truly grateful to everyone at B.O.S.S. Publishing for reading and rereading my work. Your ideas, comments, and positive feedback has transformed my work, for which I know the reader will benefit. I am thankful to my friends and colleagues who I forced to read my work way before it should have been read. But your comments and feedback has shaped the final product.

Please, understand that there are so many people to thank, I can never list you all, but the few who stand out are the usual suspects in my life. My thanks of course to my beloved daughter, Shakira, who has remained my source of constant inspiration and has kept me going when I thought I could not go on. To my parents, in this reality and the next, my siblings, David, Jenny, Ludwig, Alan, and Tracey who have rallied round me to ensure this work was completed. To my friends in the UK, Patsy, Ralph, Almina, Jane, and also, in Africa, Masinyama, Sophie and Lillian. In the United States, Judy, Kerell, Tanya, Tanisha, Michael, Mekada. Special thanks to my beloved cousin Yonette for much needed practical and moral support. A very big thank you to Sophia Morgan-Genus, because without you this book would not have been written. Because of your faith in me, I had no choice but to believe in my skills. Your unwavering support has meant I have been able to see it through to completion. Thank you, thank you, thank you.

But most importantly, to the voice within me who guided this book from beginning to end.

www.ingramcontent.com/pod-product-compliance
Lightning Source LLC
Chambersburg PA
CBHW070552120726
47909CB00007B/2319